Efraim's Eye

Efraim's Eye

by
William Peace

Strategic Book Publishing and Rights Co.

Copyright © 2012 William Peace. All rights reserved.

No part of this book may be reproduced or transmitted in any form or by any means, graphic, electronic, or mechanical, including photocopying, recording, taping, or by any information storage retrieval system, without the permission, in writing, of the publisher.

Strategic Book Publishing and Rights Co.
12620 FM 1960, Suite A4-507
Houston TX 77065
www.sbpra.com

ISBN: 978-1-61897-399-3

TABLE OF CONTENTS

Chapter 1:   Planning 1
Chapter 2:   Initiation 27
Chapter 3:   Assignment 54
Chapter 4:   Marrakech 77
Chapter 5:   Preparation 106
Chapter 6:   Efraim 128
Chapter 7:   Friday 154
Chapter 8:   Essaouira 180
Chapter 9:   Fez and Casablanca 206
Chapter 10: Readiness 231
Chapter 11: Decision 252
Chapter 12: Discovery 280
Chapter 13: D-Day 311
Chapter 14: Aftermath 334

"... the punishment shall be life for life, eye for eye, tooth for tooth, hand for hand, foot for foot, wound for wound, bruise for bruise."

Exodus 21:24

Chapter 1

PLANNING

Efraim did not consider himself as a terrorist. A terrorist, he thought, was a person of low intellect who committed suicide without knowing whether he had actually achieved his objective. Efraim, however, was a holy warrior—a very clever, indispensable piece on Allah's chessboard. He would not merely sacrifice himself for a slight improvement in the Muslim position. He would destroy dozens—perhaps hundreds—of pawns and knights in a memorable master move that would change the course of history! And he would live to see the corrupt world of the infidels thrown into chaos!

To the average Western observer, Efraim did not look like a terrorist. True, he had a heavy stubble of black beard, and he habitually wore a black-and-white keffiyeh. But his nose was small and well-formed, his eyes were a sympathetic brown, and his lips were gently curved into a secret smile. True, he was a big man—at least twenty stone, but his movements were graceful and deliberate. One would have imagined, perhaps, that he was the leader of a desert caravan, astride the first of a string of camels laden with precious merchandise, crossing a barren landscape of drifting dunes.

Efraim had a plan whose outline was now established, and step-by-step, he would add the necessary details—checking, adjusting and thinking ahead. His objective was clear—to strike at the very heart of an infidel capital, causing spectacular destruction and outrage. Many would die in sudden shock and horror. Their deaths would exact vengeance for the deaths of those who had been very dear to him. The image of their murders by the infidels was as vivid as it had been seven years earlier, but his rage had grown into a consumptive passion. *Besides,* he thought, *Does not the Holy Qur'an instruct me to 'kill them wherever you find them'?*[1] Efraim's plan involved the shattering of a great structure whose integrity was dependent on several large steel cables. When these cables were severed, the structure would fall, collapsing with a great roar and the high-pitched cacophony of screaming.

For his plan to succeed, Efram would need several shaped charges that would be similar to antitank projectiles that he had used when he had been in the army. But to cut the cables, he would need a different form of a shaped charge: a charge that cut on a line rather than a charge that penetrated at a point. This linear-shaped charge was not in routine use in armed forces around the world. It would have to be tailor-made. He would need the high explosive and a polymer to mix with the explosive so that it could be shaped. Efraim also needed to obtain the casings, detonators and liners. The liner of a shaped charge does the actual cutting. The explosive propels the charge with such force that instead of being a flat sheet of metal it becomes a concentrated, high temperature solid/liquid traveling at tremendous speed.

Efraim would need two vehicles for transportation. He would need two dedicated and committed assistants. His plan included the requirement that he obtain a European Union national identity card and several passport visas. Beyond these things, he would need money—plenty of money—for purchases and for travel. Much travel was anticipated by his plan.

To be assured that he would have access to the money he needed, Efraim arranged a meeting with Yusuf, his financial sponsor.

When they were together in Yusuf's office, Efraim knelt on the carpet facing east; Yusuf did likewise and Efraim intoned, "*In the name of Allah, the Lord of Mercy, the Giver of Mercy!*"

---

[1] This font is used whenever the language is Arabic translated into English.

They bowed deeply so that their foreheads touched the floor. They rose and seated themselves, and Yusuf rang a bell to summon a servant who brought them strong, black coffee.

Efraim said, *"I can inform you, Brother, that the plan is entirely feasible and will be implemented in such a way as to please Allah greatly."*

Yusuf responded, *"I am filled with delight to hear it. When, Allah-willing, shall the plan reach fruition?"*

"There is much to do, Brother, but I expect to be ready to strike the hammer blow in about four months. Today, however, we need to speak about finances."

"What is the sum you will require?" Yusuf asked.

Efraim reached into the small black bag slung over one shoulder, and he withdrew a much-folded sheet of paper. *"Here, I have written my estimates of expenditures for completion of the plan. You will notice that the cost of the hammer itself is modest. The most important element of cost is travel. There are several places I must visit to assemble the hammer and to move it to its destination. Some of these visits will be by air, but others will, out of necessity, be by vehicle."*

"Why, Brother, is so much travel necessary? Can you not obtain the explosive, Semtex?"

Efraim said, *"Our stock of Semtex is depleted, and the Libyans have adopted infidel ways. They no longer assist us. The Czech government now closely regulates Explosia, the manufacturer of Semtex. I have found that RDX, the explosive of choice, has a detonation rate of over 8,000 metres per second. This makes it ideal for a shaped charge."*

"And where can this RDX be obtained?"

"It is used in commercial blasting and by the military. I believe the most likely source is Afghanistan, where a

corrupt militia, the Taliban, have obtained supplies for IED's (improvised explosive devices) *from Tehran.*"

"What about Iraq? Brother, could we not use our contacts there?"

Efraim said, "I have made certain discrete inquiries. What little still exists is very tightly controlled."

Yususf looked at Efraim's estimate and commented, "I see that there are two very long trips by automobile."

Efraim nodded. "Those trips are necessary for the transportation of the hammer."

"And the two vehicles?" Yusuf inquired.

"The vehicles have distinct purposes, but both of them will be purchased used, and can be sold when the plan is complete."

"What expenses do you require for your person?" Yusuf asked.

"Only my food and lodging, Brother. You know my tastes are modest."

"Indeed I know it, Brother," Yusuf responded, "but I think the sum of fifty dollars per day should be added for your comfort."

"That is very kind, brother."

Ysuf reached into a drawer of his desk and withdrew a calculator. Reading from Efraim's paper, which lay on the desktop, he began punching numbers into the keyboard. Then, he said, "*I make out the total to be $44,400, including the fifty dollars per day for your comfort. This total includes:*

- *$6,400 for the hammer*
- *$9,500 for two vehicles*
- *$19,500 for lodging, food, and comfort*
- *$5,000 for air travel*
- *$3,000 for vehicle and petrol expenses*
- *$2,000 for immigration expenses*
- *$1,000 for gratuities for associates*

Shall we agree on a budget of $45,00? Is that a sufficient sum to punish those who killed our father and the others of our family?"

"And who killed my mother! Yes, Brother agreed!"

"I will transfer that sum to your account tomorrow."

That night, Efraim had a dream. It was one he had on many previous nights. It was after the evening prayer during Ramadan at his father's house in Basra. Many family members were present for Iftar, the ritual breaking of the daily fast. Seated around the table, in addition to his father and his two wives, were several other brothers and sisters, one set of grandparents, uncles, aunts, and half a dozen cousins. A bowl of dates was just passed around the table to commemorate the way the Prophet celebrated Iftar. It was a happy occasion. There was much laughter.

Suddenly, there was a horrendous noise and concussion. Everything and everyone disappeared. There was a great deal of dust. It was difficult to see except now it was morning. The roof of the house was gone; the walls had fallen. He was standing on the doorstep looking in. There were heaps of broken rubble and furniture. He could see half-buried bodies, torn clothes, and blood. There was his cousin, Alema, still beautiful, her face unmarked, staring at the sky through unseeing, teenage eyes. Over there was his uncle, Kadar, recognisable only by the shirt he was wearing.

Behind him, there was a noise—a clanking sound. He recognised it. It was a British Challenger 2 tank. In the dream, he started screaming with rage.

He woke up. He was sweating, and as so many times before, he thought, *"If only my brother and I could have destroyed that tank, like the other two. Then it would not have been able to fire at my father's house. If we had destroyed it, it could not have come looking for us!"*

Efraim arrived two days later in the city where the plan would be executed. There were two tasks he had to complete. First, he had to reconnoitre the site where the cables would be cut, and second, he had to find suitable associates.

To make himself less conspicuous, he had left at home his black, hooded Zaytuna cloak, his keffiyeh, and sandals. Instead, he was wearing jeans, a dark blue Gap sweatshirt and trainers. And like any tourist, he was carrying a knapsack and a camera. The camera was essential, as was the six-metre metal tape measure that he carried in the knapsack.

At the site of the cables, he sat down and seemed to be enjoying the warm spring sunshine and in tune with the tourists who were strolling about. His casual glances about him, however, were to confirm that what he did next would be unobserved. He drew out the measure stopped it, and laid it out near the cables. Then he stood up and moved away. Had anyone said to him, "Don't forget your tape measure there," he would have replied, "It's not mine. Someone must have left it there. Probably a maintenance person."

For the next hour, Efraim took pictures. He moved about, like any tourist, and most of his photographs were of scenic vistas. But some of his pictures were of the cables from various angles. And in several views, the tape measure could be seen. Once during the hour, a pair of police came strolling by. Efraim busied himself, trying to position the camera so as to get the best shot of the main tourist attraction. As the officers walked past him, Efraim gave them a friendly nod.

He had been concerned that some suspicious person would call his activities to the attention of the authorities, he would be arrested, and his photographs would be examined. But no one paid him any attention.

Before leaving the cable site, he decided it was essential that he experience the attraction firsthand. *This way*, he thought, *I'll know what it's like when the charges detonate, the cables snap, and the infidels face their deaths.*

Efraim took a room in a small hotel that had once been a private residence. The carpeting on the stairs to his room on the second floor was worn and frayed. The iron bed frame in his room had a lumpy mattress, and there was only one naked light bulb lighting the room. But the rate was well within his budget. Efraim sat at the scarred pine desk by the window, where the late afternoon light streamed in. From his knapsack, he took out a roll of drafting paper and his drafting tools. Having uploaded the photographs of the cables to his laptop, he studied them carefully. Then he made a sketch of the cable layout. Using his dividers, Efraim measured critical dimensions from the laptop screen by referencing the ruler. He added the dimensions to his sketch, and then he redrew the sketch to scale. By this method, he calculated that the cables were eight centimetres in diameter.

Allah be praised! he mused. *This is well within the capacity of the charges I had planned, and within the capability of the antitank grenades we have used. They could penetrate ten centimetres of armour.*

Having satisfied himself as to the actual arrangement of the cables, he began to sketch out the configuration and dimensions of the shaped charges. Finally, he transferred his sketches to the laptop, tore the hard copies into small pieces, and flushed them down the toilet.

He left the hotel and began to stroll through the neighbourhood in search of a suitable restaurant. A small, family-run Lebanese restaurant offered an interesting menu and was nearly deserted. He ate pickled vegetables, lamb kebab, couscous, and baklava, and he prayed to Allah that he might be permitted to make the plan successful.

As he turned a corner on his way back to the hotel, there was a woman standing on the pavement. She wore a red, sleeveless shirt—the buttons of which were halfway open—and a denim miniskirt. Her naked legs stretched all the way down to the red, ballet slippers she wore. She had a great mane of auburn hair, and her lips were glossy scarlet. *Great Allah in Heaven!* he thought, *What's this?*

She smiled. He slowed his pace. She moved her shoulders so as to display more of the swell of her breasts. "Fancy, a good time?" she asked.

He stopped and gaped at her, unable to comprehend how she could display herself so wantonly.

She smiled again and with her hand, slowly raised the hem of her miniskirt. His eyes were drawn irresistibly to the object of her gesture—a patch of auburn. "Come on, big boy, let's have a good time!" she whispered.

Efram shook his head and backed away. No! No! he stammered. He turned and hurried off. *That infidel woman!* his thoughts raced, *Spawn of Satan, trying to tempt me! Showing me her . . . her privates! May Allah cast her into the fires of hell!*

Nonetheless, Efraim found it difficult to banish her images, which seemed to be burned into his memory.

Efraim had to identify two suitable associates. Their roles were important but not vital. They would drive the vehicle away from the scene of devastation. They would impede anyone who tried to interfere with Efraim during the critical moments when he placed the charges, and they would follow his instructions. Not difficult, but they had to believe in the cause enough to die for it. In short, they had to have the commitment of suicide bombers.

Efraim had the names of five men who had corresponded by e-mail with a certain radical cleric. They had expressed a desire to fight for Allah's cause. Three had been eager to go to a training camp in Pakistan. One said he had served in the army and was proficient in the use of arms. The fact that all five wrote in passable Arabic meant that they could read Arabic, and their knowledge of the Holy Qur'an appeared to be above average. Of the five, three were Pakistani, one was Yemeni and the fifth was Somali. Efraim was slightly put off by the fact that the three who were willing to undergo training in Pakistan were also from Pakistani families. Did that mean that they saw the training trip as an opportunity to connect with family and friends in the country? Efraim also wondered about the Somali and the Yemeni who had not volunteered for training. Was it because they didn't speak Pashto? Efraim would have to investigate these points, not because he regarded the training as essential for his associates, but because willingness to undergo the training indicated a valuable level of commitment.

To meet these five men, Efraim had to travel to several other cities. While he had mobile phone numbers and addresses, he preferred to meet them at their local mosque. *If I cannot find them at their mosque, they are not true Muslims and are unworthy to serve Allah in this great cause*, he reasoned.

At each mosque, he would inquire of the imam about the prospect. He would tell the imam that he was the distant relative of the individual and that it had been suggested that he should approach the prospect about a good job that had opened within his organisation. What did the imam know about this fellow? In all but one case (a Pakistani), the imam knew the prospect. In two cases, the prospect was considered to be a good Muslim, and in the other two cases (a Pakistani and the Yemeni) they were considered to be a bit radical.

Efraim then set about the task of meeting the four prospects. He would call using a pay-as-you-go SIM card, which he had bought at a local market from a trader who shrugged when Efraim told him he had left his driver's license at home. The phone could only be traced to a Mohammed Ali—whoever he was.

The conversation with the prospect would begin in Arabic, but in all cases except the Yemeni, it became necessary to switch to English because of a lack of comfort with spoken Arabic. Efraim would introduce himself as Mohammed, and he would tell the prospect that he had been contacted by the distant imam with whom the prospect had had Internet discussions. Efraim would explain that there was an extremely important project of faith, and would the prospect be interested?

The Yemeni, whose name was Ameen Kamali, said, "*Yes, sir, by all means. Can you tell me more?*"

Efraim said, "*I cannot be precise at this time, but this is a project which will change the course of history. It is a project that will please and glorify Allah, and it will greatly elevate the status of the Muslim faith.*"

Ameen considered this briefly; he nodded his head in approval.

Efraim continued, *"Can you tell me why you did not express interest in military training?"*

"As I understand it, sir, in the camps in Pakistan, Arabs are not looked on with favour. Our language is not spoken much, and we are regarded as lower caste. But, if it is necessary, sir, for the success of the project, I will go."

Efraim shook his head. *"It is not, strictly speaking, necessary."*

"And, can you tell me, sir? Am I asked to give my life for this project?"

"Yes, and you will be among the sacred martyrs who have eternal life in the verdant garden of Heaven."

Again, Ameen nodded. *"When will this be, sir?"*

"It will be in about three months' time, Allah-willing."

"I will be ready for it, sir!"

"Very good, Ameen! I will contact you again in about two months' time. Now let us worship Allah."

Together, they knelt and touched their heads to the floor as Efraim recited the first seven verses of the Qur'an.

After meeting all four prospects, Efraim decided that the best were Ameen and one of the Pakistanis named Bashshar. He would keep in reserve the Somali named Hamzah in case either Ameen or Bashshar got cold feet. Efraim resolved that the best way to test for cold feet was to give each of them a suicide vest to try on. Before his next visit to the country, he would have several made up. They would have to look and feel like the real thing.

* * *

Efraim was now in Quetta. He had flown to Islamabad and then taken an internal flight to Quetta. It was here that he hoped to find a source of RDX, the high explosive he needed. Quetta, in the Pashtun region of Pakistan and close to the Afghanistan border, was recognised as a Taliban stronghold—not for fighting, but for logistics. If anyone needed hard currency and would have high explosives, it would likely be the Taliban.

Efraim found a small rooming house on Najiab Street near the Liaquat Bazar. A Rasheed Khan ran the house. The old wood floors were clean but undulating, his bed had a permanently sag, and Efraim had to close his window shutters to block out some of the street noise from below. Nonetheless, he was satisfied. Efraim could blend in amongst thousands of people in the area, and his instincts told him that there would be sources of vital information in and around the bazaar. Besides, just around the corner on Masjid Road, there was Komelion restaurant that served excellent aloo gosht, a native spicy stew of mutton and potatoes.

Efraim knew that the local language would be a problem; he knew no Pashto—though perhaps he might recognise the odd word. Urdu and English were the official languages of Pakistan though few people spoke Urdu in Quetta and Urdu was foreign to Efraim. So English it would have to be. But only a few Taliban spoke English, and those who did would almost certainly view an outsider speaking English with suspicion. Efraim had considered finding an associate who could speak English and Pashto. However, the associate would have to be fully trustworthy in an environment where trust was not granted unless it was earned. Besides, an interpreter just added complexity to the communication process.

So on his first evening in Quetta, Efraim sauntered through the bazaar, paying particular attention to the many fresh fruit stalls, but on the lookout, all the while, for places where men were meeting. As he ambled along the Jinnah Road, there was a place that caught his eye on the other side of the road.

Unlike most cafes, which were one stall wide—about three metres—this one was three-stalls wide, and since the shutters were rolled up, he could see inside. There were tables and chairs, but it was not a restaurant. No food was being served. Men—only men—were seated at the tables, but they were not just passing time drinking coffee or tea. They appeared to be playing games.

Efraim crossed the road and strolled slowly past, looking in. Some men were playing cards, some were playing a game with dominoes, and others were engaged in a board game like backgammon. There were loud exclamations as the games progressed, and the air was filled with heavy cigarette smoke. There was no money in evidence on any table; the Qur'an forbids gambling, but the players were clearly enjoying their games. Efraim entered and stood near a table of five card players. He listened but understood nothing except that one man—who was apparently winning was the butt of good-natured jokes from the other four.

There was a man at Efraim's elbow who had said something to him. "I'm sorry," Efraim replied in English, "I don't speak Pashto."

"Where are you from then?" the man asked in accented English. The man was tall and thin, dressed in jeans and a dark green windbreaker. His face was creased and leathery with a large bent nose and a crooked, self-deprecating smile. He had several days' growth of beard, and a tousle of black hair spilled out from under a New York Yankees baseball cap.

"I am from a country to the west of here," Efraim replied.

"Are you in Quetta on business?" the man inquired.

"Yes, but mine is not an ordinary business." Efraim made a show of looking around the room.

"You are here to meet someone," the man said.

"Yes, but I do not see him here."

"What is this man's name?"

"He did not tell me his name—only that he is associated with the Taliban."

"Ah, the Taliban. Are you for them or against them?" The man studied Efraim through narrowed eyes.

Efraim took out his passport, and showed it to the man.

"Probably you have an American passport as well," the man suggested.

For a moment, Efraim did not reply. Then slamming his right fist into the palm of his left hand, he exclaimed, rather loudly, "May Allah transport America and the British to Hell!"

The conversation ceased in the room, and many of the players turned to see who had made this declaration. Efraim's companion made a dismissive gesture to the room, and turning to Efraim, he suggested ingratiatingly, "There is a vacant table, there in the back. Perhaps I can help you."

They were seated at the table, and a morose waiter brought them two cups of very strong black tea. "So," the man continued, "You would like to meet with the Taliban?"

Efraim nodded.

"I arrange a meeting, but I need to know the subject matter. That is so that the right person or persons can be invited to attend."

"I am working—by the grace of Almighty Allah—on a project which will destroy the spirit of the British people."

The man leaned forward; his eyes were locked on Efraim's eyes. "I think the Taliban will find your project very interesting. They certainly like to understand the role they will be asked to play."

"They will act as my supplier of a key ingredient."

"And you are prepared to purchase this ingredient from them?"

"Yes, in hard currency."

The man nodded and smiled knowingly. "You have need of special explosive materials."

Eraim said nothing; the man nodded again. He looked at his watch. "May I suggest," he said, "that we meet tomorrow at the Zehri mosque just after the fajr (dawn) prayer. The mosque is just three hundred metres down the road (he gestured). And in the meantime, might I see a sample of this hard currency?"

From his pocket, Efraim removed a roll of U.S. currency. He selected a twenty-dollar bill and gave it to the man, who stared covetously at the roll of bank notes. Then the man turned, and left.

Before returning to his hostel that evening, Efraim purchased another pay-as-you-go SIM card in the souq. He did not want to cause confusion in the minds of his contacts in Quetta by using a mobile phone with a 44 (UK) country code. This SIM card had a Pakistani 92 country code.

Efraim switched off the alarm on his mobile phone. It was 5:20. Dawn prayers would be at 5:45, and he wanted to be in the mosque for the prayers. He suspected that the meeting time and place were a sort of test. If he were not committed to jihad in the name of Allah, he would not show up until after prayers. .

As he moved toward the doors of the mosque with the small company of men who had prayed with him, he saw his contact of the previous evening nod to him. Efraim fell into step with the man as he walked down Jinnah Road. Two other men were following just behind them. No words were spoken. The sun had just risen, and it cast great shadows across the dusty road. To the west, above the long parade of shops topped by living quarters, rose the mountains, tan and rocky, devoid of vegetation. Efraim's intermediary stopped, rapped on a closed shutter, and called for something is Pashto. Moments later the shutter opened with a clatter, and they stepped into an unlit café. There was more conversation between the intermediary and the café proprietor. A neon light was lit; the four of them sat at a table.

"These two gentlemen," the intermediary began, "have the connections you are seeking. Perhaps you tell them about your project."

Efraim looked at the two newcomers, neither of whom could conceivably pass for a gentleman. Both looked more like farmers with black turbans than soldiers or businessmen. The man on Efraim's right was in his early fifties with a terrible burn scar on the left side of his face. His eyes glittered, but his lips were twisted with hostility. The man on Efraim's left was twenty years younger than his associate, with eyes as black as his full beard. His demeanour seemed to suggest curiosity.

"The project involves a great act of jihad, and for that I require a special ingredient," Efraim explained. The intermediary translated this statement into Pashto and acted as interpreter during the conversations that followed.

Scarface asked, "What kind of explosive device do you require?"

"What I require is four kilograms of RDX."

The bearded one asked, "Don't you require some type of explosive device?"

"No. Just the explosive."

"What are you willing to pay for this explosive?" Scarface inquired.

"What are you willing to sell it for?"

"$10,000 in U.S. currency," Scarface replied.

Efraim gave a derisive snort and pushed his chair back. "I'm not looking for plutonium. I'm looking for RDX." He stood up, ready to leave.

"Wait! Wait!" the intermediary urged. There followed ten minutes of loud, emotional haggling at the end of which a price of $395 per kilo was agreed.

"We will meet you in Kandahar tomorrow afternoon," Scarface announced. He and the Bearded One stood up and left.

Efraim and the intermediary remained seated at the table considering each other. Slowly Efraim shook his head.

The intermediary gave a slight shrug. "They may not have what you want, but it is worthwhile to cross the border and see."

"What's your commission on this deal?" Efraim inquired.

"Five percent."

"Only five?"

The intermediary shrugged again. "It is nothing if deal not go through."

"It's also nothing it they decide not to pay you."

The intermediary glanced sourly around the deserted café, then back at Efraim.

"Any other leads?" Efraim asked; from his pocket, he removed a fifty-dollar bill and handed it to the intermediary, who could not disguise his surprise and delight.

"Yes," he said, after a few moments consideration, "There is a certain man I know of, who it is said, is expert in the employment of explosives."

"What nationality is this man?"

"He is not Afghan or Pakistani. He is from north—maybe from state in former Soviet Union."

"Does he speak English or Arabic?"

"Arabic, I don't know. He speak English."

"Well," Efraim said, "You know what I want. You talk to this man. If he is <u>quite sure</u> he can deliver the goods to me, bring me his mobile phone number, and there is another hundred for you . . . You're going to take me to the border tomorrow, right?"

"Yes, OK."

"We can talk about this man tomorrow, but just remember one thing. I don't like people who mess around with me."

Efraim had two important items of business to complete before crossing into Afghanistan. He had seen the stalls he wanted to visit the previous day during his exploration of the Quetta markets. There were five or six of them all clustered at the northern end of the market in what was also an impoverished residential area.

As he approached the first of these shops, he saw that there were quite a few customers looking at the merchandise. But as he got closer, he could see that the customers were mostly teenaged boys who wanted to make a purchase but had no money. They came to look and to handle the goods if the trader would permit it, which he did not. Efraim pushed his way to the front, and when the trader recognised a real customer, he shouted at the boys, who retreated to a respectful distance. There were plenty of AK47's, some apparently new and others in various conditions of prior use. There were even two RPG, rocket-propelled grenade launchers lying beside an open box of grenades. At the lower end of the likely price range was an assortment of locally manufactured rifles. What Efraim wanted, however, was a handgun; there were at least a dozen different models on display.

When Efraim picked up a Luger 9 mm to examine it, the trader asked a question.

"I want a small, light-weight gun. At least 9 mm," Efraim replied.

"You want revolver or semi-automatic?"

Efraim's Eye

"I want a semi-automatic."

There was a discussion of the pros, cons and prices of the various semi-automatics on display.

"I'll be back."

Anxious not to lose a sale to a competitor, the trader held up a CZ-75. "I make special price."

Efraim examined the weapon, a Czech-made .40-calibre weapon. "How much? I have U.S. dollars."

The trader consulted a small, battered calculator. "For you, $450."

"I'll be back."

"I can sell for $410! Best price!" the trader shouted at Efraim's retreating figure.

Efraim visited several stalls. He decided that he didn't trust the Czech-made weapon. He wanted a Smith & Wesson. Finally, after much haggling, he bought a Smith & Wesson .45 semi-automatic Chief's Special for $490. It was small and almost certainly had been used. Before making his purchase, he insisted that the trader prove the weapon's functionality by rapidly firing three rounds. With the purchase, he obtained twenty-five rounds of ammunition.

The second item of business was more personal. *"My brother spoke of my comfort,"* he reminded himself. *"I need some comfort, and I know where it can be found."* He took a small, three-wheeled motor taxi into the southern part of the city and into Landi Pashton Abed. Once there, he walked along Ismail Colony Street #3, which was at first glance like other commercial streets in an extremely poor area: rows of stalls on either side—some with colourful items of clothing hanging from an overhead metal structure—and a disorderly web of black electric cables crossing above in every direction. But if one looked more closely, it seemed that some of the stalls were living quarters. Efraim was most interested in those that resembled living spaces—except that none of these spaces showed any evidence of food preparation. Another strange thing was that there were a few men in evidence on Ismail Colony Street #3.

There were plenty of taxi drivers dozing in their seats, and there were a few men chatting to the many women who were waiting patiently outside their stalls. Some of the women were in their early teens, some in their sixties, but most were in their twenties, thirties and forties. They were dressed in jeans and bright-hued, embroidered tops, or saris in many colours. Efraim had not yet spoken to any of the women; instead he had reviewed the women up one side of the street and down the other side. There was one woman in a blue and silver sari who had caught his attention—not by waving or calling to him, but by her smouldering gaze from just inside a shop. She was about thirty-five, he guessed, buxom, with long, jet black hair that spilled out from under a matching blue kerchief. Her broad face was not unpleasant. She had large, black eyebrows, slightly crooked nose and full, crimson mouth.

"How much?" he asked her.

She responded with a question, the nature of which he guessed.

"Just ordinary," he said.

One of the women standing nearby explained what he had said, and the woman in blue responded. When Efraim clearly didn't understand, the woman nearby said, "Thousand rupees."

That's about ten dollars, Efraim thought. *I'll offer her half.* He retrieved a five-dollar bill from his pocket and offered it to her. She shook her head. There was evidently some thing in Efraim's manner she didn't like. He handed the woman in blue a ten-dollar bill. She took it and turned inside. Efraim followed her to the back of the stall, past a heavy, bearded man who was sleeping in a chair leaning against a post. She drew a curtain behind them and began to unwind her sari. Efraim removed his T-shirt, jeans, underpants and trainers. She turned to face him, still wearing her tight-fitting beige shirt and brassiere, but naked from the waist down, the swell of her belly and the dense black thatch at her groin were now exposed.

"Take off your shirt!" he ordered, and he moved to help her remove it.

"No! No!" she shouted, backing away. "No! No!" and she continued shouting.

The curtain was suddenly drawn aside. The sleeping man filled the doorway. "Five dollars take off shirt," he announced.

Efraim began to protest.

"You go!" the man said, pointing toward the street.

There was no chance of getting his ten dollars back. *For five dollars more, I can have what I want*, Efraim reasoned. He reached into his jeans, and from the wad of currency, he removed a five-dollar bill and handed it to the woman. The man disappeared, closing the curtain behind him.

The woman removed her shirt and brassiere, and lay down on a grubby towel that covered the single mattress. Efraim dropped down beside her and reached out to grasp her large breasts. They felt firm and swollen. As he kneaded them, his hand was suddenly wet. *Oh, Satan!* he thought. *Five dollars extra for this! It is disgusting!*

"Get up!" he ordered the woman. She was confused. "Like this!" he demonstrated, and eventually with exhortations and prodding, she was positioned on all fours on the mattress. He knelt behind her and began his business, which did not take long. With a growl of satisfaction, he collapsed onto the floor at the foot of the mattress.

The sudden grating of a chair in the room caught Efraim's attention. He turned and saw the sleeping man rummaging in his jeans. Efraim sprang on him. The force of his impact carried them both to the floor. The man had a knife in one hand, and he slashed at Efraim with it. Enraged, and ignoring the wound on his arm, with one hand Efraim seized the man's knife arm, and with the other, he crushed the man's crotch. The man screamed and involuntarily dropped the knife. With both hands, Efraim took hold of the man's head and began pounding it against the floor. There was a shout from the woman. Efraim released the man's limp body and turned to face her. She was standing two paces away, looking warily at him and still naked with her chest and belly wet. The knife was raised in her right hand.

Efraim considered the situation. "I'll leave you alone, if you leave me alone," he said. She apparently understood because she made no move—only watched him as he found the roll of bills still in his jeans. Cautiously, he eyed her as he pulled on his clothes and left.

Why do I have this obsession with women? Efraim wondered. *With their privates? The obsession grows and grows until I discharge into their privates. The Hadith of the Prophet warns that only married men may discharge into their wives. Surely in this respect, I am an evil-doer. May Allah have mercy on me! I pray that when Allah weighs my soul, He finds that my fornication is outweighed by my destruction of the infidels!*

The next morning, the intermediary met Efraim at the gaming café. They greeted each other with the traditional Muslim embrace. The intermediary said, "We drive to the border at Chaman. You pay driver. Cross border. Get another driver to Kandahar. Meet with Taliban. I go as far as Chaman. We talk now."

They approached a battered and dusty old Ford Focus. The driver was a lanky young man with an unruly mop of black hair, which was forever falling over his eyes. He moved slowly and deliberately, eyeing Efraim with suspicion. "How much to Chaman?" Efraim inquired.

"$120," the driver replied.

"Too much!"

The intermediary intervened: "The price is fair. About two-hour drive. All drivers charge $120 to Chaman."

Reluctantly, Efraim paid the driver and seated himself on the rear seat. It was not comfortable; there seemed to be a major gap in the seat upholstery.

The car left Quetta and picked up the N25 northbound near Jinnah Town. The N25 was a wide, gently curving, well-paved road with some stone guardrails. It wound through the low, worn-out foothills of the Sulaiman Mountains, and then began to turn northwest toward the border and the Bolan Pass. The car windows were covered with dust, so that it was difficult to view the landscape, which was unremitting rocky ochre, devoid of any but the hardiest vegetation. On the peaks, there were still vestiges of snow.

Efraim turned to the intermediary. "Have you made contact with the explosives expert?"

"Yes. He ready to talk to you."

"OK. Let me have his number."

The intermediary offered an ingratiating smile. "First, there is gratuity," he said.

"No. First, the expert says he can provide the ingredient, and then there is the gratuity. I told you. I won't be messed around!"

"When we get to Chaman you can call him. There's reception there. But I tell you—the price higher than Taliban."

"Why?" Efraim demanded.

"This man say Taliban product no good. Is not real RDX. He say he personally have to go and get good product."

"What is the source of his product?"

The intermediary shrugged and shook his head.

The car stopped near a makeshift canteen. The view to the west from the Bolan Pass seemed to take in all of Afghanistan: a brown plain with patches of green stretching to the far horizon. It was windy and cold.

The intermediary handed Efraim a small slip of paper. "Here is number. You call man now." Efraim checked that his mobile phone had reception; then he dialed."

A man answered unintelligibly.

"My name is Mohammed," Efraim said, "I am here with someone you have been speaking with. You told him you could obtain a certain ingredient I require."

"Yes."

"Do you understand what I require?"

"Yes, but we need to talk further about your exact requirements. I am sure it is not just three letters." Efraim paused to consider. "Besides," the man continued, "the CIA is probably listening to us. Aren't you fellows?"

"Where do you propose we meet?"

"I will meet you in Tbilisi the day after tomorrow."

"How will I find you?"

"If you are there, I will find you." The line went dead.

Efraim looked at the intermediary, thinking, *If I don't pay him the $100, he'll probably re-contact the fellow I've just been speaking to. If that happens, I won't have a contact in Tbilisi.*

Efraim paid the intermediary, put a ten-dollar bill in his passport, and walked to the border, his knapsack slung over one shoulder. On the Pakistan side, the uniformed agent took the passport and discretely removed the ten-dollar bill. He looked Efraim up and down, then, wordlessly waived him through.

For the Afghan side, Efraim inserted a twenty-dollar bill into his passport. The agent there was a surly-looking man in a grey turban. He studied Efraim's passport, having removed his gratuity, and compared it against a long list of people on a clipboard. Finding no matches, he asked, "Business?"

"I am an importer. I wish to speak to an exporter in Kandahar."

"What product?"

"Fruit."

The agent shrugged and waived him through.

At the low, brown stone café on the Afghan side, Efraim ordered a shami kabob (ground meat mixed with egg and spices, deep fried as a pancake), with bolani (Afghan bread). He waited to be approached by a driver; he did not have to wait long. Before his food arrived, a shabbily-dressed man in his late fifties with a pointed grey beard shambled up to where Efraim was sitting. "You go Kandahar?" he asked.

Efraim nodded.

"I take."

"How much?"

"$200."

Efraim shook his head. "Too much."

Aware, perhaps of his competitors crowding in behind him, the driver suggested, "$150. No one less. Is two hours."

"OK. I will come soon."

When Efraim had finished his meal, (the shami kabob was overcooked) he gave the driver a scrap of paper with the address of his meeting with the Taliban. The driver studied the paper, looked at Efraim with a frown, but he said nothing.

Down the west side of the Bolan Pass they sped, tires squealing on the hairpin turns. There were places on the outside of turns where there was a precipitate drop into the valley below, and where the protective wall had either been knocked down by a careless (and now almost certainly deceased) driver or had never been built. Efraim put an arm into the front seat and signaled to the driver to go more slowly, but the order seemed to have little effect. *I suppose he drives this road every day*, Efraim thought. *May Allah protect me!*

The A76 from Chaman to Kandahar, through Spin Boldak and Khodaydad Kalay, was another good road through more low barren foothills. At Thakheh Pol, they crossed a flood plain where a chalky river brought water down from the mountains. And at the outskirts of Kandahar, fruit orchards, flowering pink or white, and brown mud houses began to appear. The driver consulted a map and stopped outside what looked like a small warehouse, with corroded, corrugated iron walls.

"Is here," the driver said, indicating a door at the edge of the building.

"You wait!" Efraim told the driver. Was it his intuition? Was it the appearance of the building? Was it comments made by the intermediary and Tbilisi man? Efraim didn't know. He just felt that he might not be here very long. The driver shook his head. Efraim said, "I might have to go back to Chaman." At the sound of the word, Chaman, the driver's resistance ceased; it was seldom he had a round trip to Chaman in one day.

Efraim approached the door of the building, surveying its setting. There were other similar buildings nearby. No residential buildings or human activity was visible. No dogs, no cars, just the black top street, the expanses of brown earth with clumps of weeds and a few desolate trees.

Efraim tried the door. It was open. Inside, the building was dark, cool and hollow. By way of announcing himself, Efraim slammed the door. There was a voice somewhere in the recesses. Several fluorescent lights flickered on. A door opened in the rear of the building, and the Bearded One from the previous day was standing in the lighted doorway.

"Hallo!" Efraim shouted.

"Come!" the Bearded One called with a sweeping gesture.

As Efraim approached the doorway, the Bearded One stepped aside, allowing Efraim to see inside the small office. Scarface was standing behind a table. On the table was a large cardboard box, the top of which was closed. There was another table on the left-hand side of the otherwise bare room. The Bearded One stood in front of the left-hand table.

"Money? You have?" Scarface asked, placing his hands on top of the box in a possessive gesture.

"Yes. Let me see the explosive," Efraim demanded.

"First, see money," Scarface replied, with a feral smile. The smile rang alarm bells in Efraim's head. He stepped slightly to his right so as to see the Bearded One as well as Scar Face. The Bearded One was reaching for something behind him; then he was holding an AK47. "See money!" he said.

So that's your game, Efraim thought. Aloud, he said, "OK," and he dropped to one knee, simultaneously swinging the knapsack from his back. He put on a nervous smile. "OK," he said repeatedly and opened the knapsack. He reached inside, glancing anxiously from Scarface to the Bearded One. The first shot, fired from inside the knapsack, hit the Bearded One in his left shoulder with such force that it flung him back against the table. The Chief's Special was out of the knapsack and leveled at Scarface, who had turned and was reaching for something. He had just grasped the barrel of another AK47 when Efraim's second shot struck him in the centre of his back, hurling him against the wall. The Bearded One was struggling to regain his balance and to aim his weapon toward Efraim. The Chief's Special was held at arm's length with deliberate aim. The bullet struck the Bearded One just above his mouth, causing his head to jerk violently backwards; his body slumped to the floor. Efraim walked around the table to where Scarface was lying. His right arm was convulsing, as if reaching out for something. Efraim shot him through the centre of his black turban.

Rapidly, Efraim tore open the box. It was half full of sand. He turned to look at the two Taliban. They lay, face down, in slowly creeping pools of blood.

Efraim snatched up his knapsack and hurried out of the building. He pulled open the door of the taxi, climbed quickly inside and slammed the door. "Kabul airport!" he announced to the driver.

The driver raised his hands from the wheel in a gesture of surrender. "No, sir, I cannot!" And he began to whimper.

Efraim reached for his wad of currency, and, drawing out two one-hundred dollar bills, he placed them on the seat next to the driver. "Three more when we arrive. $500 total," he said.

The driver stopped whimpering. He picked up the bills and fondled them distractedly. He had heard the shots. At least one Taliban was dead. This man was dangerous. Probably CIA. The road to Kabul had checkpoints, but no Taliban control. This CIA man would certainly get through the checkpoints. He was willing to pay $500. If he drove to Kabul, the driver would make over $600 in one day. He had never made so much. His wife would be very happy. He nodded slowly, put the car into gear and began to drive away.

"Faster!" Efraim demanded. The driver complied.

Asian Highway 1, built by India, from Kandahar to Kabul was in good condition; it ran for nearly 600 straight kilometres, mostly through river valleys. The valleys were pink and white with flowering fruit and almond trees. Here and there, a farmer and his bullock were ploughing for the spring planting.

Just outside of Kandahar, they encountered an American military checkpoint. The driver stopped alongside a soldier who had an M16 semi-automatic rifle slung over one shoulder. The driver showed his license, but the soldier was clearly not interested in the driver. Efraim rolled down his window, said hello to the soldier and held out his passport. The soldier examined the passport, compared the photo to the face and asked in Pashto, "What is your business?"

Guessing the question, Efraim replied, "I am a fruit exporter. I came to Kandahar to speak with several of my producers about quantities for the autumn."

The young soldier was clearly non-plussed to be addressed in good English by someone who understood Pashto and who came from a country where Arabic was the language. He waived the taxi through.

At nightfall, there was another checkpoint outside of Kabul. Afghan soldiers and police manned this one, and it fell to the driver to translate questions and responses for Efraim. A twenty-dollar bill tucked into Efraim's passport was sourly received, and they were waived through.

On the outskirts of Kabul, Efraim had the driver stop at a bazaar where he bought a small suitcase and some additional clothing. (His suitcase and his clothing were still at the hotel in Quetta. His laptop was in his knapsack with the Chief's Special, which he wrapped in a new sweatshirt and put in the locked suitcase. He was not expecting that his checked suitcase would be x-rayed or examined on the way to Tbilisi.)

There was an Aerolyon flight departing Kabul at 11:50 p.m. for Dubai and an Airzena Georgian flight direct to Tbilisi departing Dubai at 6:10 a.m. *Not much sleep,* Efraim thought, *but at least it gets me there.* He bought his ticket, checked the suitcase, and rather than eat anything at the grubby corner snack bar, he decided to wait for whatever Aerolyon had to offer.

Chapter 2

INITIATION

The Ceremonial Sergeant, dressed in his long red robe, rapped his staff of office on the floor of Monument Hall. He shouted out, "Pray, silence for the Leader!"

The procession into the center of the hall began, led by the Sergeant, then the Leader, followed by the four vice presidents, in order of seniority, with the Administrator of the Charitable Consultants LLP at the end.

God, this is positively medieval! Paul Winthorpe mused, smiling secretly to himself. *Here, in this ancient hall, in the twenty-first century, these men—who do the same work I do—dress up in long red robes and black, floppy hats, put on an elaborate ceremony to add me as one of their members!*

The Leader, a handsome man with a full grey beard, called out, "Pray, Administrator, have you candidates for membership?"

The Administrator, alone among his red-robed colleagues, was robed in black and wearing a soft, black, Tudor bonnet and an elaborate silver chain of office. Nervously, he consulted his notes. "Yes, Leader Robert, there is Paul Winthorpe here who presents himself for membership in Charitable Consultants."

The Leader turned to face the Administrator. "Has this Paul Winthorpe been examined by the vice presidents?"

"Yes, Leader Robert, he has been examined by two vice presidents, and he has been recommended by three members of long standing. He has been practicing for thirty-four years, is a Certified Management Consultant, and a member of the Wimbledon Group of Management Consultants."

"Employment?" the Leader enquired.

"Mr. Winthorpe has been a sole practitioner for nine years. Prior to that, he was a consultant with Boston Consulting and Accenture."

The Leaderer turned to face Paul, who was standing at the front of the crowd of spectators, all of whom were dressed for a business meeting. Furtively, the Administrator motioned for Paul to step forward toward the Leader.

"Paul Winthorpe, do you wish to become a member, in good standing, of Charitable Consultants LLP?" the Leader asked.

"Yes, Leader Robert, I do."

"Then raise your right hand and say the oath."

Paul drew a card from the pocket of his suit and began to read is a loud, clear voice. He concluded, ". . . and will be at all times a loyal servant of Her Majesty, the Queen, so help me God!"

The Leader stepped forward and shook Paul's hand. "Welcome, Paul," he beamed; his air of formality had dissolved into warmth.

"Thank you, Robert. I very much look forward to it."

The Leader smiled and moved away, to be replaced by Rob Duval, who had initially proposed Paul for membership in the Charitable Consultants. Rob, wearing his infectious grin, was carrying two flutes of champagne, one of which he thrust at Paul. "Cheers! Congratulations and well done!" he burbled. "Now drink up, and I'll introduce you to some important people." Rob took a long pull at his champagne and surveyed the crowd.

"Who's that lady over there?" Paul asked, gesturing with a nod of his head toward a petite, silver-haired woman who was dressed in a fitted navy suit and a gold silk scarf. Her animated conversation with two male members had caught Paul's attention.

"Oh, that's Geraldine Paley. She's a member." Rob observed Geraldine's expansive gestures for a moment. "She is very friendly," he added. Then with a glance at Paul, he added, "But not that friendly. I think her husband works for a bank here in the City, so she has great connections in financial services."

"OK. I'd like to meet her."

"Later. I've got to get you set up with some charity work." Gripping Paul's arm, Rob threaded his way toward a man in a double-breasted blazer, who was stooped over slightly, listening to what another person was saying. "Charlie," Rob interrupted, "I'd like you to meet Paul Winthorpe. Paul, this is Charlie Brighton, who takes care of our charity practice."

Charlie Brighton, the man in the blazer, held up a finger, and said to the portly, red-complexioned man who had been speaking to him, "Duty calls, Edward. I'll catch up with you later." Then, he turned toward Paul, "Welcome on board, Paul! You've joined a splendid organisation. We've got some of the best consultants working in London. If you're a networker, this is the place to be. And we're far and away the largest supplier of pro-bono consultants to London charities."

Paul nodded. "That's one of the reasons I joined Charitable Consultants. My practice is in financial management—software, systems, and procedures—but I can afford to take a little less paid work. And I think it's about time I put something—apart from my taxes—back."

"OK." Charlie stroked his neck thoughtfully. His square-jawed face with its large dark eyes looked to be about late sixties, but his black hair had no trace of grey. "We expect to provide a million pounds worth of consultancy—about a thousand days—to charities. They just have to pay the travel expenses for our members. We try to keep assignments short—no more than seven days—so we don't end up running the charity. Right now, we've got a requirement to take on multiple assignments for Global Youth Enterprise. Would you be interested?"

Paul nodded. "In principle, yes. What is it?"

"GYE is a charity founded by the Duke of Suffolk. It provides low cost loans to young entrepreneurs who have a great business idea but who can't raise the finances required to get started. To reduce the risk of failure, they also set each funded entrepreneur up with an experienced, pro-bono, business mentor. It's worked very well here in England. There are several thousand flourishing entrepreneurs here, and they're expanding the concept around the world, with chapters in individual countries."

Again, Paul nodded. "Sounds interesting. Would I be a mentor?"

"No," Charlie Brighton shook his head, "You'd be an assessor. About every three years, GYE re-accredits each of the overseas chapters to make sure they're still doing things the GYE way. The point is that while each chapter is allowed some flexibility to fit in with the local culture, it's important that acceptable standards be maintained. Otherwise, the development banks, governments and businesses which give or lend money to GYE would stop giving and lending."

"So," Paul said, "I would be assessing a chapter for compliance with the accreditation standards?"

Charlie nodded.

"OK. Where do I go, and when do I start?"

Charlie smiled and shook his head. "You're a tough sell!" he said. "If you don't mind, I'll give your contact details to GYE. They'll set up a meeting with you, and together, you can decide on where and when."

"That's fine, Charlie. Thank you."

"Thank you!"

Paul turned to find that Rob had disappeared. He saw several faces he recognised: other Wimbledon Group members who, like Paul, were senior consultants and sole practitioners or members of small practices. But Paul was determined to make the most of the opportunity to meet new people. *I'll look for that Geraldine Paley,* he decided. *She's quite decorative, probably interesting and maybe useful. But first, some more champagne and something to eat!*

A waiter with a bottle wrapped in a white napkin filled the first requirement, and a young, Latin-looking waitress with a tray of canapés filled the second. Before she got away, Paul had taken three, stuffed choux pastries: one with salmon and chives, one with prawns and one with Parma ham.

OK. Now where did she get to? he wondered. Then he spotted her across the hall, talking to three men. Paul made his way over to the group and listened to the conversation, sipping his champagne. They were discussing a particular client—unnamed from what Paul heard—whom one of the men characterised as an absolute disaster. The son-of-a-bitch—pardon my French, Geraldine—is late paying my bills, and he almost never does what I recommend!

"I had a client like that once," someone else put in. "So I decided to recommend something ridiculous to him. I said to him, 'John, here's what I think you ought to do,' and I outlined the ridiculous solution to him. Then I said, 'You might be tempted to try such-and-such' (which was my preferred solution), 'but I feel sure you can't make it work.' Damned if the bugger didn't go for the such-and-such solution, which worked like a charm. To keep his business, I had to remind him later that I had recommended two possible solutions, one of which was such-and-such, which was more difficult, but owing to his outstanding talents as a leader he had made it work!"

There was general laughter. Geraldine turned to face Paul. She had hazel eyes, arched eyebrows, and glistening rose lips. She looked a good ten years younger than her fifty-five years. Paul shook her extended hand. "Hello, I'm Paul Winthorpe."

"Yes, I know", she said, "You're the reason for this little soiree tonight. I'm Geraldine Paley." She cocked her head to one side. "Tell me. What does Paul Winthorpe do when he's at work?"

Paul gave her the smile he reserved for special ladies. "He does absolutely splendid financial systems work for eternally grateful clients."

She raised an eyebrow and a teasing smile was beginning to play on her mouth. "Does he then?" she inquired. "And might Geraldine know any of these eternally grateful clients?"

"Undoubtedly she does!" Paul responded. "They would include Black Horse Bank, Swiss Insurance, and Securities Investments."

"Oh, I see," she said, suddenly pensive. "And what might Paul's greatest challenge have been with his eternally grateful clients?"

Paul thought for a moment; he too was serious. The three chatty men had wandered off. "I suppose it would have been Midlands Merchant Bank. They had put in a bespoke software system, which was forever crashing, and they couldn't get the reports they wanted from it. I was asked to come in and patch it up. It was hopeless. I told them they ought to scrap it and go to a shrink-wrapped system, like CometStar. I thought they'd never agree to abandon what they had, but they surprised me. They asked me to make it happen. I did, but it took me nearly a year, and it was not a fun year. I can tell you. I know they're running on CometStar now, and it's not perfect, but it's a hell of a lot better than the real mess they were in before I arrived."

Geraldine considered Paul thoughtfully. "Are you busy at the moment?"

Paul shrugged. "I'm just tidying up some odds and ends for clients, but I could do with some more work."

Geraldine nodded. She said: "You done any work for Smith Coleridge?"

Paul shook his head. "No, Geraldine, I haven't, but I've done some work for the other big trading houses, so I understand their business."

Geraldine's eyes narrowed and her lips parted; Paul felt a surge of desire. *Not that friendly!* he recalled, *Maybe she just enjoys the effect she has on men. Relax, Paul!* He focused his gaze over her right shoulder.

"I understand," Geraldine began coquettishly, "that Smith Coleridge has some serious problems with their new trading system."

Paul expressed mild interest. "Have they?"

"That's what I hear . . . You interested."

(After a moment's hesitation.) "Yes."

"OK, Geraldine. Who's the best person to approach?"

"Well, it's not their IT director. He'll just put you off. Sam Kleinfelt, the CEO, is a friend of mine. He doesn't like consultants, but he does give me some good leads. He mentioned their current problem to me. George Whitman, the Operations Director, is probably where I'd start, because he's fed up with what they've got. But you'll need to get the Finance Director—I think his name is something like Frazier—on board."

"Thanks, Geraldine. Thanks very much."

"My pleasure." She gave him a sultry smile. "If you do get some work there, my fee is seven percent." She turned to go, but she turned back. "Will I see you at the Auction Dinner?"

"Yes, I plan to be there."

With tongue in cheek, she asked, "Will I meet your wife?"

"I'm I widower, Geraldine."

She touched his arm. "Oh, I'm sorry." Her eyes searched his face.

He drew in a breath. "My wife died two years ago . . . of breast cancer."

"It's a dreadful disease! I'm sorry!" she sounded as if she meant it. She patted his arm. "See you at the Auction Dinner."

Paul wrote to George Whitman, Operations Director at Smith Coleridge. He explained that he had on several occasions worked with clients in his sector, and that he would like to have the opportunity to meet with Mr. Whitman to explain to him what he could do for Smith Coleridge. He made no reference to any problems at Smith Coleridge, but in the CV that he attached, he cited several examples of helping clients resolve bespoke software problems.

Three days later, he called Mr. Whitman, and the expected, over-protective personal assistant answered the phone:

"Good morning, Mr. Whitman's office. This is Nancy."

"Good morning, Nancy. This is Paul Winthorpe. May I speak with Mr. Whitman?"

"I'm sorry; Mr. Whitman is in a meeting. May I ask him to call you?"

"Yes. I wrote to Mr. Whitman a few days ago, and I explained to him that I have helped other companies in your field with problems they were having with bespoke trading software. I'm a senior financial management consultant."

"You say you sent a letter?"

"Yes."(Gives her the date)

(Long pause) "I'm sorry, Mr. Winthorpe, I don't believe we received the letter."

You mean you just glanced at the letter, didn't think he would be interested, and you binned it! But he replied, "Oh, don't worry. I can send you a copy via e-mail. What's your address, Nancy?"

She gave him her e-mail address, and he sent her the letter as an attachment. *The trick*, Paul thought, *is to let the PA know that you know about a problem she knows her boss is facing.*

Paul called again in two days. This time he was put right through to Mr. Whitman.

"George Whitman."

"Good morning, Mr. Whitman. This is Paul Winthorpe. Have you had a chance to look at the letter I sent you?"

"Yes, I have. You have some interesting experience. Ahh . . . I could spare perhaps an hour at 10 on Monday. That any good for you?"

"Yes, that's fine, I'll see you then, Mr. Whitman."

George Whitman was a City high-flyer in his mid-thirties: Nordic complexion and features, nervous, aggressive-defensive disposition, wearing a hundred pound Ferragamo tie, a monogrammed, Jermyn Street shirt, and real pearl cufflinks. His office on the twelfth floor of 120 King William Street was small: walnut desk, black leather swivel chair, three matching chairs, an overflowing bookcase, and one window. But Paul thought, *He probably took home at least a million pounds last year.*

"I can't promise you any business, Mr. Winthorpe, but I thought a discussion might be of interest."

"Yes, of course. Please call me, Paul . . . Would it be useful if I took you through a couple of case studies?"

From his briefcase, Paul removed a set of PowerPoint visuals, printed on white, A4 paper, and he used them to illustrate the case studies. George Whitman became involved asking questions, referring to previous visuals, jumping ahead to later visuals. He finally said. "I can see a couple of problems. First of all, our CEO doesn't like management consultants, and secondly, we would be very nervous about letting outsiders into our proprietary systems."

Paul nodded. He said, "The second one is easy to solve. I'm willing to sign an iron-clad confidentiality agreement, and you'll notice that the clients' names aren't on any of these visuals."

"Yeah, but you gave me a list of your clients."

"I think you'd find it pretty hard to match each case study to a client's name."

"Yeah, OK. How about my consultant-hating boss?"

"First of all, I think you want an ally before you go to the boss. Somebody like, say, your FD?"

George brightened "There's an idea." He reflected: "But Dick Frazier isn't going to be enough."

Paul leaned forward, "George, if the CEO knows there's a problem, and he wants it fixed, what he's going to worry about is the cost. How long will it take? And how can he be sure the problem will be solved?"

"Yeah! That's right!"

"George, all those issues can be solved. I am willing to work to a contract that will put your CEO's mind at rest."

"OK, Paul, let me think about it."

Paul, pretending that he hadn't heard George's last evasion, said, "George, why don't we see if we can meet with Dick Frazier?"

"I'm pretty sure he's in a meeting."

"OK, if he is, let's get his PA to give us a date for a meeting."

Hesitantly, George picked up his phone, and dialed. Putting his had over the mouthpiece, he said, "He can see us Friday at 10:30. Is that OK for you?" Paul nodded. "OK, Julie, we'll see him then."

George looked skeptically at Paul, who sensing the mood, asked, "How much sleep have you lost over the problem that you have, George?"

"A lot!"

"My job is to help you sleep better. One last thought, George, what is Dick Frazier's attitude toward the problem?"

"Well, he thinks it's pretty serious, and he wants to see it solved. He doesn't consider problems in terms of cost, schedule and quality of solutions; he thinks about the long term cost and benefits."

"What do you figure the problem is costing you now, George?"

George closed his eyes and shook his head. "I don't know, Paul. A lot."

On Friday at 10:30 a.m., they were ushered into Dick Frazier's office. Dick bore a slight resemblance to Humphrey Bogart: large mouth, drooping eyelids and sagging cheeks, but instead of Boggie's lisp there was a Yorkshireman's crisp drawl. The desk at which Dick sat was awash with papers, binders, folders and piles of computer print outs, but as Paul and George entered, Dick quickly stacked nearly everything in three piles on the left side of his desk. He looked up, expectantly. As George made the introductions, it was apparent to Paul that George was planning to take a back seat in the meeting. Accordingly, Paul went through his presentation, which he had altered a little to emphasize the benefits he had obtained for clients. During the presentation, Dick sat back in his chair, arms folded across his chest, watching Paul as a cat watches a songbird. Several times, Dick acknowledged a point with a nod or a gesture; finally he said, "How much would this cost us?"

Paul said, "Dick, it's difficult for me to say at this point because I don't know exactly what the problem at Smith Coleridge is."

"Bit of a chicken and egg problem, eh?" Dick said laconically.

Paul smiled. "It doesn't have to be."

"Eh?" was the response from Dick.

"I can do an analysis, and give you a report on the problem, what it will cost to fix it, and the benefits you'll get from having it fixed."

"How much would this analysis cost?"

"Nothing."

"Eh?"

Paul leaned forward. "Before I ask you to invest in me, I'm willing to invest in you because I have confidence in my abilities to make you a satisfied client."

Dick leaned back in his chair and considered the ceiling thoughtfully. Then he rocked forward and turned his attention to George. "What's your view?" he asked.

George said, "I think we ought to go for it. I'm damned tired of listening to the traders' complaints."

Dick pursed his lips. Tentatively he offered, "We've got to get Sam and Eddie on board."

"Yes. I'll set it up," George said, and he made no move to go.

"Let's set it up now," Paul said.

Dick turned a bemused face on Paul. "You're an impatient son-of-a-bitch aren't you?"

"Yeah, sometimes I am. Aren't you?"

Still bemused, Dick made a phone call. He hung up and announced, "We're with Sam at 4 next Thursday. It's his call whether Eddie is there." Then he gave Paul a clarification, "Sam is our CEO. Eddie is the prat who's responsible for our IT. If he's there, he won't be friendly."

* * *

Sarah Montgomery looked almost regal in her strapless, blue taffeta gown as she approached the entrance portico of Fusiliers House on Paul's arm. They were followed by several other couples, similarly attired in long dresses and black tie: the Charitable Consultants' Auction Dinner was a formal event which called for a suitably formal and historic venue: the home of the Honourable Fusiliers Company.

Sarah's grey hair was in a smooth, curled-under bob, which seemed to emphasize the bareness of her pale shoulders. Looking at her, one would have guessed her to have been about forty-five and a real beauty in her youth, judging by her dark eyes, prominent cheekbones and expressive mouth. One would have noted her pleasure at being there, but one would have been mistaken about her age; she was fifty-four, and with a trim figure.

Inside Fusiliers House, there were large reception rooms to the right and left with mullioned windows reaching nearly floor-to-ceiling and looking out over the expanse of green parade ground, which was tucked in amongst the City buildings. Around the walls of the reception room on the right, which was the one which Paul and Sarah entered, there were displays of military decorations and ribbons.

A waiter was standing just inside the entrance to the room with a tray full of flutes of champagne and orange juice. Paul handed a glass of champagne to Sarah, took one for himself, and surveyed the room. Rob was hurrying over with his wife in tow. There, also was Geraldine, standing next to a tall, bronzed man with a silver-haired crew cut. Rob's wife, whose name sounded something like Alicia, was very plain, reminding Paul of the Polish woman who sat behind the counter in a local shop. She wore an unflattering dress that, Paul guessed, she had selected at a local charity shop. She smiled ceaselessly, but said very little and clung to Rob's arm. Rob was his usual effusive self, expressing his great pleasure in meeting Sarah, while casting furtive glances at her impressive décolletage, which was decorated with an eye-catching, circular pendant of diamonds. "You know before dinner, we have a show to watch," Rob gushed.

"Oh, what's that?" Sarah inquired, inclining her head with interest.

"The Fusiliers Company veterans are going to put on a close order drill in authentic old uniforms. I'm told it'll be quite spectacular!"

"Oh, we'll certainly not miss that!" Sarah assured him.

Rob was explaining the intricacies of close order drill when Geraldine and her husband joined them. The husband was wearing a scarlet ribbon from which a bronze cross was suspended. He was Edward Paley, and his response to Alicia's wide-eyed query about the ribbon was, "Oh, it's a little something the Queen gave me for service to charity."

Geraldine edged closer to Paul. "Paul, how did you make out at Smith Coleridge?" she inquired.

"I have a meeting with the CEO next Thursday."

There was her sultry gaze again. "Just the two of you?"

Paul smiled. "No. The FD and the Ops Director will be there—pulling for me I hope—and the IT Director—not in the loop so far—may be there, trying to derail the train."

Geraldine chuckled. "Well done and good luck!" Then, turning toward Sarah, she inquired, "And what do you do, Sarah?"

Sarah noticed a slightly condescending tone in Geraldine's voice, but she decided to ignore it. "I'm a buyer with Debenhams," she replied. "I'm responsible for ladies' evening wear."

"Oh . . . that's a pretty big job," Geraldine's tone was somewhat more respectful. "And," she continued, "is that (she gestured at Sarah's dress) from Debenhams?" Sarah nodded. "I guess you get a pretty good discount on clothes," Geraldine offered—this time with a trace of envy.

"Yes, but this particular dress has been on display, so I just borrowed it for the evening."

"Oh, I see . . . Do you mind my asking, what does it list for?"

"I think this one is £1,200. It's a Givenchy."

Geraldine was slightly un-nerved. "How did you two meet?" she asked with a gesture toward Paul.

Sarah's eyes settled firmly on Geraldine's face. "We met at church."

"Did you? How interesting. It's nice to hear that people still go to church."

Sarah smiled insincerely. "Yes, it is, isn't it?"

Rap! Rap! Rap! It was the Ceremonial Sergeant's staff striking the floor. "Pray, exit, and join the Leader by the parade ground!" he announced.

The members, their spouses and guests moved toward the door, and as they stepped outside, the music of a brass band came alive on that May evening in the City of London. Paul stood at the edge of the parade ground, Sarah just in front of him, his arms around her waist. On the parade ground, marching in perfect order were about thirty older men, dressed in blue and red striped trousers, tight-fitting red jackets, and black shakos. Each man was carrying a rifle, and his left arm was swinging in an exaggerated arc. There was a field commander, who carried a drawn sword, at the front of the formation; the band was marching at the rear. Over the next twenty minutes, the field commander put the formation through a complex series of formation changes, involving columns, files, abrupt turns, and repositioning the rifles. Now and then, the band would stop playing, and all that could be heard was a tapping on the snare drum and the stamping of feet on the turf. But then, the drums would thump, the cymbals clash, and the band would strike up a new march. The spectators stood in a respectful, awed silence until the field commander brought the formation up facing the onlookers, and called out a command. The marchers stamped to a halt and raised their weapons in a salute; the band stopped playing and the commander raised his sword in a salute.

Applause burst from the spectators, who then walked onto the parade ground to congratulate the soldiers and hear their stories.

"I think we're at table twelve with the Second Vice President. His name is John Farrier; I don't know his wife," Paul told Sarah. They found table twelve, which to their relief had no name cards, so they could sit together after introducing themselves to the other five couples. Sarah looked around the oak-paneled Long Room, where twenty round tables had been installed. She took in the wall of mullioned windows on the south side, the many life-sized portraits of English heroes in military dress. There was even a portrait of the Queen, and high on the north wall was a small balcony from which a string quartet was playing.

Rap! Rap! Rap! "Pray, silence for the Leader."

The Leader welcomed the members of Charitable Consultants, their spouses and guests. He reminded them that the purpose of that evening was to raise money for the company's charities. He explained that during the dinner there would be a silent auction, followed by "an absolutely splendid live auction for which we owe a great debt of gratitude to very generous donors."

Grace was said, wine was poured, and conversations resumed around the table. Sarah and John Farrier, who sat on her right, examined the list of ten items that were to be auctioned silently. Of particular interest to her were a day at the Hartwood Spa and a one-week course on puddings at Leith's. She was deciding on

Efraim's Eye

an upper limit for those possibilities when the appetiser arrived: smoked salmon mousse with asparagus.

Paul was considering the list for the live auction. One item that caught his eye was the use of a villa on the beach in the Seychelles for a week. The villa slept eight. It also included a cook to prepare meals and the use of a powerboat (for sightseeing and fishing). Paul showed Sarah the picture.

He said, "This looks interesting, Sarah, but I doubt that I could fill it up. I don't have enough close friends to spend this kind of money on."

Sarah gazed at him, smiling. "Well, let's think . . . You could ask Cynthia and her boyfriend, and John and his family, and if you invited me, I'd certainly come along. That's eight. There you are!"

Paul nodded, looking slightly chagrined. "Yeah. I didn't think about my kids. Shame on me! But Sarah, Cynthia doesn't have a boyfriend, and John's kids are pretty young."

"They're eight and nine, aren't they? They'd each need a bed, and they'd have a wonderful time. And Cynthia? Well, maybe she'll have a boyfriend—or find one—by the time you're ready to go."

Paul smiled with a bit of determination this time. He patted Sarah's arm. "OK. I'll give it a go!"

Rack of lamb, roast potatoes and parcels of tied French beans arrived; St. Emilion was substituted for the chardonnay. Waiters passed baskets of assorted breads, but Sarah declined. Instead, she filled out bidding forms on the spa and the cookery course. Ten minutes later, she glanced up at the large screen that displayed the results of the silent auction. "Damn!" she muttered, "I'm under water already!" She filled out two new forms and handed them to a waiter. "That's it!" she announced. "I'm not going higher!" Her bid of £125 for the spa was holding up, but her last bid on the cookery school had been dramatically overtaken. She called Paul's attention to the screen. "Look at that!" she complained. "I bid £350 for the one week cookery course—that's seventy pounds a day—and it's already over six hundred!" Under her breath, she added, "There must be some seriously rich people here!"

Paul whispered, "Rich? Yes, probably, but I think it's more that these people are very competitive, and they like to win—in public!"

The dessert—a raspberry tart with vanilla ice cream—was accompanied by ice wine. Then came the coffee, and miniature, sweet pastries. Decanters of port were placed on the tables.

Rap! Rap! Rap! "Pray, silence for the Leader!"

The Leader called out, "The Loyal Toast!" Everyone rose, and there was a chorus of "To the Queen!" as glasses of port were raised.

The diners settled themselves in their seats; the Leader announced: "We are very fortunate to have Michael Dinsworthy, the famous Christies auctioneer, to conduct the live auction. So, I'll turn the floor over to you, Michael."

Dinsworthy stood, between the centre table and the windows, a gavel in one hand and a microphone in the other. He briefly reviewed each of the items to be auctioned, giving credit to the donor in each case. As a view of the Seychelles villa flashed on the screen, Sarah squeezed Paul's arm. "Oh, that really looks nice!"

The villa was the fifth of twelve items to be auctioned. Michael Dinsworthy showed several photos of the villa, the beach, the boat, and even the cook. He said, "Can we start the bidding at £3,000 for this lovely villa which has been so kindly donated by Mr. and Mrs. Goldman?" Several hands were immediately raised. Paul put in bids at £4,200 and £4,800, but as the bidding topped five thousand, he dropped out. During the next five minutes, there was a furious competition among three bidders, which finally ended at £8,200.

Paul shook his head. "Sorry, Sarah."

"Well, you can always contact Mr. Goldman and find out what he usually rents the villa for—certainly not £8,200 for a week."

In the taxi at the end of the evening, Sarah asked, "Paul, who was that lady with the diamond necklace? You know, the one whose husband has the OBE?" (Order of the British Empire)

"Oh, that's Geraldine Paley. She's a member, and her husband has some big job in the City."

Sarah said dryly, "I didn't like her at all. She's one of those people who have to be one-up on whomever they're talking to. I find it impossible to like people like her."

"She's the one who gave me the lead into Smith Coleridge."

"Are you sure she doesn't have some private axe to grind in giving you that lead?"

"Well, yes. I'll have to pay her seven percent of any business I get there."

"Nothing more than that?"

"No, I don't think so."

Sarah turned to face him. "I think she'd like to get to know you <u>much</u> better."

Paul shrugged. "I think she's like that with everyone. She enjoys being a tease."

"I'm not so sure about that," Sarah offered, feigning indifference.

"Well, I have no intention of taking a business relationship any further. Besides, predatory women put me off."

"Good. We agree. I think she's a nasty woman; you think she's a predatory woman."

When they arrived at Paul's house on Crieff Road in Wandsworth, he offered Sarah tea. She shook her head, and he followed her up the stairs. The large master bedroom still reflected the touch of Paul's late wife: heavy white curtains, a blue and beige oriental carpet and a white king-sized bed nearly smothered in white cushions.

"Can you help me with the zipper?" Sarah asked, kicking off her silver shoes.

"With great pleasure!"

The dress began to fall away. Paul unclasped her bra, which fell away with the dress, and he reached around to caress her. She sighed as he kissed her neck. Turning to face him, she pulled his black tie and began to take off the studs that fastened his shirt. Moments later he was naked, and she was rolling off her panty hose. In a swift motion, she shed her knickers, and with her back to him, she began to turn down the bed.

"Not so quickly, sweetheart!" he protested and swept her into his arms. "Oh, you feel wonderful!" His senses were filled with the warm softness and the lovely fragrance of her body. They stood for some moments, kissing, caressing, and embracing. He held her at arms length to look at her. Spontaneously, he said, "You really are lovely, Sarah!"

She closed her eyes and almost imperceptibly shook her head. "I know I'm not lovely. I'm too old for that. But I'm glad you think so." She turned and slid into the bed. "And actually," she added, "you're a very good-looking man."

"I'm glad <u>you</u> think so!"

The room was warm enough that they didn't need the covers. They lay on their sides, facing each other with heads on the same pillow while kissing and caressing each other. Their respective hands found what they were seeking and lingered there. Neither of them hurried, but as their excitement and passion rose, they began to feel a sense of urgency. Paul lifted one of Sarah's thighs and slid under it, so that his manhood and her womanhood were touching. Slowly and gently he entered. "Oh, Paul!" she breathed, her eyes closed, her head back on the pillow.

His hand caressed her breast and then it strayed into the dark curls at her groin. Moving slowly, he was determined to please her. She began to tremble with tension, and then with a long groan, her crisis swept over her with his release immediately following. For a time, they lay as they were. He disengaged, drawing her to him so that he could indiscriminately kiss her face, with its closed eyes and gently smiling lips. They fell asleep.

He opened his eyes, and turned his head to see the clock—8:12. He turned his head the other way and found her looking at him with a faint smile on her lips. "Good morning, sweetheart," he whispered, rolling over to face her and drawing her to him.

"Good morning," she said. The soft warmth of her body, her lingering perfume and musky scent aroused him. He slid down so that he could kiss and caress her breasts.

"Oh, Paul! Not again!"

"Yes! I can't get enough of you, Sarah."

For a time, she stroked the back of his head, luxuriating in his desire for her. He moved to slide further down the bed, but she held him against her. They began a lingering kiss; slowly and gently, he took her again.

Suddenly, he broke the kiss and cried out, "Oh, God, Sarah!" Fiercely, she hugged him as his crisis swept through him.

He gazed at her with great tenderness. ""Did you . . . ?" he asked.

She shook her head.

"Oh, Sarah . . ." It was a mixture of concern and disappointment.

"I'm absolutely fine, Paul . . . sometimes I just enjoy . . . you."

They had coffee and a leisurely breakfast in the dining room/kitchen, looking out the open double doors into the garden where an odd assortment of birds—sparrows, wood pigeons, robins, chaffinches and a blue tit—were feeding carelessly at Paul's year-round feeding station, spilling seeds on the flagstone terrace.

Sarah asked, "Are we going to church?"

Paul hesitated, "Yes, if you want to."

Sarah reached out and put her hand on his. "Do <u>you</u> want to go, Paul?"

"I find it hard to get in the right frame of mind when I'm in church." She looked at him searchingly, saying nothing. For some moments, he looked pensively down at the floor. "I feel the church let me down when Catherine was ill."

Catherine's illness and her death two years earlier had been mentioned by Paul only in passing during the six months that Sarah had known him. She said, "So your prayers weren't answered." He nodded.

They were silent for a time. "Sometimes it's like that," she said.

"I know. . . And I know that I'm being unreasonable. . . kind of blaming God . . . but . . . who else is there to blame? Sometimes I feel I'm getting past the disillusionment. I can go the church and try to rebuild what I had, but other times . . . I just get stuck in a negative frame of mind."

Suddenly, he looked at her and smiled. "Did I ever tell you," he asked, "that I started out as an altar boy, joined the choir, and when my voice changed, I occasionally sang tenor solos?"

"No. No, you didn't, but I can believe it."

"And I was a believer with a pretty unquestioning faith."

"Which has been badly shaken by your wife's death," she offered.

"Yes, but you know, during the last week of her life, Catherine was absolutely serene. Of course, the McMillan nurses were giving her plenty of morphine, but it wasn't that. It was her state of mind: she knew she was going to die, and she accepted it." Paul's eyes were glazed with tears, and he paused to get control of his emotions. "Catherine wasn't concerned for herself, at all. She was only concerned about me, Cynthia and John."

Sarah nodded; they sat watching the birds.

She said, "I don't think I told you that I had a brother who died."

"No, you didn't, Sarah. How old was he?"

"He was twenty-three. He died of meningitis, and he was in a coma for nearly a week. Pray! My God, did I pray! I <u>pleaded</u> with God!" She shook her head. "I was angry, and I thought I could punish God by turning away from him. For about three years, I didn't go to church at all. But, one Sunday, Mother asked me to go with her, and for some reason I said OK. When we were seated inside, I was listening to the organ music, and I suddenly got a compulsive urge to pray. I got down on my knees, and I said something like, 'Forgive me, Lord, I know it's not your fault.'"

Sarah paused to reflect. "I wasn't an altar attendant or in the choir, but I was a lot like you . . . It took a long time for me to build a new relationship with God." She looked at Paul. "We just don't know," she continued. "We just don't know."

She shook her head, with an ironical smile. "At Ted's funeral—over thirty-five years ago— there was a young man, a friend of Ted's I had never met . . . He turned out to be my ex-husband."

Efraim's Eye

Paul's eyes wandered over her face. Slowly and deliberately, he said, "I'm just very glad that you were at church the Sunday I decided to go."

"I am, too."

"Sarah?"

"Yes?"

"Let's go to church. Then, if you'll make me lunch at your place, I'll take you out to dinner."

"Sounds great. And what were your plans between lunch and dinner?"

"Well, I was thinking of pretending to watch cricket from your sofa while I'm actually taking a nap."

She smiled. "OK. I could do with a nap too." After a glance at Paul, she hastily added, "Not that kind of nap—a restful nap."

* * *

Sam Kleinfelt kept them waiting in his conference room for a good ten minutes. Before meeting the man, Paul couldn't decide what his motive was. Did he just want to punish a management consultant for the perceived misdemeanour of some previous consultant? Did he just want to make a point about his power? Was he hoping that the four men in his conference room would settle their differences and present him with a consensus solution?

Judging by the body language of the four around the white marble-topped table, a consensus solution seemed out of the question. Eddie Chernowski, the IT Director, had a distinctly hostile air about him. He had avoided any small talk with Paul, or—for that matter—with Dick and George. Instead, he appeared to be reading e-mails on his BlackBerry. Paul managed to engage George in a discussion of possible outcomes of the England vs. New Zealand test match. Dick, meanwhile, was perusing a pile of computer printouts, punching numbers into a calculator, and making notes.

"Sorry to hold you guys up." The new entrant was a tall, thin man in his mid-forties, with a bony face, dark eyes and black hair in a pompadour. He walked around the table, put out a hand to Paul and said, "Hi, I'm Sam Kleinfelt."

Having seated himself at the head of the table, he looked expectantly at Dick. "Your meeting, Dick."

Dick took a moment to carefully sort his papers; then he said, "Paul Winthorpe is a senior financial systems consultant who approached us on an unsolicited basis. He apparently got wind of the difficulties we're having with our trading system, and he . . . "

"We're not having difficulties," Eddie Chernowski interrupted belligerently, "we're . . ."

With firm emphasis, Kleinfelt put in, "Let Dick finish, Eddie!"

"As I was saying," Dick continued as if he were addressing unruly school children. "He has offered his services to us, and George and I thought we might listen to what he has to say." With a nod, he indicated that Paul should begin.

As his presentation unfolded, Paul took note of the body language around the table. Eddie was sitting back in his chair, no longer playing with his BlackBerry and giving the appearance of utter disinterest, but Paul suspected, from the occasional eye contact, that he was listening intently for Paul to make a mistake. George and Dick, who had heard it before, were actively listening, nodding, and putting in helpful clarifications. Sam Kleinfelt seemed not to be listening to what Paul said. Instead, he seemed to focus entirely on Paul, apparently trying to read him as a person.

After Paul summarised, Eddie asked sourly, "What makes you think you can solve our so-called problem?" He made quotation marks in the air.

Paul responded, "I can't guarantee anything at this point because I don't know enough about the issue you're having. That's why I'm proposing a two-day, unpaid analysis."

"What experience do you have with our particular software?" Eddie demanded.

"I believe you are running SuperBridge. I haven't come across that particular platform before, but I have worked with a number of other trading systems—as I mentioned. Most trading systems have a number of common features: they're configured for Windows and they're written in C+ code with an Oracle or SQL database."

Eddie attempted a pre-emptive strike: "Sam, I don't think we need this guy. He doesn't know anything about SuperBridge."

For about five seconds, Kleinfelt considered Chernowski. "Eddie, you and your team have had three months to get SuperBridge performing as advertised. Our trades are taking twice as long as they should. We can't run a business like this."

Eddie opened his mouth to protest, but Kleinfelt cut him off with a dismissive wave of his hand. Then turning to Paul, he said, "Mr. Winthorpe, in my time, I've done a lot of business with consultants. A few of them have been very helpful, but most of them were a total waste of money. Which category do you fit in?"

"The very helpful category."

"Prove it!"

"Here's a list of my clients. Call any of them and ask."

Sam said, "We might just do that. What's the output I get from this free, two-day analysis you're proposing?"

Paul responded, "I'll give you a clear description of the problem, what it appears to be costing you, and if I think I can fix the problem, a proposal for doing so."

"Are you one of these guys who collects a daily rate until the coming of the next ice age?"

"No. I can give you a firm price against clear deliverables."

"Penalty if you don't get there?"

"Yes, provided, I also have an opportunity to earn a bonus."

"Give me an idea of your daily rate."

"£1,200."

"That's pretty steep."

Paul shrugged. "You get what you pay for."

Kleinfelt looked around the table. "Any questions or comments?"

George and Dick both shook their heads. Eddie leaned forward as if to say something, but he thought better of it. Kleinfelt said,

"OK, Mr. Winthorpe. We'll check out these clients of yours, and if they recommend you, we'll arrange a date for your analysis."

* * *

Cynthia was usually late. *I guess it comes with the territory,* Paul thought as he sat at the bar at Gaucho Broadgate. *You work in the City—make lots of money—you have to work long hours.* He looked at his watch; it was 7:20 p.m.

"Would you like another one, sir?" the bar man inquired.

"No thanks. She'll be here soon." And at that moment, he saw Cynthia hurriedly push through the glass doors. She was intercepted by the maître, but having seen Paul, she rushed over, brief case over one shoulder and handbag over the other.

"Sorry I'm late, Dad. It's absolutely manic in the office." She seated herself next to Paul, and slung her bags over the back of her bar chair. To the bar man, she said, "I'll have a Malbec, please, Francisco. You know—the Opi Reserve."

Paul contemplated his daughter with an amused smile. "What's going on in the office?"

"Oh, it's the usual stuff. We're doing an acquisition for Diageo. Started out friendly, but it turned hostile and complicated. We just don't have enough people, Dad, to do the work we have in an eight-hour day."

"What time did you start this morning?"

"I was at my desk at quarter to seven. And, I'll have to go back after dinner."

"Shall we order now?"

"No, damn it!" she said emphatically, "I want to have a nice, leisurely dinner with my dad." She swung her chair to face him. "So what's new with you?"

She's a replica of her mother, Paul thought. *She has Catherine's dark eyes, wonderful mouth, and turned-up nose. She also has Catherine's very attractive figure.* He said, "Well, I have a new prospect I'm working on—Smith Coleridge."

Cynthia wrinkled her nose. I don't know much about them."

"Neither do I, unfortunately, but it seems they're having a problem with their trading system."

Cynthia made a circular motion with her glass on the bar while she considered. "You know what you might try, Dad? You could talk to the competitors of whosever software it is. They'll almost certainly have got wind of it."

"But why should they want to talk to me, Cindy?"

"I think you want to talk with their sales people. Salesmen love to talk about competitors' problems, and they also want to learn more about competitors' problems."

"You're suggesting there'll be a shared interest in whatever the problem is with the software."

"Yeah. How'd you get the lead?"

"From a lady called Geraldine Paley."

"Oh?" Cynthia arched her eyebrows.

"She's a member of the Charitable Consultants LLP."

"Strictly a professional relationship?" The eyebrows were still raised.

"Yes, Cindy. She's expecting a seven percent commission."

The eyebrows fell. "Well, in that case," Cynthia said dryly, "I hope she'll get it."

"Me. too."

Cynthia went back to swirling her wine. "How are you finding Charitable Consultants, Dad?"

"I'm enjoying it. Good people. Lots of involvement with charities. I have a meeting next week at Global Youth Enterprise to do some overseas work for them."

"Where?"

"I'll find out next week."

"Well, I hope they don't send you somewhere in the Middle East."

"Why not?"

"I just think that a lot of those people are irrational, religious zealots."

"You're talking about Muslim fundamentalists."

"Yeah."

"Well, there are plenty of flat-earth, fundamentalist Christians."

"Sure, but they don't try to lock up all their women, and preach fire and brimstone sermons about killing all the infidels. Some of those people are really scary, and we have a couple of them here in London. Not only that, we can't even send them back to the countries they came from because they'll be tortured there. I think their countries of origin have it right, and we have it all wrong!"

Paul smiled. "Next time I see the Prime Minister, I'll pass on your views."

"Please do!"

They went downstairs and were seated at a table by the floor-to-ceiling glass wall.

"How's your love life, Cindy?"

"What love life, Dad? I barely have a social life. You know this is the first time I've been out to a nice restaurant that didn't involve a business meeting in over a month?" She hesitated. "No, that's not quite right. I did go out with James Billingsley ten days ago."

"Who's he?"

"He's a friend of John's from Cambridge. You know him; he used to row at Cambridge. He's a barrister now."

"Aha."

"No ahas, Dad. He's just a friend—at least I think he's just a friend."

"Well, fingers crossed for both of you."

Cynthia made a wry face. "Speaking of fingers crossed, how's Sarah?"

"She's fine. I took her to the Charitable Consultants' Auction Dinner last week. It was a nice black tie event."

"Well, good. I'm glad. She's such a nice lady." Cynthia looked at her father pensively. "Don't you let her get away from you, Dad."

"I take it she has your seal of approval."

"Yes, she does, and you need a woman in your life—I mean a live-in woman—to keep you from getting old and crotchety."

Paul thought, *How right she is*! But he said, "I'm not getting old and crotchety!"

"Not yet, fortunately."

As they drank their coffees, Paul asked, "What do you want for your birthday, Cindy?"

"Oh, dear! Is it that time again? It seems like just yesterday I got over that awful thirty hurdle."

"Yeah. Last year."

"I don't know, Dad. I'll think about it and send you and e-mail. I've got to run."

"Love you, Cindy."

"Love you, Dad."

Chapter 3

ASSIGNMENT

The security seems a little excessive for a charity, Paul thought while a uniformed guard examined the contents of his briefcase. He had already gone through a metal detector inside the entrance at Nine St. James's Place. The detector had squawked at the stainless steel bracelet on his watch. "Why is the security so tight here?" he inquired of the guard.

The guard considered him for a moment, as if trying to decide whether Paul was obtuse or a troublemaker. He apparently decided on the obtuse option because he said, "The Duke of Suffolk has his offices here."

Paul shrugged, sat down on the maroon leather couch by the window, and reached for a copy of *The Financial Times* on the low, walnut table in front of him. As he was beginning to read the item on page two about a heightened security alert in the U.K., he heard the guard announcing him on the phone. The news item quoted the head of MI6 as saying, "Agents of al-Qaeda may attempt to slip across the U.K. border to activate previously established sleeper cells. These sleeper cells may have received training in Afghanistan, Somalia, or Yemen. We have raised the level of security alert to Amber, and we urge the British public to be particularly alert at this time."

What does he know that he's not telling us? Paul wondered. *He knows something about actual or potential movements of people linked to al-Qaeda. He has information on some sleeper cells in the U.K. I wonder how many there are and how many he knows about.*

Paul was starting to speculate about what "be alert" might entail when his thoughts were interrupted, "Mr. Winthorpe? I'm Roberta Ambola of GYE." It was a rather pretty black girl dressed in a pale green cotton shirt and beige, calf-length pique skirt holding out her hand.

Paul jumped up, shook the proffered hand, and followed her down a wide corridor. They climbed one rather grand, curving staircase, and another narrow carpeted set of stairs to the second floor. Roberta punched a code into a keypad by a dark oak door and led him to a conference room that overlooked St. James's Park through large mullioned windows. The room itself was rather grand, with white paneled walls, an ornate ceiling, and two brass chandeliers, but its contents—conference table and chairs—were more in the style of IKEA. *Probably*, Paul thought, *the Duke contributes the office, but the charity has to provide its own furniture.* Setting his briefcase on the table, Paul commented, "The security seems very tight here."

Roberta nodded. "Yes, I know. It is a bit of a nuisance for us, but you see, the Duke has his offices on the first floor, and when you own half of the best real estate in London, you probably worry about being kidnapped. Can I get you something to drink—coffee or tea?"

Roberta returned minutes later carrying two mugs of tea, a file, and her notebook. The mugs were white with the GYE logo: a young figure lifting magically off the ground. "Thank you very much for coming to see us and for volunteering to do an assessment for us," she began. "I'm the Manager of Operations at GYE, which amongst other things, means that I'm responsible for assessing our chapters, and helping them meet our standards. Our Chief Executive Matthew Andrews is going to join us in a little while. He has some particular insights and concerns about Morocco."

"So it's Morocco where you're going to send me." (Immediately, Paul had visions of a magical place with snow-covered mountains, vast deserts, oases and bazaars.)

"Yes, if that's OK."

Paul nodded. "First," Roberta continued, "let me tell you a little about GYE, and we can talk later about Morocco."

She sipped her tea, holding her mug in both hands. "We were founded by the Duke twelve years ago as an English charity. His vision was to provide employment opportunities for young people who had an idea, energy and initiative, but who could not get the financing to make it happen. The Duke also realised that to reduce the risk of failure, these young entrepreneurs needed a mentor—someone with wisdom, maturity and experience, who could provide the business guidance and emotional support the young people needed. Initially, the Duke contributed his own funds to start a kind of GYE bank, and he insisted that the interest rate should be reasonable; that is, a little higher than what a commercial bank would charge, but well below what loan sharks get."

"And what has been the experience with defaults?" Paul asked.

"In the U.K., about twenty percent of our loans don't get repaid in full. Overseas, it's about thirty percent. The difference is mostly due to cultural norms. In developing countries, there's little experience of commercial banking, and people tend to look on the funding we provide as a grant, rather than a loan that they have signed up to repay." Paul was taking notes. "The charity has been a tremendous success in England. Thousands of young people—who might otherwise be unemployed—are now working in their own business. And," Roberta added with emphasis, "each new business averages two and a half additional employees."

"OK. How did places like Morocco get started?"

"Well eight years ago, the Duke decided to expand his idea and build a network outside the U.K., so he offered his brand to interested overseas charities, provided they agreed to abide by the principles he had established in the U.K."

"So, it became a sort of international franchise system?"

"Yes, and the beauty of it was that international development banks, host country governments and the private sector began to take an interest in providing funds. They could see that the standards set by GYE assured that their funds would be used effectively in giving young entrepreneurs a real chance."

"Can you give me an idea of what your standards are?"

Roberta pulled a document with the GYE logo from her file and handed it to Paul. "They're all described here, but let me go over the key points with you. To be eligible, an entrepreneur should be between eighteen and thirty-five and unable to get other financing. There should be no requirement for collateral, and the interest rate should be reasonable. Every entrepreneur should be provided with a mentor who operates on a pro-bono basis, and gives advice for the equivalent of up to three days per month. We also expect our chapters to be run professionally with a board of trustees, strategic plan, documented and transparent management processes, annual financial audits, and local fund-raising capability. Just because it's a charity doesn't—in our view—allow for sloppy governance."

"OK," Paul asked. "What are some of the sins that chapters are particularly likely to commit?"

Roberta smiled and shook her head. "You name it; they've tried it, but some of the things that we find particularly annoying are giving preference to male entrepreneurs, charging high interest rates, insisting on collateral, charging for mentors, or finding other ways of converting the charity into a commercial bank. And if fraud is found, we'll kick them out immediately!"

"Right. And what should the staff at a chapter be doing on a day-to-day basis?"

"Well they ought to be doing a lot more than just administering their program. They should be actively seeking new entrepreneurs and mentors. They should be providing help with the preparation of business plans. Effective training programs for entrepreneurs and mentors should be in place. They've got to chase-up overdue payments, and they need to be busy raising funds. One problem all our chapters seem to have is that they'll win a big program from a development bank or their government, and then they'll stop worrying about fund-raising until that big program runs out. But then, it's too late, and often they'll have to cut staff. It's far better if they can raise money they don't need immediately and hold it in reserve."

Paul and Roberta continued to discuss details and review other GYE documents for another half an hour. "Are you OK with that? Shall I give Matthew a call?"

Paul nodded, and Roberta disappeared for a few minutes. When she returned, she was accompanied by a man in his mid-forties, wearing a top-of-the-line Marks and Spencer suit, dress shirt and tie. He was clean-shaven with a handsome, square jaw, and a look of general anticipation. Matthew was not what Paul had been expecting at all. When he thought about it later, he would have expected someone ten years younger, wearing jeans, a GYE T-shirt, and a gung-ho attitude. *Must be the Duke's influence*, Paul thought.

After an exchange of pleasantries, Paul felt entirely at ease talking with this man—as if he were a client chief executive of long standing. "So, you'd like me to go to Morocco?"

"Yes," Matthew said. "Morocco is kind of a special case, and we asked Charitable Consultants for a senior consultant with a strong financial background, and a good nose."

"A good nose?" Paul repeated, involuntarily wrinkling his own.

"Yes. I mean someone with an acute intuitive sense who can read between the lines of a situation, ask the right questions, and keep boring in."

"I'm not sure I would have described myself quite like that, but I have dealt with some pretty slippery characters on various assignments."

Matthew said emphatically, "That's what we want! In my opinion, Yusuf Al-Rashid—he's the CEO of the GYE chapter in Morocco—is pretty slippery."

"How so?"

"Well one thing he does, which I find particularly annoying, is that he almost never gives me a direct answer to a question I ask. He'll talk around the subject at great length without providing the answer I'm looking for. I think he's hoping I'll have forgotten what the question was or just give up."

"Can you tell me what some of your particular concerns are about the chapter in Morocco?"

"I can't pin them down. I just have a general queasiness. For example, we ask each chapter to report on their KPI's (key performance indicators) to us. Last month, Morocco reported that 59 of 187 outstanding loans were in arrears. The previous month, it had been 37 of 185 loans in arrears. I asked him what had happened to put so many loans in arrears. He said, 'Oh, no; that's a mistake!' but then he never came up with the corrected data."

Paul asked, "Could it be that he doesn't understand English very well?"

"That's not a problem. He got an MBA from City College of New York, and he lived in the States for two or three years. He can speak English perfectly well—although sometimes he seems to pretend he doesn't understand. I believe he's originally from somewhere in Iraq."

"Any other sources of queasiness?" Paul inquired.

"Yes. There seems to be a very high turnover of staff in the offices in Morocco. Nobody—apart from the bookkeeper—seems to be there longer than a few months. And when I ask Yusuf about it, he says, 'We can only pay charity wages. People find that they can't get by on what we pay.' So when I suggest that he pay his staff a little better, he says, 'Well that one left because he was useless.' Paul, there's something wrong when so many staff leave so soon after being hired."

Roberta put in: "I was asked to go to Morocco a couple of months ago to help them with a training program they had agreed to run. I had expected to meet with one of their employees, but he had left the organisation before I got there. Then the next day, he turned up at my hotel as I was having breakfast. He sat down at my table and looked carefully around the dining room. Then in a very low voice, he said to me, 'Miss Ambola, things are not well at AMM (that's the acronym for Young Enterprise Morocco in Arabic).' I asked him what things were not well, and he wouldn't answer. He said that Mr. Al-Rashid is a very powerful man, and 'it could be dangerous for me; Please ask Mr. Andrews to come and check!'"

For a few moments, Roberta, Matthew, and Paul sat looking at each other. Paul broke the silence, and with a smile, he said, "You know, a long time ago, I used to be in Special Forces. Haven't had much practice lately, though."

Matthew said, "No, I didn't know that, Paul, but I really don't think you'll need that experience in Morocco." Then he added, "One thing we haven't briefed you on is why Morocco is important to us."

Paul nodded. "That's a good point. It would be easy enough to just disaccredit them and kick them out. But before we get into that, did they ever run the training program, Roberta?"

She shook her head. "No, I don't think so. It was something we were trying to get them to do, but I doubt it was ever done."

Matthew said, "We'd rather not kick them out, Paul. They represent a potential model that new chapters in the Muslim world can copy . . . You know that the Qur'an forbids the charging of interest?"

"Yes, but I don't suppose GYE wants to lend money to entrepreneurs without charging interest. So what do you do?"

"Have you heard of mudarabah, Paul?"

"No, I can't say that I have."

"Well, mudarabah is one of several forms of lending which does not involve the payment of interest and is legal under the Qur'an. What happens is that the lender—in this case AMM—and the entrepreneur agree that the lender will be entitled to a certain share of the profits which the entrepreneur's company generates."

Paul considered this; he asked, "Is there some formula by which the share of profits is determined?"

"No, there isn't a formula. Agreement is reached through negotiation based on the amount of funding lent, the expected level of profits from the entrepreneur's business, and the probability that the business will be a success. The trouble is," Matthew continued, "that in our case, it is not a negotiation between equals. One of our requirements is that there is no other sourcing of funding for the entrepreneurs we support: no family money, no collateral, and no willingness of Islamic banks to lend. This immediately puts the entrepreneur at a disadvantage. Also, another of our requirements is that the entrepreneur is between the ages of eighteen and thirty-five. We want to support young people who haven't been in business before. This also puts the entrepreneur at a disadvantage because he or she doesn't have much business experience. He may have an over-optimistic view of the profits he can make, and he doesn't have the negotiating skills that someone like Yusuf, who is in his mid-forties with a business education, would have."

Paul asked, "So you're concerned that Yusuf may be taking advantage of his entrepreneurs?"

"Yes, exactly."

"But don't you require your chapters to send you audited financial statements? If he's taking advantage, he'd be making money rather than breaking even."

"We do get audited financial statements—in Arabic. And it would appear that AMM is roughly breaking even, but they've been operating under GYE accreditation only four years. So the first entrepreneurs that AMM supported four years ago are only now making profits that they would share."

"So you want me to talk to entrepreneurs and look at the contracts they've signed to determine whether they favour AMM excessively?" Matthew nodded. "But Matthew, I don't read or speak Arabic, and if AMM provides a translator, can the translation be relied upon?"

Matthew held up a hand. "If it's all right with you, Paul, we'd like to send our Director of Operations, Naomi Evensen, with you. She's fluent in Arabic."

"With a name like Evensen, how did she learn Arabic?"

"Naomi grew up in Jerusalem. Her mother is Jewish, and her father is a Swedish musician. As a child, she learned Hebrew, Arabic, Swedish and some English. She has a degree in languages from City University of London, so her English is polished, and she's picked up German, French and Spanish as well."

"Seven languages! People like that amaze me! But, Matthew, why do you need me? Naomi sounds like she could do the assessment herself."

"No. We definitely need you. Naomi has great language skills, is very good with people, and she fully understands what GYE is about. What you bring to the team is business experience and financial skills. As a consultant, you'll stay focused on the task.

If she didn't work for GYE, Naomi would probably be a musician. Don't get me wrong, she does a great job for us, but she doesn't particularly like confrontations."

Matthew excused himself, and left Paul with Roberta, who spent the next twenty minutes transferring documents to Paul and answering his questions. She told him, "This is a copy of the last assessment of AMM, which was done two years ago. This will give you an idea of the issues that were highlighted then. Since that time, we've changed the format of the reports that we ask assessors to provide. Here's a copy of our current report template."

"OK. Roberta, is Naomi your boss?"

"Yes, but she's travelling constantly. I'm here providing the home base support that she needs. She likes to travel; I don't. I've got a husband and two small children. Between the two of us, we provide the operating activity that Matthew wants."

"So I assume that Naomi is single?"

"Yes, she's single."

* * *

"This system is a bleedin' nightmare!" the trader named Rod announced emphatically to Paul. Rod's origins, Paul decided, were somewhere in east London. He didn't have a true cockney accent, but his use of wild gestures and colourful slang suggested that he had not been raised in Virginia Water.

"Show me what you're talking about," Paul asked. They were both sitting at Rod's desk in the midst of the Smith Coleridge trading room. It was noisy with telephone conversations that were not being conducted in hushed tones. Rod's desk had three side-by-side monitors on which various colour graphics were displayed. He had a Bluetooth phone headset in one ear, his right hand moved constantly over the mouse, and his left hand toyed distractedly with the headset control.

Rod said, "Look a this here! Now, I've just asked the system for the trading history of BAe. Five, six, seven, eight . . . twelve, thirteen, fourteen." A new graphic gradually appeared on the centre monitor. It showed a historic trend of BAe's stock price, together with a table in the lower right. "Fourteen seconds!" Rod turned toward Paul with obvious exasperation. "Fourteen seconds is a bloody eon! . . . I'm on the phone with a client, and I gotta wait fourteen seconds to give him an answer! He'll think I'm daft —— or bloody slow!"

"Is this the only problem you're having—historic price trends?" Paul asked.

"Hell no! It's bloody anything we ask the system for! . . . Here, now, I've asked the system to give me the trading record of a client—Mr. Hirshorn. He trades for ATA Insurance. . . . He calls me up, he tells me who he is, and the first thing I does is I call up his record. That reminds me what he's after, how much and how often. You gotta have that right away. He don't want to beat his gums about the bloody weather while you wait for the bloody system to come up with something. Here, now. It just came up."

Rod continued his demonstration with the client asking, hypothetically, about BAe shares. "So, I click on this link. We talk for a while about how ATA is doing, how his bloody mother-in-law has had a stroke, and how his bloody daughter has decided to take a gap year in Australia, and about . . . OK, here it is. Finally! See, it's showing buy. You got the BAe financials for the last couple years, and our estimates of the next couple. Then if ya scroll down, there's all this bloody text ya can read to him that explains why we have BAe as a buy. I sound pretty bloody clever when I read this to a client—kinda slow, like I'm just thinking of it. 'Cept I don't sound so clever when it takes me a quarter of a minute to think of what to say!"

Paul summarised, "So this is what's wrong with the system—it's slow. You're not complaining about the information you're getting. It's the information you want, and it's correct, but it just takes too long to arrive."

"Yeah, thas right! I mean, I can do a search on Google, and I'll get a list of over a million websites in a quarter of a second! Not a quarter of a minute!"

"How is the system in terms of its financial record-keeping and in terms of its trading execution?" Paul asked.

"Far as I know, the records are OK. Trade posting is kinda slow, but that don't matter to us on the trading floor—might be an issue for the backroom guys."

Paul talked to several other traders; their story was the same. He also interviewed two of the women who worked in Smith Coleridge's back room. They had no problems with the system. When he went to talk to Angela in the back room, she was engaged in a discussion with a young man who was apparently one of Smith Coleridge's IT technicians. She explained a major client's need for a special monthly report format. When their conversation was completed, Paul said to the technician that he was there to do some work on SuperBridge and did the technician have any experience with it.

"Naw," was the response, "It's mostly the supplier, Orion's problem, but I've heard the problem is related to Orion's graphics module, which is slow to develop a solution."

"Do you know what causes it to be slow?" Paul asked.

"I've heard that, for some reason, it requests the entire database to be updated before it extracts any data."

"That should be easy to fix."

"No, for some reason, it's not."

Paul needed confirmation and to develop a solution he could sell. He called three of Orion's competitors and told them he was an independent consultant doing a study for a big client about the pros and cons of various trading software packages. After listening to a lengthy sales pitch about the sales rep's particular product, Paul asked about any weaknesses in competitive products. All three sales reps mentioned the slowness of SuperBridge; all three confirmed that the graphics module was to blame; and all three said something about updating the entire database. Various reasons were given for this, with a consensus that this was a long-standing problem.

"Sounds like the solution for SuperBridge clients," Paul suggested, "is to un-install the Orion graphics module and put in an industry standard like Digigraph."

Efraim's Eye

The general response to Paul's suggestion was, "Yeah, but Orion wouldn't be very happy with that."

* * *

It felt good to have the whole family together in the house: John, his wife Teresa, their two boys David and Edward, and Cynthia. Paul had gone to Euston station to meet them at 7:54 p.m. on Friday when their train arrived from Manchester. "We're coming to check up on you, Dad," John said when he called. "The kids are out of school, and besides, there are some things they want to do in London."

Cynthia was already at the house when they had arrived. She and Sarah were working in the kitchen, organising dinner.

"What's for dinner, Aunt Cindy?" David asked. He was nine years old.

Cynthia replied, "We have squirrel pie, Brussels sprouts, and butternut squash followed by a lovely rhubarb pie."

David made a disagreeable face. "Squirrel pie?" he asked, dismayed.

"Yes, David," Cynthia continued airily. "You know how the grey squirrels are taking over from our lovely native red squirrels? Well, Grandpa has decided to teach the grey squirrels a lesson. He's caught some, and we've put them in a pie."

"No, he didn't!" David protested.

"Oh, yes he did," Cynthia continued undeterred. "You know, Grandpa, when he gets upset about something he takes action! Oh, and I forgot. There's turtle soup to start."

"What kind of turtle?" Edward, a skeptical eight-year-old, asked.

Cynthia said breezily, "Oh, it's just a regular box turtle. Delicious."

David carefully surveyed the pots on the hob. "There's no soup!" he announced triumphantly. Then turning to the other cook, "Sarah, what are we really having for dinner?"

Sarah could not conceal her mirth. She looked for support to Cynthia, who giggled and shrugged.

Sarah bent down and put an arm around each boy. "Your Aunt Cindy likes to have fun with you, doesn't she?"

"Sarah," Edward asked, "will you tell us what we're really having for dinner?"

"We're having roast beef, roast potatoes, and green beans. Plus, I think Aunt Cindy bought some Häagen-Dazs ice cream especially for you."

After dinner, to Paul's considerable dismay, Sarah excused herself and went home. *She could have spent the night*, Paul thought. *Why did she have to leave? She's going home to an empty house; neither of her girls are there—just the damn cats! Doesn't she like my family? My kids understand that we're sleeping together. What the hell is her problem?*

Cynthia and John were aware of their father's frustration and suspected the cause, but they knew better than to start a pointless scene by confronting him. Instead, after the boys were put to bed, they attempted to distract him. "How's work going, Dad?" John inquired when they were sitting in the living room. Teresa, in deference to family conversations, sat at one end of the couch working on a needlepoint pillow cover, one ear tuned to the conversation. She was a petite, dark-haired woman, in her early thirties, with fine features and a lovely smile.

When John had first brought her home to meet his parents, Catherine and Paul had considered her very pretty but somewhat immature. They had doubted that a relationship between their super-confident son, and this apparently scatter-brained girl could last. But that was twelve years ago, and last she did! In fact, Paul suspected, Teresa had complete domination of their household with John's influence pretty much confined to his work.

Paul said, "I've just completed an analysis at Smith Coleridge, and I'll be presenting the results to the CEO next week."

"How do you feel about it?" John asked.

"Well, John, it's not my usual kind of work. It'll involve changing out a software module, and I'll probably need some help from a real IT expert."

"Dad," Cynthia interjected, "where is that charity going to be sending you?"

"Morocco."

John was surprised. "That'll be great, Dad, except it'll be a little hot this time of year. What are you going to be doing?"

Cynthia said, "I don't think it's so damn great. They have their own branch of al-Qaeda there. Don't you remember, John, a few years ago, some fanatics set off some bombs in Casablanca and killed a whole bunch of perfectly innocent people?"

John gave a shrug, "OK, but that was years ago."

Cynthia shook her head but said nothing.

Paul explained the nature of his assignment in Morocco, and then sensing the need to change direction, he asked, "How's everything at ADP, John?" ADP, Architectural Design Partnership, was a large firm of commercial and industrial architects located in Manchester.

"Going well, Dad. We just got an assignment for a 120-story building in Doha, and my department is going to do the steelwork design. It'll be an interesting challenge because the building has an elliptical cross-section with the long axis in an east-west direction. The building will act like an airfoil, and it will have to flex in high winds. The trick will be to allow it to flex, but not so much as to cause the tenants to get seasick or to result in stress cracking of the steel."

"What are your design conditions?" Paul asked. Paul, who had obtained a first in business and finance at the London School of Economics, was no technical match for his son, who had obtained a first in mechanical engineering from Cambridge, but Paul at least understood some of his son's technical language.

"Our design constraints are a 200 kilometre-an-hour wind, from any direction, with instantaneous gusts up to 300—which meteorologists say can never happen in the Gulf—and ten meters maximum displacement on floor 120 with an acceleration not to exceed 0.5 G."

"How about resistance to collisions from 747s?" Cynthia asked with a faintly evil smile.

John at first took her question at face value, "Cindy, you can't design..." then he saw that, as usual, she was engaged in polemics, and he added, "So, we're going to put a Patriot missile battery on the roof."

Sarah returned just as they were finishing breakfast. She helped Paul clear the table and put the leftovers away. When the others had gone upstairs to get ready, Paul said, "I was expecting you to spend the night, Sarah."

"I know you were, but I thought it would be better if I went home."

"Why?"

"I thought it would be better for me not to presume too much," she said.

"What do you mean?" Paul was annoyed and a little puzzled.

"Paul, I like your kids, but I don't think I ought to be acting like a stepmother. I'm not sure they're ready for that, or that I'm ready for it."

"Spending one night here doesn't make you a stepmother. Aren't you being kind of old-fashioned?"

"Paul, this is the first time I've been in your house with Cynthia, John and his family. I've met Cynthia before and John before, but this is the first time we've all been together. I think spending the night would have symbolic significance to your kids and to me. Maybe I am old-fashioned, but that's the way I am."

"Will you spend the night here tonight?"

"No, but, if you want, you can come to my place on Monday night."

* * *

"Grandpa, can we go on the London Eye?" David asked, just as they were leaving.

John said, "I thought that you guys wanted to go to the Natural History Museum, and then to the Zoo."

"We do, but I want to go on the London Eye 'cause it's like being on a plane."

Efraim's Eye

"If we're going on the London Eye, we ought to go now because by 11 a.m. there'll be a big queue," Paul observed.

"OK, let's go now then," John decided.

"Just a minute," Teresa said, "Edward, do you want to go?"

Edward stopped, and looked at his brother. "I don't know," he said.

"Yes, you do," David insisted. "It's like a Ferris wheel, but you're inside a glass room and you go way up in the sky. You remember!"

"Oh, yeah. . . . OK."

There were only isolated puffs of high clouds in the June sky, as their capsule began to rise slowly above the river. They had hoped to have a capsule all to themselves, but, in addition to the seven of them, including Cynthia and Sarah, there were at least another dozen people: half Asian and half visitors from Europe. David stood, next to his mother, at the end of the capsule looking north. Teresa pointed into the distance. "See," she said, "there's Buckingham Palace."

"Oh, yeah. What's that?" David inquired, pointing to a large building on the north side of the river.

"That's Charing Cross Railway Station." She guided him around to the east side of the capsule.

"You see the Gherkin? It's that tall building with a rounded top; it looks like a pickle."

Edward, meanwhile, was standing, mesmerized, against the glass looking down at the river. "Boy, it's high! It's really high!"

David responded, "Eddie, it's nothing yet! Try looking down when we get to the top!"

When the capsule reached its peak of 135 metres, and their capsule was directly above the hub, Edward gazed down in fascination. "I can see tiny little seagulls down there, and the people are miniature!" he announced. "They're so far away! And there's the ice cream truck, but it's so small!"

David considered his brother who was leaning against the curved glass so as to look directly down. "Eddie, aren't you afraid to look down like that? You might fall!"

"I can't fall, stupid! I'm inside the glass."

"Yeah, but what if the glass broke?"

"It's not going to break, is it, Mom?"

As the capsule glided slowly down toward the bottom, David called, "Come here, Eddie, we can get our picture taken!" He pointed toward the momentary flashes from the structure. "See there's the camera. Don't stick out your tongue!"

Teresa was given temporary custody of the resulting photograph and was escorted by her boys to the miniature ice cream truck, where she was expected to purchase her freedom with two chocolate ice cream cones.

John, meanwhile, stood looking up at the giant wheel from its south side. Paul walked over to where his son was standing and commented, "I see an engineer's eye at work."

"Yes," John mused, still looking up, "You know, Dad, the support structure for this wheel is very different from a traditional Ferris wheel. A Ferris wheel is held up by a support structure on either side of its central hub. But they couldn't do that in this case because the wheel is suspended over the river. So this wheel is supported from only <u>one</u> end of its hub; it's cantilevered over the river. You see, Dad," he said pointing, "there are those two rigid legs which support the hub, and there's a third leg, which keeps the wheel from toppling over. The third leg is comprised of those six cables that come down from the hub at an angle and are anchored in concrete." John continued to contemplate the structure. "Cindy, come over here a minute, will you?" he called.

"What is it?" she asked standing next to him, and looking up.

"Cindy, suppose I had a really huge pair of scissors, and I cut these cables. What would happen?" he asked.

Cindy surveyed the structure, tilting her head from side-to-side. Finally, she looked at her brother, with a startled expression on her face. "I guess it would topple over."

"And into the river," he added.

"But you don't have any scissors that big!" she protested.

"I don't, but a terrorist might. I just thought that as our resident expert on terrorism, you'd like to know."

Cynthia stood dumbfounded; after a moment, Paul interceded, "How would a terrorist be able to cut the cables, John?"

"He would use what's called a shaped charge where the blast and the heat from the explosion are tightly focused." John paused to reflect for a few seconds. "I would think that about half a kilogram of high explosive in the right configuration per cable would do it. Notice, Cindy, that the other two legs—the stiff legs—are hinged, so they would not hold the wheel up once the cables are cut. They were hinged so that the wheel could be lifted into position in one piece from a barge in the river."

Cynthia was horror-struck as she looked at her brother. "You mean to tell me that a terrorist with a backpack could knock over this wheel and have it fall crashing into the river where hundreds of people would drown if they weren't killed on impact?"

John nodded. "But," he added, "he'd probably need a little time to arrange his shaped charges. Notice that the cables at ground level are surrounded by a glass enclosure so he'd either have to break through the glass or get on top of it."

"Well but, John," Cynthia remonstrated, "there are always police around here, and I'm sure they would notice if somebody climbed onto the glass."

"Yes, but they're not armed, and once he's on top of or inside the glass, it would take only seconds for him to lay out his charges."

* * *

"You think this is costing us ten percent of our trading efficiency?" Sam Kleinfelt summarised. "That's the equivalent of nearly two of our eighteen traders, and on a salary basis—not including bonus—that's well over £300,000."

"Yes, " Paul responded, "but that doesn't include the costs associated with any unhappy customers taking their business elsewhere."

"And what you're proposing is to uninstall the SuperBridge graphic module and replace it with a Digigraph module, all for . . ."

Sam glanced down at the PowerPoint graphic in front of him "Not including license fees, £34,700."

"But," Paul protested, "It's not a simple replacement, Mr. Kleinfelt. There's quite a bit of work involved in configuring Digigraph to meet your needs, in testing it live with SuperBridge, and in training your traders in its use. By the way, I think your traders will find it a lot more user-friendly than SuperBridge."

Kleinfelt turned to Eddie Chernowski, "What's your view, Eddie?"

"I think it's taking a huge risk with our system," Eddie replied sourly.

Kleinfelt lowered his head and stared at Eddie. "The bloody system isn't working!" he said slowly and emphatically, as if he were trying to make a point with someone who had limited familiarity with English.

"£35,000 is a lot of money," Eddie replied lamely.

"Is it? Dick, let me see that Orion sheet." Kleinfelt took a sheet for paper from the Finance Director. "It says here that we've spent £73,000 with Orion on their attempts to fix SuperBridge over the last three months!" He turned toward Dick and George, "What do you guys think?"

"I think we ought to go with Paul," George replied. Dick nodded.

Eddie was still shaking his head.

"Paul, I'm afraid you'll have to leave it with us for a couple of days," Kleinfelt said.

Three days later, Paul tried to reach Sam Kleinfelt without success, and the client CEO didn't return Paul's calls. Eventually, Paul reached George Whitman, who was very apologetic, "I'm sorry, Paul, but we're not going to take you up on your offer."

Paul felt anger and frustration rising within; he managed to ask, "Any particular reason, George?"

"Sam has decided to give the job to Orion."

"To Orion?" Paul was incredulous, "but you've been waiting months for them to solve the problem, which has become common knowledge in the industry!"

"I know. Sam had our attorneys call Orion's in-house counsel, threatening them with a very public law suit. That apparently panicked them. Their CEO came to see us, and promised that they would fix the problem quickly."

Paul asked, "How quickly is 'quickly'?"

"Well, Sam told them we have a proposal from an independent consultant to replace their graphics module with Digigraph."

"Oh, shit!"

"Yeah, I know, but that <u>really</u> panicked Orion. Can you imagine how their reputation would suffer if it got out that customers were replacing their software with shrink-wrapped modules?"

"Let me go back to my question, George. How quickly is 'quickly'?"

"There are three Orion engineers here now. They're loading a fix, which they say will alter the instructions on updating the entire database before calculating the graphics. If that's effective, we should have a decent system tomorrow."

"How much are they going to charge you for this fix?"

"Nothing—there's no charge, and Sam insisted that they give us a refund for the £73,000 we've spent over the last three months."

"You know, George, I feel like I've been used!"

"Believe me, Paul, I wanted to go ahead with your proposal, and I think Dick did too. If Orion drops the ball, we'll get you back in right away."

That evening, Paul recounted his Smith Coleridge tale of woe to Sarah. She said, "I suppose that's a risk of being a consultant. Some clients will use you to support their own objectives, which happen to run counter to yours."

"Well, but I think that's unethical, Sarah. It would be different if they had paid me to do that analysis—which took me three days, plus all the meetings I had with them. I feel like sending them an invoice!"

Sarah looked at Paul and shook her head. Then her eyes narrowed; she said, "Didn't you say that that Geraldine woman recommended you for this job and didn't she tell you that she's a friend of Sam what's-his-name?"

"Yes."

"And wasn't she looking for a cut of your business?"

"Yes, seven percent."

"I think she's the culprit!"

Paul was puzzled, "What do you mean, Sarah?"

"I mean that Sam what's-his-name approached his old friend Geraldine and asked her to send in a consultant who could confirm his suspicions about that Bridge-thingy. And I'll bet that he promised her a nice little stipend if the consultant performed well. So," Sarah finished triumphantly, "Geraldine got the fee for your analysis!"

Paul was horrified. "No! She wouldn't do that!"

"Yes, she would! I told you she is a nasty woman, and you admitted that she's a predatory woman. But she's not after your body; she's after your money!"

"Oh, Sarah, I think that's a bit much!" Paul shook his head. "Geraldine is a member of Charitable Consultants, and that would be totally contrary to the code of ethics!"

Sarah gave him her warm smile. "One of the things I love about you, Paul, is that you trust people, and you assume that their intentions are honourable, which shows me that <u>you</u> are honourable and trustworthy."

* * *

Paul spent the better part of two days preparing for the assessment in Morocco. He got a Lonely Planet guide, and read the history, culture and traditions of Morocco. While the sights to see and places to visit were tempting, he set all of that aside for when there might be some free time available.

He read the report of the previous assessment of AMM that had been completed in 2009, and he found it disappointing: very long on generalisations and quite short on specific facts and figures. The general tone of the report seemed almost obsequious in its praise of the "vital work being done by AMM to relieve chronic unemployment amongst young people in Morocco." He knew that the use of Charitable Consultants by GYE was something new, and he wondered whether previous assessments had been done by 'business advisers' or by 'management consultants'. He raised this question when he was on the phone to Roberta; she told him that prior audits had been carried out by 'volunteer retirees', and that GYE was not particularly happy with some of the reports.

The previous report did mention two 'concerns' with AMM: that the board of trustees was more an advisory body than a governing body and that there were no procedures manuals to document day-to-day activities. In response to e-mails that Roberta sent of Yusuf two weeks before his departure, Paul received copies of AMM's board of trustees meeting minutes, which had been translated into barely comprehensible English. Paul had the impression that the board activity was focused on discussion rather than decision-making.

Paul sent an e-mail to Yusuf saying that he looked forward to meeting Yusuf and his team. He also attached his CV *He might as well know at the outset that I'm not a 'volunteer retiree'*.

Roberta booked Paul's flights to and from Marrakech, his hotel room, and arranged for a car and driver to be at his (and Naomi's) disposal. "Naomi will pay for the meals for the two of you, but if there is any other expense, like telephone calls, you can report that when you get back to the U.K., and we'll reimburse you," Roberta told him.

About a week before his departure, Paul received an e-mail from Yusuf, which detailed who he and Naomi would meet, where and when. A copy of the e-mail had been sent to Naomi, who, according to Roberta, was in India at the time. Yusuf's schedule had large gaps in it: late starts, early finishes and long lunch hours. It also provided for at least a one-hour meeting with Yusuf every day. *Oh, no you don't!* Paul thought.

He send an e-mail back to Yusuf, copying Naomi and Roberta, in which he requested an earlier start, later finish, shorter lunch breaks, and said, "I would like to meet with four more of your entrepreneurs, and three more of your mentors. I will select them on arrival. I would also like to meet with all of your current staff, representatives of the Inter-Saharan Development Bank, two major Moroccan commercial banks, the Moroccan Ministry for Employment, and three of the five companies which are currently providing funding to AMM. I think it will not be necessary to take up your time every day, just the morning of the first day of our visit and perhaps two hours during the afternoon of our last day. I look forward to meeting you and working with you. Shukran bezzef (Thank you very much), Paul Winthorpe."

The next morning Paul received an e-mail from Naomi that read, "Hi, Paul. It's great to have you on the assessment of AMM, and I look forward to helping you any way I can. Roberta sent me a copy of your CV. Wow! It'll be great to have a real professional on the job. Your e-mail to Yusuf requesting the additional meetings was right on target. He wouldn't let us out of the hotel if he thought he could get away with it. It'll be interesting to see his response. I'll be in Cairo on Sunday and Monday, so I should get to Marrakech on Tuesday. Shall we have dinner together? Roberta has booked rooms for us at Riad el Norj. Shall we meet in the courtyard at 7:30 p.m.? Your photo was with your CV; mine is on the GYE website. Kind regards, Naomi."

Paul went straight to the GYE website. There at the top of the staff page was a photo of Matthew Andrews, followed by a brief biography. He scrolled down the page until he came to Naomi Evensen, Operations Director. She looked to be about thirty-five, and a lot like Kate Moss. *How does a Jewish girl get to be blonde?* Paul wondered, non-plussed. *Well, she bleaches her hair.* But her complexion and blue eyes suggested otherwise. *Or,* he mused, *now I remember, she has a Swedish father.* Naomi had been with GYE for three years. Before that, she spent four years with Care International in Paris; prior to that with a small charity in Gaza. She was educated at City University, London, speaks seven languages, and her interests include violin, flute and sociology. She grew up in Jerusalem.

Chapter 4

MARRAKECH

The driver bowed deferentially. He was a small man with a dark complexion, black nervous eyes, and a neatly trimmed moustache. In spite of the heat, he was wearing a dark jacket, navy trousers and a clean, white T-shirt. "My name Mohammed, Mr. Winthorpe," he announced in his staccato voice. "I take you to hotel. Car this way. Please come."

The car was a black Mercedes four-door sedan that looked to be at least ten years old. The back seat was comfortable, however, and the air conditioning worked. "Is this your car, Mohammed?" Paul inquired.

"Yes, sir."

"And are you going to be our driver while we are here?"

"Yes, sir. Inshalla." (God willing). Paul was to learn that in Morocco a great deal seemed to depend on the willingness of God.

They sped down a divided road; on either side, there were occasional walled houses and fenced plots where goats and sheep grazed listlessly. The landscape was flat and brown, the houses, dusty.

Now and then, they passed small groups of children, dressed in their unkempt uniforms, making their way home from school: the boys kicking a football; the girls, walking together, wearing dark headscarves.

As they approached Marrakech, the houses on either side abutted one another and the central median was irrigated so that the white and rose oleander grew more abundantly.

"Here is big, new shopping centre," Mohammed observed with a gesture toward what looked like a transplanted American shopping mall, with a large car park, palm trees and more oleander. Then the high, ochre stonewall of the city loomed on their right. "Down there is the Djemaa el-Fna."

Paul asked, "That's the big open square where everything happens?"

"Yes, sir. Many things happen there."

"And is it safe at night?"

"Djemaa el-Fna very safe. Side alleys not so safe. You tell me where you want go. I take you there."

Paul asked, "How is the restaurant in the hotel, Mohammed?"

"I not know, sir. I never stay there. Is small. Other people say is OK. You want go out, I give you my phone number, so I pick you up. . . . Here is hotel now, sir."

The car was stopped in a wide street, where vendors of baskets had piles of goods on display. Paul got out and looked around; there was no hotel in sight. An old woman approached with two armloads of baskets. Mohammed intervened, "La! La!"

The woman looked offended, and began to remonstrate with Mohammed, who in turn patiently explained something to her.

"I don't see the hotel, Mohammed," Paul remarked.

Mohammed removed Paul's suitcase from the boot of the car. He locked the car and turning to Paul, he said, "Down this little street, sir." There was no street sign on either the wide street or its narrow offshoot. Nor was there any indication of a nearby hotel. When Mohammed approached a heavy wooden door, which was marked only with the number sixty-three, Paul began to feel ill at ease. Mohammed rapped loudly on the door and stood back. Sensing Paul's uncertainty, he said, "Is here."

The door opened, and a wizened man in baggy black trousers, a long black shirt and a maroon fez stood back and bowed slightly. Paul stepped across the threshold and found himself in a splendid garden courtyard. There were four large orange trees, that were laden with fruit, and a fountain gurgled in the midst of them. Geometric walkways were paved with blue and white ceramic tiles, and resting on the tiles, here and there, were large pots filled with ferns, ivy and white lilies. To his left, Paul saw a tile-lined rectangular pool of water about five feet deep. The swimming pool? Looking up, Paul could see the sky above the second story.

"Welcome! You must be Mr. Winthorpe." It was a man's voice with a French accent. The man himself appeared from an alcove. He was deeply tanned, wearing a white polo shirt, tan shorts and sandals. "I am Julian Perot, your host. Let me show you Riad El Norj. We can attend to the paperwork later!"

Mr. Perot explained that he and his wife, Yvonne, had bought the building, which had been abandoned nine years ago. He said, "It was, like all riads in Marrakech, once a grand family home with a living area on the ground floor, bedrooms on the first floor, and a terrace with servants quarters on what would be the second floor. We have eight bedrooms, each ensuite. For staff, we have a cook—who is quite good—two maids and a porter. Through this door we have the lounge, through that door is the dining room, the kitchen is there, and there is a small hammam in that corner."

"What is a hammam?" Paul asked.

"It is a sauna where one can scrub oneself and apply various oils. There are lots of public ones in Marrakech for men or women. Ours is small—for at most two people—if you want to use it, you'll need to reserve it with me or Yvonne so we can make it ready."

The room to which Paul was shown was small but luxurious in its decorations: the large bed was covered with a satin amethyst spread and half a dozen white cotton cushions. There were colourful tribal carpets on the tile floor, and heavy chocolate curtains hung at the windows that looked out into the atrium. The bathroom was more Spartan: there was no shower enclosure; just a huge showerhead in one corner and a drain set into the stone-tiled floor. The towels and bathrobes looked inviting. The bedroom air conditioning was blowing softly, and Paul saw that his suitcase had been placed on a stand. *OK. Very okay*, he thought, *Let's see the view from the terrace*.

The narrow, winding stone staircase in one corner of the building led up to the terrace on the north side of which was a single-story building, which Paul took to be the servants' quarters. In the centre, one could look down into the atrium and the courtyard below. Looking to the west, the roofs of Marrakech, with satellite dishes and antennae, reached out into the distance, where the sun coloured a band of clouds orange and pink.

To the east, the perspective of roofs was unbroken except for one structure: the great tower of the Koutoubia Mosque. Paul knew that Koutoubia was the largest mosque in Morocco, and he had read that it, like all mosques in Morocco, was closed to non-Muslims. *Strange*, he thought, *that mosques in Turkey and India* (which he had visited) *should be open to Christians, but here, they are closed.* He had read that the closure was the result of desecrations committed long ago by disrespectful Christians. *But*, he pondered, *if there are any two places where religions have been in conflict, they would be Istanbul and Delhi.* Turning to the south, Paul could see the peaks of the Atlas Mountains—not so far away—and he thought he could make out the last vestiges of snow on the higher peaks.

Paul settled himself in a comfortable leather armchair, having selected a picture book, *'Beautiful Morocco'*, from the shelves in the lounge. The room was large with a fireplace at one end, and it had been decorated with the same colourful, native fabrics. There was no one else in the room as he began to peruse the book, but moments later the same small man, dressed in black and topped with the maroon fez, slipped silently into the room. Standing deferentially to one side of Paul, he inquired in halting English, "Would like drink, sir?"

"Yes, I would." He was aware of the Qur'an's strictures regarding alcohol, so he asked, "What do you have?"

Silently, the porter produced a card and handed it to Paul. It listed various spirits, imported and domestic beers, and wines, by the bottle. The price range was startling: from a hundred dirhams for a Scotch—nearly £8—to ten dirhams for a bottle of Casablanca pilsner. "How is the Casablanca?" The porter raised his hands in a gesture of ignorance.

"I'll have a Casablanca."

When the beer arrived, it was cold and good. Paul was absorbed in the photographs of the Atlas valleys: stark burnt red rock slopes with foaming torrents of pale green water.

"Hello, Paul,"

He turned to see a slim, blonde girl with blue-grey eyes, looking down at him, a slight smile on her lips. "Oh, hello, Naomi," He jumped to his feet. "I'm glad to meet you at last."

She settled herself on the sofa opposite him, her legs folded under her and her brown leather sandals on the floor. She was wearing a long, Laura Ashley, flower-print dress with short sleeves and a high neckline. Her purse—a small, brown leather sack with red, silk rope ties—lay by her sandals.

"Good evening, Ms. Evensen, can I get you something to drink?" It was a stout European lady with a French accent. *This must be Yvonne*, Paul thought.

Naomi tossed her head, considering. "Can I persuade you to switch to wine, Paul?" she asked.

"Yes, you can."

"Red or white?"

"It doesn't matter. Is there a good Moroccan wine?"

Naomi turned to Yvonne; there followed a brief conversation in French, ending with "OK," and then, "Shall we eat here, Paul?"

"Yes, why not?"

"Do you prefer chicken or lamb?"

"Lamb."

Another conversation in French, after which Naomi turned her attention to Paul. "We're going to have mezze to start—that's an assortment of small appetizers and salads. Then tajines—yours is lamb, mine is chicken, couscous, and bastilla—that's a sweet Moroccan pastry for dessert."

"Sounds fine. How was your trip?"

"Oh, it's all the same. I don't like airplanes, but I love meeting new people. Would you believe it we have a new female chief executive of the GYE chapter in Egypt—an Arab, female chief executive!"

Paul smiled. "I guess that is quite an event. How did she get the job?"

Naomi hesitated. "I guess I had something to do with it. I met her at a conference in Alexandria. She was an administrator in the local Red Crescent office. Very bored, but bright and ambitious. Our Cairo chief executive had quit, and I persuaded the chairman to interview her. With a little help from two of the board members who happen to be female—one in government, the other in the university—she got the job, and she's off to a great start!"

Paul nodded. "Very good."

Naomi leaned forward. "Do you think so?"

Paul was slightly startled. "Yes, I really do. I think the Islamic world could benefit greatly from a larger female touch. In fact, I think England could also benefit from more meaningful involvement of women."

Naomi considered this. "I take it that you're married, Paul."

"I was. My wife died two years ago."

"Oh, I'm sorry. How did it happen?" What could have seemed like an invasive question instead came across as a genuine expression of sympathy.

"She had breast cancer." She looked at him expectantly; he continued, "She noticed a lump in her breast one morning. She went to the GP right away. They did a mammogram and a biopsy, and . . ." He broke off.

She nodded. "There are some cancers that can't be beaten, no matter what you do."

That sat in silence for a few moments, interrupted when Yvonne came in with the wine. "Would you like me to pour the wine for you now, or at the table? We're ready for you."

Naomi asked, "Shall we go in?" Paul nodded.

The dining room was long and narrow with two tables placed end to end. Paul and Naomi sat at the end of the left-hand table; there were two couples at the far end of the other table. A maid in a long-sleeved white shirt, apron and kerchief came in and set down a tray that was covered with small dishes. Naomi explained, "That one is pickled cauliflower, these are cheese balls—probably goat cheese—that's an aubergine puree, this looks like raw peppers and onions, that's some kind of marinated fish, and I haven't any idea what those are. Oh, and this is pita bread."

The idea of an assortment appealed to Paul; some of the dishes he liked; others failed an initial taste test. "You have an interesting background, Naomi," he said.

She looked up. "You think so?"

"Yes. What was it like growing up in Jerusalem?"

"Looking back, it seems quite normal to me. I had all kinds of friends: Jews, Arabs—even a few Christians. We didn't differentiate until we got to be teenagers. In fact, I don't even know today whether some of my Muslim friends are Sunni or Shia—probably Sunni, but I don't know for sure."

"What kind of a school did you attend?"

"I'm sure you know that as a female whose mother is Jewish, I am considered a Jew. So, my mother insisted that I go to a Hebrew school, and my father—I think reluctantly—agreed, but he insisted that it couldn't be an orthodox school. So at school, I learned proper Arabic. It has quite a lot in common with the Hebrew we spoke at home, and a little English. I played the violin and the concert flute. At home, we also spoke Swedish."

"How did your parents meet?"

"My father was second violinist with the Royal Stockholm Philharmonic Orchestra, and they came to do a series of concerts in Israel. My mother was a very promising young violinist with the Israel Philharmonic, and I suppose she was what you might call a classical music groupie. She was certainly beautiful and aggressive. Anyway, she met my father at a reception, and here I am." She smiled.

Paul looked slightly puzzled. He asked, "Just like that?"

"No. I've abbreviated the story somewhat. They got married, and they argued about whether she would relocate to Sweden or whether he would take up residence in Israel. What decided it was that the Israel Philharmonic offered him a violinist's position, and the Israeli government was willing to give him a permanent visa. My mother says that she would not have found a violinist's position in Sweden, but I know he disputes that. I also know that he wasn't happy living in Israel."

"But he's still living there?"

"No. He's living is Stockholm and back with the RSPO. When the First Intifada broke out in 1987, he was very upset. I was twelve at the time. My father didn't agree with the Israeli government's position on Palestine and living in Jerusalem at the time could be dangerous. He signed his Israel Philharmonic pension rights over to my mother . . . and he left." There was sadness in Naomi's voice and in her face.

Paul asked, "Do you still see him from time to time?"

She shook her head. "Well, yes, I try to see him once a year, but he's not very happy and he can be difficult. He's still angry at my mother—after all these years—for refusing to at least let me go to Stockholm with him. And he's angry at me for staying in Jerusalem, and . . ." Naomi trailed off.

Paul suggested, "But how could he have expected you to leave your mother at the age of twelve?"

"Oh, it's not just that. He's also angry that I gave up my music to work for charities. He reminds me of 'all the hours I put in to teaching you the violin, and you threw them all away!'"

"But it's your life, Naomi! Who can say that you're not making the world a better place by working for GYE than you could have done by playing the violin beautifully?"

She looked up. There were tears in her eyes. "Thank you for that, Paul. Thank you."

The maid had cleared away the mezze and brought out the cone-shaped, terracotta dishes. When the cones in which the tajines had been baked were removed, the main course of steaming meat, vegetables and broth was exposed.

Naomi asked, "How is your tajine?"

"It's all right, actually. I don't think this is lamb—more like mutton—but it's tender, and the flavour is very good."

"I have the impression," she said, cynically, "that in most of the non-Western world, lamb stops being lamb at the age of about six."

They went on to talk about various work experiences, and where they lived. Naomi said she had a small flat in Notting Hill. "But it doesn't see you very often," Paul suggested.

"I know, but it's small, and I get a pretty good deal on the rent. What do you do in your spare time, Paul?"

"Oh, I read. In the summer, I like fly fishing, and the rest of the year, I'm a Chelsea football fan."

"Are you? My boyfriend is an Arsenal fan."

"The Gunners. What does your boyfriend do, Naomi?"

"He's sort of a farmer."

"Oh! Where does he farm? Not in Notting Hill, I guess."

"No. He works on a kibbutz in the Sharon Valley, Galilee."

Paul thought he had misunderstood. "Your boyfriend works on a kibbutz in Israel, and when you're not on an airplane, you live in Notting Hill?"

Her smile betrayed her amusement at his confusion. "Yes."

"Sorry, but how does that work?"

She shrugged, "It works well enough. I get to Israel two or three times a year for a week or so. We're very good friends, and I don't want to make the same mistake my parents made by forcing the relationship to be in a particular location."

Paul was tempted to challenge her: to understand how a relationship like that could work in practice, but her love life was really none of his business, so he changed the subject.

Later, however, he thought, *If I were her boyfriend, and I had a beautiful girl like her, I wouldn't like it at all if I saw her only three weeks a year. I'd move to Notting Hill or I'd ride airplanes with her—whatever it took!*

Breakfast the next morning included a pitcher of fresh orange juice, goat's cheese, assorted olives, pancakes, fresh peaches, baskets of just-baked Moroccan pastries, and, of course, strong coffee. *Different, but very good!* Paul thought.

When Naomi joined him, she was wearing a white cotton blouse, embroidered with tiny blue flowers, and a long, pleated cotton skirt. Her hair, which was still damp, was tied at the nape of her neck with a blue ribbon.

They said their morning greetings, he poured her some coffee, and she surveyed him. "You don't need to wear a tie, Paul. In fact, in North Africa, most businessmen don't wear a suit unless it's a formal occasion."

"OK. I can dispense with the tie, but I do want to look like a European businessman, so I think I'll stay with the suit."

"OK." She smiled indulgently, and took a sip of her coffee. "We ought to talk about AMM."

"Yes. I guess you've met Yusuf?"

"I have, and I don't like him very much—probably because he looks at me in a certain way—if you see what I mean."

Paul nodded. He thought, *Who wouldn't?* But he said, "What we could do is for you to play the very kind, but distant, business woman, and for me to play the hard-assed—pardon the expression—nit-picking, auditor . . . "

Naomi added, ". . . who's sort of a father-figure/protector."

Paul said, "Yes. I think it's important—in case we give AMM a clean bill of health—that Yusuf feels warmly toward GYE, and if there's anybody he chooses to dislike that it be me."

"That's a good point. Has he come back to you with additions to the interview schedule?"

"No. I haven't heard a word from him."

"Figures. During the last assessment a couple of years ago, he used the same tactics: stall and delay, betting that we would give up and go home. He was right. We did. This time, I think we ought to stick it out, and get the information we need to make a valid decision about accreditation. I'm assuming, Paul, that you could stay on a couple of extra days?"

"Yes."

* * *

Naomi asked: "You know where to go, Mohammed?"

"Yes, ma'am."

They passed through the walls of the medina at the Bab Nkob gate and moved west into the New City, with its wide, tree-lined boulevards, shops, hotels and offices. Turning down a side street, Mohammed stopped the car by a wall beyond which a dark brick building and tall cypresses could be seen. This was clearly a wealthy residential area.

Naomi pressed a button beside a heavy wrought iron gate, which served to protect a steel-clad door. Paul looked up at the barbed wire that topped the wall, and at the scarred, metal garage door to his right. "Security's kind of tight here," he observed.

Moments later the steel door swung open, and a thin, bearded man dressed in black with a black and white keffiyeh worn as a scarf around his neck. The man made no response to Naomi's greeting in Arabic; he unlocked the gate, stood back and let them enter. Inside, the walkway spanned a rather dreary, colourless garden of sparsely planted shrubs and tall trees. A second door opened as they approached the building. A servant woman in a dark cotton robe and headscarf bowed as they entered.

Approaching from the rather dim interior, a man called out, "Enter, my honoured guests!" He was of medium height with a dark, leathery complexion, trimmed beard and dark eyes. His white shirt was open halfway to his waist, revealing the glitter of gold. "Naomi, it is so good to see you!" He bowed deeply, and turning slightly, he announced, "You must be Paul. I am Yusuf Nuh Al-Rashid, Chief Executive of ash-Shbab Mshrw Maroc, or as you like to say in Great Britain, AMM. We are a charity very pleased to be affiliated with Global Youth Enterprise. Please come in. Will you have some coffee?" He clapped his hands and the servant re-appeared miraculously. Raising an index finger, he gave her clipped instructions in Arabic.

Paul said, "I would prefer a glass of water, if that can be arranged."

"Yes, of course!" Yusuf said. "You have been to our offices before, Naomi, and we are very pleased to have you with us again." Turning slightly toward Paul, Yusuf went on, "This is actually my home, and in order to disperse the maximum amount of funds to our entrepreneurs, we have the AMM offices over here, in what was once the lounge. At one time, this was actually the home of a French diplomat, and as you can see, it is built in the riad style on three floors with a central courtyard, and fountain, which unfortunately, is not working at the moment."

Naomi and Paul were ushered into a beige undecorated room in which the central features were a dark, antique desk, and a black oval conference table surrounded with old wood and leather armchairs. There was a scattering of frayed tribal rugs on the floor.

"Now, then," Yusuf continued, "I propose to begin your visit with a presentation outlining our vision of the future of AMM. Just last week, I gave this presentation to our board of directors, who have given it their unanimous endorsement."

Paul interrupted, "Before we hear your presentation, may we get some clarification of our agenda and schedule for this visit?"

"Yes, of course, what did you have in mind?"

Paul opened his briefcase and pulled out a printed e-mail, which he passed to Yusuf. "You may recall that I sent you this e-mail, asking that certain meetings be added to our schedule."

"Ah, yes," Yusuf was stroking his beard. "I have been very busy, and I have asked Latifah to attend to this. I will ask her." He clapped his hands and called, "Latifah!"

The door at the far end of the room opened and a young woman wearing a white headscarf, long, dark shirt and jeans entered the room.

"Yes?" she asked deferentially. There was something about her body language, which suggested resignation as well.

Yusuf held out the e-mail to her, and what followed was an exchange in Arabic. Yusuf turned to Paul, "I'm sorry, but do you happen to have a copy of the schedule we sent you?"

Paul leafed through a file and extracted a single sheet. "Yes, here it is."

Yusuf laid the schedule next to the e-mail, and pointing back and forth between the documents, he issued instructions to Latifah. Now and then, Naomi would interrupt with what sounded like suggestions or alterations to Yusuf's instructions.

"Now," Yusuf looked up at Paul, "You say here you wish to select the entrepreneurs and mentors you interview on arrival.

How do you propose to do that? Many of these people are very busy; we know them and can save a lot of wasted effort trying to arrange meetings with people who haven't got time for meetings."

"Yes," Paul said, "I understand, but we think it is very important to interview a random sample of people, so that the results are not skewed favourably or unfavourably."

Yusuf suddenly turned on Naomi, "What means 'skewed'?" he demanded.

Naomi explained in Arabic that it meant that the results might be distorted. Yusuf was clearly offended. Naomi went on to explain that Paul was not suggesting that AMM would intentionally distort the results, but that it could happen accidentally. Slightly mollified, Yusuf shrugged and said, "You will just waste a lot of your time and Latifah's time."

"Why don't I stay with Yusuf and listen to his presentation, while you, Paul, go and help Latifah with the entrepreneurs and mentors?" Naomi suggested.

Paul followed Latifah into the adjacent, small office, which was crowded with three gray, steel desks and filing cabinets. At one of the desks, an older woman with a deeply lined face was sitting. She, too, wore the ubiquitous dark headscarf. "This is Yaminah, our bookkeeper; this is Mr. Paul from GYE," Latifah announced. Brief deferential bows were exchanged.

Paul asked, "Latifah, have you got a list of AMM's entrepreneurs?" Latifah sat at her desk, and on screen, she brought up an Excel spread sheet with seventy-six rows. "But, Latifah," Paul protested, "AMM's last report of GYE mentioned a hundred and eighty-eight entrepreneurs. Where are the other hundred and twelve?"

Latifa, clearly flustered, brought up a second Excel spread sheet, which she quickly merged with the first one. The combined spreadsheet had one hundred and ninety rows. She said, "This one in English is for Inter-Sahara Development Bank."

Paul scanned the list, looking for Marrakech addresses. "Latifah, I'd like to have appointments with this one, this one, this one and this one."

Latifah turned toward Paul. "OK, Mr. Paul, I take care of it." She clearly expected him to re-join the meeting with Yusuf.

"Latifah, I'll stay here while you make the calls. That way I can help you arrange individual meetings and then we can do the mentors."

This was not what Latifah wanted to hear; she sat looking at her monitor for several moments before she picked up her phone. Over the course of the next hour and a half, the additional meetings were arranged, but it took twenty-three calls to book four entrepreneurs, and fifteen calls to get three mentors. Each unsuccessful call prompted a defensive explanation from Latifah: "He must have changed his phone number. I guess she doesn't live there any more. He must not have paid his phone bill. TelecomMaroc has problems in that area."

Very strange! Paul thought, *She seemed very nervous, and she only spoke to twelve people out of the thirty-eight she called. Something peculiar is going on here.* But he thanked Latifah and returned to Yusuf's office, where he found the chief executive holding forth in front of a projection screen, a pointer in one hand and the remote control in the other.

Yusuf was explaining, with great enthusiasm 'AMM's 2015', the vision and strategy for providing 1,500 entrepreneurs with loans and making 750 trained mentors available to help the entrepreneurs. The financials were based on a grant from Morocco's Ministry of Employment of twenty million dirhams, a new loan from the Inter-Sahara Development Bank of thirty million dirhams, and charitable grants from various companies that aggregated fifteen million dirhams. A further essential feature of the strategy was the sale of training and mentoring services; these services totaled sixty million dirhams.

My God! Paul thought, *This is wildly optimistic! He's talking about raising the equivalent of about fifteen million pounds over the next five years. Over the last five years, AMM has raised about two million!*

Paul said, "Yusuf, the sixty million from the sale of training and mentoring services, are you saying that you're going to start charging entrepreneurs for these services? If so, that would be contrary to GYE's basic principle that these services should be free."

"No, no, Paul. These are services we would make available to the general market. Young entrepreneurs who qualify for a loan would receive these services for free. But we have identified that many mature businesses have needs for these services."

"Sixty million dirhams is a lot of money," Paul said.

"Not actually so much, Paul. We have gone over the figures with Demoitte, the big consultancy that is represented on our board. They consider that the AMM brand is well-positioned to offer these services in Morocco."

"And regarding the other grants and loans you mentioned, how confident are you of being able to achieve those numbers?" Paul asked.

"Well, we are in touch with the government and the ISDB on a weekly basis. They are very enthusiastic about participating in a project to assist 1,500 new entrepreneurs! And many of the companies I mentioned are on our board."

Yusuf paused triumphantly, looking first at Naomi and then at Paul. "So you see," he summarised, "AMM is on its way to becoming one of the largest and most outstanding chapters in GYE! Now, may I suggest that we go to lunch? There is a very good restaurant, Essaada, around the corner, and I am very pleased to have you as my guests."

They were seated in a booth toward the rear of Essaada. Naomi and Yusuf were discussing the menu. Now and then, one or the other would turn to Paul and ask, "Do you like snails?" (He did.) and "Do you like pumpkin?" (Not too much.)

During this discussion, Paul sat watching Naomi. *God, she's pretty* crossed his mind. She wore almost no makeup—only a hint of eyeliner and a creamy-rose lip-gloss. She had a habit of leaving her lips slightly parted and puckered while she was listening. *It just makes you want to kiss her*, Paul thought. *Her chest is pretty modest: both in size and in that she doesn't emphasize it, as a lot of women do.*

The conversation turned back to AMM and Paul decided to ask how AMM dealt with mudarabah. "Ah, you know about mudarabah, then," Yusuf replied. "As you have learned, the Holy Qur'an forbids usury, which to the charging of any interest on money lent. AMM deals with mudarabah in a simple and charitable negotiation with our entrepreneurs."

"Yes, I see," Paul said, "but in those countries where the charging of interest is permitted, the interest rate charged by commercial banks becomes the benchmark. The advice of GYE to its chapters is that they should charge an interest rate that's comparable to that charged by commercial banks. In Muslim countries, there is no similar benchmark as far as I know. So my question is, what evidence can you show us that the mudarabah contracts you have with your entrepreneurs represent a concession in relation to the contract that the entrepreneur could arrange with an Islamic bank?"

"Well, first of all, our entrepreneurs would not be able to arrange a mudarabah contract with an Islamic bank. One has to have proven financial status to borrow money from an Islamic bank. From a money lender –yes, of course—but the terms would be quite onerous and would probably amount to half the profits from the business for many years."

"But, I thought the whole point of the Qur'an's prohibition on charging of interest was to avoid the situation where the lender profits from the borrower's need."

"That is correct, Paul, but the true followers of Allah know what is just, and do not permit themselves to be overcome with greed. I think that Christians face a similar challenge in obeying the Fourth Commandment: Remember the Sabbath and keep it holy. I have read that the Amish people in America go to church every Sunday, they read the scriptures and do no work. Other people never go to church; instead, they play golf all day on Sunday."

"So are you saying that compliance with the Qur'an is a matter of interpretation?"

Yusuf appeared to be genuinely shocked; he looked around to determine whether anyone might be listening to the conversation.

Efraim's Eye

"No, not at all!" he said emphatically, "I am saying that true followers of the Prophet and worshipers of Allah know in their heart what is correct!"

Paul nodded, appearing to concede the point to Yusuf. "I suppose the same observation could apply to Christians."

Yusuf shrugged, indicating his disinterest in Christian dilemmas.

"But," Paul continued, "we still haven't answered the question about evidence of the charitable nature of your mudarabah contracts."

"If you want evidence, I can show you the actual contracts."

"They will be in Arabic?"

"Yes, of course. But this beautiful lady here can read them to you."

"I think it will be sufficient if we make copies of the files of three or four entrepreneurs."

Yusuf frowned, and said nothing for several moments; then, he said, "If you are assuming that we file documents under the name of the entrepreneur, you are mistaken. We find it more convenient to file by subject matter."

"OK. But under the subject matter 'Contracts', you have a file for each entrepreneur, don't you?"

Yusuf nodded. "Yes, of course, and we can provide you with copies of three or four of those."

"And," Paul continued, "under the subject matter 'Business Plans', you have a file for each entrepreneur?"

Sensing some kind of trap, Yusuf studied Paul for a moment; then, he conceded, "Yes. That is the way our files are arranged."

"That's fine," Paul said, "What I'd like to have is—for three or four entrepreneurs—their business plan and contract files."

Yusuf protested, "But these files are unrelated! They will only confuse you!"

Paul considered the chief executive for a moment; then he said, "On the contrary, Yusuf, the files are very much related. The business plan will reveal the expected future profits of the business and will likely indicate something about the probability of profits over time."

"I think you will find this very confusing, and I insist that before you reach conclusions, you will review your findings with me."

"I have no problem reviewing findings with you," Paul suggested with a smile, "provided you have no problem allowing me to select the entrepreneurs."

Yusuf's face wore a look of resignation. "You are making things unnecessarily difficult."

"Difficult perhaps, but necessary," was Paul's response.

"Why is all this necessary?" Yusuf demanded.

"It is necessary, because there is no other way to do a thorough assessment, and that is what I have been asked to do."

"I am beginning to think that GYE no longer trusts me and is preparing to discredit me and all the excellent work I have done for GYE over these last years."

Paul leaned forward. "Yusuf, I can assure you that GYE does not want to discredit you or any of its chapters. As to the issue of trust, I am here to <u>prove</u> that AMM is fully trustworthy. So if you are, as you say, completely trustworthy, you have absolutely nothing to fear."

Yusuf sat sourly for some moments; then, he motioned for the waiter.

"Yusuf," Naomi put in, "May I ask you something?"

Yusuf brightened. "Yes, of course, my dear."

"What happens to payments made under the mudarabah contracts to AMM?"

Surreptitiously, Paul gave Naomi a thumbs-up for the initiative of asking this important question; she caught the signal and smiled slightly.

"Oh, well, that is easy, my dear," Yusuf replied expansively. "There is a separate bank account into which those funds are deposited."

"And what happens to the funds?" Naomi asked.

Yusuf smiled. "They are lent out again."

On their return to the AMM offices, it was agreed that Naomi would work with Latifah to obtain copies of the agreed entrepreneurs' files. Paul was with Yusuf in his office, reviewing the schedule of planned meetings.

With the review complete, Yusuf leaned back in his chair and contemplated the ceiling. "Paul," he asked, "what are you expecting to get out of this assessment of AMM?"

"I'm hoping to provide GYE with an accurate appraisal of AMM."

"No, I'm asking what your personal expectations are."

"My personal expectations are about being professional and thorough."

"So, you are completing this assignment on a pro bono basis?"

"Yes, GYE is just paying my travel expenses."

"Paul, do you mind if I ask what your normal daily rate is?"

"I normally receive £1,200 a day."

"So for five days, including travel time, you would normally get £6,000?"

"Yes."

Yusuf nodded, apparently lost in thought. "That's not very much," he mused, "In one of my commercial businesses, I paid a consultant 100,000 dirhams—that's about £8,000—to complete a study which supported my position regarding a major project."

"Do you have many commercial businesses, Yusuf?" Paul asked.

"Yes. There are three businesses. They all involve various aspects of security for the Moroccan military and government. . . . But returning to the subject of consultancy, I believe that consultants who provide a good service to me should be well-paid."

"Yes, of course," Paul said. He looked at his watch. "I think we have that call to the Inter-Sahara Development Bank now, Yusuf. Do you mind if we use your office?"

Paul and Naomi placed a Skype call to Mansur ben-Tanoos, a project manager at the ISDB in Cairo. He had responsibility for overseeing a number of development projects, including the funding of 1.5 million in U.S. dollars provided to AMM —half of the funding was as a loan; the other half was a grant. It was contractually required that AMM obtain matching funds for the grant portion.

Mr. ben-Tanoos said that the ISDB requires reports on the status of its funded projects every three months, an annual funding audit, and a closing assessment by one of its consultants.

Paul said that they had seen copies of the monthly reports, and that he was having difficulty reconciling the numbers reported to ISDB with what should have been similar numbers reported by AMM to GYE. Mr. ben-Tanoos said that the bank was not concerned about "numerical discrepancies as long as they are not major." He went on to say that the ISDB was pleased with the young entrepreneurs project that AMM had recently completed "because the number of young people who have been given help in starting a successful new business is very impressive, and sets a very good example in Morocco, but also in the larger Arab world."

Paul asked whether the ISDB had any concerns about AMM as an organisation. Mr. ben-Tanoos replied that the recently completed closing assessment had identified some concerns about management processes being "somewhat lax, but we tend to judge the organisations by the results they achieve, rather than their management processes."

Naomi asked whether the ISDB was considering funding a further project with AMM.

"Yes," Mr ben-Tanoos responded, "We are open to receiving a new proposal for funding next year."

"Have you thought about how much funding might be available?"

"This is always the difficult question," the ISDB project manager replied. "A great deal depends on the bank's strategy for next year which hasn't been finalised. But provisionally, we are talking about a number like fifteen million dirhams over a period of five years. This would represent a slight increase over the size of the project just completed."

"Do you know whether anyone from ISDB has ever come to Marrakech to see firsthand what goes on at AMM?" Paul asked.

"Unfortunately," Mr. ben-Tanoos replied, "our travel budget does not permit these kinds of meetings. Of course, Mr. Al-Rashid is always welcome here in Cairo, and in fact, he has been here several times. As to firsthand appraisal of the NGO's we support, we depend on our consultants, and on organisations like GYE to advise us on the effectiveness of our NGO's."

As the call was concluding, Yusuf knocked and entered. "Your four o'clock meeting with the entrepreneur is here," he announced. Then, he asked, "How was the call to Mr. ben-Tanoos?"

Naomi looked over at Paul, who responded. "It was quite useful. One thing that did come up was that he said the ISDB is considering further funding of fifteen million dirhams over the next five years. I believe you said that they were considering thirty million."

Yusuf shrugged. "Mr. ben-Tanoos is not fully connected with the key decision-makers at ISDB, so he is not aware of their thinking. Sheik Rajih Quereshi, the Senior Vice President of Human Development at the bank, has personally assured me that he has set aside thirty million for AMM."

The entrepreneur with the four o'clock appointment was a reedy, young man with dark, intelligent eyes. His name was Qasim Muhib Nazari—about twenty years old. He was dressed in stained, grey cotton pantaloons, a dark brown shirt, a grey skullcap and plastic sandals. He spoke no English, so Naomi conducted the interview. He told her that he came from a farming family living south of Marrakech close to the Atlas foothills. He had dropped out of school at the age of thirteen, and had worked with his father on his family's three-hectare (seven-and-a-half acre) plot of land.

Qasim's father had died five years ago, but the young Nazari had struggled on, growing cauliflower and tomatoes, and raising chickens and goats. He came to realise, however, that these traditional outputs were unlikely to make him enough money to attract a good bride. From a neighbour, Qasim had heard that a new farmer's co-operative had been established at Al Fassia, just south of Marrakech. When he went to see this co-operative, he learned that it was exporting fruit to Europe, and that there was a particular interest in exporting pomegranates because of their health benefits. He also heard that pomegranate seeds were an important ingredient in various recipes and that parts of the plant were prized for their medicinal properties. Nazari's investigations convinced him that pomegranates could be grown on his somewhat arid land. With the co-operative willing to pay four to eight dirhams per fruit, depending on size and quality, growing pomegranates seemed financially attractive.

However, Nazari needed money to acquire young pomegranate plants, and he had approached AMM for a loan. His business plan was based on the purchase of 100 plants at a cost of 5,000 dirhams. The expectation was that in three years his plants would produce ten fruits each with a gross value of 6,000 dirhams, with production growing each year thereafter.

Paul asked, "Ask him what has actually happened, Naomi."

There followed an extended discussion is Arabic.

"Good news and bad news," she told Paul. "Qasim says that his production is better than expected. Sixteen hundred fruits last year. Their size and quality are good, averaging seven dirhams each. The bad news is that he has to pay AMM fifty percent of his profits for five years. Moreover, he has planted fifty new plants last year, and this year he planted about eight hundred seedlings. He figures that by the time the five years is up, he will have paid AMM over 25,000 dirhams."

Paul was dumbstruck. "That amounts to about one hundred percent interest per year! Can't he deduct his operating costs and some kind of a salary for himself in arriving at the net profit figure?"

Naomi turned back to Qasim, who began to shake his head repeatedly.

"He says," Naomi explained, "that the contract doesn't allow him to deduct a salary, and his operating costs have all been attributed to his vegetable and livestock production, which he needs to keep going for the time being."

"Ask him if he feels cheated by AMM," Paul demanded, and he watched as Qasim responded to Naomi's question with a shrug of his shoulders.

"He says he does feel that AMM took advantage of him. But he says that he never could have started the business without the loan from AMM, and that in just over three years, the profits will be all his and that he'll become a rich man with two thousand trees, a new house and a beautiful wife."

"Yeah, but this isn't right, Naomi. This venture was all Qasim's idea. He was the one who made it work, but Yusuf lent him £500 and gets £2500 for essentially no effort and very little risk!"

Naomi shrugged. "I know," she said.

The entrepreneur they met at five o'clock had a somewhat different story to tell. His name was Abdul-Bari Mahmoudi; he was short, and overweight, but with a happy-go-lucky disposition, arriving fifteen minutes late for the meeting. The discussions began in English, but it soon became apparent that Mahmoudi's vocabulary was insufficient. He would pause to think, and then insert an Arabic phrase. When Naomi shook her head and asked him a question in Arabic, he stared at her incredulously.

Paul thought, *I know what he's wondering. He can't figure out how a pretty, blonde, Western woman can possibly speak fluent Arabic.* After this anomaly was explained to him, Mahmoudi adjusted his black turban, sat down on the proffered chair and began his story. His father had died two years ago and had left him a shop full of tourist knick-knacks: wooden carvings, pashminas, post cards, metal trays, etc. The shop was in the souq, but it was tucked away in a back alleyway, amidst vegetable and clothing sellers.

This inauspicious location meant that the shop made barely enough money to support his mother, father and Abdul. His older siblings had no interest in the shop. On his father's death, Abdul decided that either he should carry different merchandise, or he should move the shop. He decided to do both. His plan was to sell the shop with all its stock, as a going concern, and purchase a new, vacant shop in a better location. As there were always young men from wealthy trading families looking to get a toehold in the souq, he had no trouble selling.

Desirable properties, however, seldom came on the market, but they were passed between generations of the owning family. After several months of investigation, Abdul identified four shops in good locations that he felt might come on the market for various reasons. He deemed it inadvisable to directly show his interest to any of the owners; instead, he would regularly invite the owners of neighbouring shops for a coffee. In the course of these meetings, Abdul would off-handedly inquire about business in the particular shop. One morning, his dogged patience was rewarded with the news that the young owner of a shop in question had decided that being in the souq from 8:30 a.m. until 9:30 p.m. was not for him. Besides, he did not have a proper trader's mentality. Instead, he had decided to work in his uncle's construction firm as an office manager.

Abdul approached the young man with a coffee and listened with friendly indulgence to his complaints about his business. Eventually, Abdul told the young man that, if he wanted to sell, he had a family friend who might be interested, but that the friend was in an advanced state of negotiation to buy another shop. The young man confirmed his interest in selling, and Abdul produced an uncle, who was prepared to act the part of the buyer. In the discussions that followed, the uncle prized from the young man his trading history, which was not particularly favourable. The uncle informed the young man that he liked the location of the shop, but the trading history put him off, and, since he was ready to by another premise, the young man would have to accept a discounted price.

For an hour, the young man and Abdul's uncle exchanged offers with Abdul acting as the mediator. Several times, when the uncle threw up his arms in disgust and walked away, Abdul was able to urge the resumption of negotiations at a lower price level. Finally, the uncle told the young man. "I just want the premises, not your stock. You say that your stock is worth 220,000 dirhams. I am prepared to come with the cash tomorrow as long as you take

220,000 dirhams off the price!" The young man protested that the 220,000-figure represented the retail value of the goods, and that he could not value the goods at more than their aggregate cost of 110,000 dirhams. There were more frantic, heated discussions. Several times, Abdul took his uncle aside, ostensibly to reason with him on the young man's behalf. Eventually a deal was agreed on a premises-only basis at a discount of 168,000 dirhams for the stock.

Abdul then swung into action on the second phase of his strategy: acquiring his stock. He had decided that he would sell only women's jeans. This would make his shop quite different than others that offered a wide range of women's clothing. Abdul believed that women—particularly young women—who wanted jeans would come to him because he would have a wide range of styles and sizes. Customers were more likely to find what they wanted at his shop. Initially, he thought he would need about four brands, three styles per brand in forty sizes: 480 items, one to three of each at an average wholesale price of 250 dirhams: about 240,000 dirhams worth of stock. He could pare that figure down, and his uncle had offered to lend him 90,000 dirhams.

He approached AMM for a loan of 110,000 dirhams, which would cover the initial stock of his business. The loan would also cover the installation of a small changing space. He prepared a rather pessimistic business plan, which made no mention of the loan from his uncle, and which forecast relatively low levels of profitability. In the negotiations with Yusuf that followed, AMM was asking for thirty percent of the profits for ten years. Abdul agreed to this provided that he could terminate the loan contract upon payment to AMM of a total of 200,000 dirhams before the end of the second year. Yusuf, considering this very unlikely, agreed.

Abdul paused and looked from Naomi to Paul, expecting their encouragement to continue the story. Naomi held out her hands, palms up, and must have said something like, "Well, tell us the results!"

Abdul said that in the first year of trading, just completed, he had made a net profit of 204,000 dirhams. He explained that the real figure was considerably higher, but that he had made an arrangement with an accountant to certify the 204,000-figure. So he paid AMM 61,200 dirhams, and he intended to pay AMM an additional 138,800 dirhams within the next year. This additional payment would represent considerably less than 30 percent of his expected second-year profits.

Paul said, "So the moral of the story is that two can play this game."

Abdul looked quizzically at Naomi, who explained Paul's comment.

Grabbing Paul's hand to shake it, Abdul exclaimed, "Yes! Yes! You are very right, Mr. Paul!"

Back at the Riad El Norj, Paul and Naomi examined the business plans and contracts they had requested. One entrepreneur—probably an experienced mountaineer—had proposed the establishment of a company to provide tourists with climbing experiences in the Atlas Mountains. Another was preparing to start an Internet service business in his home near Youssoufia. A third person—Naomi identified her as female—wanted to begin trading as seamstress; she wanted to borrow money to purchase a Singer computer-controlled sewing machine with which she would make and custom-embroider formal dresses for wealthy clients.

The contracts in each case were detailed, lengthy and subject to shariah law. Paul noticed that as well as a formal signature page, each page of each the contract was initialed by both the entrepreneur and Yusuf. In the case of the seamstress and the Internet entrepreneur, there was a provision that in the case of late payment, AMM reserved the right to "take possession of property in addition to that purchased with the proceeds of the loan." The mountaineer had an additional provision that his father would guarantee repayment of the loan.

Naomi commented, "Those provisions are far in excess of what we normally allow our chapters to do."

Paul noticed that the lowest percentage of profits to be paid to AMM was 20 percent, and that the minimum period during which

Efraim's Eye

the share of profits was to be repaid was three years; the longest was seven years.

"In my opinion," Paul said, "this is not charity lending. It borders on extortion."

Naomi paused and looked across the lounge. "What do you think Yusuf will say tomorrow when you criticise his contracts?"

"I think he'll probably say that by being certain of being repaid, AMM is able to lend the money to new entrepreneurs, and that this is what makes possible his vision of helping 1,500 entrepreneurs."

"Paul, I wonder whether we ought to have a chat with Omar Saleem."

"Who's he?"

"He's the ex-employee of AMM who told Roberta that things were not right at AMM."

"Do you have his phone number?"

"Yes. I think it's in an e-mail from Roberta." Naomi examined her iPhone for several minutes.

Then she put it up to her ear, and began to speak in Arabic. "Is tomorrow right after breakfast alright, Paul?"

"Yes, sure."

There was more conversation in Arabic. "He wants us to promise that we'll never tell Yusuf that we've met with him."

"OK. No problem."

Naomi went back to her phone. She looked up. "He wants to know if it's alright for him to bring Mosa Mitri with him."

"Who's he . . . or she?"

"He's another ex-employee of AMM."

"Fine."

"They'll be here at nine tomorrow morning." She sat for several moments staring at a tapestry on the far wall. "I don't feel good at all about this, Paul."

"We've got to find out what's going on, Naomi."

"I know, but I've got a bad feeling."

"Premonition?"

Slowly, she nodded. "We've got to be very careful, Paul."

She suggested that they have dinner in Djemaa el-Fna. They walked along the Rue Sidi Boulabada, which even at 8 o'clock was teeming with people, and on into the great square. The northern quadrant of Djemaa el-Fna was brightly lit with many lights, and there seemed to be numerous open tents filled with people and human noise. Paul stopped to take it in.

"Do you know about this?" Naomi asked.

"No. What is it?"

Naomi smiled. It was the amused smile of a child who knows a secret of which her parent is unaware. "It's where we're having dinner. At number 67."

She took his arm, leading him past snake charmers who were squatting on the pavement and playing a simple flute for the lethargic cobras swaying in front of them. They passed fortune-tellers, men with monkeys on chains, and knots of men who were intent on some game of chance being played on the stones at their feet. When they entered the lighted area, the pandemonium there assaulted Paul's senses. There was a great hubbub of hawkers touting their individual eating areas, the smells of fried food, and spices, and swirling crowds of people moving about to inspect what was on offer.

Several times, a tout accosted Paul, "You eat my restaurant, sir! Very good chicken!" Paul would shake his head and try to move on, but the touts were not deterred—following, shouting, cajoling. There were individual areas that had been cordoned off. Each area had its own tables and chairs, its own lighting, at one end its own open-air kitchen, and its number on prominent display.

When they had made an almost complete circumnavigation of the restaurants, they came to number 67. Its tout took Paul by the arm, and attempted to steer him into the seating area. Paul disengaged himself and turned to Naomi, who began to shout in Arabic to be heard above the din. Tout 67 considered her in astonishment, then he bowed and pointed toward a vacant table. She shook her head and pointed toward another table adjacent to the makeshift kitchen. The tout shrugged, seated them, and shouted for a waiter.

Naomi smiled at Paul. "It's a little noisy, Paul, but they have very good fried fish and chips, and an excellent salad of diced vegetables. I like this table because I can watch them prepare the food."

"I don't suppose they have any beer," Paul said, feeling the need for a bit of solace.

"Not here. They'd be in big trouble."

A metal tray was set down abruptly in front of them. On it were various sizes of fish that had been coated in spicy flour and deep-fried. Alongside the fish were crunchy, savoury, fried potato slices, and there was a large bowl of red and green salad. Apparently, they were expected to eat with their hands, but Naomi called the waiter, who brought individual metal plates, knives, forks and napkins. "This is absolutely amazing!" Paul said. "And the food is really good."

Naomi looked up. "If you came here tomorrow morning at 6, all this would be gone." Her sweeping gesture took in the entire restaurant quadrant.

"You mean they'll tear all this down later, and put it back up again tomorrow evening?"

"Yes. Exactly."

Chapter 5

PREPARATION

On arrival in Tbilisi an hour and ten minutes late, Efraim was short-tempered, but he forced himself to be the patient, important businessman. At immigration control, he was confronted with numerous questions about the purpose of his visit, where he would stay, for how long, etc. He knew nothing of the Georgian language; the first immigration officer spoke no English, and he was handed off to another. He had no visa (although the airline told him he could obtain one on arrival.) After explaining the purpose of his visit, which was to identify potential machine shops which could provide certain mechanical parts his company required, he asked the officer, "May I offer you a gratuity for your assistance with my visa?"

"Yes," the officer said with a sideways glance at Efraim, "a modest gratuity would be acceptable."

And his eyes widened when the fifty-dollar bill was presented.

With the visa stamped in his passport, Efraim informed the officer, "I am very late for my first meeting." He glanced at his watch. "Unfortunately, the specifications for the products we require and several important samples are in my suitcase. Could you possibly expedite me through customs?"

The immigration officer accompanied Efraim as a VIP through customs, and gratefully pocketed another fifty dollars.

At the information counter in the arrivals hall, Efraim inquired of a young woman, who spoke passable English about modestly priced hotels. After reviewing several alternatives with her, he selected the Kapan Kovi Hotel on the right bank of the Mt'k'vari River, and in the Armenian/Persian quarter of Tbilisi.

Efraim's Eye

In a taxi on the way to the hotel, Efraim considered, *How am I going to make contact with Tbilisi Man?* Of course, he still had the man's phone number, but he distinctly remembered the man telling him, "I will meet you in Tbilisi the day after tomorrow, and if you are there, I'll find you." *Oh!* Efraim suddenly realised, *that means tomorrow, not today. I got here very quickly. He's going to take an extra day.*

At the hotel, Efraim put his suitcase in the closet of his room, having transferred the Chief's Special from the suitcase to his knapsack, which he always carried slung over his left shoulder. On the third floor, the room had a single window looking out onto a quiet side street and facing an antique brown apartment building with blue wooden cantilevered balconies. A heavy green fabric decorated with burgundy roses covered the double bed and was repeated for the curtains. There was earthy carpeting on the floor, an upholstered easy chair, an antique television, a scuffed pine desk and matching chest of drawers. *Quite satisfactory* was Efraim's appraisal. The en-suite bathroom was of less interest to Efraim as his habit was to wash himself with water from a sink once a week.

As he approached the hotel dining room, there were three men just leaving. One of them stopped and said something to Efraim. The man made a disagreeable face, pointed to the dining room, and shook an index finger at Efraim.

"Not good?" Efraim inquired.

"No. Don't eat," the man replied.

So Efraim found a café on the right embankment, overlooking the tree-lined river. *This is a strange city*, he thought. There were grim, old grey buildings with elaborate brickwork, mouldings and wrought iron window gratings, mixed in with newer construction in vivid colours of red, blue, orange and pink.

After a breakfast of strong black coffee, matsoni (sour yoghurt) and adjarian khachapuri (a flakey bread, stuffed with melted cheese and topped with an egg), Efraim returned to the hotel.

Having logged onto the wifi on his laptop, he searched for "metal fabricators Tbilisi" in both English and Arabic.

There was nothing.

He spoke with the hotel manager, who performed the same search in Georgian. Aha! The photos of some of the factories on the Georgian websites looked promising, and the manager wrote down the names of several companies, their general managers, addresses and phone numbers in English. (The Georgian alphabet bears no relationship to the English alphabet in form or pronunciation.) The three most promising companies were in the Nadzaladevi area. Efraim walked across the river and took the metro north to Eristavi Street.

The first factory on Efraim's list, and the most promising from the photos on its website was Tbilisi Custom Steelworks, Its general manager was Barric Giorgadze. At the main entrance, Efraim paused to survey the building, which stretched almost a full block along Eristavi Street. It probably had been built originally of patterned grey and black brick just after the First World War. There were sooty stone gargoyles above each of the windows, but the ground floor windows had been bricked shut. Only the first floor windows appeared to be in use.

Inside the main entrance was a once grand lobby, that had been permitted to fall into disrepair. The plaster columns, walls and ceiling were no longer white; rather, they were soot-smudged, cracked and peeling. To the right, there was a small, jerrybuilt wooden office with a window that looked out into the lobby. Inside the office was a white-haired man, seated on a wooden chair, chin against his chest and snoring loudly.

Efraim rapped on the window. The man woke with a start, rose painfully, and slid aside the window.

He said something to Efraim, who removed a business card from his jacket, and handed it to the man. "I want to see Mr. Giorgadze, please."

The porter (if that's what he was) made several remarks.

"I want to see Mr. Giorgadze, please." Efraim held up his right hand and rubbed his thumb against the tips of his fingers, to indicate that this was not just a social call.

The porter made a brief statement and then petulantly considered Efraim, who pointed meaningfully to the telephone on the porter's battered wooden desk.

The standoff continued for perhaps half a minute longer. Finally, the porter shuffled over to the desk, picked up the telephone and dialed. There followed an extended conversation between the porter and whoever was at the other end of the line during which the porter referred frequently to Efraim's business card. The porter hung up and pointed to an old office chair that stood outside his office.

Ten minutes later, a tall man with an expansive waist, wearing a well-worn navy polyester suit and off-white shirt appeared. "Giorgadze," he announced.

"Mohammed Al-Buktar," Efraim replied, offering the general manager one of his business cards.

Mr. Giorgadze, a man in his fifties with a florid complexion and oversized, bushy moustache and eyebrows studied the business card. It announced that Mr. Al-Buktar was the purchasing director of North African Marine Systems Ltd., with an address in Cairo.

The general manager turned his attention to Efraim. "OK," he said, "What you want with Tbilisi Steelworks?"

"My company has a requirement for several, custom-made fittings that we must supply to the Egyptian navy, and we haven't found a competent Egyptian supplier."

"How you find us?" Mr. Giorgadze inquired.

"I am here in Tbilisi sourcing some items for another contract. I thought while I'm here, I should look for a supplier for the navy fittings. So, I asked the hotel manager if he could recommend a very good metal working company, and he recommended you."

"Where you staying?"

"At the Tbilisi Marriott."

Suitably impressed with this bit of information, Mr. Giorgadze said, "You come my office."

The general manager's office on the first floor had a row of internal glass windows that looked out onto the factory floor. The windows did little to shut out the hammering, the shouts, and the occasional screech of metal on metal from the floor below. Mr. Giorgadze had bookshelves filled with black lever arch file boxes, a standard grey metal desk covered with files, and half a dozen assorted chairs. "You sit," he directed, "I get coffee." Putting his head outside the door of his office, he bellowed something in Georgian. "You have drawings?" he asked of Efraim, as he pulled up a chair across the table.

From his jacket, Efraim produced a neatly folded paper that he spread out in front of Mr. Giorgadze. The general manager studied it, running a large index finger along the dimensions and the English language labels. "What for?" he asked, looking across at Efraim.

"I'm afraid I can't tell you that," Efraim offered apologetically, "for two reasons: first, because the Egyptian navy is very secretive about these things, and secondly, because they haven't told me."

Mr. Giorgadze seemed to accept this. "What is material?"

"They want the large curved casing in titanium."

Mr. Giorgadze shook his head. "Titanium difficult. Why they want?"

"Because it's lighter and very strong."

"Take extra time get titanium."

"How much extra time?"

"Maybe three weeks."

"I believe that's OK."

The general manager pointed at the cross section of the casing on the drawing. The casing was about 30 centimetres long curved on a radius of 40 centimetres. It had a deep, C-shaped cross section. "How this shape formed?"

"It can be bent or machined or welded—whichever is easiest for you—but the material must maintain its strength."

"These pieces at the ends," he asked, pointing to the closures at the ends of the casings, "can be welded?"

"Yes, and the eyes on the end pieces can be steel, screwed into the end pieces."

Mr. Giorgadze nodded. He pointed to the liner. "This titanium also?"

Efraim's Eye

"No. That piece should be tungsten."

"You want pure tungsten? Is very expensive."

"They would prefer a tungsten alloy: nickel, cobalt or iron—whatever is available." *He can probably guess,* Efraim thought, *that this is some kind of a weapon.* (Tungsten alloys easily penetrate steel because of their high density and strength.) But Mr. Giorgadze made no comment.

Efraim pointed again to the liner. "Notice how it slides into the grooves which need to be machined into the casing. That way, it closes the casing. There is one other item I should point out. There is a hole in the back of the casing. That should be threaded to accommodate a bushing of about one centimetre. I will have to let you know what is the inside diameter of the bushing." (Efraim was referring to the hole in the casing through which the detonator would be inserted.)

"Very strange," Mr. Giorgadze commented. "Is electric cable going through bushing?"

"I don't know, Mr. Giorgadze."

The general manager shrugged. "How many you want?"

"We want six. Can you do them?"

"Yes. You want price?"

"Yes, please."

Mr. Giorgadze got up from his chair, slid open one of his windows and bellowed something to the shop floor below. Moments later, a squat, heavily bearded man in black-stained dark green coveralls came into the office. He sat next to the general manager, and the two of them conferred at length with frequent references to Efraim's drawing. The foreman (if that's what he was) rose, gave a deferential nod to Mr. Giorgadze, and left the office. Retrieving a calculator from his desk, the general manager sat writing numbers in a tattered notebook. Then, he looked up. "That will be 1,500 Georgian Iaris."

"That's for all six," Efraim asserted, hopefully. The price he quoted was about $900.

Mr. Giorgadze scoffed and shook his head. "Each one."

"It's very expensive!"

There was a shrug. "Is titanium and tungsten. If steel would be three times less."

Efraim paused to consider. "How would the weights of each unit compare: titanium versus steel."

Mr. Giorgadze thought for a moment. "If steel, each unit weigh 3 kilos. If titanium, it weighs half."

That means with the steel, explosive and the cables in place, I've got to lift over twenty-five kilos. With titanium, it's more like sixteen kilos. It's also easier to position the lighter charges. I think the $3,600 extra is worth it. Efraim asked, "Is that your best price?"

"Yes."

"OK. I'll be back."

"Don't bother speak to competitors."

"Why not?"

Mr. Giorgadze shrugged. "This is Tbilisi."

Efraim approached two competitors. In the first case, after he gave his name, no one—not even a sales person—was available to see him. In the second case, he gave a different name and a sales manager met him, but as soon as the drawing was unfolded, he announced that his firm could not do it. "Why not?" Efraim asked.

"You are customer of Tbilisi Steelworks."

So they have a kind of cartel here. No one is allowed to take anyone else's customers.

Efraim returned to Mr. Giorgadze with whom he reached agreement on a slight discount for payment in U.S. dollars, but the entire amount had to be paid in advance. He was told he could collect his order, which was confirmed on company stationery in Georgian, on about June 15.

The following morning, Efraim went to the dining room at his hotel, the Kapan Kovi to see for himself what the buffet breakfast was like. Based on his brief survey of the greying scrambled eggs, overcooked sausages dripping with grease, and the bread (on which spots of black mould could be seen), he again opted for the right embankment café. While he was watching the creamy green river roll by, his mobile phone rang. "Mohammed here," he announced.

"This is Anton. We spoke two days ago. Where are you?"

"I am at the Chalaubani Café on the Right Embankment."

"OK. Take a cab to the Iliani Hotel. I will meet you there. I am wearing a dark blue jacket." The line went dead.

He certainly doesn't stay very long on the line. He is probably afraid of his conversation being intercepted. But it's not like tracing a call, which can take time. With a mobile phone, the whole conversation—no matter how short—can be recorded by the intelligence services. Maybe he just wants to avoid giving away avoidable clues.

At the Iliani, there was a man in a blue windbreaker sitting on a couch in the lobby reading a newspaper. Efraim could not tell what language the newspaper was written it; he assumed it was Georgian. The man was in his late thirties, of medium height, but with a powerful upper torso. He had sandy hair, a sharp nose and penetrating hazel eyes. Efraim sat down beside the man and introduced himself.

Anton said, "We have to go somewhere else soon, before they have a chance to track us."

Efraim nodded. He looked up as a tourist in front of him with a camera apparently took a picture of several friends behind the couch. Efraim sprang to his feet and growled at the man, "I don't want to be in your pictures!"

"No, no!" the man protested, "I was taking a picture of my friends over there." And he quickly moved away.

Anton said, "Come! We get a taxi. We go to my hotel."

"You're not staying here?"

"No." As they got into a taxi, Anton confided, "I'm staying at the Vere Palace Hotel on the other side of the river."

When they arrived at the Vere Palace, a newly built European style four-star hotel, Anton said, "We can go to the bar."

Efraim retorted, "I don't drink alcohol!"

"No, no, of course not! We can have coffee or something." He looked at his watch. "It's not yet 10 o'clock. It will be quiet in the bar, and we can talk."

The barman brought them their orders: a Turkish coffee for Anton, and a mint tea for Efraim. He then disappeared discretely behind the bar.

"Now," Anton began, "I understand you are looking for RDX, or something similar. Perhaps you could tell me about your project."

"Before I tell you anything about my project, tell me, why should I be talking to you?"

Anton offered a brief laugh, and then, putting his right hand on his chest, he said, "You know of Adnan Khashoggi?" Efraim nodded. "Well, I am like his understudy, shall we say. I have contacts in various places. And these contacts are able to source certain important products that my clients require. So I meet with the client; I understand his specifications and his budget. I find what the client wants, and I collect his down payment. I obtain the product, deliver it to the client and collect the balance owing."

"Whom do you work for?"

"I am what I suppose you would call a freelance."

"What sort of mark-up does your business operate on?"

"On that point, it is quite difficult to generalise. It depends on several factors: the rarity of the product, the various risks I take in obtaining it, and the amount of time I have to spend on the project."

"Have you acquired RDX before?"

"Yes."

"For who have you acquired it?"

"I'm afraid it is my policy never to mention the names of my clients. But I also have a policy to keep my clients very well-satisfied with my services."

Efraim and Anton sat considering each other for several long moments.

Finally, Efraim said, "I require four kilograms of RDX."

"And what is the application?"

"A shaped charge."

"Four kilograms will make a very large shaped charge."

"There will be several shaped charges."

"Used against one target?"

"Yes."

"And what is the nature of the target?"

"I have a policy not to mention the identity of a target until after it is destroyed."

"I take it that you have destroyed other targets successfully."

"Yes. You have read about them in the newspapers, but my name was not mentioned at the time."

"Your name is not really Mohammed." Efraim shook his head. "You asked who I worked for; I told you I am freelance. For whom do you work? Is it al-Qaeda?"

"I, too, am freelance."

"What motivates you as a freelance? For me it is money. I doubt that it is money which motivates you."

"I am motivated by revenge."

"Revenge for what?"

"Revenge for the killing of thirteen members of my family: my father, my mother, a brother, two sisters, my grandmother, two uncles, an aunt and four cousins."

"Who did this thing?"

"They were evil, infidel, crusader Christians."

"Where did this happen? Was it Europe, or the Middle East, or the old Soviet Union, or . . ."

Efraim simply shook his head. "When it is done, I will tell you. . . . Now, you tell me, what is the source of RDX?"

"At the moment, I have a very reliable source in Chechnya, just across the border."

Efraim was unable to conceal his surprise. "Chechnya?"

Anton nodded. "The ultimate source is Russia, but my sources in Russia are not completely reliable. There is a Chechnyan who can always meet my clients' requirements, but he is a little bit expensive."

"How expensive?"

"Well, for a shaped charge, I assume you require powdered RDX, rather than a solid." Efraim nodded.

"You are prepared to pay in dollars?" Efraim nodded again. "The price for powdered RDX is one thousand dollars per kilo."

Efraim shook his head. "The going price for RDX is four hundred dollars per kilo."

Anton gave Efraim a sideways glance. "That is the price of imaginary RDX. Real RDX is priced at one thousand dollars per kilo."

"How do I know it is real RDX?"

"We will arrange a test explosion for you."

"And detonators?"

"We will include four detonators in the package."

"I need seven."

"All right. We'll include seven."

"There is also the polymer I will require to mix with the RDX to make PBX (polymer bonded explosive). I need to be able to shape the explosive when it is mixed with a warm polymer, and have it set at room temperature."

"There are literally dozens of different PBX formulations."

"I know," Efraim said, "I need to meet with someone who understands different PBX formulations and can supply me with the right polymer."

Anton considered this. Then, he said, "You meet me at this hotel tomorrow morning, and we will go to Chechnya. In the meantime, I will speak to my contacts about the supply of polymers."

"How do we get into Chechnya? I don't have a Russian visa."

"You don't need one. I have my motorbike, and I know how to get in the back door. Would you like to have dinner with me here at the hotel? If so, we can each pay our own expenses."

Efraim thought, *I want to know more about this Anton. Is he really what he says he is?* He said, "OK."

"I'll meet you here in the lobby at eight."

For Efraim, the dinner at the Vere Palace was not satisfactory. When he arrived, Anton told him, "There's been a change in plans for tomorrow. I have made contact with a man who has experience making PBX, and he can get the polymers you need. He is employed by the national oil company in Azerbaijan. He is going on a business trip, and the only time in the near future he can see us is tomorrow."

"Where would we meet him?"

"In Baku."

"How do we get there?"

"It's a quick flight from Tbilisi, and visas are arranged by the State Oil Company."

Efraim was doubtful. "How does an oil company employee know so much about explosives?"

Anton offered an indulgent smile. "Oil companies use shaped charges to fracture the walls of a well to increase the flow of oil. My contact is Manager of Special Drilling Operations."

"And what is this man's fee for the services I require?"

"His charge is $900 for two hours of tuition and two litres of polymers."

Efraim made a sour face.

"And," Anton continued, "there is also my service fee."

"Which is?"

"Let's say $750 dollars plus travel expenses. I will have to accompany you. If I'm not with you, he won't see you."

Efraim frowned. "I'll pay you the $750 when I have the RDX. Otherwise, two litres of polymers are of no use to me." Anton nodded and shrugged. Efraim asked, "When will we see this Chechnyan?"

"The day after tomorrow."

When they were seated at a table in the dining room, a waiter approached. Anton asked Efraim, "Would you like a soda or some juice?"

"A Coca-Cola, please."

Anton gave the waiter their order. Shortly thereafter, the Coca-Cola was set in front of Efraim and a glass filled with ice and a clear liquid was set in front of Anton. Judging by the way Anton sipped at it, it wasn't water. During the course of the meal, Anton ordered two more of them. Efraim thought, *This man, too, is an infidel, but at least he may be able to help me implement the plan.*

Efraim was concerned that the meat dishes on the menu did not meet halal standards, and when he inquired, Anton simply shook his head. Efraim ordered a vegetable soup, an omelette, and fresh fruit. Anton, to Efraim's jealous annoyance, ordered a shrimp cocktail, roast beef and tiramisu. *As an infidel, he lives as he wishes now, but in the life eternal, he will be amongst the flames.*

Anton further annoyed Efraim by trying, in roundabout ways, to learn more about the plan: Had Efraim ever been to this country or that country? Did Efraim think Catholics were more sinful than Protestants? Had Efraim ever served in the military? Where was that? Etc.

Efraim rebuffed, "I am not prepared to tell you about my private life." When Anton persisted in questioning him, Efraim gave evasive answers and asked, by way of reciprocating, "Where are you from? Where do you live now? Are you married?" It was an unedifying standoff.

Several times during the meal, Anton's mobile phone rang. The conversations were always short, and it seemed to be with the same person. With a client like Efraim, Anton was talkative; with this person, he was reserved and formal like talking to a boss.

By the time he returned to the Kapan Kovi hotel, Efraim was thoroughly suspicious of Anton. *He seems more like a spy than a rogue arms dealer. Why would an arms dealer want to know about my target? I think he'd probably rather not know. And all this secretiveness about our meeting, was that really necessary? He leaves his mobile phone on the table. If a security service wanted to find him or us, they could fix our position from the signals from the mobile phones. He's not what he presents himself to be, but we'll see about tomorrow.*

The flight from Tbilisi on Azerbaijan Airlines took and hour and twenty minutes. They took a taxi to downtown Baku to the

State Oil Company offices in a modern glass and steel building on Gurban Abbasov Street on the west bank of the Caspian Sea. Anton's contact, Mr. Arseny Djavadov, fit Efraim's mental image of a soviet bureaucrat: dressed in an expensive but ill-fitting suit, clean-shaven, grey-haired, with dark, nervous eyes and narrow lips. He also seemed somewhat ill at ease, and his English was very poor. Mr. Djavadov and Anton seemed to have a common language—was it Russian?—but there was no warmth or familiarity between them.

After he was introduced, Mr. Djavadov inquired, "What you want with polymers?"

Anton explained in the common language.

"But what you going to explode?" the bureaucrat asked.

"That is proprietary information," Efraim responded.

A conversation between Djavadov and Anton followed. Watching, Efraim wondered, *Is he going to produce any polymers?*

Finally, Djavadov picked up his phone, dialled, and issued instructions. He sat at his desk, and scribbled something on a small sheet of memo paper, which he tore off and gave to Anton. After thanking the bureaucrat, Anton nudged Efraim "The gratuity."

Efraim removed an envelope from his pocket and handed it to Djavadov.

Out in the street, Anton hailed a taxi. "We're going to a warehouse for the tutorial and to pick up the polymers."

Driving through Baku, Efraim had the impression of a wild, grubby city. It seemed a jumble of old, Soviet-style edifices and cheap, modern, high rises with much construction, and busy, dirty streets. There were few trees and no parks. In the distance, he could make out the tall, black steel structures of clustered oilrigs. Here and there were small, black lakes, seemingly of oil, which contrasted with the dusty emerald of the Caspian.

The taxi came to a stop outside a large white sheet metal warehouse that was set back from the south shore of Boyukshor Lake, a few miles north of downtown Baku. Once inside, they were introduced to a technician in white coveralls. The technician, whose name was Farid, was an enthusiastic young man, evidently well-educated, he spoke quite good English. He explained that he had responsibility for the plastics section of the laboratory, which was located in the warehouse.

Efraim said that he wanted some advice on mixing a powdered explosive with a polymer so that when first mixed, it could be moulded into a shape, which it would retain.

"Yes, OK!" Farid responded, "You don't want to work with a hot polymer, correct?"

"I would rather not heat it," Efraim responded, "unless the heating is to less than two hundred degrees Centigrade."

"And you want to keep the polymer content less than ten percent, right?"

"Closer to five, if possible."

"Five is not possible, because there is no bonding, but with seven or eight percent, one can achieve good bonding of the explosive particles into a solid mass at room temperature."

"OK," Efraim said, "Tell me how to do it."

"I will demonstrate the technique here in the laboratory using fine, inert silicon powder."

Farid recommended the use of Miravar and Bramothol, two liquids that when mixed in the right proportions would form a rubbery mass at room temperature. When heated to 150 degrees Centigrade, the rubbery mass would assume a very fluid state. He explained that eight percent, by weight, of the fluid would be sufficient to bond ninety-two percent powdered explosive.

As a part of Efraim's tuition, Farid coached him through the process of producing a solid, polymerised ball out of 250 grams of the powdered silicon.

Efraim examined the small, brownish yellow sphere. "It's very solid, but also slightly elastic," Efraim threw the ball onto the floor; it bounced up about a foot before coming to rest.

Farid shook his head. "I don't recommend that you do that with actual explosive." He handed two plastic bottles to Efraim: one litre of Miravar and half a litre of Bramothol.

"No, of course not, and thank you." Efraim's brain was searching for a way to ask the question, "Farid, if you happen to have the RDX here, I would pay you handsomely for it because it would save me considerable trouble."

Anton interrupted vehemently, "No, he doesn't have it!"

Efraim wheeled angrily on Anton to silence him.

"No, sir," Farid responded hastily, "It is kept in another warehouse to which I have no access. When we are preparing charges, they bring us only what we need."

Efraim confronted Anton angrily in the taxi on the way to the airport. "If the State Oil Company has RDX, why did you not arrange to obtain it on this trip? Why is it necessary that we go on a wild goose chase into Chechnya tomorrow?"

"Because the State Oil Company does not want to find itself implicated in any unusual explosions. These days, manufacturers of high explosive put chemical tags into each batch they produce. Each explosion can be traced to the company which supplied the explosive."

"And what about the Chechnyan?"

"It's not his problem."

"But the explosion will be traced to his supplier."

"Yes, but a large supplier can always produce excuses like theft or hijacking or diversion from munitions."

In thinking about this discussion later, Efraim decided that there was something about it that did not ring true. Where was the Chechnyan likely to obtain RDX? Anton said it was from a large supplier. What large suppliers were within reach of a Chechnyan? Most likely, the Russian military, or a Russian oil or mining company. Efraim doubted that a Chechnyan would have access to Russian natural resource companies. But, access to the military, yes, because of the Russian military occupation of Chechnya. Were the Russian forces in Chechnya likely to be careless in their handling of high explosive? Very doubtful. Something about the trip to Chechnya began to Efraim to feel like a set-up. Was he being set up for another robbery?

Possibly not because Anton had promised a test explosion. Still, robbery was a possibility. Efraim thought of a means of minimising the chances of a robbery, *Could it be a sting?*

What sort of sting?

That evening, Anton insisted that Efraim be his guest for dinner. In other respects, the meeting was much like the previous night. Anton tried various unctuous lines of questioning to discover Efraim's intended target. Efraim decided that it was best if he let it slip that his target was not part of the former Soviet Union. Eliminating the former U.S.S.R. as a target might remove a possible incentive <u>not</u> to supply the explosive.

For his part, Efraim repeatedly emphasised that he would not be messed around, and that he expected to be back in Tbilisi the following evening with four kilos of RDX and seven detonators. He even told Anton the story of the Taliban's attempted robbery.

Anton said, "We are not like the Taliban. We keep our word. We said we would help you get the polymers, and you have them."

"Then, you will probably not object, if just before we depart tomorrow, I show you the funds I will owe you, put them in an envelope with my name on the outside, and put the envelope into your mail slot at your hotel?"

Anton smiled. "You are afraid you will return empty-handed."

"Exactly."

"You will return with four kilos of RDX and seven detonators. So, I can wait until tomorrow afternoon to collect my money."

Efraim nodded and got up from the table. At the doorway to the restaurant, he looked back at Anton. He was speaking on his mobile phone.

The next morning, Efraim was riding pillion on Anton's 350cc motorcycle as they headed north out of Tbilisi along the Aragvi River. The valley was lush green with forest hillsides on each side, and the river itself boiled over its rocky bottom. After an hour, the road that was well-paved became steeper as it followed the winding river into the hills. Looking ahead, Efraim could see a snow-covered mountain in the distance. At about two hours, Anton turned off the main road onto a dirt track, which appeared to serve occasional small stone dwellings set in high mountain meadows, where sheep were grazing. The road was potholed and the going was slow. Then the road ended abruptly at a forest.

Anton stopped the motorcycle. "The border is just ahead. We have to walk for a while."

There was a narrow, dirt path leading into the forest. Anton walked alongside the motorcycle, letting the clutch out now and then as the machine propelled itself up the hill. After 700 or 800 metres, the summit seemed to have been reached, and the path descended, twisting and turning for about a kilometre. Then, it opened into a high meadow with four shepherds cottages.

"We are in Chechnya," Anton announced. He pointed to a cottage, "Our contact is waiting for us there." The cottage Anton indicated was close to the forest, and standing next to it, only a few metres from the nearest trees, was a battered, black Toyota pick-up truck.

"Why couldn't he have brought the stuff to us, if he's so close to the border?" Efraim asked.

"Borz has to be very careful. Many people want to kill him. Here in these mountains, he feels safe."

The cottage had a low, rough-beamed ceiling. There was one room with a cast iron stove, bare plank floor, an old wooden table, chest and chairs. At the table, there was a man in dark coveralls, wearing a black beret. He was probably in his mid-forties, but his unkempt, greying hair, and deeply creased face made him look older. The man, Borz, rose and embraced Anton warmly. The two of them ignored Efraim as they stood, apparently sharing reminiscences. It was apparent that the two men knew each other well, personally, and Efraim thought, professionally. *What is the professional connection? This man Borz does not look like an arms dealer.*

Eventually, Borz turned his attention to Efraim. As Efraim looked at him, he saw the face of a hard man: dark, scrutinising eyes, a white scar down one cheek, and a narrow mouth, lost in black stubble.

"You want some explosive?"

"Yes," Efraim said, "I require four kilos of RDX."

"For what purpose?"

Efraim stepped angrily toward Borz. "That is my business."

Borz contemplated Efraim; there was silence in the room. "We are not prepared to provide explosives for use in the Russian federation."

Efraim stared at Borz; then, he said laconically, "I am under the impression that Chechnyans not only provide explosives, they set them off in the crowded parts of Moscow."

Borz swore and spat on the floor. "Some of us are loyal to Mother Russia," he said savagely.

So that's the connection! Efraim thought, *It's Russia!*

Borz returned to the table and sat down. "We wish to know in which country the explosives will be employed."

Efraim shook his head.

Borz swore again, and slammed his fist on the table.

Efraim turned and strode to the door. "This is pointless, Anton! Let's go!"

Anton stepped toward Efraim. "Just a moment, Mohammed! We will give you what you want. Can you repeat what you told me that the Russian federation is not your target?"

"Yes. The Russian federation is not my target."

There was a brief conversation between Anton and Borz, who got up from the table and left by a rear door. When Borz returned, he was carrying several packages and a box. He set them on the table. The packages were tightly wrapped in clear plastic with Cyrillic lettering, and were the size of sugar or flour packages. Their contents were white. Borz pushed four of the packages toward Efraim, and said, "four kilos." He opened the box, emptied its contents on the table, and counted the objects, which resembled short pencils with wires attached at one end. "Seven detonators."

"How do I know this is RDX?" Efraim asked.

Anton picked up one of the packages, and pointed to the centre of the label. "It says so right here in Russian."

Efraim glanced from Anton to Borz and back to Anton. "The test explosion?"

Efraim's Eye

Borz nodded, reached for one of Efraim's packages, and began to open it. Efraim replaced the package that Borz had taken with another one. "Four <u>complete</u> kilos," he said.

Borz frowned but said nothing. From the chest, he removed a blue earthenware mug and poured some of the white powder into it. He went outside and returned with a handful of earth that he packed onto the white powder. Into the earth, he inserted one of the detonators and clipped a black object—the size of a matchbox—to the detonator leads. "OK," he announced and went outside.

He placed the mug on a tree stump fifty metres away, and returned to Efraim and Anton. Removing a mobile phone from his pocket, Borz dialled a number. Suddenly, there was an intense flash and a very loud crack from where the mug had been. Efraim had expected to be hit with tiny fragments. There was nothing. When they walked to inspect where the explosion had taken place, there was nothing. The stump was gone. Where it had been, there was a shallow smoking hole in the ground.

"OK," Efraim said, turning to Anton, "I'm ready to go back to Tbilisi where you can get your money."

Efraim carefully placed the four packages and the detonators into his knapsack.

At the edge of the forest, Anton started the motorcycle again, and began walking alongside it up the hill. When they were near the summit, Efraim announced, "Wait a minute. I've got to take a piss," and he walked to the far side of a large tree. When he had finished, he nodded at Anton, and began to follow him up the hill.

The shot struck Anton in the centre of his back. He was flung forward by the force of it, and fell, face down onto the path. He made a plaintive sound for a moment, trembled and was still. Blood began to stain the path. Efraim had fired with the Chief's Special pressed against Anton's back so as to muffle the report.

The motorcycle had fallen over; Efraim switched it off. He dragged Anton's body, feet first, well into the forest. He found Anton's mobile phone and put it in his pocket. Searching Anton's leather jacket, he found the wallet. Inside were about a dozen, one hundred Georgian Iaris notes. There was also some sort of identity card in Cyrillic lettering with Anton's photograph. In one corner of the card was what Efraim recognised as the Russian flag. He returned the wallet to Anton's jacket pocket. *I am not a thief.*

Then, Efraim scattered leaves over the blood-soaked dirt of the path. He pushed the motorcycle the rest of the way up the hill, and then made his way cautiously down the hill, squeezing the brake when necessary to slow the machine's silent progress. Near the meadow on the Georgian side, he pushed the motorcycle into the forest, out of sight. He crept down the path, keeping himself invisible to anyone in the Georgian meadow.

Cautiously, Efraim looked out into the meadow. *Just as I thought. There is a welcoming committee.*

There in the meadow were several olive drab vehicles, including two jeeps parked nose to nose, blocking the dirt track where it passed between two cottages. There were also three or four men in camouflage dress and carrying AK-47's lounging by the jeeps, and looking up hill toward the path.

Once again, Efraim crossed the border and made his way cautiously to a spot opposite the Toyota pick-up truck. There was no evidence of Borz. *He's there, though. His truck is still there, and he certainly doesn't live there.*

Efraim scooped up a generous handful of leaves. Stealthily, he moved to the rear of the pickup truck, put his and Anton's mobile phones into the truck bed and covered them with leaves. Then he sat down, out of sight in the forest, to wait

Neither phone rang. Efraim's was on silent; he guessed Anton's was too, but there may not be any reception. Ten minutes later, Borz emerged from the cottage, got into the truck and drove north down the dirt road.

For the next six hours, Efraim alternated: one hour watching the Chechnyan meadow and one hour watching the Georgian meadow. No one came into the Chechnyan meadow. *That's good,* He thought, *Borz has gone home taking those phones into an area where they can be tracked.* As dusk fell on the Georgian meadow, the waiting military seemed to have a conference. An officer was explaining something to his men.

He made a sweeping gesture toward the north. *That's where they think we've gone.*

Fifteen minutes later, all of the military vehicles moved down the track and out of the meadow.

Efraim waited for another two hours. All was quiet. It was dark, but there was a three quarter moon and no clouds. *Shall I walk and get a lift from some passing truck, or shall I ride? They think I'm in Chechnya; I'm going to ride.*

Moving along the dirt track on the motorcycle, Efraim would stop every mile or so, turn off the engine and listen. There was neither a sound nor evidence of people. Before getting onto the highway, he removed the license plate, and streaked the machine with mud. Then, at high speed, he made his way to Tbilisi.

Once in Tbilisi, he parked the motorcycle in May 26th Square, and left the key in the ignition. *Whoever picks this up will eventually have some explaining to do.*

He went to the Vere Palace hotel, where he claimed his envelope. At the Kapan Kovi Hotel, he collected his suitcase, which contained the polymer liquids, and he checked out. At the airport left baggage counter, he placed the suitcase containing the four packages, the detonators and the two bottles of liquid into storage for one month.

Then he checked into a hotel near the airport, and the following morning, he flew home.

Chapter 6

EFRAIM

Omar Saleem looked nervously about him as he sat in one corner at the end of a couch in the lounge of Riad El Norj. For such a big man with a dense black stubble on his face, his nervousness was incongruous. "Mr. Paul and Miss Naomi, you must promise never to tell anyone in Morocco that we have met today," he said.

Paul said, "Of course, Omar. We promise, but we would like to understand the risk you are apparently feeling. Can you tell us what your concerns are?"

Omar Saleem paused and considered Paul for a moment. Then he said, "You know that Yusuf Al-Rashid has connections to the Moroccan military?"

Paul nodded. "He told me yesterday that he has several companies which are involved in security for the Moroccan military."

Omar raised an eyebrow. "He used the word security?"

"Yes, I think so."

Omar leaned forward, and said almost under his breath, "The word security may have a different meaning for you than it does for Mr. Al-Rashid."

Paul said nothing, but the wrinkles on his forehead expressed his puzzlement.

"For you," Omar continued, "the word security may have a passive connotation as in protecting things and keeping them safe."

Paul nodded.

"For Mr. Al-Rashid, the word has a more active connotation as in coercion and enforcement."

"Are you saying," Paul asked softly, "that Mr. Al-Rashid's companies may be involved in reprisals against enemies or even torture?"

"Mr. Paul, you are aware of the situation in the Western Sahara?"

"Well, I know that there is a military confrontation between Morocco and the Polisario nationalists in Western Morocco, and I know that in November 2010 the Moroccan military entered Western Sahara to drive 12,000 people out of a refugee camp."

Omar nodded. "There have been hostilities between Morocco and Polisario for thirty-five years—much of it under cover."

"So, is your concern that you could find yourself treated as a Polisario agent?"

"I do not wish to find myself in the Galaat Magouna Prison."

Paul nodded. "I understand."

Omar continued, "There is also the brother of Mr. Al-Rashid."

"What about his brother?" Naomi inquired.

"His name is Efraim Nuh Al-Rashid. He is a few years younger than Yusuf, and I believe he has a different mother."

"A half-brother?" Naomi asked, "What about him?"

"He lives with Yusuf, but it is not clear what he does. Some people say he owns a shop in the medina. I have never seen him there. Other people whisper that he is an agent with the Moroccan secret service. I only know that he is a very large man, and that he makes very nasty speeches in a mosque."

"So," Paul summarised, "your concern is that Efraim may be an enforcer for his brother Yusuf."

Omar shrugged uncertainly. "Maybe. He could be." He picked up his neglected coffee cup; Paul noticed that his hand trembled slightly.

Naomi said, "Omar, please rest assured that whatever you tell us today will remain within the confines of GYE in London."

Omar nodded and slowly seemed to gather himself. "Things are not right within AMM," he said.

"What things?" Naomi asked.

Omar bent over and removed a beige manila file from the battered leather case he had brought with him. He extracted what appeared to be a report and gestured at the cover. "This is the ISDB report on AMM's young entrepreneur project." Paul and Naomi watched as Omar leafed through the pages of the report. "It is in English."

"Yes, I know, we've seen it," Naomi said.

Omar ignored her comment. "Here," he said, laying the report on the table, "it says that AMM has lent money to 187 young entrepreneurs." Briefly, he looked from Naomi to Paul, who nodded. "That is a lie," he continued, "There are at most about seventy-five entrepreneurs who actually received loans."

"How do you know that?" Paul asked.

"Because I used to work there and I had access to the files."

Naomi said, "But that suggests that something must have happened to the rest of the money."

"Of course." The three sat looking at one another for some moments. "But," Omar continued, "the money wasn't returned to the bank." There was another pause. "Because that would have been mentioned in the report. In fact, if you multiply the 187 entrepreneurs by the average loan size mentioned in the report, and you add the amounts for administration, training, etc, shown in the report, the total you will come to equals the total of the ISDB loans and grants. All very much in order."

Omar looked up. "Ah, here now is Mosa Mitri. He was my predecessor at AMM."

Greetings were exchanged. The old porter appeared with a fresh pot of mint tea, bowed, removed the empty pot and disappeared. Mosa Mitri, in contrast with Omar Saleem, was a thin man, clean-shaven, with an assured disposition. He had a large, sharp nose and narrow, watchful eyes. Like Omar, he wore a faded dress shirt, jeans and trainers.

Omar said, "These people from London have assured me that our discussions today will never be repeated to anyone from Morocco." Mosa nodded impatiently. "And I have called to their attention the shortage of entrepreneurs."

"And mentors?" Mosa asked.

"No, I was just getting to that when you came in."

"That report (Mosa gestured toward the report which lay on the table) says there were eighty-two mentors. At most, there were half that number."

"And the funding for the other half went into Mr. Al-Rashid's pocket?" Paul added.

"Of course." In a sardonic tone, he added, "It's a much more efficient way to get your hands on the money. You have half the training and recruitment expense, and you work your unpaid volunteers twice as hard."

"But," Naomi protested, "why didn't the outside auditor who wrote that report for the ISDB find these deceptions?"

Mosa eyed Naomi speculatively for a moment. "I believe the expression in English is 'you scratch my back and I'll scratch yours.'"

Naomi was shocked, "He was bribed?"

Mosa shrugged. "There is also the matter of double-counting expenses."

"How does that work?" Paul asked.

"Suppose you have an invoice from a training company for training sessions for mentors," Mosa began. "What you do is charge that invoice against grants from three private sector companies. All three companies will think they've paid for the training, but only one has. The funds provided by the other two just disappear."

"But," Paul protested, "That sort of thing should be discovered during an audit."

"Well, it isn't," Mosa retorted, "Probably because the audit isn't very thorough."

There was a long moment of silence. Paul asked, "Does either Yaminah or Latifa know what's going on?"

"Probably," Omar said.

Mosa disagreed. "Yaminah <u>certainly</u> knows! In the name of the Prophet, she's the bookkeeper! Latifa probably knows, but I think she hopes she has misunderstood. Such a trusting girl!"

"Why doesn't Yaminah quit like you have?" Naomi wanted to know.

Omar shook his head. "Her husband has been very ill. He's unable to work. They have five children. She said something to me once about how she had medical insurance. That's probably the hold that Yusuf has on her."

"He tries to get a hold on everyone," Mosa added, "When he can't get a hold, and he thinks someone is in a position to hurt him, he acts."

"So you guys didn't quit," Paul suggested.

"No, I was fired," Omar confirmed.

Mosa said, "So was I."

"Why?" Naomi wanted to know.

"Because he knew that I knew too much, and he said it was time I found someplace else to work. I tried to complain to one of the board members about the way I was unfairly fired. I never said anything about what was really going on—as Omar has probably told you that would have been a big mistake. I got nowhere. Yusuf just told the board member that I was a worthless employee. But afterwards . . . afterwards . . . there was a dead rat in my post box. It had been decapitated."

Omar said, "The same thing happened to me."

"In Italy," Paul said, "the Mafia used to send informants a dead fish to warn them that they would 'sleep with the fishes.'"

"That's the idea," Mosa responded dryly. Then he surveyed the two Westerners. "We haven't given you fingerprints or a smoking gun."

Paul said, "No, but you've given us the incentive to dig deeper and uncover the hard evidence."

"Inshallah."

"What are you guys doing now?" Paul asked.

"I'm working in the sales department of a company that exports Moroccan carpets," Omar replied. "Believe it or not, when the company insisted on talking with my former employer, they got a good report."

Mosa said, "The same thing happened to me except that I'm a loan officer at Shahzad Rameel Bank."

* * *

"How were your meetings yesterday with the entrepreneurs?" Yusuf inquired when Paul and Naomi were served more coffee in the CEO's office.

Paul answered, "They said you drive a very hard bargain."

"Actually, I am very lenient and relaxed in the discussions I have with entrepreneurs."

"I don't think the two we spoke with last night would agree with that."

Yusuf shrugged. "What they fail to understand, and what you haven't seen yet are the contracts where money is lent, the business starts up, the business loses money, and the entrepreneur disappears without paying AMM any money at all. We have quite a few of those, believe me. I can show you one or two like that. As it happens, you selected two entrepreneurs who have made some money. It all balances out in the end."

"But, in my opinion, your contracts very strongly favour AMM."

"In what way?"

"Well, for example, in the event that an entrepreneur is late in making payments, AMM has the right to confiscate property which has nothing to do with the business for which the loan is granted."

Yusuf shook his head. "Confiscate is the wrong word, I think. Better to say 'take temporary possession.' Besides, we have never invoked that provision. It is there just as a reminder to our borrowers to keep their payments up to date. You see, Paul, in Morocco, many of these young entrepreneurs seem to believe that AMM is a charity that has provided them not with a loan, but a grant. Unless they are reminded that they might temporarily lose their radio, we would cease getting payments altogether!"

"So, are you saying that provisions like this are the norm for commercial banks in Morocco?"

"Yes, of course!"

Paul made a mental note to meet again with Mosa Mitri to hear his views on normal terms from commercial banks.

"Tell me, Yusuf," Paul continued, "What actions does AMM take when one of your borrowers is delinquent on his or her payments?"

"Well, when a business fails to make any profits, our hands are tied. We will talk to the mentor who is involved to get his view of the situation, but if it is no good, we simply have to write off the loan. Sometimes an entrepreneur will have a slow first year or two, and again, we will talk to the mentor to understand the problem. But in cases like that, we just have to be patient, and of course, AMM will make a far lower return than we all had expected."

"Have you had any entrepreneurs who take the position that the contract amounts to usury, and that because their business is more successful than expected, they are paying AMM what amounts to a usurious interest rate?"

Yusuf shook his head vehemently. "No sharia court would ever accept that argument!"

"I noticed that the contracts are subject to sharia law. So you would never use the Moroccan civil courts?"

"No. They don't have jurisdiction. Now, if I may suggest for Naomi to meet with Latifa for her discussions. Yaminah will be ready to meet with you, Paul, in half an hour, but in the meantime, she had to go to the bank."

When Naomi had gone to the other room to meet with Latifa, Yusuf closed the door behind her and paced about his office, apparently lost in thought. He said, "Paul, have you considered further our discussion of yesterday?"

Immediately, Paul knew what was meant, but he decided not to make the conversation easy for Yusuf. He said, feigning incomprehension, "Which discussion was that, Yusuf?"

"Well, you know, you were kindly telling me that you are thinking of completing the review of AMM for GYE on a pro bono basis. You mentioned, by way of comparison, a daily rate of £1,200. I explained that I am accustomed to paying the very best consultants, like yourself, Paul, an equivalent amount, and of course, to ease the tax situation, I have paid my overseas consultants directly into their account. Naturally, as far as GYE and Her Majesty are concerned, your work here at AMM is on a pro bono basis. Yesterday, we mentioned an assignment duration of five days including travel time. If we were to consider a duration of seven days, that would equate to £8,400."

Yusuf seated himself in the ornately carved chair at his desk, and considered Paul silently for a moment. *God I wish I had a tape recorder*! Paul thought, but he said nothing.

"Of course," Yusuf continued, "you would certainly not wish to say anything which is untruthful about AMM. It is clear that we have some opportunities to improve our office procedures as the report to ISDB suggests. My only concern is that AMM continues to operate under the GYE umbrella."

"Why is that so important, Yusuf? Your organisation appears to be very successful."

"We are successful exactly because of our association with GYE, which has a very strong brand."

"I see. Well, let me think about it, Yusuf. I can give you an answer tomorrow." Paul thought, *Tonight, I'm going to look for a small tape recorder in the souq, and bring it with me tomorrow*.

Yusuf said, "Time and state of mind are very important, Paul. We have a saying in Morocco that one should not knock more than twice on the door of opportunity, because the rains will come and drown the foolish man." Yusuf's tone of voice and his body language suggested that this was not a casual statement.

Is it a threat? Paul wondered; he said, "I'll keep that in mind. Oh, by the way, Yusuf, would you be kind enough to make me an appointment tomorrow to see the financial auditor of AMM?"

"You have the audit report. What is the need to meet with them?"

"The report is in Arabic, and I'd had some questions I'd like to ask."

"Miss Evensen can translate the report of you; it is self-explanatory."

"I can make the appointment myself, but as a courtesy to you, I'm giving you the opportunity to make the appointment."

Yusuf nodded sourly.

When Paul entered the small, Spartan office, he found that Naomi and Latifa were seated together at Latifa's desk. They were deep in conversation regarding a file that was open before them.

Paul approached Yaminah, who, as on the previous day, was wearing a dark, cotton head scarf, a knee-length black shirt that was buttoned to her throat, and navy twill trousers. Her face looked very tired, with its shadowed eyes, crow's feet, and creased brow. There was not a trace of makeup, and Paul thought, *She looks old before her time.* And yet the light in her large, dark eyes was bright; her nose was modest and her mouth, straight. *She used to be an attractive woman.*

"Good morning, Yaminah. Is this a good time for us to talk?" She smiled faintly and nodded. All the files were cleared from her desk and her monitor was in sleep mode. "Can you tell me what your duties include?"

"I work mostly in financial area," she said. Her English was spoken slowly with a heavy accent. "Latifa (she nodded toward her colleague across the room) mostly do filing and work with entrepreneurs and mentors."

"So you pay all the bills?" Paul prompted.

"Mr. Al-Rashid pay bills. I log invoices on system and print cheques. Mr. Al-Rashid sign. Sometimes he pay electronically. I tell him user name and password; he never remember."

"Does anyone else have to sign AMM's cheques?"

"No. Only Mr. Al-Rashid."

"Can you show me your system?"

Yaminah woke up her monitor and clicked on a desktop icon. "Is old system. We use only for payables. I wish for new system." When the file opened, Paul saw that it was in Arabic. With a slight smile, Yaminah offered, "I think you are not reading Arabic."

Efraim's Eye

"No. Unfortunately I am not, but let me summarise. This system . . ."

She interrupted . . . "is called Abacus."

"Abacus provides an electronic record of all your expenditures, but I suppose you also keep paper copies."

"We keep also bank statements."

"You have one bank account?"

"We have twelve bank accounts in AMM. There is one in dirhams and one in Euros for the ISDB project <u>loans</u>. There is one in dirhams and one in euros for the ISDB project <u>grants</u>. There are two more in dirhams for loans or grants from Moroccan government. Two more in dirhams for loans and grants from private sector. Also one in sterling and one in Euros for private sector grants. There is account in dirhams for AMM expenses. Another one for loans repayment by entrepreneurs."

"Yaminah, wouldn't it be possible to have just three accounts: one in dirhams, one in Euros and one in sterling if you also had multi-currency software that could handle individual projects?"

"Yes."

"Why doesn't Mr. Al-Rashid get the software?"

"He says we not need it." There was a defensiveness and finality in Yaminah's tone that persuaded Paul not to pursue the question further.

"So you have to reconcile twelve bank accounts every month?"

She nodded. "Is not so bad. Some accounts no activity."

"But you have to prepare income statements every month, and I suppose there are balance sheets that have to be drawn up."

She shook her head. "Mr. Al-Rashid prepare reports to ISDB and government, and auditors prepare some report. I not do financial reporting."

"How does Mr. Al-Rashid know the financial status of AMM?"

"Mr. Al-Rashid very smart man," she said with a touch of asperity.

"OK. Well, how about the income side of things?"

"When funds come in from ISDB, or government or private sector, I record in spreadsheet, and deposit in bank.

When entrepreneur sends cheque, Latifa records in spreadsheet. I take to bank and deposit."

"I'd like to see the loan repayment bank statement. Can you show it to me, please?"

Yaminah opened a file drawer and took out a beige manila folder. She put it on her desk and opened it. Paul recognised the format, and the numbers were legible, but the text was not. "This column is deposits?" he asked running his finger down the page. She nodded. "And this is withdrawals?" Another nod. "How many pages are one month's activity?" he asked.

"From here," she said, "to here," pointing at places on two pages.

Paul ran his finger down the deposits column. "Thirty-two deposits . . . That's not very many considering you have one hundred and eighty-seven entrepreneurs." He sensed that Yaminah was suddenly uncomfortable.

"Many entrepreneurs just starting business. Some not profitable. Some not paying every month."

To Paul these sounded like conjured excuses. "These numbers here are withdrawals? . . . Ten in the month. What are they for?"

"Those are loans to new entrepreneurs."

"And this one here? It's for 300,000 dirhams."

"Transfer to another account." Her answer was a little too quick.

"What account would that be?"

She shook her head vehemently. "I not know. Mr. Al-Rashid make transfers."

Paul continued to study the page. *Why the hell wouldn't she know?* he wondered. *She sees all the bank statements. It would be easy enough to spot a 300,000 withdrawal here and a 300,000 deposit there. The figures would stand out. . . . Unless the deposit was made into an account she doesn't see.* "Yaminah, would you make me copies of these three pages?" he asked, clasping the three pages between thumb and forefinger.

She continued to sit where she was, as if she hadn't heard.

"Or I can make the copies, if you prefer."

She stood, took the file, and walked across the room. Moments later she handed him the copies without a word.

"Yaminah, I understand your husband has been ill. I'm sorry."

She considered him coldly for a few seconds, and then her lips began to tremble. "My husband has very bad osteoarthritis. He have much pain and difficulty moving."

"That's terrible. Does he take medication?"

"He try many medications. They not work. Now, he take ibuprofen, but not good for stomach." She shook her head and continued, "He ask doctor for morphine, but I say no! . . . . Is no way back from morphine."

Paul nodded. "I understand that in severe cases like your husband has, surgery is sometimes effective."

"My husband have both knees and one hip replaced. Now other hip very bad." She sat down again at her desk and stared at her monitor. Then, she turned to face Paul. "This job very important for me."

"I understand. You are supporting a large family."

Her hands were folded with resignation in her lap. "My husband not able work. Have five children. Oldest fifteen. She not go to school. She take care my husband."

Paul could only nod. "That's very difficult."

Again she looked at Paul. "What you recommend about AMM?"

"I . . . I don't know yet, Yaminah. We . . . we have at least one more day of work to do."

"Is possible to say AMM need make this and that change, but AMM OK?" Paul considered his answer. She continued, "You not say AMM no good'!" Paul could see that Yaminah's hands were tightly clenched. Her dark eyes held his. "If AMM no good, I not have a job. There not any job in Marrakech for woman bookkeeper. I have to work in hotel as cleaner. Then I not have insurance for my husband." Her face was strained with barely contained desperation.

Paul reached out with both his hands and took hers. They sat, juxtaposed, but together for several moments. "I understand, Yaminah."

"Paul, we're due to make that call to Mr. Chieraux now." It was Naomi, who had finished her discussions with Latifa. "We can use the phone in Yusuf's office."

When they had moved the speakerphone onto the black tabletop and were seated close by, Naomi asked, "What do we want to ask Mr. Chieraux about?"

"Well, what I want to ask him about is what investigations of AMM he completed before he wrote that report for the ISDB. The problems he reports on are all relatively minor, and he seems not to have discovered any major issues."

"He's been the ISDB's consultant who reviews AMM for several years now. Maybe he felt he knew all there was to know."

Paul grinned at Naomi. "Or maybe his level of curiosity is particularly low for selfish reasons."

Naomi considered Paul for several moments; she said, "Is it your nature to be so suspicious of everyone, Paul?"

He sensed that she was only partly jesting, and he decided to take her seriously. "I think that as a financial consultant, I'm trained, and clients expect me, to question anything that isn't obviously OK. But, in my private life, with family, friends and acquaintances, I tend to accept everything that isn't obviously wrong."

She smiled, and there was the hint of a tease. "Isn't that a bit schizophrenic?"

"Aren't we all a bit schizophrenic?"

She was grinning now. "I'm not!"

"I'll bet you are! I just haven't found it yet!" She laughed aloud. "Besides, Naomi, we're not talking about brain pathology. We're talking about applying different values in different situations."

"That sounds pretty pathological to me!"

It was Paul's turn to laugh. Then he considered her seriously for a moment. "Are you telling me that none of your values is situational?"

"Yes! Exactly!" They looked at each other for several moments. Then she asked, "What are you thinking, Paul?"

"I'm trying to figure out whether you're naïve or an extraordinary person."

"Oh, I can tell you that!"

"I know you can. Let's call Mr. Chieraux."

Mr. Chieraux took the call in his home office in Bordeaux. After the initial introductions were made by Naomi, Paul asked, "How did it happen that you were asked to prepare the report on AMM, Mr Chieraux?"

"I have been working for the Inter-Sahara Development Bank for some years now, and as a consequence, I am on what you might call on their approved list. I was referred to Mr. Al-Rashid, who found me acceptable, and I have been performing the annual assessment each year thereafter."

"Do you have a set of standards which recipients of ISDB funds must meet?"

"There are no objective standards, if that is what you mean. One must bear in mind, Mr. Winthorpe, that 1.5 million dollars is almost—as finance directors like to say—a rounding error—for the bank. Their main concern is that their funds are put to good use."

Paul glanced at Naomi, and shook his head in frustration, but she was occupied with an elaborate doodle in her notebook. "Well, Mr. Chieraux, is there a customary process you would follow in completing this kind of assessment?"

"Of course, I go to their offices and I speak with the employees and the managing director. I also review certain files."

"Which files do you review?"

"Well, I review their list of borrowers, and I examine the training records of the mentors."

"Individual training records?"

"Oh, no, there is nothing like that. I review the master list of training courses held. That list shows the names of the personnel who received the training."

"Do you review the financial records?"

"No, that kind of work is done by the auditor."

"Do you interview members of the board of trustees?"

"No, that is not necessary."

"Do you interview entrepreneurs who have or have not received funding?"

"We are not interested in entrepreneurs who have not received funding, but I interviewed four or five funded entrepreneurs."

"Did you select the interviewees?"

"No. The interviews were arranged by the AMM staff."

"And the mentors?"

"I met three or four of them."

"Mr. Chieraux, as a part of your assessment, do you cross-check important information you receive from an assessee with information received from independent sources?"

"What do you mean, Mr. Winthorpe?"

Naomi looked up from her doodling and was suddenly paying attention. Paul continued, "Well, for example, when an assessee tells you he lent money to one hundred people, do you check his bank statements to see that there were actually one hundred disbursements?"

There was a pause at the other end of the line. "No. No, we wouldn't do anything like that. In the first place, it would be quite time consuming, and the bank provides funding for only a three-day assessment. And also, such an effort would create an adversarial attitude between the bank and their client. They much prefer to have a trusting environment."

Paul asked, "Mr. Chieraux, you've been doing this kind of work for several years, I suppose?"

"Twelve years to be exact."

"During that time, have you ever encountered a case of fraud?"

There was another pause. "Of course. Yes. Over the years there have been one or two, I suppose."

"One or two out of how many?"

"Well, I don't know exactly, but there have been quite a few."

Wordlessly, Paul made a gesture of surrender. Naomi was frowning, and Paul saw that she had a copy of Mr. Chieraux's report in her hands. She suddenly asked a question in French, as she

Efraim's Eye

thumbed through the report. During the discussion that followed, Mr. Chieraux's tone seemed to Paul to become defensive.

"Au revoir, Mr. Chieraux, é merci beaucoup." She hung up.

"What was that about?" Paul asked.

Naomi said, "I asked him how he was able to visit Marrakech, do his assessment, return to Bordeaux, and write his report—all in three days."

"Good question, Naomi. What did he say?"

"He said that the three days he mentioned was just his time allowance for Marrakech, and that he got another two and a half days to write his report." She thumbed the report again and looked at Paul. "How long would it take you to write a report like this? It's almost a hundred pages."

"I couldn't write a report of a hundred pages with all original material in just two and a half days."

"Maybe it's not all original material."

"Oh, who's getting suspicious now?" he teased.

Naomi flushed. "Well, there was something about the way he answered questions, particularly my questions, that bothers me."

Paul smiled. "A woman's intuition."

Naomi glared at him. "You don't have to belittle it! There is such a thing you know!"

"Hey, Naomi," Paul held up his hands. "I wasn't belittling it. In fact, I know about women's intuition. I've lived with women for about thirty years."

Naomi was suddenly confused. "Which women?"

"My wife and daughter. Oh, and there was also my mother."

Naomi was mollified. "Oh, OK." She sat down and began to scan through the report more carefully.

Paul said, "I'll go tell Yusuf he can have his office back." But when Paul returned, he said, "He's gone out somewhere. Shall we call it a day?"

Naomi didn't respond. She seemed to be absorbed in her reading. "Am I losing my mind?" she asked. "I think I've read a lot of this before, but I know I haven't read this report before."

Paul sat down, opened his notebook and began to add to his entries for the day.

"Es salaam alaykum." (Peace be with you.) It was a deeply resonating baritone voice. The greeting was uttered by a burly man dressed entirely in black and wearing a black and white keffiyeh. The man, who had just entered Yusuf's office, had a heavy black stubble, flecked prematurely with white, large dark eyes, and gleaming white teeth.

"Wa alaykum salaam," (and peace be with you) Naomi responded automatically, but she was studying the man carefully.

"Asmeetek?" (What is your name?) the man asked, abruptly

"Esmee Naomi Evensend," Naomi replied.

The man frowned, lowered his head and stared at Naomi. There was a brief exchange in Arabic. Then, he suddenly asked in heavily accented English, "Where you learn to speak Arabic?"

"In Jerusalem."

"You are not a Palestinian girl. You are a Jew." His tone was accusatory.

"I am Jewish. Who are you?"

"I am Efraim Nuh Al-Rashid," he said emphatically, as if no further introduction was necessary.

He's not exactly very friendly, Paul thought, *About six foot four and at least twenty stone. He would be a good choice for a rugby lock!*

Paul said, "You must be Yusuf's brother."

"Yes." No further discussion of this point was required. "And you are?"

"Paul Winthorpe. I am here to complete an assessment of AMM on behalf of GYE."

"You are a Christian." Efraim made the word 'Christian' sound derogatory, like 'leper'.

"Yes, I am a Christian." Later, Paul wondered why, given his religious ambivalence, he had made so forthright a statement. *Was it to challenge the arrogance of Efraim?* "And you, I suppose are a Muslim?" he added.

Efraim drew himself up, emphasising his stature. "I am a believer in the true Islamic faith, a worshipper of the One God, and a devout follower of his Prophet, Muhammad."

"I'm glad to hear it," Paul said, with just a touch of sarcasm.

"So! We have a Christian crusader and a Jew woman coming here to tell us of the true faith how to conduct our business!"

Paul protested, "Efraim, this is not a religious exercise."

"So you say, but you wish to corrupt our ways with your usury, your City of London values and our socialist principles. You are a crusader in a suit!"

Paul didn't know whether to laugh or be angry. He said, "Efraim the last crusader died about eight hundred years ago."

"Not true! There are crusaders by the thousand in Afghanistan and in Iraq! There are hundreds more in Saudi Arabia, Yemen, Qatar and the Emirates!" He strode to where Naomi was sitting, his dark bulk towering over her. "And why are you here?" he demanded of her.

Paul could see that Naomi was visibly frightened. "She is the operations director of GYE, and she is here to assist me in the assessment of AMM."

"I am asking you!" Efraim insisted, poking Naomi's shoulder with a finger.

Suddenly, Naomi was out of her chair, facing him, her face drained of colour. "Don't you dare touch me!" she hissed. She backed away from him as if he were a cobra with its hood extended.

For a moment there was absolute silence and no movement in the room: Paul, seated, but ready to act; Naomi, trembling, her arms clasped across her chest; and Efraim between them, radiating hostility.

Softly, Paul said, "What can we do for you, Efraim?"

Efraim said nothing. He suddenly turned and left the room, closing the door noisily behind him.

Naomi moved to where Paul was sitting. Paul stood and put his arms around her protectively. Wordlessly, she clung to him, her head against his chest. "God, he's awful!" Then, "Let's go, Paul."

"Password is 'ElNorj123'." Naomi was speaking to herself as she sat on the couch at Riad El Norj with her white Sony VAIO laptop in front of her. "There," she said, "Connected . . . There's an e-mail here from Roberta." She looked up at Paul. "She wants to know what's going on."

"Tell her everything's fine," Paul suggested.

Naomi gave a derisive snort. "I'll answer it later. . . . Here we go." She started to read from her screen: "ash-Shbab Mshrw Maroc is the Moroccan chapter of Global Youth Enterprise giving young entrepreneurs a boost up the ladder of success." She picked up her copy of Mr. Chieraux's report. "It's absolutely word for word the same! He just copied his report from the website! He copied the pages on young entrepreneurs and the pages on mentors. He's copied the About Us pages. Just about everything!"

"So that's how he does it," Paul remarked, still making entries in his notebook.

Paul's offhand tone irritated Naomi. "Paul are you listening to me?" she demanded.

"Yes, of course."

"Well, don't you think it's awful?" she insisted.

"Plagiarism is always the mark of a poor consultant, but it doesn't really concern us."

Naomi was annoyed. "Why not?"

"Well, we didn't hire him; the bank did."

"OK, but don't you think somebody ought to tell them that they paid for a plagiarised report?"

"You can tell them. And, when you're sending the e-mail to Mr. ben-Tanoos, would you ask him what the bank's rules are about withdrawals of funds from the loan repayment account?"

"Why?"

"Because this afternoon I asked Yaminah to show me the bank statement for the loan repayment account. There was one withdrawal for 300,000 dirhams that she said Yusuf transferred to another account—she didn't know which one."

Naomi stared at him. "300,000 dirhams?"

"And there were ten other withdrawals in the month, which she said were for new loans, but I don't believe her."

"Why not?"

"Because all the withdrawals were for the same amount: 30,000 dirhams. What are the odds than ten different entrepreneurs take out loans in identical amounts in the same month?"

Naomi closed her eyes as a look of resignation crossed her face. "I feel sick," she said.

Half an hour later, Naomi was sipping at a mug of tea and still working on her laptop. Paul was nursing a Scotch and soda. He was preparing a To Do List for the following day.

"Here he is! That horrible creature!" she announced.

"Who's that?"

"Efraim."

"You found him on Facebook?"

She scowled. "I found his website."

"What does it say?" Paul was starting to show some interest.

"It's in Arabic."

"And?" he prompted.

She sat reading intently and scrolling down for several minutes. She shook her head. There was a look of revulsion on her face. "It's all bigotry and hatred," she said. "'Christians are crusaders intent on subjugating Islam. We must take the war to them. Jews have invaded Palestine, intent on making the Palestinian people their economic slaves. We must push them back into the sea.'"

She was quoting from the website. "Oh, and here it says that he will be speaking during Friday prayers at the Bakkali Mosque—that's tomorrow."

"Here in Marrakech?"

"Yes."

"Everything pretty much closes down on Friday afternoon doesn't it?" he asked.

"Yes . . . You aren't thinking of going to listen to him are you? He won't be speaking in English!"

"Yes, I know, but I think it would be interesting to see his speaking style. Is he a budding Islamic Hitler? I'd also like to see how the faithful in the mosque feel about him."

Naomi made a distasteful face.

"Okay," he said, "How about this? We can go to the mosque near the end of the service—if that's what it's called. That way, I can peek in and get an idea of his style, and we can judge his effect on the faithful." She gave a concessionary shrug. "Oh, and I almost forgot Naomi, I'd like to go to the souq tonight to pick up a tape recorder."

"What on earth for?"

"Yusuf tried to bribe me twice now. I'd like to have a recording of him trying to close the deal tomorrow."

"You must be kidding."

"Unfortunately, I'm not.

Revulsion showed on Naomi's face. "What did he offer you?"

"£8,400."

Her eyes were wide open in surprise. "In exchange for what?"

"For recommending that AMM retains its GYE accreditation."

Naomi continued to gaze at him. Then the wisp of a smile appeared. "I have an idea," she said.

"What's that?"

"Let's get him up to ten thousand. We'll split it. You copy your report from the website, and we'll all live happily ever after." She chuckled.

He reached across the table and patted her hand. "Let's go to the souq."

"What's with the headscarf?" he asked as they were leaving the Riad El Norj.

"It's so you can get a better price on the recorder."

"What does the headscarf have to do with the price of a tape recorder?"

She said, "They don't make tape recorders anymore. They're all digital memory."

"Not true. Sony is still making the Walkman. That has a record feature."

"You want to go into Yusuf's office tomorrow with the tape drive on your Walkman grinding away in your pocket?"

Paul laughed. "OK. What does the price of a <u>digital</u> recorder have to do with your headscarf?"

"I don't want to look like a blonde, New York girl who's out with her dad on a shopping trip. That would certainly drive the price up."

As they entered the din and confusion of the souq, Naomi made inquiries of several traders. "This way," she said, threading her way through the jostling crowds of people of every age and economic circumstance: tourists, old men bending over their canes, young men carrying huge bundles, children on bicycles, women linked arm-in-arm. They were all resolutely moving this way and that, bumping into each other, and engaged in shouted communications with the watchful traders. Here was the smell of spices; there it was the scent of fried delicacies, or the reek of tobacco smoke.

Naomi stopped at a shop and surveyed the merchandise on display.

"Please to come in, missus," the proprietor said with a bow. She ignored him and continued to look. Then she said something in Arabic as an aside to the trader. He responded, bowing more deeply and disappeared into his shop. When he reappeared, he approached Paul with a box. "Here is excellent digital recorder. Very good price."

"Too big," Paul said, "Should be small. Like this." He held up his hands to demonstrate. The proprietor made a sound signaling his understanding and returned with a smaller box. Paul opened the box. Inside was a recorder about the size of a small mobile phone. He found the panel on the box where the specifications were written in English. "How much?" he asked, rubbing a thumb against his fingers.

"Very good price. Is 700 dirhams."

Paul shook his head. "Too much. You have cheaper one?" He made a display of looking past the proprietor into the shop. A moment later, the proprietor was back with a different box. "Is cheapest one," he said.

"How much?"

"Is very good price. Is 400 dirhams."

"I give you 200," Paul said, holding up two fingers.

The proprietor threw up his hands in desperation. "Is Sony. Very good quality. For you, I accept 350."

"No. Too much." To Naomi, he said, "I think we'll have to try that other shop."

Immediately, the proprietor was at Paul's side. "You tell me what you pay," he pleaded.

"220."

"Oh, sir, 290 is very best price."

Paul considered the cracked ceiling of the little shop. "250! Nothing more!"

The proprietor's mournful expression was gradually replaced with a reluctant smile. "OK, sir, 250," he confirmed.

They were back in Djemaa el-Fna, with its brightly lit restaurant area. "Where shall we have dinner?" Naomi asked.

"Please, not at number 67 again."

"How about one of those rooftop restaurants?" Naomi suggested, with a gesture toward one of the open, first floor restaurants overlooking the square.

Paul considered this. "I think it would be kind of hot and noisy," he said. "Isn't there a hotel down this alley? I feel like a quiet, air conditioned dinner."

After walking several hundred yards down the twisting alley, they came to an imposing, white, French-style building with a columned portico. There were taxis and rickshaws drawn up in front. They entered the Western-style lobby of the Hotel d' Marseilles. To the right of the reception desk, there was the sign pointing to the Concorde restaurant. Paul said, "This is what I had in mind."

Naomi studied the menu posted on a stand by the entrance. She shook her head. "This is definitely out of GYE's expense reimbursement range!"

"My treat. See anything you like?"

She looked up at him. "Yes, a few things."

"OK. Let's go."

Efraim's Eye

They were seated at a table by the glass wall that looked out on the garden. On one side were the cool, white linen tablecloths topped with small vases of pink carnations. Beyond the glass was the hot, humid garden with its lemon trees, rose bougainvillea, and a fountain. Naomi had removed her headscarf and her blonde hair cascaded over her shoulders and navy dress shirt.

The sommelier approached them, deferentially placing two wine lists on the table. Naomi briefly scanned the list, and ordered for herself in French. Paul considered the list, and finally asked the sommelier, "The amontillado sherry is from Jerez?"

"Yes, sir."

"I'll have that. On the rocks, please."

Naomi was amused. "You like things to be just right."

He shrugged. "Yes, I guess I do. Don't you?"

"Sometimes. Other times, I like to go with the flow, and see what happens. It makes life a bit of an adventure. For example, I ordered a chardonnay. I haven't any idea what he's going to bring me." She smoothed the tablecloth with her right hand, which like her left was devoid of any jewelry. "You got a good price on that recorder."

"Do you think so?"

She nodded. "I never get the best price when I'm in the souq—not because I don't like to bargain. It's just that I think: this poor man has a family to feed, and I'm trying to take money away from him."

Paul smiled. "You're a very nice person, Naomi."

"No, I'm not! I hate that Efraim! He was horrible! If I were a nice person, I would see some good in him."

"Maybe Saint Peter wouldn't see any good in him, either."

"How can people be so horrible? I'll bet he thinks that women should not work or be educated—that they should stay at home, taking care of the children, cooking, and taking care of the man's needs."

"It seems to me that for some Islamic fundamentalists, there's a hatred that builds up and up until they are no longer able to think logically, and their values shift dramatically."

"Why is that, Paul?"

"I suppose it depends on the individual. Maybe it's a sense of injustice, or jealousy and frustration. I think they tend to brood on their grievance until it gets larger and larger in their minds."

"But it's not really based on religion."

"I understand the Qur'an is pretty clear about killing innocent people: you're not supposed to do it, but they refer to other parts of the Qur'an where it talks about jihad—holy war—and justify it that way. I think the hatred comes before the justification. I think it's always been that way with people."

She smiled admiringly and nodded.

The sommelier brought their drinks. Naomi asked him in English, "Where does this chardonnay come from?"

"It is from Meknes, miss." She took a sip, nodded at him, and he moved away.

Paul asked, "Where is Meknes?"

"It's north of here near Fez. It's the major wine-growing area. Want to try it?"

Paul took a sip from her glass. "It's quite good actually."

"Not as good as the French, but it's less than half the price. May I try your sherry?"

"Yes, of course."

She sipped. "Very smooth and nutty. Not too sweet though."

Paul leaned back in his chair. "Let's see where we are with this assessment. First of all, we have the accusation that AMM has falsified the records of loans to entrepreneurs and has misappropriated funds. But we have no proof of either point, although I had a suspicion of non-existent entrepreneurs during my meeting with Latifa. And we have the accusation that AMM charged the same expense to two or three donors."

"During my meeting with Latifa," Naomi said, "I found out that AMM has no operations manual. Everything seems to be done on an ad hoc basis. The record-keeping is atrocious, and the files are a mess. She had difficulty finding files I asked to see, and the ones I was shown had important records missing."

"We also learned from entrepreneurs that Yusuf drives a very hard bargain on the contract terms for mudarabah. So hard, in fact, that he seems to treat the contracts less as instruments of charity and more as money-making ventures for AMM," Paul added.

Naomi offered, "Then we have the fact that AMM is housed in Yusuf's home, rather than in a separate office."

"We've heard Yusuf's plan for the next five years," Paul said, "and to say the least, it's very optimistic! There is some doubt about ISDB's level of contribution. And we have Yusuf's apparent attempt to bribe me."

Naomi added, "We suspect he also bribed the ISDB's consultant! And also, the ex-employees are terrified of Yusuf and his awful brother."

"Naomi, I didn't tell you yet that Yaminah said that Yusuf has absolute control of all AMM's finances, and there is no financial manual. She pleaded with me desperately not to remove the accreditation from AMM. She's afraid she'll lose her job, which she says she absolutely has to have to take care of her ill husband and her family."

Naomi shook her head. "The poor woman!"

"And then," Paul added, "there is the matter of the withdrawals from the loan repayment account."

"We can't possible re-accredit AMM, Paul."

"But the problem, Naomi, is that we don't have hard evidence of <u>anything</u>."

"I know. But what can we do?"

Chapter 7

FRIDAY

Naomi was not her usual confident and relaxed self at breakfast the next morning. Her hand shook, and she spilled some coffee. "Are you OK, Naomi?" Paul inquired.

She sat for a moment with her untouched coffee in front of her, her eyes fixed on her clenched hands.

"I had a horrible dream last night," she said slowly and softly.

"About what?"

"About that awful Efraim." She closed her eyes and then opened them wide as if to erase the memory.

"What happened?"

Naomi stared at her coffee. "I was at home in my bed on Meir Shamam in Jerusalem, and I heard this awful banging downstairs at the front door. Then I heard a crash as the front door was forced open. I knew who it was. I called out to my mother, but there was no answer. Then, I heard him coming up the wooden staircase. Thump, thump, thump—his heavy feet on the stairs." Her palm struck the table with each thump. "I heard him shouting something. Then I heard him yell, 'Where is the Jew girl?' I didn't know what to do. I was sure he meant to kill me. My bedroom door had no lock; neither did the bathroom. I couldn't hide in the closet—he would find me! Suddenly, I thought—under the bed! He'll think I've run away. I slid under the bed just as my bedroom door burst open. He shouted, 'Where are you, Jew girl?' There was a lot of crashing as he moved furniture and opened doors to look for me. I was so terrified. I just huddled under the bed. There was a ripping sound and the bed shook, again and again. He was stabbing my bed with a huge knife, and suddenly, I saw the blade where it penetrated the mattress. I screamed and woke up."

"That's pretty awful, Naomi." He reached across the table; she reciprocated, taking his hand.

Paul asked, "Have you ever suffered violence when you were a child?"

"No, not really. Oh, there was one Palestinian boy from a trading family. He was a couple of years older than me, and physically very big. He would pester me when I walked home from school. He'd make suggestive comments and follow me. Sometimes he would poke me, trying to get me to react. I told my mother about it. She reported it to the police, and it stopped." She looked up at Paul. "In Israel, if the police tell you to stop doing something, it's very unwise to continue—particularly if you're Palestinian."

"You needed a couple of Israeli policemen in your dream."

She nodded. "I guess the only real violence I've seen apart from television news was at Yad Vashem—the Holocaust museum in Jerusalem. Have you seen it?" Paul shook his head. "The photographs, the videos, the personal effects. My God, it's so awful, Paul! I was about eleven when my parents took me there. Before I went, I knew about the Holocaust, of course, but it was remote in time and place, and somehow, it didn't involve me. After that day, the Holocaust was no longer remote; it struck a powerful chord in me. For about six months after I went to Yad Vasheem, I used to have nightmares about it. Sometimes, to get away from the terror I felt, I would slip into my parent's bed."

She pushed her coffee away and poured herself some orange juice.

She looked up at Paul. "How can one people be so hateful against another?"

"You mean the Nazis against the Jews or the Muslims against the Jews?"

"Both. I mean the Nazis were sick, but there was plenty of complicity on the part of normal people. And the Muslims? If you read the Qur'an, there are frequent mentions of the Jewish people. We have the same ancestors, most of the same prophets, the same traditions and many of the same laws." She paused. "And the same God!"

"But you don't share the same Prophet."

"And as far as I know, that's just an accident of geography and, I guess, of history. Mecca is about 700 kilometres from Jerusalem. The tribes of the Arabian Peninsula were polytheistic—either traders or nomads. In 600 AD, Judaism was the well-established religion of the Israeli people, and we were already monotheistic. Why did we need this new religion that Muhammad was preaching?" She shook her head. "Anyway, why can't people focus on what they have in common, instead of what makes them different?"

Paul said, "I think it's human insecurity which makes us long to be better than the other person or group, and to better we have to be different."

"What makes us so insecure, Paul? I don't think I'm insecure."

"Except when Efraim is coming after you with a knife."

She expelled a gust of breath and gave a shrug of acceptance. Paul relented, "You are a secure person, Naomi. I think it's just that the world is a pretty chaotic, unpredictable, and sometimes hostile place. We have every reason to be insecure."

She placed two of the pancakes on her plate, spread them with peach preserve and began, distractedly, to eat. After several minutes she said, "Remind me, Paul, what are we going to do today?"

"Well, first of all, I think we need to have a come-to-Jesus meeting with Yusuf."

Naomi was amused. "That's an interesting expression. What does it mean?"

"I think the expression originated with the evangelical Protestants in the American south. Originally, it referred to the need for repentance, but its use was expanded to refer to any meeting involving the need to make an important change in behaviour. I think we need to tell Yusuf that his brother's behaviour is unacceptable."

"Good. What else?"

"I want to try to get Yusuf to repeat his offer to me—while you're not in the room. Then we have meetings with two members of the board of trustees, and Yusuf was going to arrange a meeting with the auditors. Also, I'd like to meet again with Mosa Mitri."

"Why do you want to meet with him?"

"I'd like to get a clearer picture of what the commercial loan alternatives look like. You remember he said that he was now working as a loan officer. We can meet at his office."

Naomi picked up her iPhone. "Shall I call him?"

"Yes. Please do."

There was a brief telephone conversation in Arabic.

She said, "At about 4:30 at the Shahzad Rameel Bank branch office on Rue Imam el Ghazali."

Yusuf was not his usual effusive self. He sipped distractedly at his mint tea, then he pushed it aside. "Paul, your meeting with PFC Maroc is at 9 this morning. Your meetings with the members of the board of trustees are at 10 and 11. Friday afternoon is prayer time in Morocco, but I can be available to meet with you at 4 this afternoon for our final session."

Naomi said, "Thank you, Yusuf. Now, I have to go and see Latifa for a few minutes. There are a couple of things which we didn't quite finish yesterday."

When Naomi had closed the door behind her, Paul said, "I have given further consideration to our conversation of yesterday, Yusuf, and I am ready to reach an agreement with you."

Yusuf seemed puzzled. "What conversation was that?"

"The conversation where you said that you could make my assignment here more rewarding than a pro bono assignment if I am able to arrange a continuation of AMM's accreditation."

Yusuf frowned. "I don't remember any such conversation. Certainly, I would never offer a financial inducement for you to recommend something that you don't agree with."

The clever bastard! Paul thought, *He suspects I have a tape recorder*! Paul said, "Oh, well, I must have misunderstood, and I apologise to you, Yusuf!"

Yusuf smiled insincerely.

For some minutes, they discussed the normal working hours in Morocco on Friday afternoons, until Naomi returned.

"There is something quite important we wanted to speak with you about, Yusuf," Paul said. Yusuf said nothing; he simply studied Paul, who continued, "Your brother came to see us yesterday, Yusuf."

"Oh?"

"He was rude and very unpleasant."

Yusuf folded his hands on the desk in front of him. "Perhaps he didn't understand who you were. We sometimes . . ."

Paul was irritated and interrupted, "He understood perfectly who we were because I told him who we were, and his English is nearly as good as yours. We are here on GYE's business, which has nothing, whatever, to do with religion."

"Oh, I see. My brother is a very religious man, and he can sometimes jump to conclusions."

Paul leaned forward. He spoke slowly, trying to keep the anger out of his voice. "We expect two things from you, Yusuf. First, we expect a sincere apology on behalf of your brother, and we expect that you will inform your brother that GYE does not accredit chapters that permit visitors to be treated the way we were treated yesterday."

The room was silent for nearly ten seconds. Then Yusuf, without looking at Paul said, quietly: "I apologise on behalf of my brother, and I will inform him not to take any action which threatens the accreditation of AMM."

Naomi said, "Thank you, Yusuf."

Then Paul added, in a more conciliatory tone, "While we have a few minutes, do you mind if I ask what kind of work your brother is engaged in?"

Yusuf shrugged slightly. "This is an area which can be best described as enforced confidentially. Even our late father—may Allah have mercy on his soul—who would normally be conversant with such matters, would be unable to provide a proper answer to your question. Perhaps it is best to say that, from time to time, Efraim works for the Moroccan government."

"On the military side?"

Yusuf extended his hands, palms up. "Who can say?"

Paul decided to continue his offensive. "We Googled your brother last night."

"You did what?"

"We put his name into the Google search engine."

"Ah, and you found nothing."

"On the contrary. A search in Arabic yielded some chilling results, particularly for a Jew and a Christian."

"Oh, but you must not be alarmed about that. Efraim often speaks in the mosque, and one radical group—the one whose website you found—tries to put words in his mouth. Efraim himself is quite a moderate Muslim."

"Does he have any business ties with this group?"

"Who can say?"

When they were in the car, and Naomi had given Mohammed the address of PFC Maroc, she commented angrily, "What a load of rubbish about his brother! Saying he's a 'moderate Muslim.'" Her fingers made quotation marks in the air.

"What were you expecting, Naomi?" Paul asked.

"Well, I thought Yusuf would be shocked when we told him about his brother's behaviour."

Paul said nothing; he just shook his head.

Naomi studied him for several moments. Suddenly, she asked, "You don't think that Yusuf instigated that outburst from his brother, do you?"

"Possibly."

"Oh, God, I feel sick again!" For a time, she sat looking out the window, then she asked, urgently, "Did you get the recording?"

"No. He said he didn't remember any such conversation. He must have guessed I was ready to record him."

Naomi shook her head. "He's very clever."

She turned to face Paul. "I had an interesting conversation with Latifa. I told her you wanted to hear Efraim at the mosque this afternoon. She said, 'But Mr. Paul doesn't understand any Arabic.' So, I told her I was thinking of going with you, and she said, 'But you can't go together. At the mosque, the men's section is separate from the women's section. Besides,' she said, 'you're obviously not a Muslim.' I told her I was thinking of wearing a headscarf. She said, 'that's not good enough. You'll have to wear at least a half niqab.'"

Paul asked, "What in the world is a half niqab?"

"It's a head covering that leaves only your eyes showing."

"Blue eyes, in your case."

She shrugged, and continued, "Latifa told me she would lend me one of her half niqabs, and then she said, 'But Naomi, you don't know the conventions of the mosque. You need someone to go with you.' And then she said, 'I'll go with you!' I asked her if she was afraid of Efraim. She said, 'No, not as long as I'm on the women's side.' So, she's coming with us this afternoon, and she said you should borrow a keffiyeh from Mohammed."

The reception area at PFC Maroc was Spartan. There was a low, and rather battered wooden table with no newspapers or magazines, four, slightly unsteady wooden chairs and a large, colour photograph of King Mohammed VI on an otherwise blank wall. They were not kept waiting long, however. A young man, who was dressed in a light grey suit and white shirt, and who identified himself as Amal, showed them to a meeting room and took their coffee orders. Amal was shortly joined by Faruq Qaderi, an overweight man in his fifties with an imposing moustache, who explained that he was a partner of PFC Maroc and the Amal was one of his associates.

Naomi explained who she and Paul were and thanked them for their time. The discussion then switched to English. Paul asked, "How did you find the financial affairs at AMM?"

Faruq said, "As our report says, we found everything to be in order during the day that Amal and I were there."

"You were there for just one day?"

"Yes, just one day."

"I suppose you have frequent discussions with the staff of AMM during course of the year," Paul observed.

"No, we just visit AMM once a year."

"But, they must have sent you quite a lot of financial information before the day you were there?"

"No. The Inter-Sahara Development Bank does not require that we be sent advance information, and Mr. Al-Rashid prefers that we do the examination on his premises."

Paul was puzzled. "But, Mr. Qaderi, how can you audit twelve bank accounts in one day?"

"We do not, Mr. Winthorpe. We are required by the ISDB to audit only their two accounts in Euros, and this is not a complex assignment."

"Well," Paul asked, "Is there a separate audit of the other ten bank accounts?"

Faruq made a palms-up gesture. "Not to our knowledge, Mr. Winthorpe."

Paul turned to Naomi. "Do you know of any other audit of AMM?"

She said, fingering a copy of the audit report. "No, this is it."

"Well, but did GYE know that this audit report covers only two of twelve bank accounts?"

Naomi shrugged. "I don't know a thing about audits, and our financial controller can't read Arabic."

Paul turned back to Faruq. "Can you explain to me, Mr. Qaderi, why the ISDB doesn't wish to have their dirham accounts audited, as well?"

"I think their interest is in the euro accounts, because that is the currency in which they disburse their funds."

"But AMM doesn't disburse any funds in Euros—except perhaps rarely. How can the ISDB be certain that the funds are not misappropriated?"

"Oh, well, we do check that disbursements from the euro accounts are made against legitimate invoices or against foreign exchange transactions where the proceeds are in dirhams deposited in an ISDB account."

"OK, but you don't audit the dirham accounts so you can't say that funds aren't misappropriated there."

Mr. Qaderi shrugged.

"Doesn't the ISDB care about possible misappropriation of its funds?" Paul asked.

Mr. Qaderi was thoughtful for a moment. "I think, Mr. Winthorpe, that there are several factors at work here. First, as you know, Morocco is a Muslim country where theft—misappropriation as you call it—is a very serious matter. In some Muslim countries, theft is punishable by the amputation of a hand. So, there tends to be a fundamental trust that accompanies financial transactions. Second, the ISDB is more interested in the results it achieves for its money. As I understand it, AMM has been very successful in making loans to a number of entrepreneurs. And, finally, there are financial considerations for the ISDB to consider. If my firm were to audit the ISDB dirham accounts—which are considerably more active—our fees would have to increase by a factor of nearly three."

When they were seated in Mohammed's old, black Mercedes, and en route to the office of AMM's chairman, Paul was still shaking his head. "I can't believe it! It's like a game of football at Stamford Bridge, where all the Chelsea fans are delighted that we're winning ten nil at half time. What the fans don't know is that the referees are ignoring any and all infractions committed by the home team!"

Naomi found the analogy somewhat amusing. "I suppose we ought to mention this—the audit situation I mean, not the football—to Mr. Al-Zahari."

"It'll be interesting to see if he knows anything about it," Paul said.

Mr. Al-Zahari as Director of Public Affairs of OilMaroc had a spacious office overlooking the Jardins de l'Agdal. He seated Paul and Naomi on either side of his place at the head of his glass-topped meeting table. After a polite inquiry about Matthew Andrews, GYE's CEO, "whom I have now known for several years now", he asked about the status of the assessment of AMM.

"We probably need two more days to complete our work," Paul replied.

Mr. Al-Zahari was surprised. "This is quite a long assessment, then."

"Yes," Paul said, "We've found that we can't rely entirely on the data we've been given before we started."

"Oh?"

"For example, we now understand that the audit which was commissioned by the ISDB is not a complete audit of AMM."

"In what way is it incomplete?"

Paul replied evenly, "It covers only two of AMM's twelve bank accounts."

"Twelve bank accounts?" For a moment Mr. Al-Zahari thought he might have misunderstood.

"Why do they need so many?"

"We're not entirely sure. But it would be fair to say that if AMM had the right financial software they could make do with three accounts, at most."

"And is this software very expensive?"

"Not really. There are shrink-wrapped packages that have Arabic and English capability for less than 500 dollars."

"I see," Mr. Al-Zahari temporarised. "You say there are twelve bank accounts?"

"Yes. May I ask, sir, what sort of financial reports the board of trustees receives from Mr. Al-Rashid?"

"Well, at our quarterly meetings, we customarily receive a report of disbursements and new income."

"And is there much discussion of these reports?" Paul asked.

"The discussions would take five or ten minutes. The report is only one page."

Paul glanced at Naomi, who said, "Mr. Al-Zahari, I'm getting the impression that the AMM board sees its role quite differently than GYE sees the role of a GYE chapter board."

"Oh, I don't think so, Miss Evensen. We are all promoters of AMM; we're all active as fund-raisers, and we control the destiny of AMM."

Naomi leaned forward. "In what way does the board control the destiny of AMM?"

Mr. Al-Zahari looked slightly exasperated. "Well, through our quarterly meetings, of course!"

Naomi looked at Paul, who thought for a moment, and then asked, "A hypothetical question, Mr. Al-Zahari. Suppose that

100,000 dirhams went missing from an AMM account, how would the board discover it?"

"Of course, we would expect Mr. Al-Rashid to tell us about it."

"And if, for some reason, Mr. Al-Rashid was not aware of it?"

"Well, it that case, we would expect the auditors to . . . I see what you mean."

Paul decided not to allow the chairman to evade the issue further. He said, "There are essentially no financial controls at AMM."

Mr. Al-Zahari appeared to be suddenly concerned. "What do you mean?"

"I mean that there are no written procedures that set forth how financial transactions are to be processed. The CEO has one hundred percent authority to make any disbursement, and . . ."

Mr. Al-Zahari interrupted, "You're not expecting that the board check every disbursement, are you?"

Naomi responded, "No. But we do expect that the board will put in place and enforce proper management controls."

Mr. Al-Zahari shook his head in confusion. "But we're talking about a small charity here."

Paul made a gesture of conciliation toward the chairman. "It doesn't really matter whether we're talking about a small charity or a large oil company. There are people involved. Mistakes happen. Things can go wrong. GYE believes that the board of a charity has the same responsibility as the board of an oil company: keeping the ship afloat and off the rocks."

Mr. Al-Zahari leaned back in his chair and looked out his window toward the distant mountains. Then he sat forward, his chin on his clasped hands, and looked at his two visitors. "I suppose," he finally said, "that there would be an appetite for more active control of AMM by some of the board members."

"And you?" Naomi asked, "how would you feel about it?"

The chairman tilted his head from side to side. "I certainly could do what you're asking, and I have the time. One thing I do not want to see is that AMM loses its GYE accreditation."

Efraim's Eye

"I'm afraid that is what would happen if the board did not take an active role in the governance of the organisation," Naomi said.

Mr. Al-Zahari closed his eyes and shook his head. "That would be a catastrophe! The government of Morocco would no longer fund us. Probably ISDB also would drop us, and we would struggle to raise funds from private companies."

There was something about Mr. Guy Labossiere that Paul liked immediately. Was it his slightly accented, but impeccable English? His tailor-made, natural linen suit? Or his clean-shaven good looks, reminding Paul of a particular cricket commentator whose name he couldn't remember?

"I'm not happy with the way things are at AMM," Mr. Laboissiere said. *That's it!* Paul thought, *He's direct. He says what he thinks.* "I'm not sure," Mr. Laboissiere continued, "that Yusuf Al-Rashid has the right skills to be a general manager. He's bright, he speaks very well—several languages—he's an excellent salesman, and he's very good at fund raising. But sometimes, he comes across to me as being manipulative or devious. He's not someone I'd like to work for."

"You know that there are essentially no management controls in AMM?" Paul asked.

Mr. Laboissiere gave a brief shiver. "Yes, I know. I've mentioned it to Al-Zahari several times. It's really up to the chairman to get a grip on things." He paused. "I don't think he wants to have a confrontation with Al-Rashid. He's afraid—as we all are—of losing Yusuf. That's the problem. Yusuf is AMM."

After a brief silence, Naomi offered, "But, Mr. Laboissiere, GYE can't continue to accredit a chapter that has poor management controls. If we did, and something went wrong, we would lose our credibility with the banks, governments and private contributors who rely on the integrity implied by our brand."

Mr. Laboissiere nodded. "I understand. Demoitte is working behind the scenes to improve the situation. I have persuaded Yusuf to work with us on a joint project called Transformation 2012, which is aimed at the creation of operating procedures for AMM."

"How is the project progressing?" Paul asked.

"In a word, slowly. Yusuf always has three or four urgent issues that need to take priority."

Paul asked, "What is your take on AMM 2015?"

"I think it's pretty optimistic."

"Yusuf told us that Demoitte had signed off on the numbers."

Guy Laboissiere shook his head. "No. You see, this is the problem with Yusuf. He hears what he wants to hear. I told him that Demoitte would review the numbers and get back to him in the next few weeks."

"But, in the meantime," Naomi put in, "I think when he meets with the bank or the government, he's using the numbers you say are optimistic."

Mr. Laboissiere conceded with a slight nod. "Yes, I know, Naomi, but this is a classic fund-raising technique. You outline this wonderful project, and you exaggerate the funding commitments already received in order to persuade new contributors to get on board. It works."

Naomi asked, "Do you know anything about Yusuf's brother, or I should say: half-brother?"

"No. I didn't know he has a brother. What about him?"

"He came to the AMM office yesterday. Apparently he lives with Yusuf. He was hostile: anti-Semitic, anti-Christian. On the Internet we found him as a radical imam."

"That's interesting. I know nothing of the brother. But apparently, Yusuf is quite religious. He went on the Hajj last year."

* * *

Naomi gave an address to Mohammed. "We're going to pick up Latifa. Have you asked Mohammed if he has a keffiyeh you can borrow?"

"Yes. He says he has one. I'm going to look a little incongruous in a dark suit and a keffiyeh."

"No, you won't!" Naomi said. "You'll look like a distinguished visiting businessman. Probably Lebanese."

The car pulled up in a side street, walled on either side, where a group of unwashed boys was playing football with what looked like an old tennis ball. "Back in a minute," Naomi said.

She got out of the car, spoke to one of the boys, and disappeared through a gate in the left-hand wall. Five minutes later, two veiled Arab women, dressed all in black, came out through the same gate. They opened the car door and got in. They were Latifa and Naomi.

Under Latifa's directions, the car made its way west toward the airport and then south down Avenue Al Masjid into a poor residential area, where they stopped. "It is better we walk from here," Latifa announced.

They got out of the car, and Mohammed removed a plastic bag from the boot. Taking out a black and white keffiyeh, he wrapped it expertly around Paul's head. Then, he wound a similar brown and white keffiyeh on his own head. He locked the car and motioned Paul to follow him.

Paul said, "You can wait for us here, Mohammed."

"No, sir, I go with you. Is necessary."

They set out along the crumbling pavement. Two men followed at a respectful distance by two women. From a loudspeaker, ahead and slightly to their left, they could hear the drawn-out baritone voice of the muezzin's call to prayer.

The Bakkali Mosque was set at the back of a small square, where traders who were now closed for business, had their various stalls. The mosque itself was a simple, grey concrete structure topped with a whitewashed dome and the golden crescent moon pointing skyward. There was no minaret.

The women disappeared through a portal on one side, while Mohammed approached a large concrete basin near the entrance. There was an open tap pouring water into the basin. Mohammed scooped up water to splash his face and rubbed his hands. He stood aside, waiting for Paul to copy him. Having nothing to dry his face and hands, Paul watched what other men did: they simply wiped the water from their faces and shook the excess water from their hands. Inside the main portal, there were shelves that were already filling up with shoes. With their shoes removed, Paul and

Mohammed moved into the prayer hall and seated themselves on the carpeting about two-thirds of the way back from the qiblah wall. At the centre of the qiblah wall was the minrab niche, which pointed the way to Mecca. Looking around, Paul saw that the whitewashed walls were completely unadorned, except for some verses from the Qur'an that were painted on the qiblah wall in black Arabic script. To his right, Paul saw that there was a women's section of the prayer hall that was made separate by a sturdy rope cordon. He thought he could see the two dark figures of Naomi and Latifa toward the back.

The prayer hall was nearly full. Suddenly, Paul saw Yusuf seating himself near the front of the hall, having exchanged greetings with several men around him. *I can't let him see me*, Paul thought, drawing one corner of the keffiyeh so that it covered his nose and mouth.

A large figure, dressed in a white robe and a green-and-white keffiyeh stood ponderously near the minrab and surveyed the faithful. It was Efraim. The muezzin made one last call to prayer, and Efraim strode toward the raised pulpit. He raised his arms, said something in Arabic, which all the faithful repeated and leaned forward so that their foreheads nearly touched the carpet.

Efraim began to speak. His booming voice needed no amplification. His arms were constantly in motion: reaching up, reaching out, and reaching down. He spoke with great emotion. It wasn't all anger. Sometimes he seemed to be leading his audience toward a conclusion with a series of logical points. Reaching into his pocket, Paul turned on the little recorder. He glanced sideways at Mohammed, whose face seemed to be frozen in a look of disapproval. The man on Paul's other side seemed to be paying no attention at all; he seemed to be occupied with his own thoughts.

The faithful sat in orderly rows, listening or in the one case, pretending to listen. They uttered no sound either of approval or of censure. Efraim's harangue—for that is what it was—went on for about forty minutes. Efraim stepped down from the minbar briefly, and sat on a chair, facing the faithful. After a few moments, he resumed his place at the minbar and began to deliver what seemed like a summary of what he said earlier. Again, he stepped down; he raised his arms high and called out a phrase, which the faithful repeated, bowing down again.

The muezzin sang another call to prayer, and for the next fifteen minutes, the faithful recited scriptures led by Efraim, which culminated in each case with the deep bow of reverence.

Mohammed and Paul (still shielding part of his face) slowly edged their way out of the crowded prayer hall. Glancing around him, it was hard for Paul to decide what the reaction was to Efraim's sermon. Most people just moved along silently, saying nothing to those around them. Looking back toward the qiblah wall, Paul saw Efraim and Yusuf standing together with a small group of men. They seemed to be engaged in an animated discussion. Taking hold of Mohammed's arm, Paul asked, "Mohammed, can you take a picture for me?" He handed his mobile phone to Mohammed, indicating the small group.

"No, sir, not in mosque. Is forbidden. When they come outside, I will do it."

In the small square outside, little groups of the faithful were loitering. To one side, Paul saw Naomi and Latifa waiting. He went over to them. "Mohammed will be with us shortly. I asked him to take a picture."

"Of what?" Naomi asked.

"Of Efraim and Yusuf."

Naomi was alarmed. "Won't Yusuf recognise Mohammed?"

Latifa said quickly, "I book Mohammed for you. Yusuf not know Mohammed at all."

Mohammed, obviously quite pleased with himself, joined them. He said, "I tell them I like take picture of them in honour of great sermon preach by Efraim to glory of Allah. They very happy. I take several pictures."

When they were seated in the car, Naomi pulled off the niqab and allowed her blonde hair to spill out.

"What did he say?" Paul asked.

"More of his hateful venom. This time it was focused on Christianity—how it has tried to corrupt the true religion with its worship of a second god. How it has corrupted the world with its pornography, its insane media, and its denial of the laws of Allah. He said that the true believers should resist Christianity with every possible resource. He didn't actually use the word destroy, but he came close to it. It seemed like a recruiting pitch for terrorists. He didn't promise anyone twenty-four virgins in paradise, but maybe he will next time."

"Authorities should stop that," Latifa said. "Is very bad."

Mohammed was nodding agreement in the front seat. "Is very bad," he echoed.

* * *

"So," Yusuf asked, "what conclusions have you reached?"

"We haven't reached any definite conclusions yet," Paul said. "We're planning to spend two more working days in Morocco."

Yusuf leaned forward in his office chair, frowning. "And, what are you proposing to do during this time?"

"We'd like to visit the AMM offices in Fez and Casablanca," Naomi said, "We had those visits listed on the original agenda."

Yusuf's frown deepened into a scowl. "Yes, but they are just local offices. They do not set any policy; they do exactly what we do here. Besides, the manager in each of those offices is new."

"The visits to Fez and Casablanca will confirm that your two local offices do <u>exactly</u> (Paul put an ominous emphasis on the last word) as you do here. Besides, it will give us an opportunity to meet with members of the local boards."

Yusuf looked back and forth between Paul and Naomi. "One can't be sure that the managers will be available on Monday and Tuesday."

Paul said, "I'm sure that if you ask them to be available, Yusuf. They will be pleased to meet with us. Why don't you give them a call now?"

Reluctantly, Yusuf made the calls. "Ms. Nahyan in Fez will be expecting you on Monday and Mr. Sidqi in Casablanca will see you on Tuesday." Yusuf's face retained its sour expression.

He asked, "Will I see you then on Tuesday afternoon or Wednesday morning before you depart?"

"It depends," Paul said. "There is one further meeting that we need to have in Marrakech with Mr. Tasneen of the Moroccan Ministry for Employment. You'll recall that I had asked to meet with them, and in your presentation, you mention Mr. Tasneen as your key contact there."

"He will have gone home by this time on Friday afternoon."

"We can leave the arrangement in your hands, Yusuf. We can meet with Mr. Tasneen after three on Tuesday afternoon or first thing on Wednesday morning."

Mosa Mitri's office at Shahzad Rameel Bank was very small: only large enough for his battered metal desk, his plastic chair, two similar chairs, and a filing cabinet. The scuffed walls were in need of repainting, and the only decoration, affixed to the wall behind him, was a large calendar with a view of the Atlas Mountains. Mosa's desk, however, was orderly, with a pile of files in one corner, next to the phone. "How is your assessment progressing?" he asked. He seemed genuinely glad to see them.

"No definite conclusions yet, Mosa," Naomi responded, "We strongly suspect that you are right in what you told us, but we haven't yet found independent proof."

"It may be very difficult. That Yusuf is a clever one, and I don't have the smoking gun."

Paul nodded. "We know that, Mosa. What we wanted to talk to you about this afternoon is commercial bank loans. We'd like to understand the differences between what AMM offers entrepreneurs and what Shahzad Rameel Bank might offer them."

"OK." Mosa Mitri considered the ceiling of his little office. "Well, in the first place, the Shahzad Rameel Bank does not engage in mudarabah with individuals. Mudarabah, which is known in Islamic banking as a joint venture, would be used only in the context of financing large corporate projects. I am involved in retail banking, serving individuals who want to buy a house, or a car, or furniture, or appliances. The method we use to finance consumer purchases is referred to as murabaha, or cost plus, in Islamic banking. What happens is that the customer selects the house or the car he wants. He negotiates the price and makes a down payment of say 20 percent. Then we, as the bank, pay the balance, and we take the title to the car or house, as surety. We arrange for the customer to pay us a certain amount per month. When the loan is paid off, we transfer ownership of the property to the customer. There is no interest involved, because it is cost plus."

"Right. But how is the amount of the plus in the cost plus determined?" Paul asked.

"It is based on the size of the loan, its duration and the risk the bank takes. Bear in mind that the Qur'an prohibits profiting from only lending money. In taking title to the property, the bank assumes risk of loss. Generally, the plus factor is quoted to the customer as a lump sum or as a percentage mark up. We will negotiate the plus factor with the customer within limits." Mosa paused to smile. "I know what you're going to ask, so I might as well tell you now. A customer buying a house under a murabaha contract would pay more than if he could get a percentage rate mortgage as you have in the UK. Not a great deal more, and he's happy because he has an opportunity to own his home in a way that is compliant with Islamic law."

"Mosa, I noticed that AMM's mudarabah contracts are all subject to sharia law," Paul commented, "Whom does this favour: AMM or the entrepreneur?"

"Morocco is one of the countries where civil and sharia laws coexist to an extent. I would say that Sharia law would probably favour AMM. There is no jury and only one judge in a sharia court. Rules of evidence are quite restrictive, and judges make decisions based on jurists' manuals and collections of legal opinions. There is no codified law or system of precedents."

Naomi asked, "Who can be a sharia judge?"

"Usually, they are appointed, but they have to be trained and pass an examination."

"Could Efraim Al-Rashid be a sharia judge?" she asked.

"I don't know. I suppose it's possible."

Naomi closed her eyes and shook her head.

Feeling the need to summarise, Paul said, "Mosa, I'm getting the impression that your bank's lending practices are considerably more favourable to customers than AMM's."

Mosa smiled. "I take it that you have been reading some of the contracts." Paul nodded. "What you say is true, but the comparison isn't really valid. As Yusuf probably told you, a bank like Shahzad Rameel would not lend to a young person without security."

"So it's a case of, 'if you want to make your dream come true, AMM can help you, but we want a big piece of your rewards,'" Paul suggested.

Mosa shrugged, then he asked, "Are you two nearly finished with your assessment?"

"No." Naomi responded, "We're going to Fez and Casablanca on Monday and Tuesday, and we've asked Yusuf to set up a meeting with Mr. Tasneen at the Moroccan Ministry for Employment."

Mosa looked puzzled. "But he doesn't work there any more."

"When did he leave?" Naomi asked.

"About a month ago. He used to be one of my contacts. He called me to tell me he had left the Employment Ministry that he was looking for a new opportunity, and whether I knew of anything."

In the car on the way to Riad el Norj, Naomi said, "It's very strange that Yusuf didn't seem to know that Tasneen has left the Ministry for Employment."

"I agree. I guess we'll find out more next week."

Naomi turned her attention to her iPhone. "Oh, there's a message here from Mansur ben-Tanoos at the ISDB. He's responding to my e-mail about disbursements from the loan repayment bank account. He says, 'Normally, disbursements can be made, after the project has been completed, for the purpose of making new loans.'"

She looked over at Paul. "But the ISDB project has only just completed. Didn't you say that there were disbursements over a year ago?" Paul nodded. "And didn't you say that at least one of the disbursements wasn't a loan?"

"Yes."

"Oh, and here he says he'll look into the questions you have raised about Mr. Chieraux's report."

"There you go," Paul said, "One wrong is about to be made right!"

"Bollocks! I'll bet he doesn't do a thing about it."

Paul could not suppress a laugh. "Naomi, am I turning you into a cynic?"

She turned to look out the opposite window, hiding her smile. "Yes, you are!"

* * *

"Yvonne, I'd like to use the hammam before dinner," Naomi announced to the proprietor's wife when they arrived.

"Yes, of course, Miss Evensen. I'll turn the heat on and make sure everything is in order." She hurried off.

Naomi turned to Paul. "You coming?"

Paul was uncertain. "It's a Turkish bath, right?"

"Yes. It'll do you good."

"OK."

Paul opened the door of the hammam and stepped inside. The heat and the cloudy steam were almost overwhelming. At first, he found it difficult to breathe. He sat down on a wooden bench, and tried to orient himself. He could make out Naomi on the other side of the little room. She was all pink. *My God*, he thought, *She hasn't got any clothes on. Is this right?* He looked down at his dark blue plaid swimming trunks.

Her voice came out of the cloud ahead. "Paul, how are you going to scrub yourself properly when you're wearing a swimsuit?"

"I didn't know the convention," he said.

"Well, I think that in a small hammam like this, the convention should be that cleanliness takes precedence over modesty."

"OK." He removed his swimming trunks and sat down again.

They sat in silence for a time. The cloud and the intensity of the heat began to diminish.

"Ready for a little more heat?" she asked.

"I think so."

She stood, and, taking a dipper from a bucket on the floor beside her, moved to the centre of the space. She was indeed all pink. There was the dank, blonde hair that fell over her shoulders, and nothing else. *I guess she shaves*, he thought.

She poured the water onto a metal basket filled with stones that stood on the floor between them. There was a loud, prolonged hissing, and a burst of steam rose from the basket, quickly obscuring her.

Paul began to sense his body relaxing in the heat. He was sweating profusely, and it felt cathartic. About every ten minutes, Naomi splashed water on the hot stones, refilling the small space with steam.

"OK, it's time to scrub," she announced. Reaching into a wicker basket on the bench beside her, she took out a plastic bottle and what looked like a small bundle of hemp. "Here, you can do my back." She handed him the bottle and the hemp. "What you should do is put a little of this lotion—I think it's a combination of natural soaps and skin conditioners—on this scrubber, and rub briskly." She turned her back to him.

Confronted with her back, he paused momentarily to consider her. There was no mistaking her femininity: the swell of her hips, the roundness of her bottom, and the lovely smoothness of her skin. He poured lotion on the hemp and was about to begin when he saw that her hair was cascading down her back. Gently, he separated it, left and right, and put it over her shoulders. "Sorry. I forgot," she said.

He began to scrub her back, with long sweeping strokes, holding her shoulder with his free hand so as not to push her away. When he reached her bottom, he changed to shorter, curving strokes. He thought he heard her giggle. He knelt and returned to long strokes for the back of her legs. *God, she has beautiful legs*, he thought, *They're shapely and smooth—no knots of muscle.*

"OK," she announced, "I'll do the rest. Turn around, and I'll do your back."

He complied. She began with his upper back, rubbing, applying more lotion, as he had done and working her way down to his calves.

Now and then, between scrubbings with the hemp, she would smooth his skin with her hand. Her touch was positively magical.

"Turn around," she ordered, "I can do your chest." She faced him, a faint smile on her lips. The lovely mounds of her breasts were crowned with small rosy nipples. She began at his collarbone, and began to work down.

"Oh!" she exclaimed. She covered her mouth, and sat down.

"Sorry," he offered, resuming his seat opposite her.

She chuckled, "No, it's my fault."

"Yes, it is," he agreed.

She laughed aloud. "Look, here's some more lotion and another scrubber, which you can use to finish where I left off." She handed them to him. Remaining seated, he scrubbed his chest, stomach and legs.

"I'm done," she announced, her scrubbing completed, "There's a shower just outside."

"You go ahead. Shall I meet you for a drink in the lounge in about an hour?"

"Yes."

When she came into the lounge, Naomi was wearing a pale blue, sleeveless, linen shirt, and a long, navy skirt. The skirt covered her legs, which she had folded beside her. Her hair, still slightly damp, was in two long braids that fell across her shoulders.

Yvonne came in to take their drink orders. Naomi frowned, trying to recall. "What kind of sherry did you have the other night, Paul?"

"Amontillado."

"Yes. I'd like some of that, Yvonne, if you have it, with ice, please."

Paul nodded. "Two, please."

Yvonne inclined her head slightly. She asked, "How was zee hammam?"

Naomi said, "It was excellent, Yvonne, just what one needs after a long day."

Paul watched Yvonne depart. He thought, *She probably is thinking that, but she's French so she doesn't really care.*

Paul said, "You know, at my gym there's a sauna, and I've never used it."

"You go to the gym very often?" Naomi asked.

"I go three or four times a week for an hour or so." Naomi raised her eyebrows. "If I didn't," Paul continued, gesturing to his waist, "I would put on two or three stone all right here."

"Good for you." She thought for a moment. "I'd like to belong to a gym, but I'm never home enough to use it, and I'm pretty sure I wouldn't use a sauna. I don't like the dry heat, but there's something about a Turkish bath or a hammam with all that steam that makes me feel good."

Paul nodded. "I think I must have sweated half a litre, but I feel really good."

"You look very well."

"So do you."

Their drinks arrived. Naomi took a sip and gave a nod of satisfaction. "That's really good. I think I've had sherry only once or twice before. It was that dry kind that has an astringent taste, and I didn't like it. Thank you for introducing me to this (she said the word slowly) amontillado."

"I'm glad you like it."

"You know," she said, reflecting, "I think that Latifa is a brave girl."

Paul asked, "Do you think she knows what's going on?"

"Yes, I do, and she doesn't approve of it at all, but she needs her job. I think she'd like to help us if she can see a way not to get fired."

"I wish we could help her find that way."

They sat for a moment in companionable silence. She shook her head. "I can't get that man out of my head."

"Who's that?"

"Efraim." She paused for a moment. "Have you seen films of Hitler giving one of his rants?"

"Yes. All the extravagant gestures and wild facial expressions?"

"Exactly. Do you suppose that Efraim intentionally copied Hitler's style?"

"Well, he certainly has a lot of Hitler's intolerance."

They sat talking about Efraim, about Yusuf, and whether they would ever find proof of wrongdoing at AMM for perhaps half an hour. Yvonne brought them another glass of sherry and explained the choices for dinner. They both ordered brochettes: lamb for Paul and chicken for Naomi to be preceded by the usual array of mezze.

Paul ordered a bottle of Meknes cabernet. Over dinner she told him some of the remembered events from her childhood in Jerusalem. He sat opposite her, his chin on his hands, listening in rapt attention and admiration.

They decided to split a bastilla, a sweet pastry with cream and nuts. Naomi ordered a Turkish coffee, which Paul declined. "Do you have calvados?" he asked Yvonne.

"Yes, of course."

When his snifter of calvados arrived, he sipped it and smiled at Naomi.

"OK. Something else I've got to try." She took a sip, smiled back and nodded at Yvonne.

With the calvados in hand, her conversation drifted back to Efraim: "How did he become what his is? Did his mother beat him? Was he raised by a hateful uncle?" She did not believe that a child could naturally become the monster she perceived Efraim to be.

For a time they sat in the lounge, looking at the Moroccan picture books. Then Naomi got up, said she was tired, gave Paul a peck on the cheek, and went upstairs.

Later that night, Paul was suddenly awake. There was someone in the room. A slight, pale figure had slipped almost soundlessly past the door. The figure made no threatening movements. He tried to see through the gloom. Like a butterfly shedding its chrysalis, the figure dropped its robe. It was Naomi. She lifted the bed covers and climbed in beside him. She was trembling.

"What's the matter, Naomi?"

"He tried to attack me."

"You've been dreaming."

"It was horrible."

Still trembling, she clung to him. Gently, he stroked her hair, which cascaded across her face and shoulders. There was peaceful, utter silence in the room. She laid on her side, against him, her head on his shoulder. He kissed her forehead, and stroked her back. Gradually, he felt the tension seep out of her. There was the faint scent of her perfume. He felt one of her breasts against his chest.

"Thank you, Paul."

Desire swept over him. "I want you Naomi."

She said nothing. She stroked his chest, and her hand strayed down across his belly. "Oh!" For some time she continued to hold him. "Do you have a condom, Paul?"

"No, but I've had a vasectomy, and . . . and I have no . . ."

"No STDs," she finished the sentence for him.

She continued to caress him. Then deliberately and languorously, she slid on top of him. Reaching down for him, she guided him. She gave a little groan of pleasure and began to move. He was almost passive, knowing that his time was later. He caressed her face, her breasts, her back, and her arms. "God, you feel lovely!"

She gave soft mewling sounds as her passion flamed higher, and the pace of her movements increased.

Then, suddenly she convulsed, buried her face at his throat and gave a long sighing groan. He could hold out no longer, wrapped his arms around her, and succumbed to the surge of ecstasy.

They floated down, lay on their sides, her back against his chest, pressed tight against him and his arms still around her. She felt blissfully safe. They fell asleep.

Chapter 8

ESSAOUIRA

Paul woke up. Daylight was seeping into the room. Naomi had turned over to face him. She was caressing him and making barely audible murmurings. In the distance, he could hear the drawn out call of the muezzin to prayer. *It must be about six o'clock*, he thought. He put his arm around Naomi's shoulders and drew her closer. In addition to the faint fragrance of her perfume, there was a rich, musky scent. *This girl will drive me crazy.* He kissed the top of her head, and with his free hand, he stroked her warm bottom.

Mmmm.

"You're awake," she said lazily.

"Yes. Did you sleep all right?"

"I slept like a child. No dreams. Just warmth and comfort." He pushed off the bedclothes and looked down at her.

"What are you trying to do?" she protested, "make me cold again?"

"I want to look at you."

"There's nothing much to see."

"Oh, yes there is."

He felt her warm breath on his chest. "You're ready, Paul."

"Yes, I know," he said.

Playfully, she said, "And I'm ready, Paul."

He sat up, and she pulled him down onto her.

"Oh, yes. It's lovely." She looked up at him, and he could sense her eager anticipation. He moved with deliberate slowness, savouring her. But she bucked against him, urging a faster pace.

Her fingers gripped his bottom. She was moaning in little gusts against his shoulder.

"Oh, God, Paul," she panted, "I'm going to come!" She breathed a long, warbling cry, which only finished at the end of a second breath. She pressed her cheek against his, kissing indiscriminately.

Her panting began to subside. "You came didn't you?" she asked.

"Yes. It was wonderful."

She giggled. "I thought so, but I was preoccupied."

"Were you?" he asked, teasingly, "Well, that's good!"

He pulled up the comforter and with his hand, gently brushed her hair onto the coverlet and out of her face. It lay on the white sheet like a cascade of gold.

"Mmmm," she murmured.

They fell back to sleep.

"I'm hungry!" she announced, sitting up in the bed, "What time is it?"

Paul consulted his watch. "8:43."

"Goodness! We have to get going!" she sprang out of bed.

"What's the hurry? It's Saturday."

"They stop serving breakfast at ten on Saturday."

Paul shrugged. "What are your plans for after breakfast?"

"I thought we might go to Essaouira."

"Where's that?"

She sat on the edge of the bed, considering him. "It's on the Atlantic coast, about an hour and a half from here. I've never been there, but it's supposed to be really nice." Her face assumed a slightly insolent look. "I think we can have some fun there."

"Oh, I'm sure we can!" She bent down and picked up her robe.

He said, "You can shower here, if you want to."

She shrugged. "I've got my shampoo and all that stuff over there. I'll meet you in the dining room by 9:45."

Paul was having his second cup of coffee and had nearly finished reading the section on Essaouira in his guidebook, when she came in. She was dressed in white cotton trousers, and a red-and-blue striped polo shirt, with an Italian logo. Her hair was tied at the nape of her neck with a white ribbon. She poured herself a cup of coffee and surveyed what was on offer on the table.

There was something slightly different in her manner today, Paul noticed. There was a certain sensuality, a certain womanliness that he hadn't seen before. Their eyes locked wordlessly for several moments. There was a slight smile on each of their faces. Their unspoken messages were the same: "I admire you. You're wonderful."

"How are the pancakes?" she asked.

"Well, they were all right a while ago, but I think they've gotten cold."

"Okay. I'll ask for some fresh ones . . . What does the guide book say?"

"It sounds very interesting. It says it's a fishing town with fortified walls designed by the same architect who designed Saint Malo in Brittany. But inside the walls it's distinctly Moroccan with many narrow alleys, and intriguing shops. Lots of artists there and people just go to hang out. It's quite windy, being on the coast. There's a beach and plenty of good seafood restaurants."

She nodded, approvingly. "Hotels?"

He handed her the book. There's this one here, Riad del Mar, which sounds very nice, and it's not too expensive."

"Let me go get my laptop and look it up."

"Why don't you have your breakfast first, Naomi?"

She sipped her coffee while her laptop was connecting. "Here we go. Riad del Mar. Oh, it's got rooms with a sea view and a rooftop restaurant for breakfast. Rooms look nice. Five hundred dirhams double, bed and breakfast." She smiled a cunning little smile and giggled. "If we each get a receipt for two fifty, GYE will think we made a good choice. Let's see what Trip Advisor says. Okay. There are eighteen four-star reviews, two five stars, a couple of threes and one one. This woman sounds like a chronic complainer, 'The towels were too small, my eggs were cold, the porter was slow collecting my luggage.' Shall we go for it?"

"Yes."

"I'm going to call them." She picked up her iPhone. "I want a sea view room."

* * *

The porter turned the key to room 253 and pushed the door aside. The room was very dark, and it had a faintly musty odour. Moving across the room, the porter drew aside the curtains, swung open the windows, and unlatched the window shutters. Light and a fresh breeze poured into the room. Naomi went immediately to the window stood transfixed. "Look at that! It's spectacular!"

Paul stood beside her. There below them, the restless, tossing sea, was churning over half-submerged rocks, and surging against the city walls. In places, the sea was an ominous dark blue; near the white crests of the waves, it was a shimmering emerald green. They heard the gentle roar and booming of the surf, mixed with the fervent cries of swooping sea birds. Now, there was the fresh smell of seaweed and salt. The Atlantic Ocean stretched out to the distant horizon, where it met a pale blue sky. For several minutes they stood, mutely gazing at the scene before and below them.

"It's going to be wonderful hearing the sea at night," she said. Then turning to him, she said "Let's go to the beach!"

She began to attack the one suitcase they had brought with them, laying on the bed, in separate piles, her things and his clothes.

"Do you suppose there's a beach cabana where we can change clothes?" she asked.

"I should think so. It's a public beach. Lots of people use it. They've got to have somewhere to change. We'd probably be arrested if we walked through town in our bathing suits."

"What does the guide book say?"

"It doesn't."

They left the hotel. He carried two towels and their swimsuits in a hotel laundry bag. She scanned the map that they picked up from the front desk. "We have to go here," she said, pointing at the map. "But, this town is a maze. We're going to get lost."

"I think I know the way. We go down this little street to the end and turn left, on the main street, then turn right and left."

She looked at him doubtfully, but she took his arm.

The streets were narrow and paved with cobbles or slabs of stone. The entire city was closed to vehicular traffic; only pushcarts and bicycles accompanied the many pedestrians. The stucco buildings—shops and residences—were painted in various earth tones, and began at the edge of the streets. On the main street, there was an abundance of activity: little shops, with their goods on display, tiny cafes with two small tables and chairs outside where customers chatted lazily in the bright sunshine. The city was scrubbed clean and had a festive, relaxed and welcoming atmosphere.

Paul said, "I think the square by the main city gate is down this street. I remember that little woodworking shop when the porter took us to the hotel."

They plunged into a narrow, dark alley—almost a tunnel—with buildings closing off the sky, above. The alley swerved left and right before in opened out onto a busy square, with large cafes, hotels, and individuals hawking their wares to passers by.

"Very good, Paul!" She consulted the map. "The beach is down that way."

Crossing the square, they came to the sea front. Outside the protection of the city walls, the wind tugged at them as it blew in from the limitless ocean. Many gulls wheeled and cried in the air above, but many more were perched on the ground, avoiding the wind as they slowly moved about looking for food. Passing through a crowded car park, they came to the sea wall and the north end of the beach. Before descending, they surveyed the panorama in front of them. The beach was very wide, ochre sand, curving south and west in a broad arc. Lines of gentle white surf were rolling in across the shallow slope of the shore.

People and animals dotted the vast expanse of the beach. There were camels and horses intended for riding. The people were in the water, stretched out on the sand, playing football, or just walking along the damp shoreline.

"I don't see a cabana, Paul. Where are we going to change?"

Paul pointed toward an awninged building with tables and chairs at the eastern edge of the beach. "Let's go to that café and order a mint tea. We can change in the loos there."

Naomi reappeared in a royal blue, one-piece suit, cut high at the legs, with a spiraling white stripe. She had also put on a plain white cotton blouse. Paul smiled and shook his head as she sat down.

"What?" she asked.

"That's very becoming."

She was pleased. "I'm glad you like it. . . . Shall we go for a swim?"

The water was surprisingly cold for a late June day. It was also murky with large strands of brown and green seaweed drifting in it. As they walked further out to where the water was clear, there was also a strong northerly current running along the coast. No one was swimming in the deeper water. Naomi paused, chest deep, looking doubtful.

Paul said, "I think this beach is mainly for sunbathing, socialising and getting your feet wet, not for swimming."

"I'm happy to sunbathe, if you are."

They moved out of the water and onto an unoccupied patch of dry sand. No sooner had they spread their towels than a big man in ragged trousers and several days' growth of beard approached them, towing a camel.

"You want camel ride?" he asked.

"No thank you," Paul said.

"Is very good camel—very good price."

"No thanks."

"For you, I make special price. Only fifty dirhams for half-hour beach ride."

Paul shook his head and went back to arranging his towel, but the man persisted. Naomi was sitting on her towel. She and the camel driver exchanged brief words. The man looked hurt and walked away.

Curiosity overcame Paul. "What did you say to him?"

She stretched out on her towel. "I asked him if he spoke Arabic. He said, 'Yes.' Then I asked him what part of 'No, thank you, he didn't understand.'"

Paul lay on his stomach, considering the exchange with the camel driver. *She wasn't the least bit concerned telling him to buzz off, and yet she's terrified of Efraim. Why would that be? That camel driver was an ugly looking cuss; I wouldn't want to be up against him in a dark alley. Course the same could be said for Efraim. What accounts for the difference? I wonder if it's a social class thing. The camel driver is a peasant, while Efraim . . . No, I think it's more about power and status. She knows she can tell the camel driver to buzz off, and he'll go, whereas, Efraim tells her to buzz off and she goes.*

The sun was quite warm. Paul turned over onto his back. Finally, he asked, "Naomi, have you got any sunscreen?"

"Yes, there's a little tube in my handbag. You'll have to put it on yourself."

At first, Paul was slightly hurt, but then he realised what she was saying. He found the sunscreen and began to apply it, smiling to himself.

She looked up at him. "What are you grinning about?"

"I was just speculating on the various levels of punishment here."

"What punishments?"

"Well for an unmarried couple putting sunscreen on each other's backs versus an unmarried couple making love in private."

She chuckled. Then she said, "Actually, it can be pretty serious, you know."

"What can?"

She sat up. "In the tribal areas of Pakistan, an unmarried woman can be killed for making love to the wrong man, and it's not the authorities, but it's her family who'll kill her."

"But that has noting to do with the Qur'an."

"No. It's a cultural thing; it's about family honour."

"I remember you're interested in sociology. Can you explain to me how people develop crazy norms like that?"

She had turned to face him and was gesturing energetically. "I'm no expert, Paul. I just find sociology very interesting. . . . To answer your question, you have to go back into ancient tribal history several thousand years ago. At that time, men were the key members of the tribe, and their status was determined by several measures: the number of sheep and goats they owned, the number of wives and concubines they had, and their power—power in the tribe, power in times of conflict, and power over their possessions. Naturally, a man with five beautiful wives was more important than a man with five ugly ones. And a man whose daughters were chaste and married men he selected was more powerful than a man whose daughters fooled around."

"So are you saying that a man's honour can be more important than the life of his daughter?"

Wordlessly, she nodded.

"God, that's depressing," he said and lay back down. He felt her hand seek out his, and for perhaps half an hour, they lay in the sun, a yard apart, holding hands.

"I'm getting hungry!" Naomi announced. She sat up and looked around. "What time is it?"

"It's 2:10."

"No wonder I'm hungry! Aren't you?" Paul nodded. "How about that place over there—next to where we changed?"

Paul consulted the guidebook. "It says that 'for great seafood at a reasonable price, there's nothing better than the fish grills between the main city entrance and the car park.'"

Naomi stood up. "Yeah, OK." She pulled on her white trousers. "I'm ready."

Paul buckled on his sandals and put on his green polo shirt. He was still wearing his green plaid swimming trunks, and he looked down at himself critically. "What do you think? Should I go change again?"

"No. They could pass for shorts, and some of the tourists are wearing shorts. You look fine."

As they approached the fish grills, there were wispy clouds of smoke carried away on the wind, and then they could smell the cooking fish. The fish grills were arranged in a semi-circle around a grassy area adjacent to the car park. Each stall was numbered, and there must have been ten of them, each with its own tables and chairs on the pavement between the grassy area and the building where the cooking staff was busy at work. Just outside each kitchen was a display of the seafood that particular stall offered, and, waiting like a predator, was the stall tout, who took customer orders and arranged seating. Naomi and Paul stood in the grassy area, appraising the situation, just out of reach of the individual touts, but still bombarded by their invitations.

"Number eight looks pretty popular, and they seem to have a large display of fish," Naomi opined.

"OK, let's go for it."

At the display, the tout called out the names of the various fish and shellfish, each with a card displaying the dirhams per kilogram of that particular choice.

"*I'll have this one,*" Naomi said, pointing to a display of sea bass. "*No, that one's too big; the one next to it.*"

Reluctantly, the tout put the smaller fish into a cardboard cone, weighed it and turned to Paul.

"You have lobster, sir? Very good lobster. Is fresh."

"No, thanks. I think I'll have some of these shrimp and some of these whitebait." Again, the size of the portion had to be reduced from what was initially selected by the tout.

"*Can I have a salad?*" Naomi asked.

"*Yes, ma'am. Very good salad . . . I bring.*"

Paul said, "I'll like a salad, and do you have French fries?"

"Yes, sir. I bring fries."

"And a beer?"

"No beer, sir. Is water, Coke, Sprite, and lemonade."

Their drink selections made, they were seated at a table where they could watch the passersby. Most of the people coming and going along the sea front were middle-aged tourist couples, overweight and armed with cameras slung from their shoulders. There seemed to be a lot of pedestrian traffic around the fresh fruit and ice cream vendors over by the sea wall.

Efraim's Eye

"Shoo!" Naomi spat out. "Shoo! Go away! Seer fhalek!"

A grey and brown cat scurried out from under their table, quickly taking refuge under an adjoining table.

"You think the cat speaks Arabic?" Paul asked.

Naomi glared briefly at Paul. "All Moroccan cats speak Arabic."

"What have you got against Moroccan cats?"

"I don't discriminate. I have a terrible cat allergy—particularly to dirty ones like that! There's another one over there—just behind you! God, there are cats all over the place!"

There were, in fact, at least six cats in the immediate vicinity, waiting for morsels of fish to fall from the tables. Naomi beckoned to the tout, said something to him, and he disappeared, briefly. When he reappeared, he had a can of aerosol, which he sprayed under the table and at any cats nearby. The cats vanished.

Paul said, "When the cats go, the sea gulls move in." Now, there were three large, white gulls standing brazenly next to their table, and moving their heads to take in the prospects for food.

"I don't mind sea gulls. I think they're rather pretty." She reached out toward one of the gulls with a closed hand. The bird took a step closer to see what was in her hand, and when he saw that there was nothing, he took three steps back. "Pretty clever, too," she said.

A waiter set heaping paper plates in front of them.

"These look really good!" Naomi said, reaching out and taking a small fish from Paul's plate. Paul feigned irritation, and made as if to smack her hand.

She giggled, "I'll give you some of mine!" And taking a forkful of her fish, she fed it to him.

"This is really good!"

"Mine is, too!"

"Sorry you didn't take the larger fish?"

She inclined her head uncertainly. "I'll have some ice cream later."

But later, at the fruit vendor's stall, there were tempting mounds of cherries, strawberries, oranges and bananas. Naomi said something to the vendor, who nodded his head in agreement. She selected a cherry, ate it, threw the pit over the sea wall, and then selected a strawberry.

"Cherries!" she announced, "and they're better than ice cream!"

They sat on the sea wall, dipping their hands into a one kilo bag of cherries, and watching the world pass by.

"What's down there?" she asked, gesturing to her right.

"I think it's the harbour."

"Shall we go have a look?"

They walked down a cobble-stoned road, a big whitewashed building on their left. Paul peered in through a large open door. The stone flooring was littered with plastic baskets and boxes; two men in white coats were hosing down the floor. "This must be the fish auction house."

Naomi read the plaque by the door. "It says that the auctions begin at five a.m., Monday through Saturday. Licensed vendors only."

They walked on through a portal, and suddenly there was the harbour before them. The stone sea wall formed a barrier to the ocean on their right; a similar wall marked the eastern limit of the harbour. Between the walls were scores of large, motorised fishing boats moored together in neat rows and columns.

"Fishing is a big business here," Paul commented.

As they walked around the landside of the harbour, they encountered small groups of fishermen spreading out their tangled nets, or working to effect repairs.

"I'm going to ask these guys where the best seafood restaurant is," she said. One of the men pointed in the direction from which they had come. Naomi shook her head, and explained something. One of the men pointed in the opposite direction, toward the far end of the harbour.

"He said it's called 'Chez Sam', and it's down there. Shall we go have a look?"

Standing alone on a small spit of land at the southern end of the harbour was an unlikely single story, dark-shingled building.

Efraim's Eye

It looked not unlike a building one might expect to find along the coast of New England. Above the door was a white painted sign 'Chez Sam'. They studied the menu posted by the door.

"Oooh, it looks good," Naomi proclaimed. Paul nodded. She made a reservation for 8 o'clock

"I'd like to have a look in the artists' section of town," he said, pointing on the map, "which is here."

Naomi was amused. "So are you a collector, Paul?"

"No, I don't know good art from bad unless it's on display in a museum. But I do like to watch artists at work. It seems so easy, but it's a skill I could never have."

In the artists' quarter, they found many paintings on display from vivid seascapes, to bustling street scenes, to unflattering portraits. There were artists, too, but none was at work on his trade. They were all standing next to their creations waiting to entice prospective buyers.

Paul's attention was diverted to the woodworking shops, where exquisite marquetry boxes of various sizes and shapes were on display. Many of the actual craftsmen were at work at their benches in the rear of their shops, fitting tiny slivers of different woods, or smoothing and polishing their nearly finished creations. Mostly, Paul watched the craftsmen while Naomi inspected the finished goods, but in one small and musty shop, a strange piece on a top shelf caught Paul's eye. He took it down and inspected it. It was a dark wooden cylinder, about sixty centimetres long and three centimetres in diameter. It was inlaid with lovely flourishes of pale wood. Naomi, sensing his sudden interest, came over. "Oh, my gosh! It's a flute!" She put it to her lips and played a quick octave.

The proprietor stepped alongside them. "That is an antique piece. It is thuya wood," he said.

Paul explained to Naomi. "Thuya is a rare hardwood with beautiful grain. The guidebook says the demand for it is going to make the trees extinct."

Naomi examined the flute carefully, and she played it again briefly. "Beautiful tone," she said, putting it down.

"How much is it?" Paul inquired.

"Three thousand dirhams, sir."

"I'll give you two thousand."

"Paul!" Naomi interjected, "What in the world do you want with a flute?" He ignored her.

"I'm sorry, sir. Three thousand is the price. A musician offered me three thousand several weeks ago, but he hasn't been back to collect it."

"OK," Paul said.

He paid the proprietor, and handed the flute to Naomi. "You're crazy, Paul!"

He shrugged. "Maybe a little bit."

"Why did you do that?" she asked, still incredulous.

"Because I want to hear you play."

"Thank you," she said, looking away so that he couldn't see the emotion she suddenly felt.

They walked on for some distance, examining boxes, salad bowls, and carved figures.

"Naomi, I'm feeling all salty and sandy. I'm ready for a shower."

"OK. Let's go to the hotel."

In the room, Naomi seated herself at the desk and mirror. She watched herself as she played short riffs on the flute. It was as if she and her instrument were making their acquaintance: she assessing its capability, and it testing her skills. Every now and then, she would smile at herself in the mirror, and then look down at the instrument, which she held, lovingly, in her hands.

Paul stripped and immersed himself in the deluge of the shower. For him, the shower always had renewing properties, and it felt wonderful to rinse away the sand, sun lotion and salt. Suddenly, the shower curtain was drawn aside, and a naked Naomi stepped in. "Hi, mind if I join you?"

"No. No, of course not." He didn't know what to do with his hands. He wanted to embrace her, to touch her, but perhaps she just wanted to share the shower.

"Aren't you going to use the soap?" she asked, looking up at him. Water was streaming down her face. He bent, and kissed her forehead.

"Yes. Yes, I was. Where is it?"

"Here," she said, handing him the small white bar. "Well?" she asked.

He was suddenly very happy. He hugged her to him; she felt slippery, warm, and wonderful. He rubbed the soap over her back.

She stepped back. He started with her shoulders and neck, then lingering, her breasts. She smiled and then giggled. His hand guided the soap across her belly. When he touched her, she squealed and pushed him away. Kneeling, he washed the front of her legs.

"OK. Turn around," he ordered. Slowly and admiringly, he washed the roundness of her buttocks.

"You like my bottom?" she asked.

"Yes, I do. You're lovely."

"OK. My turn."

She started as before with his back.

"OK. Turn around."

The soap swirled across his chest, and his stomach. "Hmmm," she murmured, soaping him, "I like you."

He was amused. "What's to like?"

She looked into his eyes, her lips parted in desire. "When he's like this, he excites me." When he said nothing, she asked with a gesture, "How do you like me?"

"Well, she's kind of hidden—sort of secret." She laughed. ". . . and she's very sweet."

Scarcely dry, they tumbled onto the bed.

"No," she said, "I want you on top."

Minutes later, his crisis overtook him; he cried out. "Oh, God, Naomi!"

Feeling this, the urgent passion within her burst, and she breathed a long groan of satisfaction.

For some minutes they lay, facing each other, floating in fulfillment, listening to the surf outside the windows, his hand stroking her hair and her hand resting against his cheek.

"Naomi, I want to hear you play."

"Oh, gosh. It's been such a long time since I played or practiced on the flute."

"Would you like to play?" She nodded. "Well, you've got a very eager audience here."

She got up, picked up the instrument, and stood looking out to sea, lost in thought. She put the flute to her lips, took a deep breath and began to nod her head to an internal cadence. The notes began to flow. Paul sat up, captivated by the girl at the window. Her slender naked figure bent to the feelings of the music. Her face and upper body were coloured golden pink by the sinking sun. Her hair swung as she tilted her head to emphasise a phrase. She seemed to live only for the music she was playing. *This is really beautiful,* he thought, *She's a very talented girl!*

Paul lost track of time; he didn't expect it to end, but with an emotional burst of notes, it ended. He wanted to applaud, yet he didn't wish to interrupt the trance she was in, still staring out to sea, the flute by her side.

Slowly, she turned toward him.

"That was absolutely wonderful," he said.

She shook her head. "I really need to practice."

"What was the piece?"

"It was a messy version of *Queen of the Night* from *The Magic Flute*."

He asked, "Why don't you spend more time with your music?"

She looked dejectedly at the floor. "You sound just like my father."

"Naomi, I'm not your father! I just want to understand. You're a very talented musician."

"I guess," she said slowly, "it was just my rebelliousness. What do the Americans call it? Cussedness."

"There is another expression for it."

"I know. Cutting off your nose to spite your face." She looked at him, appealing for understanding. "But I really feel it's our duty as human beings to try to make the world a better place. Does that just sound too idealistic?"

"No. No, it doesn't. Wouldn't it be possible to do both?"

"What do you mean?"

"I mean combining your music and charity work."

She came and sat next to him on the bed. Idly and pensively, she stroked his arm. "Maybe. I don't know." She smiled at him. "Thank you for the flute, Paul. Thank you very much."

They walked along the ramparts of the city wall. To their right, a glowing red sun was half submerged in the Atlantic. She was wearing a simple white dress with a full skirt that billowed in the wind. Her hair streamed out in front of her. He had to lean back slightly to offset the force of the wind, and his thin cotton trousers flapped about his legs.

She laughed and pointed at a small flock of sea birds that was being carried by the wind. "They have to go where the wind takes them."

Seated at a table by the window of Chez Sam, they could look out onto the harbour, which was covered with little white crests. The fishing boats tugged nervously at their moorings. A waiter brought them menus.

"What are you going to have, sweetheart?" he asked.

She put her menu down and looked at him. "Before he left for Sweden, my father used to call me that."

Anxious to disassociate himself from her father, he asked, "Doesn't your boyfriend call you sweetheart?"

"No. He says 'my beauty'."

"When was the last time you saw him?"

"About three months ago."

"That's a long time." She shrugged. "How would he feel about you being with another man?"

She considered him, a slight smile on her lips. "He wouldn't like it, but he knows, as I know, that there are temptations in life, and sometimes it is better for us to give in. Being apart for so much of the time, there can't be any formal commitment. If there were, it would end in tears."

Paul was pensive. *For her, that makes a lot of sense*, he thought, but he said nothing.

Her hand stole across the table and touched his. "Is there somebody back in London?" she asked.

He nodded.

"What's her name?"

"Sarah."

"My mother's name is Sara." She paused. "So Sarah would be mad at me?"

"No, she'd be mad at me."

"Why?"

What a daft question! He said, "There's no formal commitment between us. We're just really good friends, but . . ."

". . . but she would feel betrayed." He nodded. "Do you feel you've betrayed her?"

"No. Not, really. If I had it to do over again, I wouldn't want to change a thing!"

She smiled. "Neither would I."

She squeezed his hand. "I think the difference between Isaac, my boyfriend, and Sarah is expectations. It's clear in Isaac's case; it's assumed in Sarah's case."

He nodded. *She's quite clever about people.*

She considered him. "Do you feel a little better, Paul?"

He gave a slight smile. "Yes. Yes, I do."

She picked up her menu again. "Now, what are we going to have for dinner?"

At the Riad del Mar, she hung up her white dress, shed her underwear, and lay on the bed, her eyes following him around the room. At last, he lay down beside her, facing her. Lightly, he stroked her cheek. She reached for him.

"I'm afraid he needs a little rest," he whispered.

"In that case, I'll say good night to him, and see him in the morning," she whispered back.

As they lay sleeping, all that could be heard were the murmur of the sea surf, the gentle gusting of the wind, and their peaceful breathing.

Paul woke to an exquisite sensation. He was no longer sleeping, and he had Naomi's undivided attention. The dusky light of early morning was coming through the open windows. At his side was Naomi's lovely bottom. "Mmmm. Hmmm. Ummm," she mumbled.

"Let me have you," he whispered.

One of her thighs passed over his face, and then he could feel her firm, small breasts against his belly. He drew her to him, and then he was drowning in a sea of pleasure, feeling her urgency and intoxicated with her musky wetness. They reached the peak together: trembling, groaning, and clasping.

She lay with her head on his chest; gradually, their breathing was recovering.

"How did you like it?" she asked.

"It was luscious."

She giggled. "The same." She stroked his chest. "Do you think we were naughty?"

"No. Not at all. It was lovely."

"It probably isn't Kosher."

"Do you care?"

"No. I don't, really." She gave a long, gentle sigh. "You know there are over six hundred rules you have to follow to be a good Jew."

"That's quite a lot."

"Yes, and some of them are contradictory." She resumed her stroking. "How many rules do good Christians have to follow? Isn't it just ten?"

"Actually, it boils down to just two."

She raised her head to look at him. "What are they?"

"One is to love God with all your heart and soul and mind. Two is to love your neighbour as much as yourself."

"Well, if somebody isn't your neighbour, you can cheat them and beat them up."

"Oh, no! Jesus taught that all human beings are neighbours."

"Oooh, that makes it pretty hard then."

"Not as hard as six hundred."

She giggled and pinched his nipple. He reached for her thigh, just above her knee, and squeezed.

She burst into gusts of laughter. "Don't! That tickles!"

"You started it!" He raked his fingers down her sides. She was laughing uncontrollably and squirming frantically, trying to escape his tickling. She rolled off the bed and stood up, ready to escape to the bathroom. They were looking at each other, both smiling. He held out a hand to her.

"Come back to bed. I won't tickle you any more."

She lay down beside him, her body pressed against him, and after a time, they fell back to sleep.

The wind rattled the green canvas awning that covered the roof restaurant. They were sitting side-by-side so that they could look out to sea. A waiter had cleared away their breakfast plates of fruit and pastries. Naomi was sipping her coffee pensively. She turned slightly to face him. "Do you love me, Paul?"

Unprepared as he was for that question, Paul knew that there could be only one answer. "Yes, yes, of course, I love you."

Naomi's head tilted, and her gaze fell to the tablecloth. Uncertainly, she asked, "Why do you love me?"

Instinctively, Paul knew that his answer must not include the word beautiful or one of its synonyms. He said, "You're a very sweet idealist, Naomi. You are a woman with great talents as a linguist, as a musician, and in dealing with people. But for me, best of all, is your *joie de vie*. Life is a great, pleasing adventure for you, and it's delightful to be with you."

For some moments, Naomi gazed at him, apparently repeating his words in her mind. She asked, "So you think I'm a sweet, talented, adventurous woman?" She pronounced the word woman awkwardly, as if it were a term unfamiliar to her.

He smiled. "For a four word summary, that will do."

Paul knew the answer to the reciprocal question. She loved him as a daughter loves, and he had awakened her latent brilliance as a lover. But for her part, she had wanted to know whether she, herself, was a person who could be loved.

She took his hand in hers, and they sat, quietly gazing out to sea, each lost for some time in his or her own sunny thoughts.

"More coffee, miss?" the waiter asked.

Naomi shook herself as if recovering from a trance. "Umm, no, thank you. Paul?"

"No thanks." He considered her, fondly. "What are we going to do today? Is Mohammed going to drive us to Fez?"

"No, I think it's too long a drive to be cooped up in the car. He can drive us to Marrakech, and we can take the overnight train."

"Can't we fly from Marrakech?"

"No. I checked. Fez has flights from Casablanca and Europe only." She pushed back her chair.

"Let me go get my laptop."

Moments later, she was re-seated at the table. "Let's see. The train company is ONCF. The overnight train from Marrakech to Tangier leaves at 9 p.m. and arrives in Fez at 6:10 a.m. That's not too bad. First class fare is 360 dirhams. Then if we don't want to sleep in seats," She looked up at Paul, "I don't! Then we have a choice between a compartment with two bunk beds and a shared compartment with four bunk beds."

"Let's go for the comfortable option."

"OK. That's 450 dirhams, per person, extra."

Paul said, "So the total, per person, comes to about sixty pounds. That's pretty cheap! Then, how do we get to Casablanca and back to Marrakech?"

"We can either fly or take the train on both legs."

"That means we could fly to Fes via Casablanca late today."

"Yes, I guess it does," she conceded. "Let me see." For several minutes, she tapped at her keyboard. "A couple of problems. First, there are no afternoon flights from Marrakech to Casablanca, and the fares are pretty steep. The total for the two legs comes to 2,234 dirhams, per person."

"That's about one hundred and seventy pounds. The train it is. Can we fly back to Marrakech?"

She returned to her laptop. Shaking her head, she announced, "Royal Air Maroc only has morning flights from Casablanca to Marrakech and Atlas Blue has nothing. It isn't too bad, though, because we can take the train to Casablanca tomorrow afternoon—about three and a half hours—and then take the train down to Marrakech on Tuesday afternoon—about four hours."

"OK," he said, "We'll see some of the country, instead of just clouds."

"I'll make the reservations. Where do you want to stay in Casablanca?"

"You pick it."

"Let me see the guidebook." For several minutes she leafed through the guidebook. Then with an enigmatic smile, she tapped away at her laptop.

"OK, we're all set. What do you want to do today, Paul?"

"Well, it's Sunday, today, and I was thinking it might be nice to at least look in on a church. I think I saw a small sign for one yesterday."

Naomi leaned toward him, confidentially. She said, "You know, I've never been inside a Christian church."

He was surprised. "You haven't?"

"No, never."

"Would you like to see what it's like?"

"Do I have to wear anything special?"

"No, nothing. I mean, you have to wear clothes, but what you have on would be fine."

"Naomi, the adventurer, says yes!"

The small church, probably the only one in Essaouira, Paul guessed fronted a little square a short walk from the Avenue Sidi Mohamed Ben Abdallah. A single, sonorous bell was ringing from the whitewashed steeple. The ancient wooden doors at the front portal were open, and two old women were climbing the three steps to the entrance. Tacked to one of the doors was a notice in French.

"It says that there are services on Sunday in French at nine and eleven and in Spanish at ten," Naomi reported. She looked at her watch. "Quarter to eleven. Shall we go in?"

She took Paul's arm as he walked down the central aisle of the vaulted nave. It was cool and quiet; their footsteps resounded on the stone floor. Above the altar that was draped in fine white lace hung a life-size wooden crucifix. The polished body of Christ reflected the lights of the candles. Behind the crucifix, high in the rear wall of the apse, there was a single, round, stained-glass window that depicted a lamb with a banner.

Naomi whispered, "Is this a Catholic church?"

"Yes, I'm pretty sure it is. The one way you can tell for sure is to find a light where the host is stored. Yes, there, to the right of the altar. Do you see the little amber light next to that little brass door in the wall?"

"Yes."

"That's the tabernacle, where the host is kept."

"What's the host?"

"During the service," Paul whispered, "we take communion, which is what Christ did with his disciples during the last supper. He offered them bread and wine, which he said, were his body and blood. And he asked them to repeat the communion in memory of Him. The host is the bread, Christ's body, which is kept in the tabernacle, and the light, which burns 24 hours a day, is to honour Christ."

From the rear of the church, an organ began to play. Naomi listened attentively, her head down. "Bach. G major," she whispered, and, not being able to restrain herself, she looked behind her for the organist. "Not much style," she whispered to Paul, who managed to suppress his amusement.

He confided, "She probably plays the same piece every Sunday at eleven."

After a time, an ancient, white-robed priest appeared, a little bell rang, and the service began. Paul understood almost nothing of what the priest said, but the order of the service was fixed in his memory: he stood, sat, and knelt at the right moments, and Naomi simply followed his lead.

A feeling of peace and gratitude gradually came over Paul. Perhaps it was the atmosphere: the shaft of coloured sun light falling from the window, the scent of incense and candles, the distant, dark recesses of the church, the modulated tenor of the priest and the baritone of the organ.

Perhaps it was the presence of the lovely, surrogate daughter and lover next to him. Or maybe it was the feeling that he had come to this home again, after two spiritually barren years. As the priest began his homily, his mind wavered, and a prayer formed, *Oh, Lord, forgive me for having pushed you aside and wrongly blamed you. Help me, Lord, to find the way back to You.*

The priest was standing in front of the altar, facing the congregation, with a silver chalice in his hand. *Oh, my gosh,* Paul thought, *What should I do? I haven't been to confession in two years! Should I take communion or not?* As he rose to his feet, a sense of rightful belonging came over him. To Naomi, he whispered, "I'll be right back."

As they walked through the alleyways of Essaouira toward fish grills number eight, Naomi was recounting what the priest had said during his homily. She said, "His theme was that the first shall be last and the last shall be first. He gave quite a few examples of that, most of which were unfamiliar to me, but he mentioned one about the disciples who wanted to sit on Jesus' right and left in heaven. But Jesus said he couldn't do that, and he told the disciples whoever wants to be important should serve the others." She looked over at Paul. "I think that's a really nice thought. It seems to me that there are too many people who are trying to be powerful or to have lots of money and they do it at the expense of others. Just think how much better the world would be if the wealth and power were spread more evenly."

Paul considered this thought. "You know, Naomi, Jesus said, 'the poor will always be with you.'"

"Why did he say that?"

"Oh, I think there are several reasons. First of all, while God may love us equally, some people are brighter and more talented than others, and they have the capacity to earn more than others. If their earning advantage were taken away, what incentive would they have to earn? Also, think how dull a place the world would be if everyone were on the same salary. I'm not saying that we shouldn't have charitable instincts. We should! Our charitable instincts are perhaps the ultimate test of our humanity. So, Jesus was right."

Naomi considered what Paul had said for a while. Then, she asked, "Are you saying that God allows people to be poor as a test for the rest of us?"

"Oh, Naomi, you're incorrigible!"

She stopped, and faced him irritably. "No, I'm not! Answer me!"

"Naomi, I don't know what God allows or doesn't allow. I believe He's all-powerful, and he could allow or disallow a lot of things. But, he doesn't choose to. He allows human beings to just be. I believe some things in life are God's test. I don't know why. And I know that it is wrong for us to test God because any test of Him is an expression of our doubt."

She stood looking at him for several moments, the annoyance gradually melting from her face, and replaced by a wistful smile. "OK," she said.

He held out his hand to her. She took it, and they walked on.

The tout recognised them, shooed the cats away, and seated them. "You want same yesterday?" he asked. They looked at each other.

"Yes," Paul said.

"What I don't understand," Naomi said, "is why, at one point people were saying, 'we believe in one God, the Father Almighty,' and yet there is that huge sculpture of Jesus on the cross, and the whole service seems to be about Jesus."

Paul nodded. "I guess it's not an easy concept, and I think I read somewhere that the reason Muslims reject Jesus as God is that if there are two or three gods, they will be at war with each other—working at cross purposes."

"I think a lot of Jewish people have the same problem."

"OK, but the assumption in this argument is based on human nature and human experience that kings don't share power very well. If one sets that argument aside and thinks of perfect beings, why can't perfect beings share power perfectly, as if they were one?"

"So you believe that Jesus is God?"

"I believe that Jesus is part of God." She shook her head slightly, still mystified. "I'm not trying to convert you, Naomi. I'm just trying to explain."

"Well then, explain to me all this stuff about communion, bread and wine."

"Jesus wanted his followers to do what he did on the night before he was crucified. He knew that they would be left without him, and he wanted them to remember him and his teachings by sharing a symbolic meal together. The meal would not only help cement their relationship to him but with each other."

Naomi said, "That's actually quite clever." She threw a bit of bread to a sea gull. "Have you ever been in a synagogue?"

"Yes, but I really didn't learn much from the visit."

"OK. After lunch and after cherries, I'll take you to a synagogue."

The synagogue was a single-story, beige stone building hidden away in the depths of the mellah, the old Jewish quarter. Its door was open, but there was only one man with a white beard, dressed in black, who was seated on a bench by the door. He was reading something aloud, bowing and nodding rhythmically as he read. Naomi took a white cotton skullcap, a kippah, from a basket, and gave it to Paul. "Here, put this on. It shows that you fear God." She put one on her own head.

"Do you have to wear one, too?" he asked.

"No, but it feels appropriate."

She led him by the arm to the centre of what was a modest space with rows of perhaps twenty benches. She said, "The benches are facing east, toward Jerusalem, and toward that large wooden cabinet, which is called the Torah Ark. That's where the Torah scrolls are kept. The Torah Ark is like the Ark of the Covenant, where Moses put the Ten Commandment tablets. We have in common with the Muslims that we both face our holy cities during worship."

She gestured toward a raised platform with a podium. "That's the tebah, where the Torah is read. And over there is the ner tamid lamp that is always lit like the miraculous menorah in the Jerusalem Temple. It's a little bit like your tabernacle light. The large menorah on that stand is a symbol of Judaism; God told Moses how to make it. That one looks like the real thing. It burns olive oil."

A very wide and elaborate chair with its seat high off the floor caught Paul's attention. "What's that chair?"

"It's the Elijah chair. It's used during circumcision ceremonies." She beamed, tongue in cheek.

"You'll notice, Paul, one other difference. There are no sculptures or illustrations of the human body. That is considered idolatry." She looked around. "You see this is all one space. An orthodox synagogue would have a separate area for women as the Muslims do."

"What's the ceremony like, Naomi?"

"There are three prayers that are performed daily and are required for men, optional for women. There are morning, afternoon and evening prayers; sometimes the latter two are combined. There are readings, prayers and blessings from the Siddur, the Jewish prayer book. An extra prayer, the Musaf, is inserted on Fridays and Jewish Holidays. There is a fifth prayer, the Ne'ilah, that is said on Yom Kippur. Many of the prayers are chanted or sung. On Shabbat or Jewish holiday, there is usually a cantor to lead the prayer service. If there are less than ten people present, prayers are considered individual prayers. With ten people or more, a minyan, it is considered a community prayer, which is the best form of prayer. I could go on, but it gets quite technical."

"There seem to be a lot of commonalities between Jewish and Muslim worship."

"Yes, there are."

Paul looked around the near-deserted synagogue. "What do Jewish people believe?"

"We believe in the same God that you believe in."

Chapter 9

FEZ & CASABLANCA

They had had dinner at a crowded Spanish restaurant near the station. The service was frantic, and the atmosphere was, as Naomi put it, "like the Pamplona bull run," but the tapas and rioja were surprisingly good.

The train was of recent vintage, clean, and on-time departing, but slow.

"The guidebook says the distance from Marrakech to Fez is 460 kilometres," Paul had said, "With nine hours travel time, it means the average speed is just over fifty kilometres per hour. That's about thirty miles per hour."

"Well, if the train was faster, it would get there in the middle of the night. That wouldn't be good. Besides, I rather like the slow clickety-clack."

The train porter had showed them to their compartment, where the bunks were made, the washbasin had hot water, and the lavatory was hidden behind a curtain. Shortly after departure, a conductor had checked their tickets.

"I think it's warm in here," Naomi had announced. She called the porter, who examined the thermostat, and shrugged. "He says the air conditioning may not be working."

They were sitting on their respective bunks, reading what they had purchased at the Marrakech station: Paul, the *International Herald Tribune*; Naomi, the French issue of *Cosmopolitan*.

She put the *Cosmopolitan* down and examined the window. Paul shook his head. "No, sweetheart, it won't open."

Frustrated, she took off her shirt, jeans and sandals.

Efraim's Eye

"Uuh, Naomi, don't you think you ought to draw the curtains?" Paul asked.

"No, not particularly. I can't see out with the curtains drawn."

"Yes, but people can see in. Do you want them to see you in your beautiful underwear?"

"They'll only get a quick glimpse." There was a provocative tone in her voice.

"But when the train stops at a station?"

"In that case they'd get a real eye-full." She looked at him wide-eyed.

"Are you planning to get completely naked?"

Her look turned sultry. "Yes, aren't you?"

He paused. "Yes, but not now."

She came and sat very close to him. Her eyes were on his face, her lips moving wordlessly. Slowly, she reached behind her, unfastened the catch, and moved her shoulders forward. He could not resist looking down at her uncovered pink and creaminess. She took a deep breath.

"I've changed my mind," he said. He stood up, drew the curtains, locked the door, and began to undress.

The train was just under an hour late arriving in Fez. They had taken turns using the washbasin before arrival, and while less than fully satisfactory, they at least felt partially refreshed. Walking through the modern station interior with its grey marble floors, its huge golden lamps, and exiting through the enormous keyhole portal, they hailed a taxi.

Naomi spoke to the taxi driver. To Paul, she said, "The AMM office is in the new city. I sent a text to Adiba Nahyan that we'd meet her in her office at 8. So we have time for a little breakfast."

The cab dropped them off at a café. The driver got out and, pointing and gesturing, he explained to Naomi where the office was located.

When they were seated at a table in the café, she said, "The driver said it's just two hundred metres from here."

Paul said, "You are a real road warrior, Naomi."

"What do you mean?"

"I mean, you're a professional traveller. Look at you! Fresh as a daisy. One would think that last night you slept in a stationary hotel bed for eight hours. Didn't the rocking of the train keep you awake?"

She shook her head. "I can sleep in a car, on a plane, a train, or a boat—doesn't matter. As long as I'm feeling safe, warm, and fairly comfortable."

"I'm spoiled. I like my bed to be stationary and quiet."

She looked down at her coffee. "Last night was lovely, Paul, really lovely."

"Yes, it was."

"For selfish reasons, I'm going to make sure you sleep on the train to Casablanca."

Adiba Nahyan was in the office when they arrived promptly at eight. She was a large, very plain woman in her late twenties. The effect of her wide nose and mouth was offset by the light in her active dark eyes and her gracious manner. She was dressed in baggy, brown trousers, a forest green sweatshirt, and a matching headscarf that was tied at the nape of her neck. She bustled about the office, making mint tea and inquiring about their trip.

"How did you get the job here?" Naomi wanted to know.

"A friend of mine applied for loan from the office here. Before she got loan, manager here left. I not sure why." Adiba's English was halting but clear. "My friend tells me this and asks if I interested. I interested because of divorce. I call Marrakech and speak Mr. Al-Rashid. I tell him I like job. I speak English and graduate university. He ask if I have experience of office. I tell him yes, I work in husband office. So I go Marrakech and speak Mr. Al-Rashid in person. He say, 'OK you hire.'" Adiba paused, beaming at her visitors.

"And how do you find the work here, Adiba?" Naomi asked.

"I like very much working here in office. Is very important give loan to entrepreneur. Very good for Morocco, and very good for entrepreneur!"

Naomi nodded. "How did you find the office systems when you started working?"

Adiba leaned forward, "Systems. What systems you speak about?"

"I'm thinking about the general procedures in the office: the forms, the paperwork, the records, the filing—that sort of thing."

"Was big mess! I call Latifa, and she explain me what she do. She send me forms. I look forms, and I make better." She beamed again at her visitors.

Paul asked, "What kind of office work did you do for your ex-husband?"

"I office manager."

"And what was your ex-husband's business?"

"He have small personnel company. Provide temporary workers to construction companies."

Paul asked, "How is Mr. Al-Rashid as a boss to work for?"

Adiba made a sour expression and shook her head, but said nothing.

"We will not repeat anything you say, Adiba, to Mr. Al-Rashid or anyone else," Naomi assured her.

"I not like." Adiba looked anxiously at Naomi.

"It's all right, Adiba, you can tell us."

"Mr. Al-Rashid very selfish. He make very hard contract with entrepreneur." Paul and Naomi nodded their agreement. "And he pay me less when I come to office late. Sometime my bus late. I work extra time, but he no care."

"Anything else?" Paul asked.

Reluctantly, Adiba responded, "Mr. Al-Rashid want list of entrepreneurs."

Naomi was confused. "Why would he ask for that? He knows who your entrepreneurs are, because he negotiates the contracts with them."

"No. He not know. Some entrepreneurs have no good business plan. I not recommend for loan."

Paul was nodding. "So he asked you for the information on all the entrepreneurs who applied to you: their names, contact details, and a brief description of their proposed business?"

Adiba nodded but said nothing.

Naomi turned to Paul. "Why would he need that? GYE doesn't want the names of people who aren't approved for negotiation. We just want the number of applicants, so why would he want it?"

"Because," Paul said dryly, "he wants to include their names on the list he reports to the development bank."

Adiba murmured her agreement; Naomi stared at Paul, wide-eyed: "So that list of one hundred and ninety entrepreneurs that Latifa showed you included people who never got loans?"

Paul nodded. "Probably."

There was absolute silence in the room for several moments. Naomi began to flush red with anger. "That's fraud!" she declared. Her hands were balled in fists.

Paul gave a slight shrug. Naomi turned on him. "What do you mean acting so dismissive? You're supposed to be the auditor!"

Gently, Paul said, "Naomi, we haven't proven anything yet."

Still angry, Naomi spluttered, "Well we can get Adiba to . . ." Paul was shaking his head, and she trailed off, but she still held Paul's gaze, doggedly and angrily. Finally, she said, "Paul, promise me one thing." She paused for effect, "That we're going to get that bastard Yusuf!"

"Probably."

"Not probably, damn it! I want to hear you say definitely!"

Paul looked at the ceiling for a moment. "We'll definitely get him, Miss Evensen."

Adiba sat looking from one to the other and looking very uncomfortable.

Naomi asked, "What's the matter, Adiba?"

"You be careful!"

Naomi was still energised with anger. "Careful of what?"

"You know Mr. Efraim Al-Rashid?"

"Yes. What about him?"

"He very dangerous man. Latifa, tell me."

"What did she tell you?"

"When I go Marrakech, I go lunch with her outside. She tell me she believe Yusuf cheating. She ask Yusuf. He say no. Next day, Efraim stop her on way home. Tell her keep mouth shut, or be very sorry." Paul and Naomi shared knowing negative glances. Adiba shifted uncomfortably in her chair; she asked, "You know about bombing here in 2007?"

"Yes."

"Police still looking for one man. Is big man with beard. I see police picture. Look like Efraim Al-Rashid."

Paul asked, "How do you know?"

"I not know certainly. I see him one day in Marrakech office when he there."

"And the police picture, was it photograph or sketch?"

"It was sketch."

"Haven't you reported your suspicions to the police, Adiba?" Naomi asked. Adiba shook her head vigorously. "Why not?"

"Mr. Al-Rashid very powerful—maybe also with police."

Naomi frowned, and was about to protest when Paul said, "This is something that you and I can work on later, Naomi." He paused, and looked around the small office with its two desks, two barred windows, filing cabinets, and scuffed walls. "For now, I think we ought to focus on Adiba's work here."

For the next hour and a half, Paul and Naomi examined the work that was being done in the AMM Fez office. The record-keeping was exemplary. Adiba's enthusiasm for her work was very evident. She had been able to recruit nearly thirty mentors; she admitted, however, that she had not been able to provide them with adequate training. As a result, the entrepreneurs complained about the usefulness of the guidance they had been given. Adiba said she had identified an organisation that could provide training for the mentors, but Al-Rashid had vetoed the training for cost reasons.

Adiba showed them a list of forty-one applicants for loans. She had put twenty-eight of them forward to Al-Rashid for negotiation of a loan contract, and twenty-four had actually received contracts. She said, "I have twenty-four of one hundred and ninety entrepreneurs. How could Casablanca and Marrakech have one hundred and sixty-six? To me, it not make sense."

Naomi looked up from her note taking. "Why not, Adiba?"

"Because Fez territory of AMM include more than one third population of Morocco. My territory include Rabat, Meknes and Mediterranean coast."

Naomi sat with her pen poised. "Adiba, could you have gotten more than forty-one applicants?"

"Oh, yes. I here one year. Before me only ten applicants."

"How did you get thirty-one applicants, Adiba?" Paul wanted to know. "I mean how did you publicise the AMM program?"

"Is not hard. I speak to newspapers. I speak on radio." She beamed with delight: "I go on television one time! I say: 'I coming to Rabat next Thursday. If you interested, you meet me at 7 p.m. at civic centre'. Then I tell them about program. They fill out application. I look. If OK, I ask come to Fez. I discuss; I decide."

Rakin Qaderi came to the office at 10:45 a.m. He was a portly man in his mid-fifties with a sallow complexion, and a moustache which that almost obscured his mouth. He was perspiring profusely, and mopped his face repeatedly with a green bandana; nonetheless, the collar of his shirt was soaked. The owner of a local electrical parts distribution company, he was pleased to be associated with AMM.

"When I was young," he offered, "I want my own business but was impossible for me. I have one-year college education. I had to work for my uncle in his business. For fifteen years, I work as salesman. I think I will be salesman until I die. One day uncle have heart attack and die—right in shop! So I run shop, but I cannot own shop. It belongs to uncle's family. But I make agreement with widow and sons. For ten years, they get half of profits, then shop is mine. I very lucky!"

Paul asked, "How did you get to be a mentor at AMM?"

"Adiba ask me if I interested. She come to Chamber of Commerce meeting to speak about AMM. I think is very good what this woman try to do. I try to help."

"Did you have any training?" Naomi asked.

"No training."

Paul inquired, "How many entrepreneurs have you worked with?"

"I work with two."

"How have you gotten along with them?" Naomi asked.

"Is difficult. They thirty years younger than me. Think differently. I try to teach what my uncle taught me." He studied Paul for a moment; then he said, "I know what make good business."

"I'm sure you do," Paul said, "and what I think you're saying is that you haven't been sure of how to pass your knowledge on to the young people so they can benefit from it."

"Is correct. I speak with other mentors. They have same problem."

There was a reflective pause.

Naomi turned to Paul. "You know, Paul, GYE has a curriculum which covers how to be a mentor. The course doesn't teach how to be a businessperson; it covers how to advise a businessperson. It's all about interpersonal skills."

Rakin was nodding enthusiastically. "I like study this course."

Alim Al-Hamdani, when he arrived at noon, was nothing like Rakin. Tall, reserved, and beautifully attired in a grey silk suit and cream dress shirt, he seemed out of place. He sat at one of the desks, cleared a space in front of himself, and looked over his sharp nose expectantly at Paul. Naomi also made a slight deferential gesture toward Paul, who with these prompts, thanked Mr. Al-Hamdani for coming and explained the purpose of the meeting. Paul asked, "Would you tell us about the role of a local director of AMM?"

"Do you ask, Mr. Winthorpe, what it is or what it should be?"

"We would be interested in your views on both points."

"Ah, well, what it is, is nothing, really. One carries the flag, so to speak, for AMM when requested with various local officials and others of influence. What it could be, were the role to be defined in a certain way, is quite important."

Paul asked, "How might the role be defined to give it this importance?"

"Ah, that is a matter for Mr. Al-Rashid."

Paul thought for a moment. "Mr. Al-Hamdani, how did you come to be a local director of AMM?"

"Ah, yes, well, I have had certain business relations with Mr. Al-Rashid over the years, and he asked me to sit on the local board here in Fez. One might say that I owed him a favour."

Paul was doodling in his notebook while he listened. "May I offer my views on what the role of a regional director might be?"

"I would be most interested."

Paul said, "Setting aside the important roles of fund-raising at a high level and supporting the regional manager—where I believe you are already active—there is the management of relationships with entrepreneurs."

"How so?"

"As it stands now, Adiba decides which entrepreneurs should be passed on to Mr. Al-Rashid for contract negotiations." Al-Hamdani nodded. "I wonder how you would feel about being involved in discussions with potential entrepreneurs and Miss Nayhan during which the business plan would be reviewed, and suggestions would be given to the entrepreneur on possible improvements to the business plan. At the moment, the review of business plans is a pass-fail process, partly because Miss Nayhan had relatively little business experience. It seems to me, though, that the advice of a senior executive like you to an entrepreneur could be invaluable in making his project more promising."

"Yes, I think you may be right."

"Also, there is the matter of contract negotiations. These are all conducted by Mr. Al-Rashid. To free up his time for other pressing matters, could these negotiations not be concluded by an executive, such as you, on behalf of AMM?"

Mr. Al-Hamdani adjusted himself on his chair; he looked distinctly uncomfortable for a brief moment. "Well, such a change would naturally require the approval of Mr. Al-Rashid . . . " Then, he sat forward, and narrowed his eyes, he said, "But should GYE mandate such a change to AMM, I would, of course, be eager to follow your instructions."

* * *

The train rattled over the points outside Fez on the way west toward Meknes and the Atlantic coast.

"Paul, what are you proposing we do about Efraim, and his possible connection to the bombings in Casablanca?"

"Naomi, I'm sorry I cut you short in the meeting with Adiba, but I sensed she didn't want to be involved in any way. I'm not sure it's a good idea for us to go to the police either. I have the impression that there is—or could be—too much transparency about this kind of issue within the police. What could happen is that Efraim gets wind from a source in the police department that he is being linked to the bombings. He finds out who originated the linkage, and he takes action."

"OK, Paul, but we can't just ignore it. What if he decides to organise another attack?"

"I think we ought to go to the British embassy. That way, if Efraim learns he's being investigated, he won't immediately blame GYE. He may think that it's MI6, or some busybody British resident or tourist."

Paul leaned back against the slightly rocking seat and closed his eyes.

"Before you take a nap, Paul," Naomi said, "tell me what you thought about our meetings today."

Paul looked out at a small group of children waving on their way home from school, and in the distance, neat rows or trellised green vines climbing the hillsides. "I liked Adiba. She's the right person for the job: organised and conscientious. She makes things happen. Regarding Rakim, I think what needs to be done is to train a few trainers in AMM, using the GYE mentoring course. There are bound to be a few mentors who could learn how to train their colleagues, without buying expensive training courses. Alim, well, I couldn't really tell what motivates him, apart from preserving his self-esteem. And I don't know whether he could really do a fairer job than Yusuf in negotiating contracts, but I do know that we've got to find a way to block Yusuf from doing it."

The Casablanca Hotel, part of the Monarch chain, was reminiscent of a newly built Hilton. It had a hammam, or rather two hammams: one for men and one for women. As soon as they had checked in, Naomi donned a white bathrobe and shower slippers. Giving Paul a saucy look, she asked, "Will you miss me?"

"Yes, indeed!"

Paul took his time undressing and heading for the men's hammam. There were three middle-aged, overweight, businessmen sitting naked on an opposite bench engaged in animated discussion. The space was not particularly hot or steamy: the men seemed to be more interested in their discussion than in the benefits of the Turkish bath. Paul picked up the water ladle, and asked, "May I?"

One of them replied with an Arabic accent, "Yes, of course. Sorry, we're not paying attention."

The room filled with steam, so that the men were lost to view, and their conversation seemed distant. Shrouded in his own hot cloud, Paul relaxed and let his mind wander. *What is going to happen with Naomi? Two more nights. Is she going to London with me? It might be nice, but somehow I doubt it. She's beautiful. She's sweet, intelligent, and wonderful in bed. I suppose I'm in love with her. Would she ever marry me? Would I ever ask her? Would it work if we didn't get married? No, it wouldn't, not as far as I'm concerned. If we did get married, would it last? Would it last? That's the question. And what would my kids think of her?*

For a time, Paul dozed. When he awoke, the steam and the men were gone.

When he returned to the room, Naomi was sitting at the dressing table with a roaring hair dryer. He stood behind her, watching her in the mirror as her hair flew about, the rise and fall of her breasts, and her critical expression as she concentrated on her task. She put the hair dryer down and began to brush vigorously.

"I had three men in the hammam with me. Who was with you?"

"No one. No one at all." She stood and faced him, slipping the robe from his shoulders. "You could have been with me." She pressed her nakedness against him. "Paul, let's go have dinner. It's kind of a special dining room. And then . . ." His hands caressed her bottom and drew her to him. She breathed, "And then we'll come back here and do lots of lovely things."

The dining room was just off the modern, marble, glass and cream-walled lobby. Above the entrance was a sign in large white script: Rick's Café Americain.

Paul said, "Oh, my gosh, let me see!"

"It's not the original," Naomi whispered, "The original is on a Warner Brothers lot somewhere, but I thought it would be fun."

Inside was the vaulted ceiling from which was suspended the large, Arabic, vase-shaped light, the beige carved archway, balustrades, the grey stone tile floor, the potted plants, the tables covered in white cloths, and the bamboo chairs. There was even an upright player piano decorated with marquetry inlays. The maître was an older man wearing a double-breasted, white jacket and bow tie—not exactly Humphrey Bogart, but close enough.

The player piano was playing "It Had to Be You." They were seated at a table by a bamboo screen. "This is really fun," Paul said.

Naomi was pleased. "I thought you'd like it."

Paul was getting into the fantasy. "I think you could pass for Ilsa."

Naomi looked doubtful. "I'm certainly no Ingrid Bergmann."

"Well, not exactly the same, but . . . Say, Ilsa, haven't we met somewhere before? Was it Paris?"

Naomi started to giggle, "I think it was Marrakech, actually, Rick."

"It seems like yesterday."

"Yes, it does. Tell me the story, Paul. I forget."

"Well, Rick—Humphrey Bogart—and Ilsa—Ingrid Bergmann —were lovers in Paris. Ilsa was married to Victor, a Czech resistance leader, whom she believed had died in a Nazi concentration camp. But Victor had escaped the concentration camp, and he rejoined Ilsa after Rick had left Paris for Morocco. Ilsa and Victor travel to Morocco, trying to escape capture by the Nazis. Ilsa comes here . . ." Paul gestured around the room. ". . . and she meets Rick again. She explains about her husband, and she admits that she still loves Rick, but she is desperate for Victor to find a way out of Morocco. Meanwhile, Rick has obtained two letters of transit that permit the holders to travel to neutral Portugal and on to the U.S. Victor meets Rick and tells him he is aware of Rick's love for Ilsa; he urges him to take her to safety."

"How does it end?" Naomi asked, almost breathlessly.

"At the last minute, Rick bundles Ilsa and Victor onto a plane for Portugal. In the final scene, Rick and Louis—the Casablancan chief of police—walk off into the mist, vowing to join the resistance."

Naomi doodled with her finger on the tablecloth. "How did you feel about the film, Paul?"

Paul sighed. "A little sad. I identified with Humphrey Bogart, and I wanted him to go off with Ilsa. But I could see that it was important for Victor to be saved, and of course, his wife should go with him. So I was torn. How did you feel, Naomi?"

"Much the same. I liked Humphrey Bogart a lot, and I feel he made the right decision, in spite of the love that he and Ilsa had for each other."

For a few moments, the piano stopped playing; then, it began "As Time Goes By."

The Casablanca office of AMM was just off Boulevard Moulay Ismail in an industrial section of the city, not far from the port. It was on the second floor of an older but rehabilitated building that had been subdivided into offices, mostly occupied by charities. Mr. Tariq Sidqi welcomed them to the small office that had lighting from two skylights and was decorated with travel posters of Morocco. He was a slender man of medium height with a sharp nose and chin. His hair was cut short and flecked with grey. His expressive hands with their long, narrow fingers were in constant motion. Paul wondered if he were gay.

Mr. Sidqi had been working in AMM for about four years. He thought very highly of the charity and of Yusuf Al-Rashid. "He is very good manager for AMM. I like work for him."

Paul and Naomi asked the usual questions about business processes and the numbers of entrepreneurs and mentors. The files and records that were available appeared to be in good order.

But some of the files had been "transferred temporarily to Marrakech". Included in this transferred category were files on twenty-seven entrepreneurs and on fourteen mentors. Remaining in the Casablanca office were files on twenty-two entrepreneurs and eleven mentors.

"Mr. Sidqi, why were the files transferred?" Naomi inquired.

Mr. Sidqi shrugged. "Mr. Al-Rashid want inspect them."

Paul asked, "When were they transferred?"

Mr. Sidqi studied a skylight. "I think it was last week sometimes."

Paul decided to open a new subject. "Mr. Sidqi, Mr. Al-Rashid has told us that he has difficulty keeping employees in AMM, but here you are, you've been here for four years. How do you find the compensation?"

"Oh, is OK. Not much money, but this is charity." Then, with a conspiratorial wink, "Sometime, Mr. Al-Rashid pay me bonus."

"I see," Naomi said, "and do you do much work outside the office?"

"Oh, yes! I go raise funds for AMM. I find new entrepreneurs and new mentors."

The local board member, Mr. Kaliq Bishara, asked Naomi and Paul to go to a nearby café. "I like to buy you very best mint tea in Casablanca!" he explained.

At first, Mr. Bishara, who apparently was a senior manager in a large, French-owned insurance company, was very enthusiastic about GYE, and what it could do for Morocco. He went on and on about how wonderful it was to give young people a chance to make their dreams come true—that the loans and the mentoring were the key to making the dream come true.

"But," Naomi protested, "You haven't said much about AMM. AMM is the charity in Morocco; GYE is far away in London."

Mr. Bishara stirred his tea thoughtfully. He considered his guests and went back to stirring his tea. For a moment, Naomi thought he hadn't heard her question and was about to repeat it.

"I tell you something," he began. He looked somewhat apprehensively from Paul to Naomi and back. "I do not want you to repeat to anyone what I am going to tell you. You understand?"

Paul said, "We understand. We will keep what you say in confidence."

Bishara continued: "Al-Rashid called me on Friday and asked me to meet with you. He asked me to tell you how happy I am to be working with AMM Casablanca. I am happy, but only a little bit. We are not achieving what we could achieve. Mr. Sidqi is a nice fellow, but he sits in his office all day. He should go out and tell the world how great is AMM. Entrepreneurs and mentors should be queuing up. We should be receiving offers for much money. Some is happening, but not much."

Mr. Ibrahim Hajjar looked like a modern Moses. He had a mane of white hair and a full, white beard. His large, dark eyes looked out benevolently across a large nose. He was wearing immaculate canvas trousers and a soft leather jacket over a blue dress shirt. He explained that he had started out after university writing software for computer games, started his own gaming company, had sold it, and was now working as a "kind of consultant to Maroc Telecom, but I'm also developing some crazy new applications for Nokia." He went on to say that he was currently a mentor to three entrepreneurs and had worked previously with two others.

"Have you had any mentor training?" Naomi asked.

He shook his head. "No, I was not offered training, but for me, was not a problem. You see, Miss Evensen, to be a business mentor one needs three things: business experience, good communication skills and a real commitment to the success of the young person. I am sixty-two years old. I have had much experience in business—some good, some not so good—but I stored it up here. (He pointed to his temple.) I like very much to talk to people. I try to be sincere. At age sixty-two, I have some wealth, and I like very much to create some more Ibrahim Hajjars."

Paul and Naomi smiled. "Ibrahim," Paul asked, "would you be willing to teach a course for other mentors at AMM?"

"You have course materials?"

"Yes."

"OK. I may follow Ibrahim's script rather than AMM's script. But OK. Mentors will learn."

* * *

The train had begun to gather speed as it clattered through the tan and white suburbs of Casablanca on its way to Marrakech. In the distance, Paul could make out the tall, stone tower of a mosque.

"Naomi, do you think that Sidqi is gay?"

She stifled a laugh. "He's as queer as a three shekel note. Couldn't you tell?"

"I'm never completely sure about that sort of thing. I find that women are much better at spotting gay men."

"I assume you can spot gay women."

"I don't know. I think Catherine could usually tell."

"Oh, Paul, you're hopeless! Anyway, trust me, he's gay and a nice guy, but pretty lazy. Why do you ask?"

"I was trying to think if there could be any connection between Sidqi being gay and his excellent relationship with Al-Rashid."

"Oh, I see. Well, I don't think that Al-Rashid is gay—either one of them. But . . . (she paused to consider) . . . I don't think the Prophet was very keen on homosexuality. Gay people have problems in this culture. Maybe . . . maybe Yusuf provides some kind of protection for Sidqi in return for his enthusiastic support."

There were six people they hadn't met before in the meeting room at OilMaroc. Mr. Al-Zahari, as chairman of the board of AMM, sat at the head of the table, with Paul on his right and Naomi on his left. Guy Labossiere of Demoitte had seated himself next to Paul. They had shaken hands with the other board members, and Paul was arranging the business cards in front of him to correspond to the seating arrangement. That way, he would be able to mention each individual's name when questions were asked. *An impressive group of people,* Paul thought. *All these people are at least director or vice president, and all represent multinational or big Moroccan companies"*

Mr. Al-Zahari opened the meeting with a welcome; he then called on each of the attendees to introduce him or herself. Besides Naomi, there was only one other woman present. The chairman thanked Paul and Naomi for taking the time to brief them on their preliminary findings. He emphasised the value of GYE's accreditation of AMM in terms of its credibility and ability to raise funds.

Paul thanked the board for the meeting, and he told them that he and Miss Evensen would meet later that afternoon to give the same oral report to Mr. Al-Rashid. Paul said that the assessment of AMM had revealed several important deficiencies. First, was the lack of agreed and documented financial controls. This lack of controls made the charity vulnerable to fraud, though he hastened to add, they had found no direct evidence of fraud. He pointed out that there was no comprehensive audit of the books of AMM. Secondly, he reported that there was no written operations manual. "Thirdly," he said, "and perhaps most important in terms of our meeting this afternoon is that the governance of AMM does not meet the standards set by GYE."

The lone female board member, the human resource vice president of a large bank said, a little defensively, "Your last comment sounds like a criticism of this board."

"Yes, Ms. Amari, I'm afraid it is. GYE expects the boards of its chapters to function much like the board of a bank, setting the overall strategy, controlling in broad terms what is done, how it is done, and examining the results actually achieved."

Ms. Amari looked around the table. "Isn't that what we do?"

"No, Haifa, we're more of a talking shop," Guy Labossiere interposed. "What Paul is talking about is establishment of policy for matters such as how we raise funds and how funds are spent."

There was further discussion on this point until it gradually became clear that what GYE expected was a complete change in the role of the board.

At one point, Paul said, "It's not only a different role that we're asking the board to take, we're also asking you to see ourselves entirely differently—Mr. Al-Rashid works for you."

Efraim's Eye

A board member who had been quiet until that time suddenly said, "He thinks we work for him!"

Heads were nodding around the table.

Paul said, "What we're asking you to do involves more work and more risk, but it will also make AMM a better, more valuable charity. Are you up for it?"

There was a moment of silence as board members exchanged glances. The quiet member, the IT director of an insurance company, turned toward the chairman. "What are your thoughts, Hatim?"

Mr. Al-Zahari pushed his chair back and laced his fingers behind his head. "When I first met Paul last week, we discussed this matter, and I realised that I haven't provided this board with the leadership it has needed. At this point, I am willing to step aside, or if you wish, continue as your chairman if you'll give me a prod from time to time."

Guy Labossiere said, "I move that we re-appoint Hatim Al-Zahari as chairman of the board of ash-Shbab Mshrw Maroc."

"Second!"

Every hand was raised.

"Motion carried!"

"Paul, can you explain to the board what GYE will do next?" Mr. Al-Zahari asked.

Paul responded, "When I return to London, I will prepare a draft of my report for review by Miss Evensen and by Mr. Al-Rashid during a teleconference. The report is then finalised and I'll present it at a meeting of the Accreditation Board in three weeks time. The board will decide whether to reaccredit AMM, or whether to deny or suspend accreditation. That decision, along with any action items will be communicated in writing to Mr. Al-Rashid and the board."

After a long moment of silence, Haifa Amari said, "Paul, may I emphasise the importance of GYE accreditation to the future of AMM? Please, please, don't withhold accreditation!"

Naomi intervened, "Everyone at GYE, including the Accreditation Committee, knows how important accreditation is to our chapters. But it's important to understand that if the GYE brand name and our accreditation are to have any value, the process has to have teeth. If it doesn't, it will become impossible for all of our chapters to raise money."

Yusuf was in his office when they arrived. "This is Mr. Tasneen of the Moroccan Ministry for Employment. I believe you wanted to meet with him. I have an appointment, but I shall return in about one hour."

"Thank you, Yusuf," Naomi said, "we'll meet with you later."

Mr. Tasneen was a rather handsome, clean-shaven, young man in his late twenties. He seemed to have a perpetual smile and a sunny disposition. He was dressed in a grey polyester suit and a white shirt. Having seated himself in Mr. Al-Rashid's chair, he gestured for Paul and Naomi to take the seats in front of him. The three exchanged business cards.

Paul said, "Thank you for coming here, Mr. Tasneen, we could just as well have gone to your offices for this meeting."

"Oh, it's no inconvenience. I just concluded another meeting in this area."

Naomi asked, "Could you tell us about your role in the Ministry for Employment?"

"Yes, of course. I am deputy assistant to the head of the Youth Employment Section." He paused to gauge the effect of his words. "Youth Employment, as you will understand, is responsible for the development of strategies and programs to reduce the level of youth unemployment in Morocco. Currently, the level of unemployment among young people, aged sixteen to thirty is thirty-four percent, and this constitutes a threat to social stability."

"Does the figure you mention include both males and females?" Naomi asked, looking up from her notes.

"The figure of thirty-four percent is for males only."

Paul asked, "What would the number be if females were included?"

Mr. Tasneen studied the ceiling for a moment. "I don't, at the moment, recall the figure, but it would be somewhat higher."

"And," Paul continued, "does thirty-four percent cover only those people not in full time employment?"

"No, it covers people who are not in any employment or education."

Paul made a note. "Quite a serious problem."

"Yes, and this is where the charity AMM and Mr. Al-Rashid have been so helpful. The program offered by AMM not only provides employment to young entrepreneurs, but the expectation is that after two years of trading, the average young entrepreneur will offer employment to three other young people. And more people will be added as the business grows."

"And so your ministry has been providing funding to AMM?"

"Oh, yes! We have provided nearly two million dirhams over the last three years!" He smiled broadly at the visitors. *That's about fifty thousand pounds per year,* Paul thought. "And for the future?"

"We are setting aside twenty million dirhams, perhaps more!"

Paul also studied the ceiling, "A ten-fold increase!"

Mr. Tasneen nodded.

Naomi said, "It sounds as if you're quite happy with the work AMM has done."

"Yes, very much so! Nearly two hundred entrepreneurs, and soon we'll be adding one thousand five hundred more!"

"How was your meeting with Mr. Tasneen?" Yusuf asked on his return.

Paul said, "He certainly thinks highly of AMM."

"Ah, yes, well, he has been a loyal supporter." He studied Paul and Naomi for a moment. Then he asked, "And how was your meeting with the board? Just as positive, I hope."

There was silence in the room for a moment, broken only by the sound of Naomi's pen busily at work. Paul said, "Well, there is much to be done, Yusuf, in order for AMM to retain its accreditation."

Yusuf nodded slightly. Paul went through the same litany of changes he had outlined to the board, but adding more detail, including the need for AMM to adopt written personnel policies and to move to its own offices.

Yusuf pushed his chair back and studied the far wall as if the answers to his concerns were written there in fine print.

"There is no way we can afford to lose our accreditation." He paused. "I have been thinking that AMM should hire additional staff. That will surely solve the problems you mention about personnel policy, operations manual and financial manual. And I agree, of course, that AMM should have its own head office—as we do in Fez and Casablanca—so that is just a matter of finding the right premises. As I think I mentioned, the office is here only because it represents a savings to AMM. The audit of AMM's accounts is certainly not a problem. I have not called for a full audit just for cost reasons. Perhaps Demoitte would perform the audit on a pro bono basis. That leaves only the matter of governance by the board. What was their reaction to your proposal?"

"They recognise that the role GYE wishes a board to assume represents more work and more risk, collectively, but they are keen to go ahead."

"Well, there you are then! So I look forward to seeing your draft report in about ten days?"

"Yes, we'll send it to you by e-mail and arrange a call to discuss it."

"I don't get it," Naomi said when they were in the car on the way to Riad el Norj. "Why didn't he fume and rant and rage? We basically told him his charity needs to start over—that it's rubbish."

Paul shook his head. "I don't know. He's a very complex, clever individual. Maybe he felt that ranting and raving would only confirm our suspicions and lead us to toughen up the report. He might be thinking that by being accommodating, he will induce us to write a more lenient report."

"Maybe so. And that Tasneen guy? Something about him gets my alarm bells ringing. I know!" She glanced at Paul triumphantly. "I'm going to call his number and see if he really works at the Ministry for Employment!"

She retrieved the business card from her case and punched the number into her iPhone. There was a brief conversation in

Efraim's Eye

Arabic. She put the phone down. "The operator says he's no longer employed there. Mosa was right!"

* * *

At the hotel, they scrubbed one another in the hammam. Naomi broke away to check the door. "There's no lock on it," she reported.

"Later then."

As they sat in the lounge, sipping sherry, Paul asked the question whose answer he was dreading. "Where will you be going tomorrow, Naomi?"

Matter-of-factly, she replied, "I'm flying to Madrid and on to Buenos Aires."

"So will you be in Argentina for a while?"

"For a few days. Then I've got to check on Uruguay, Paraguay and Bolivia."

Paul shook his head in wonder. "How do you manage your clothes? I mean you always look so nice. Do you ever get tired of wearing the same clothes?"

She laughed. "I would get <u>very</u> tired if I had just one suitcase of clothes being washed over and over! But I have a deal with GYE that for any month I don't return to London, they pay me a thousand pounds, after tax. It's actually a good deal for them because my return airfare would usually be more than that. So anyway, every few weeks, I go on a shopping spree to replace items I'm tired of. The old items go to charity. Madrid airport is a great place to shop."

"Do you think you'll ever stop being a nomad? I'm beginning to think you must have some Bedouin blood."

She was silent for a moment, gazing at the floor. She shrugged and said quietly, "I don't know, Paul." Then brightening, "Let's go to that Concorde restaurant in the Hotel d' Marseilles again. I think we both liked that."

They both liked it again. Paul was able to throw off the cloak of sadness he had been feeling and emulate Naomi's joyful living for the moment. He complimented her, teased her, laughed with her, treasured her, and when he made love to her later, he did so joyfully.

"Before we go to the airport, Mohammed, we need to stop at the British embassy."

"Yes, sir."

"Who are we going to see there?" Naomi asked.

"I spoke to a Major Bancroft. He's the assistant military attaché, and he said he could see us."

"Why are we seeing a military person? Shouldn't we see someone on the commercial side?"

"Well, I just felt that the military are more likely to make the right connections and get action."

Major Thomas Bancroft appeared to be in his mid-thirties; he wore the summer khaki uniform, neatly pressed with two rows of decorations on his left breast. He was blonde, blue-eyed, with a neatly trimmed moustache and a foxy nose. Clearly, he hadn't been expecting a female visitor, but he was polite and deferential to Naomi.

Paul said, "Miss Evensen is a colleague of mine at Global Youth Enterprise. It's a charity helping young people start a business."

The major nodded. "I believe you said that you were in the British Army, Mr. Winthorpe?"

"Actually, I joined the Army and moved to the SAS. I spent three years in Northern Ireland."

"Were you an officer?"

"When I left the service, I was a captain."

"Ever have any regrets about leaving the service?"

"Yes and no. I missed the camaraderie and the gung-ho spirit, but Northern Ireland seemed like an unending hell hole at the time."

"You said you might have a lead on the identity of a terrorist."

"Yes, there is a man named Efraim Al-Rashid—I don't know if that's his real name—he's apparently the half-brother of the man who runs the GYE charity in Morocco. He preaches jihad at a mosque here in Marrakech. One of the employees of GYE told us that he looks very much like the missing suspect in the Casablanca bombings."

"Have you gone to the police?"

"No, we haven't. We have concerns about this man's possible connections to the police."

"OK. Have you got a picture of him?"

"Yes. There are several pictures, here, on my mobile phone; I can send them to you. Also, you may want to have a look at this website." Paul handed the major a slip of paper.

Major Bancroft studied the images on Paul's phone, then he turned to his computer and typed, "www.bakkalimosque.ma/imam." After a few moments, Arabic text appeared on his screen. For several minutes, he sat reading the text. Then he picked up his phone and dialed. What followed was a conversation in Arabic. He covered the mouthpiece of the phone and asked, "Have you got anything else, Mr. Winthorpe?"

"Yes," Paul said, "We have here a recording of him speaking at the mosque last Friday." Paul handed the small recorder to the major. Major Bancroft spoke again on the phone, obviously referring to the recorder. Then he gestured toward Naomi and Paul while speaking. Naomi held up her hands in negative gesture. The major, clearly surprised that Naomi followed his conversation, covered the mouthpiece again and spoke with her in Arabic. After he had hung up, he said, "I didn't realise that Miss Evensen spoke Arabic. She told me that you have some concerns about being identified to the Moroccan authorities."

Paul said, "Yes. We know Mr. Al-Rashid. He is well-connected in Morocco, and if his actions match his words, we don't want him looking for us, and we don't want the name of our charity connected to any investigation."

"Understood. May I borrow this?" He held up the recorder. "You gave me your business card, and I'll send the recorder to you after we've downloaded it."

When they were in the car again, Paul asked, "Do you know who Major Bancroft was speaking to, Naomi?"

"No. I couldn't tell. Probably, it was somebody in the Moroccan military." She turned to Paul. "I didn't know you were in the SAS."

"It was a long time ago, Naomi."

She looked out the window at the passing houses and nodded.

Naomi's flight to Madrid departed before Paul's flight to London. She had checked her suitcase; her boarding pass and passport were in her hand. "I better go, Paul," she said.

For a long moment, they embraced wordlessly.

"Love you, Paul," she said.

"I love you, Naomi."

She turned and walked through the departure gate.

Chapter 10

READINESS

At home, once again in Marrakech, Efraim went immediately to the Bakkali Mosque to give thanks to God for his success on the trip. The mosque was nearly deserted, but Efraim knelt in front of the minrab niche and began to pray. He prayed, *"Thank you great Allah for Your many blessings and for the success I have achieved during my trip. Your might has preserved me from my enemies: the Taliban and the Russian spies. Your gracious wisdom has been bestowed on me so that I could avoid their evil traps and snares. Thank You for guiding me to Tbilisi Steelworks where the great hammer to glorify You is being made. Thank You for leading me to Baku and for granting me the knowledge and the supplies with which I will make the great weapon to glorify Your name. Thank You for supplying me with the explosive powder and the detonators that will destroy the heathen infidels. Thank You, great Allah, for granting me a place of supreme importance in Your grand Islamic design!"*

As Efraim was leaving the mosque from the main portal, he encountered several of the faithful coming to pray.

"Peace be with you, Imam," one of them said.

"The blessings of Allah be upon you," Efraim replied.

Another of the faithful said, *"You have been away for some time, Imam, on an important mission, I suppose."*

"*You are correct. It was a mission of great importance to Allah. But it is not yet complete. I will have to be away from Marrakech twice more to complete the mission, Allah willing.*"

"*Your mission will—I am sure—glorify Allah and reflect the perfection of Islam,*" the first one said.

A third person said, "*I am sure your mission has great humanitarian importance, Imam. Can you tell us more about it?*"

Efraim nodded benevolently. "*It is indeed a mission of great importance, but Allah has spoken to me. He has warned me not to unveil the mission until it is complete.*" And he strode away.

The third of the faithful said to the other two, as they looked after their departing imam, "*He is a man of great religious fervour, but I find little kindness in him.*"

Yusuf was eager to meet with Efraim to hear about his trip. When they had met in Yusuf's office and said their prayers together, Efraim said, "*I have assembled all the components of the hammer, Brother. Praise be to Allah!*"

"*Where are these components, Brother?*"

"*They are in Tbilisi.*" When Efraim saw the surprised look on Yusuf's face, he explained, briefly, the reasons for this.

"*So you had no luck in Pakistan or in Afghanistan?*"

Efraim nodded. "*In fact the Taliban tried to rob me of my funds.*"

"*May the devil take them! How much did they rob you of, Brother?*"

"*They got nothing and they are dead!*"

Yusuf was startled; he considered this. "*You didn't . . .*"

"*Yes, Brother, I killed the devil's spawn!*"

"*But Brother,*" Yusuf protested, "*the Holy Qur'an tells us 'Do not kill each other for Allah is merciful to you.'*

The Holy Book also says, 'Never should a believer kill another believer."

"Aye, Brother, but in the fifth sura (chapter), *the Holy Book also announces, 'We decreed to the children of Israel that if anyone kills a person—unless in retribution for murder or spreading corruption in the land—it is as if he kills all mankind.' Reflect, Brother! The Taliban are not believers. They are murderers who kill their neighbours, and they are thieves who spread corruption. They deserved to die, and they are now lamenting their sins and their non-belief in the flames of hell!"*

Yusuf was not convinced by his brother's religious arguments, but he was prepared to excuse the killing of the Taliban on the grounds of self-defense. There was something else that quite perplexed Yusuf. *"Tell me, why the Russian authorities were prepared to provide you with explosives to use against a Western target. They must know that this duplicity will be discovered!"*

"It was a sting, Brother! I did not tell you yet, but the Russians were out to trap anyone who is prepared to buy their explosives. Probably they have the same trap laid out for anyone seeking to buy enriched uranium."

"What transpired?"

"I narrowly escaped capture, and I was forced to kill a Russian spy."

Yusuf studied Efraim with concern. *"I am anxious, Brother, that you do not step too far and attract the wrath of Almighty Allah!"*

Efraim shrugged. *"The spy was an infidel, and if I had not killed him, I would be rotting in a Russian prison."*

Yusuf judged that it was best to change the discussion, so he inquired about Efraim's future plans.

He listened and nodded as Efraim gave a summary of his intentions.

Then Yusuf commented, "*Brother, there are two people here on business for our charity. Should you encounter them, it is best if you treat them with courtesy.*"

Efraim sneered, "*I have already met them. There is a Jew girl and a Christian capitalist. The girl is very strange. She has the appearance of an angel, but I feel the devil radiating from her. We do not need them to tell us how to run our charity!*"

"*Brother, they are People of the Book* (the Qur'an's name for monotheistic worshipers in other Abrahamic religions). *But, more important, they have the power to remove the accreditation from our charity.*"

"*Let them! We don't need their accreditation!*"

"*You are mistaken, Brother! Without their accreditation, we will no longer obtain bank loans or corporate contributions. Should that happen, funding of your activities will cease!*"

There was silence in the office as Efraim considered this. After some moments he said, "*I will stay clear of them.*"

Efraim judged that it was best to do what he had to do next in Morocco, rather than in England. So, in the souq, he bought three, white canvas vests in different sizes. They were the type of vests that fishermen wear with plenty of pockets to hold lures and other fishing tackle. He also bought two metres of matching fabric, fifteen bars of soap, twelve kilos of children's glass marbles, and six metres of electric wire.

Efraim took these items to an old seamstress who worked in the poor fringes of the souq. "*Ancient mother, I have a piece of work for you to complete, and I will pay you fairly for your work.*"

"*What is this work, Imam?*" she asked, looking askance at the pile of goods he had placed on her workbench.

Efraim took out a sketch that he had made of the finished product. "*I wish you to add pockets to these vests, as I have shown in this drawing here.*"

The old woman put on her glasses and studied the sketch. *"This is a jacket for a suicide bomber!"* she exclaimed, looking up in horror at Efraim.

"No, Ancient Mother, it just looks like such a garment. These are only costumes for a theatre group." Efraim opened the packages of soap and marbles. *"You see here, Ancient Mother, instead of explosives, there is soap, and instead of ball bearings, there are children's marbles. However, to the actors and the audience, they will seem, as you say, like a bomber's jacket."*

The old woman shook her head. *"I do not approve of making a joke of such dreadful things!"*

"I agree with you, Ancient Mother!" Efraim said, *"The play is a serious work—no one laughs—it emphasises the sin of such actions. In the third act, the bombers repent and take off their jackets. As a consequence, Allah forgives them."*

The old woman looked at Efraim thoughtfully for a few moments. Finally, she nodded. *"Two hundred and fifty dirhams per jacket. How shall I place the wire?"*

That's very expensive! Efraim thought, but he said, *"Use your imagination Ancient Mother. It should look real."*

As he rode the bus back home, he thought, *the Holy Qur'an says we are always to tell the truth, but if we do, it is impossible to complete Allah's Plan.*

When Efraim arrived in the UK, he checked into the same hotel—on the northern edge of the Soho area—he had used previously. It was a part of London where he could blend into the crowds. There was also the Lebanese restaurant he liked as well as several others which offered halal food. At the same time, it was an area of unfamiliar contrasts: wealthy hedonists strolling to restaurants and theatres close by seedy sex shops. Efraim liked to think that some of the people who were dressed in their evening finery would be amongst those who met their doom at his hand.

He thought, *These people care about nothing but their worldly pleasures. I shall see them cascading down to hell!*

To Efraim, the sex trade in Soho was a source of fascination and revulsion. In Morocco, such activities were banned, and in no other country had he seen such a profligate display of human vice. *All these women will certainly burn in hell for their lewdness, their displays and their . . .* He didn't name the acts they committed, but he saw the acts clearly in his mind, and they made his groin ache.

That night he had a dream—a recurrent dream. He is in a small, dark space. There is a large washing sink and a door to the hallway just behind him. There are several metal buckets on the floor at his feet, and he can feel the damp clothing brushing against his right shoulder. In front of him is another door, open just two centimetres. He leans forward to see what is in the other room. It is vacant, but he can wait. In the room is the grand, enameled hipbath with its higher, curving backrest at one end. There is also a porcelain sink, a white dresser, matching stool and a freestanding towel rack. His patience is rewarded by the arrival of the maid, carrying a huge ceramic pitcher. The maid empties the pitcher into the bath, and she leaves, closing the door behind her. Wisps of steam rise from the bath.

His mother enters and refills the pitcher at a tap below the sink. She pours water into the bath, putting the pitcher down several times to test the water. She is satisfied with the temperature. She removes her grey Pleiku tunic, folding it carefully and draping it over the towel rack. She removes her sandals and unbuttons the white flared-leg trousers, which are also folded and placed on top of the tunic. He leans forward in anticipation. She grips the hem of her heavy jersey top, and pulls it over her head. Her large breasts have come into view. Last to be removed are the long, white jersey drawers. There, at last, is the black thatch. His heart is pounding is his throat with excitement. She turns to view herself in the mirror to the left, lifting her breasts, inclining her head from side to side, and then passing her hands across her belly to her groin. Clumsily, he eases himself from the confines of his trousers. She seats herself on the stool and takes a sponge from the bath. Languidly, she begins to wash herself, her legs spread wide. The sponge is dropped back in the bath. Her hands and his are busy. He can see her gleaming pinkness.

Suddenly, the searing culmination overtakes him, and with in involuntary spasm, his leg upsets a bucket. At the clatter, she leaps to her feet and flings open the door.

He wakes, stammering newly invented excuses, but no excuse could save him from the caning he received from his father—a caning so severe that it raised permanent white welts. And no excuse could mitigate the withdrawal of his mother's affection.

After dinner that evening, Efraim walked down Shaftsbury Avenue toward Piccadilly Circus, and turned down a side street into the less salubrious section of Soho. A buxom, blonde woman was standing in a doorway, smoking a cigarette. She was wearing pink hot pants, a sleeveless scooped neck T-shirt, and silver high heels. She winked at Efraim, and when he paused to take her in, she beckoned him with a forefinger and smouldering look. Efraim's mouth opened to say something —he didn't know what—but nothing came out. She was blonde and had large breasts. He could see her nipples. He felt the surge of lust radiate from his loins.

"Follow me, big boy!" the blonde commanded. She turned, stepped inside and began to climb a flight of stairs.

Mesmerised, Efraim followed.

At the top of the stairs, she pushed open a door and entered. He followed; she closed the door behind them. In the room, lit by a three-lamp ceiling fixture, there were a large bed with stained pink sheets, a dresser and two wooden chairs.

"Forty quid," she announced as she kicked off her shoes.

"I give...I give...twenty...twenty-five," Efraim stammered.

The blonde put her hands on her hips. "It's forty, or you can go jerk off."

Efraim inclined his head in acceptance.

She pulled the T-shirt over her head and slid the shorts down her legs.

Efraim recoiled in surprise. "You . . . are not a real blonde!" he said, pointing at her crotch.

"That's right, big boy. I don't bleach my pussy . . . You goin' to get undressed, or you just here to look?"

Efraim suddenly noticed a gold object hanging from a chain between her breasts. "Take it off!" he ordered.

She looked at him. "Take what off?"

"Take that off!" he repeated, pointing at the gold object.

"My crucifix? That stays on. That's my good luck charm."

"Take it off!" he shouted, and he suddenly lunged at her, taking hold of the chain. She kneed him in the groin, just as he snapped the chain, and the crucifix fell to the floor.

"Ooooh!" he was bent double in pain.

"Help! Help me!" she yelled.

The door burst open, and a wiry man in a black shirt and jeans surged in. Pausing for a moment, he demanded, "What's the problem, Rosey?"

"He was trying to steal my crucifix, and he broke my necklace!" Warily, Rosey reached down to pick up the crucifix.

"OK, buddy, clear off. You owe the lady forty quid for breaking her chain."

Efraim shook his head, angrily. He was still trying, in considerable pain, to stand up straight. Suddenly, the man struck Efraim a hard kidney punch in the side with the edge of his hand. Efraim slumped to the floor in agony.

"You go back to work, Rosey," the man ordered, "I'll take care of this som bitch."

Rosey pulled on her clothes and quickly left. Some minutes later, Efraim also departed, still in pain and with forty pounds less in his pocket.

He was raging inside at the humiliation he had suffered. *I must get even, he thought, that bastard infidel devil took advantage of me when that Satan's spawn of a woman attacked my privates! But the Chief's*

Special—the weapon that Allah gave me—is in Tbilisi. I could not take the chance to bring it with me.

Efraim considered how he might punish the man who had humiliated him. He knew that finding a gun would be difficult. Could he buy a knife and slit the man's throat? Yes, he could do that!

But a voice inside told him that there would be risks in attempting such an attack—that the attack might be thwarted—and he could be arrested and imprisoned. He told himself: I must stay focused on the plan!

Efraim called Ameen Kamali, the Yemeni whom he considered to be the best choice among the possible associates, and arranged to meet him in Luton, where he lived, on the following day. Realising that he could not meet Ameen in a public place, Efraim reserved a room for half a day at the Nice Night Hotel, a modern budget motel in downtown Luton.

Efraim asked the Yemeni, *"Are you prepared to participate in this great project of faith that we spoke about previously?"*

"Yes, sir, I am. Can you tell me more about it now?" Ameen Kamali asked.

"The time has not yet come when I can reveal the glorious scope of the project, but the time is approaching when I can do that. What we must do today is ascertain that you have sufficient faith in the Lord Allah, the Merciful, to glorify him in martyrdom and to be welcomed into Heaven."

"Yes, sir, I am eager to enter Heaven as a glorious martyr."

"Then there is one item of preparation that we can complete today. Tell me, what is your jacket size?"

"Sir, I wear a thirty-eight regular."

Efraim opened the suitcase he had with him, and removed one of the jackets that had been altered by the Ancient Mother.

"See if this fits, Ameen. Be careful of the wires. Do not pull any of them out."

Ameen put on the jacket and closed the buttons in front. The jacket was very bulky and heavy. While it fit reasonably well, it limited the freedom of his movement. Ameen stood in front of the mirror in the hotel room, inclining his head from side-to-side as he appraised himself. He smiled at his own image, and looked down at the jacket. *"Where is the button that I must push?"*

"That has not been installed as yet. We do not wish to have a premature detonation."

"No, of course not. Is this my jacket then? Should I keep it with me?"

"No, that's not necessary. It is your jacket. I will mark it with your name and keep it with the others."

"How many others are there, sir?"

"There will be at least three of us."

Ameen nodded. *"You are planning to be a martyr also, sir?"*

"Yes, of course!"

Efraim arranged further meetings with the Somali, Hamzah, and Bathshar, the Pakistani, for the next day. Hamzah assured Efraim that he would be alone in his council flat in Brixton, and Bathshar would meet Efraim in the lobby of the Nice Night Hotel in High Wycombe in the afternoon. Efraim was very pleased with himself: he had one very committed associate in Ameen and could choose one of the remaining two.

After dinner that night, Efraim was walking back to his hotel when he encountered the auburn haired woman once again. She did not seem to remember his rejection of her or recognise him; again she asked, "Fancy a good time?"

Her sleeveless red shirt was open even more than he remembered; the swell of her breasts and her nipples were very evident.

He paused to take her in: the flaming red hair, the crimson lips and the long bare legs.

She slowly raised the hem of her miniskirt, revealing her auburn hair. "Come on, big boy, let's have a good time."

Efraim's testicles were still sore from the previous night's attack, but his libido was rampant. *I must do this woman!* he thought, motivated both by physical need and the desire to reprove himself.

"How much?" he asked.

"Fifty quid."

"I give you forty—what I paid last night."

"More work for me, if you came off last night. Forty-five. Take it or leave it."

Efraim took it.

She was enthusiastic. She seemed to appreciate him as a man. She had, he thought, the most beautiful body that a woman could have: wide hips, long smooth legs, firm breasts, and pale skin. True, her face was very plain and creased, revealing her age of over forty, but her face expressed her apparent pleasure.

"Stay with me tonight," he commanded.

"That's a hundred quid extra," she replied.

Very reluctantly, he shook his head, and she departed.

Damnation! he thought, *why do I have this need of unclean women? She was beautiful, but she is surely unclean! She is Christian. She is an infidel! She sells her body. She is therefore unclean. The Holy Qur'an says, 'Unclean women are for unclean men. Clean women are for clean men.' I am not an unclean man! I am a clean man! Yet I have never had a clean woman! It must be the devil who tempts me in this way.*

He fell to the floor and began to pray fervently, *O Great Merciful Allah, cure me of this obsession with unclean women!*

Nervously, Hamzah welcomed Efraim into his tidy two-room flat. There were sheer, white curtains at the windows, and a prayer rug, facing southeast in the centre of the room. Efraim began the discussion much as he had with Ameen. When he removed the vest from the suitcase and handed it to Hamzah, the nervousness was more apparent. Hamzah's face was glossy with perspiration, and his hands were trembling.

"Try this one on for size," Efraim instructed.

Hamzah held the jacket at arms length and asked, "Is there explosive in it?"

"Yes, of course. Try it on!"

Gingerly, Hamzah slid his arms through the armholes. Then he froze, stooped over under the psychological weight of the jacket. Slowly, he looked around the room until he caught sight of his own image in a mirror across the room. His whole body began to shake, as if he were about to have a convulsion. He rushed to the kitchen sink and vomited. For some moments, he stood retching, bent over the sink. Then, slowly and carefully, he removed the jacket, and holding it by the collar, he gave it back to Efraim. "I can't do it," he said.

Efraim sneered at him, brusquely took the jacket, and manhandled it roughly back into the suitcase, while Hamzah looked on, trembling with fear.

"May the devil take you, coward!" Efraim admonished, as he slammed the door behind him.

Bathshar was waiting for Efraim in the lobby of the Nice Night Hotel. As he tried on the jacket in a room, Bathshar was neither eager nor emotional; he was resigned. "Will my name be mentioned on television and in the newspapers?" he asked.

"Of course!" Efraim told him.

"And will they speak of me as a great martyr in the mosque?"

"There is no doubt of that!"

He looked past Efraim as he asked, "Is Heaven just as the Qur'an says it is, where one can recline on couches in a beautiful garden and be waited on by lovely girls?"

"That is God's promise!"

Efraim had his two associates. Now it was time to retrieve the hammer from Tbilisi. But first, after dinner, he walked his usual route back to the hotel. "Why should I change my chosen path to avoid an infidel woman?" he reasoned. He had not decided what he would do when he met her, but secretly, he knew that he would give her one hundred and fifty pounds to spend the night with him. But she was not there. *Perhaps Allah has heard my prayer, and has decided to remove her from my temptation.*

The next day, in Croydon, Efraim perused the used car lots. What he wanted was an older, prestige car that was still in good condition. He wanted a prestige car for several reasons: when he crossed a border, he wanted to be recognised for what he was—a man of substance and not a refugee. As there was a long trip ahead, the car should be comfortable, and it should have large wheels. He bought a fourteen-year-old, black Range Rover for £3,995. It was a diesel-fueled car with a full service history and 109,000 miles. The external finish was excellent. The leather upholstery was in good condition, and it was air-conditioned.

Efraim took the P&O ferry from Dover to Calais. He showed his (forged) Greek national identity card to the French immigration official in Dover. From Calais, his route took him past Reims to Dijon, where he spent the night in an autoroute motel. The next day, he went past Geneva, and into Italy, where in Piacenza, he stopped for the night at an autostrada albergo. On the third day of his trip, Efraim reached Ancona, on the Adriatic coast, where he boarded the overnight ferry for Igoumenitsa, Greece.

The following day, late in the evening, he arrived at a small motel just outside of Kesan, Turkey, having showed his passport with the Turkish visa. He crossed the Bosporus and reached Ankara on the sixth day. The seventh and eighth days were spent driving east on relatively poor Turkish roads. At the Georgian border, Efraim showed his passport with the Georgian visa and drove on to Tbilisi after a nine-day trip of over 5,000 kilometres.

Efraim was keenly aware that, by that time, he was probably a wanted man in Georgia. Even if the authorities had not discovered Anton's body, they would have recovered his motorcycle, and would have concluded that Efraim was involved in Anton's disappearance. Then, too, there were all of Anton's secretive phone calls: what had he told his boss about Efraim? Finally, there was Borz, with the two mobile phones in the back of his truck. What, if any, connection did Borz have with the authorities?

All these thoughts led Efraim to the conclusion that it would be unwise for him to stay in downtown Tbilisi. He decided to search for accommodation near the Varketili metro station, which was the last metro line station not far from the airport. It was also the line that ran north and closest to Tbilisi Steelworks.

He parked the car near the Varketili station, and approached a group of high school aged boys who were on their way home. "Excuse me," he said, "can you help me? I don't speak Georgian. I'm trying to find accommodation in this area."

The boys consulted amongst themselves. Then, one of them turned to Efraim. "You want to rent an apartment?" he asked.

"Yes. A small apartment with a garage for my car."

There was another consultation. The boy said, "There is a shop called Kakheti where they arrange property rentals. You go down this street," he continued pointing, "and at the second intersection, you turn right. You will find Kakheti after one hundred metres on your left."

Five minutes later, Efraim entered Kakheti, and as he did so, a small bell above the door jingled. There was no one in the shop, but the walls were covered with photographs of houses and apartment buildings.

An old woman with a dark, wrinkled face and white hair in a Betty Davis style came into the shop. She said something in Georgian to which Efraim replied, "I am looking for a small apartment with a garage to rent."

The old woman muttered something and left the shop the way she had entered. Moments later a girl of about twelve in pigtails and a blue and grey school uniform entered from the rear of the shop. A woman who was probably her mother followed her.

"May I help you?" the girl asked. She looked at Efraim with a mixture of curiosity and self-confidence. The mother said nothing; she regarded him with her arms folded.

"Yes, I hope so," Efraim replied to the girl, and he repeated his request.

There was a brief dialogue between mother and daughter, at the conclusion of which the mother stepped forward and pointed sequentially to several photographs. The girl read aloud, in English, the particulars of each apartment to which her mother pointed.

Having listened carefully, Efraim asked about two of the apartments, and when he received an answer, he asked the girl, "May I see this one, please?" He pointed to a beige brick building of two stories where the ground floor was a series of garages.

"Yes, of course," the girl said. There followed a three-way conversation in two languages about how to get there. The issue was resolved when Efraim announced that he had a car and would gladly drive them there.

The apartment was about one kilometre away in what Efraim judged to be a working class neighbourhood with a series of shops on the main road. The garage was clean and vacant. The apartment above it consisted of a bedroom and living room/dining room/kitchen. There was a small bathroom with a shower. Furnishings consisted of off-white, IKEA-style bed, couch, table, and chairs. There were even green curtains decorated with daffodils.

Efraim signed the minimum contract for six months rent and gave the woman a deposit plus two months rent in advance of four thousand iaris (about fifteen hundred pounds). *Expensive, but essential,* Efraim thought, *and, leaving early, I won't get my deposit or the second month's rent back. But, I have under spent my travel budget.*

At the nearby shops, Efraim bought a pair of white workman's coveralls, a green hard hat and a lady's, straight-haired wig in chestnut. The woman in the hair dressing shop had difficulty understanding why a man would want to buy a lady's wig, but he finally got her to understand that it was for his wife who had cancer. Returning to the apartment, Efraim shaved off his beard, cut his hair and put on the wig, which he had shortened and tied in what he judged to be a masculine ponytail.

Dressed in the coveralls and hardhat, he was no longer recognisable. Surveying himself in the bathroom mirror, he considered his disguise to be *Excellent!* Efraim now felt that he could appear with reasonable safety in public. He assumed that the photograph taken by the tourist when Efraim had first met Anton had been circulated to the police. That photograph would have showed a bearded businessman, not a hard-working craftsman who carried the tools of his trade in his coverall pockets.

At the airport, Efraim placed a phone call from a public phone booth to Mr. Giorgadze at Tbilisi Steelworks, who informed him that his items should be collected at 10 a.m. tomorrow. Mr. Giorgadze wanted to know whether Mr. Al-Buktar was still staying at the Tbilisi Marriott? *They've planned another sting!* Efraim thought. *Why arrange a particular time for collection? Why ask if I'm staying at the Marriott, unless they want to track me? Also, if the casings will be available tomorrow morning, they're probably ready now. Besides, its four days after the promised date.* He decided that urgent action was required.

From the airport's checked baggage area, Efraim collected his suitcase that contained the RDX, the detonators, the Miravar and Bramothol, and some additional clothing.

At 2 a.m. he drove to Tbilisi Steelworks and parked at the rear of the building. It was absolutely quiet in the area. There was no sign of life; the building was nearly dark. Efraim could see no external evidence of an alarm system. At the back of the building, there was a large shutter door for goods in and goods out. This door was closed securely as was the smaller personnel door beside it. Further along the building, however, was an apparently disused door with an external padlock. Removing the hacksaw from his coveralls, he cut through the lock, entered and closed the door behind him. No alarm sounded. He found himself inside a vacant metal cage that was probably used to store high value items at one time. The metal door of the cage was padlocked on the inside, but the cage had no ceiling, only ten foot high-wire walls. Efraim put on his gloves, and grasping the wires, he pulled himself to the top. Carefully, he let himself down. Still no alarm.

The factory stretched into the gloom, fifty metres in each direction. There were low-wattage night-lights about every twenty metres, but they revealed only the outlines of major machine tools and the aisles.

Efraim took out his torch, switched it on and began to search. There was no sign of his casings in the right hand end of the factory. He reasoned that all six would be together and in plain sight. A cursory review of the left hand end also revealed nothing. *They've got to be here! I've got to look!* he thought.

He began opening cabinets and looking on shelves. Back at the right hand end of the factory, one particularly large steel table had two full-sized shelves beneath it. The first shelf had only a collection of old castings. He had to bend over to shine his light onto the lower shelf. There they were! At the back of the lower self!

Efraim found a large piece of cloth. He put the finished casings and liners on the fabric, tied the ends together and hoisted the parcel under one arm. At the rear personnel door, he found that it could readily be unlocked from the inside. He exited, locking and closing the door behind him. At the abandoned door through which he had entered, he put the padlock back in place, so that a casual observer would not notice that the lock had been disturbed.

Efraim kept himself busy the following day. At a shop, he bought several pots in which he could merge the polymers and heat them gently on his cooker until the liquid became very fluid and mixed easily with the RDX powder. Wearing rubber gloves, he scooped the newly made PBX into the casings, having sealed off a small space for the detonators. He slid the liners in over the carefully formed and tightly packed PBX. He surveyed the six curved metal boxes. *There is the hammer—almost ready! Time now to rest for an hour or two.*

He completed his work in the garage, and he thought he would sit outside—perhaps he would meet a willing, clean woman. There was a wooden, communal bench outside his apartment, so he sat and watched the passers by.

Several men nodded affably in his direction and passing school children waved to him shyly.

A man approached the apartment next to Efraim's, but seeing Efraim sitting on the bench, he came and sat next to Efraim.

The man, who was dressed like Efraim in craftsman's clothing, said something in Georgian.

Efraim said, "Sorry, I don't speak Georgian."

"Oh. My English very bad. Where you from?"

Efraim studied the man for a moment. There was nothing about the man to suggest that he was anything other than a local Tbilisi craftsman—probably a carpenter. "I'm from Morocco," Efraim said.

The man was surprised. He said, "So you speak Arabic and English?"

Efraim nodded.

"You move in yesterday?"

"Yes."

"What kind of work you do?"

Efraim said, "I set up and repair kitchens in Arabic restaurants."

"Work is good?"

"Yes."

The man shook his head. "My work very bad. I laid off today. No work. No money."

Efraim considered the man thoughtfully. Suddenly, he had an idea.

"My problem," Efraim confided, "is that my passport has been stolen. My company urgently needs me on another job. It will take a week or two to get a new passport. In the meantime, I'm losing a lot of money because I can't get to the job."

The man studied Efraim for a long moment. Then without a word, he rose and went into his apartment. *Damnation! It didn't work,* Efraim thought.

The man returned and sat down again; he studied Efraim's face for a moment. Then, he held out a little maroon booklet to Efraim. "Do you think this like you?" he asked.

"Yes. A little. The hairstyle is the same. Shape of the face is similar. Eyes are the same."

"I sell this to you," the man announced. "Help you get out of Georgia. You have other passports?" Efraim nodded.

"If you buy, you get work. I have money."

Efraim studied the Georgia passport. "How much you want?"

"I want one thousand laris."

"Is too much. I can wait. I pay you two hundred dollars."

The man considered this offer. He had no immediate need of his passport, and he could get a replacement, claiming it had been stolen. "You pay me two hundred fifty dollars, we have deal!"

They shook hands, and exchanged the passport for the currency.

Thank you, Allah, for this kindness You have shown me! Efraim thought. *At the Georgia border, they will be carefully checking all foreign passports, but they know that this man they seek, Mohammed, is not a Georgian.*

That evening, Efraim moved the Range Rover into the garage and closed the door. He removed the spare tyre, deflated it, and levered the tyre off the rim. Carefully, he arranged the six shaped charges around the inside of the tyre. Then, he levered it back onto the rim and stowed it again in the spare wheel well. It looked perfectly normal; one could not see, without touching it, that the tyre had been deflated.

At about 4 am, Efraim got up and removed the license plates from a car that was parked in the street. He replaced his U.K. plates with the stolen Georgia plates, having carefully hidden the U.K. plates in the Land Rover. He wanted to be as much a Georgian as possible.

By quarter to five, he was on his way.

At the border, there was a long queue to cross into Turkey. *They are certainly searching for me!* he thought. As he drew closer to the immigration officer's booth, he could see that people and their passports were being carefully scrutinised. *Calm and confident! Calm and confident!* He told himself.

Finally, as he drew closer to the officer, he noticed that the dark blue, uniformed official was armed with a holstered pistol. *I don't remember that they were armed before.* The officer, in his early twenties, with a ruddy complexion, a blonde moustache and pale blue eyes, seemed hesitant, as if he were new on the job. He said something to Efraim in Georgian. Efraim smiled, nodded and handed him the passport. The officer carefully studied the passport and bent down to examine Efraim. He pointed to the passport photo and asked Efraim a question in Georgian. Efraim gave him a shrug and a self-deprecating smile, waving over his shoulder to indicate that the photo had been taken years ago.

The officer asked Efraim another question in Georgian. To this, Efraim responded by holding his windpipe in the fingers of one hand, while he waved the index finger of his other hand. The officer considered this briefly, and asked a question which, to Efraim, sounded as though he was seeking confirmation. Once again, Efraim took hold of his windpipe, and then he drew his right index finger across his throat, indicating that he had had an operation.

The officer gave him a sympathetic look, handed him back his passport, and waved him through.

Efraim arrived back in the U.K. nine days later, having re-installed the UK license plates and disposed of the Georgian plates. Near Crawley, he rented a lock-up garage, and at a builder's merchant, he acquired a metal chest, padlock, heavy braided wire and U-clamps. The shaped charges were stored in the locked chest in the garage.

He sold the Range Rover for £3,495 and he bought a ten-year-old, white Ford Escort van for £1,295. Then he took the van to be painted to his specifications. On the floor of the garage and referring to his earlier sketch at the target, Efraim laid out a full-scale template of the cable layout. He used sections of three-inch pipe, the ends of which he cemented to the floor, to represent the cables. Then, he checked and double-checked that he had the right spacing between the cables and that he had the right offset for the two, outermost cables. Next, he laid the shaped charges on the floor, each next to a target cable. Finally, he coupled the shaped charges into a circuit, using the braided wire that passed through the eyebolts at each end of the shaped charge and was secured by the U-clamps.

Because of the offset of the two outermost cables, Efraim had to add two restraining sections of wire, one inside each of the outermost cables. These two sections assured that the physical recoil of all shaped charges would be minimal when they were detonated.

All the next day, Efraim practiced putting in place the actual linked shaped charges on the template. He tried various sequences of the required tasks, seeking the minimum elapsed time. His best time was fifty-six seconds, not counting time to lift the charges into their elevated position. Raising the charges from ground level would, he estimated take fifteen seconds at most. Within another fifteen seconds, he expected to be sufficiently clear of the target that detonation would have no effect on him. He was satisfied about his preparations to that point. On D-day minus one, he would install the detonators into the shaped charges and connect them to their impulse generator that he had assembled from components bought at three electronics shops.

Before flying back to Morocco, he had to meet the auburn-haired one again. For two hundred and fifty pounds, he had her for a day and two nights.

When he was on the easyJet flight, he began to consider how he could make the relationship with her more dependable. *Could he remain in England after D-day? This seemed unlikely. Could she be persuaded to come to Marrakech? Perhaps, but he would have to share her. Was he prepared to share her? Well . . . Was he prepared to marry her? Yes, but was she prepared to marry him?*

He could no longer think of the auburn-haired one, Shauna, as an unclean woman. For Efraim, she had become clean, and he refused to think about what the Qur'an said about her. The more he thought about her, the less he could recall certain passages from the Qur'an, and the less he thought about the Qur'an.

Chapter 11

DECISION

The EasyJet flight from Marrakech to Gatwick was about sixty percent full. Paul was able to get an aisle, exit row seat, which at least offered space to stretch out his legs, even though the back didn't recline. There was a retired English couple returning from a Moroccan holiday, to his left in the same row. After hearing about their desert camel safari from Merzouga, and their hike up the "incredible" Todra Gorge, Paul was able to close his eyes. But sleep eluded him. Diligently, he tried to plan his report writing, but the persistent ache would not be banished. Two Bloody Marys only sharpened his feelings and dulled his reasoning.

You're in love with her, Paul, let's face it! She's so lovely; such a pleasure to be caught up in her adventurousness. She took twenty years off my life with her sweet young body, her joyful sensuality, and her need for protection. . . . Where will she get the protection she needs in Buenos Aires? . . . There won't be a Paul Winthorpe there. . . . Am I kidding myself? . . . No, I don't think so. She's not at all promiscuous and much more at ease with women than with men. . . . I think what she'll do is what she's always done: make sure her environment is OK and then explore it to her limits. . . . God, I miss her already! . . . Does she miss me? . . . I wonder. . . . She said she loves me . . . And yet . . . and yet she didn't kiss me or even wave goodbye . . . What can I do? . . . How can I find out what she's really feeling? . . . I could call her. No. . . . No, she won't know what to say . . . She'll think I know how she feels . . . How does she feel? . . . She loves me with all her precious naiveté . . . and . . . and she's also afraid . . . Afraid of what? . . . Afraid that somehow I'll destroy her world.

He took the local train from Gatwick to Clapham Junction and a taxi from Clapham Junction to Crieff Road, Wandsworth. His mood lightened slightly on returning home. It was comfortable and familiar. The garden, he noticed, needed weeding, and the climbing nasturtiums were threatening to spread their red and gold flowers across the paved patio. *Saturday or Sunday,* he thought. In the master bedroom, he opened a window and put on an old pair of khaki shorts and a faded blue polo shirt.

Paul returned to the garden table with a gin and tonic and the latest issue of the *Economist*. But world political and financial issues were of little interest.

What was he to do about Naomi? He relived the eight days he had spent with her, almost minute by minute, in his mind. *I remember,* he thought, *how she could braid her hair in a matter of seconds without even glancing in the mirror, and it looked wonderful—like a young girl.*

But there were no new conclusions—except for one. It was not a new conclusion that he loved her, or that she, in some way, truly loved him. His new conclusion was that if he pursued her, it would only frighten her more.

And what about Sarah? he wondered. *Well, I don't have to do anything. I never promised her anything.* But this conclusion left him with an uneasy feeling. *Do I really think I can pretend that nothing's happened? That's not really honest. But if I tell her I've been with another woman, she may say 'goodbye.' And I really don't want to lose Sarah! Why do I feel that way? Because I'm very, very fond of Sarah, and, in many ways, she's my kind of woman.*

The next morning he thought, *So, I've got to tell Sarah, and I've got to be truthful. If I'm not, there's no chance of any relationship with Sarah.*

Sarah was very glad to see him. They sat in the garden at his house with an open bottle of sauvignon blanc in front of them. She asked him about the trip to Morocco, and he told her about Djemaa Al-Fna in Marrakech and Rick's Café Americain in Casablanca as well as about Yusuf, Efraim and his suspicions regarding each of them. She sensed his reserve, and she asked, "You don't seem very happy, Paul. Did something go wrong?"

He took a deep breath, and without looking at her, said, "Sarah, I have a confession to make."

Sarah cocked her head slightly. "What is it, Paul?"

"I've been with another woman, Sarah."

She studied his stricken face, and she understood that he hadn't just been in the company of another woman. For a long moment, she searched for a response within herself. There was anger and grief, but also the strong desire to understand. "Who was this woman?"

"Her name is Naomi Evensen. She works for GYE, and she met me in Marrakech to act as interpreter."

She noticed his use of the present tense of the word to be. Not that she 'was' Naomi Evensen; she 'is' Naomi Evensen. "What happened?" she asked.

Paul glanced briefly at her face. *Oh, God,* he thought, *I've hurt Sarah so much!* "She came into my room one night."

Well, at least he didn't start it, Sarah thought. "What was she doing in your room?"

"She had had a nightmare about Efraim, and she was frightened."

"How old is this woman?"

"About thirty-five."

"So, she got into bed with you, and you screwed her." It was a statement, more than a question.

Paul nodded. "Is she single?" Another nod. "And pretty?" He nodded again.

During the long pause that followed, Sarah looked at her hands, which were lying as if lifeless in her lap. "This woman has designs on you, I suppose. She meets an attractive, reasonably wealthy widower from London, and she says to herself, 'I think I'll latch on to that!'"

Paul shook his head. "No, I don't think so, Sarah. She was really trying to escape her fears."

"But," Sarah said bitterly, "she wasn't afraid of getting in your bed again and again."

"No," Paul conceded, "No, she wasn't."

"And you," Sarah was angry now, "You couldn't believe your good fortune!" Her words came out in a torrent. "You had this willing young bimbo with her big tits, and her wet pussy to fuck whenever she could get it up for you!"

Paul shook his head.

"No?" she demanded, "what do you mean 'no'?"

"It wasn't like that, Sarah."

She leaned toward Paul and said, slowly and savagely, "What was it like then? You tell me!"

For a moment, Paul considered. "She's a naïve idealist who grew up in Israel—a musician turned charity worker—and she has small breasts."

The earnestness with which he spoke startled Sarah, and his words echoed in her mind: naïve idealist, grew up in Israel, musician, charity worker, small breasts. Sarah's impression of the situation suddenly shifted. Quietly, she asked, "Are you in love with this woman, Paul?"

This was the question he had been dreading. Carefully, he said, "Yes, but I'm not sure it would ever work."

Sarah's lips were trembling. "Why not?"

"She's in South America, and I don't know if I'll ever see her again."

Sarah was startled by this change in direction. "In South America? What's she doing there?"

"That's what she does for a living. She looks in on GYE chapters around the world."

Sarah shook her head, trying to take it in. Then she asked, "Is she in love with you?"

"I suppose she is, but there's no future plan or commitment."

"On her part or yours?"

"Both."

There seemed to be nothing more that either of them could say. They sat in silence, their eyes wandering around the garden, submerged in their own thoughts. Finally, Sarah rose from her chair. Tears began to spill down her cheeks. "I need some time to think, and I suppose you do too." Her hand rested momentarily on Paul's shoulder. Then, she turned and left.

The following morning, Paul threw himself into writing the first draft of his report. He was both helped and hindered by the report template that Roberta at GYE had sent him. It was helpful in that it provided a clear guide; but it was also a hindrance in calling for responses to questions that were, in AMM's case, peripheral. The report was organised into subject matter sections: corporate governance, financial controls, operational controls, fund-raising, service to entrepreneurs, provision of mentoring, adequacy of staff, etc. Each section contained individual quality statements where Paul was expected to insert a comment about AMM's compliance with the statement and an overall assessment: good, satisfactory or unsatisfactory. For example, the first statement under financial controls read: "There is a complete audit of the chapter's books by an accredited financial auditor on an annual basis." Paul's response was, "Only one of AMM's twelve bank statements is audited by PFC Maroc annually." And his assessment was "Unsatisfactory."

But many of the statements required a full paragraph response, so what started out as an eight-page form became fifteen pages by the time Paul had completed it. His approach was to go first through the report, inserting a short response to each statement. Then opening his notebook in which there were eleven pages of hand-written notes on AMM, and beginning at the first page, he typed facts and conclusions from his notes into the appropriate section of the report. This was a laborious process that took two full days. When the insertions were complete, he read through the entire report, making editorial changes as he went.

Now he thought, *I've got to send it to Naomi for her to look at.*

"Hi, Naomi," he wrote, "Here's my first draft of the report on AMM. Your comments, corrections and additions would be most welcome."

How am I going to sign the e-mail? he wondered. *I can't sign it "Love, Paul", and it wouldn't make any sense to sign as 'Kind regards, Paul.' So what should I do?* Finally, he decided to sign it "Paul", and to insert two additional sentences, "Hope your trip to Argentina is going well. Believe it or not, I had tango lessons at one time, but I'd probably get booed of the dance floor now."

Before he went to get coffee the next morning, Paul opened his Outlook inbox. There was a message from "Naomi Evensen". When he opened it, he read, "Hi, Paul, Thanks very much for sending me the report, which is excellent—your usual great work! Would it be possible—maybe somewhere toward the end—to put in a hint to the Accreditation Board about Efraim? If he is what we think he is, and that becomes public knowledge, it would be good if we could say 'we told you so.' Got my shopping done in Madrid. Haven't seen a live tango yet. I'm pretty sure it's well beyond me, but maybe you could teach me. Naomi."

Paul took his coffee out into the sunlit garden. He felt absurdly happy that Naomi had not only responded promptly but had told him something personal about herself (her shopping in Madrid), was complimentary ("your usual great work"), and mentioned something about their future ("maybe you could teach me"). *God, sweetheart, I would love to teach you anything I knew!*

As the day wore on, he had to remind himself that nothing of substance had actually changed.

Toward the end of the report, in the "Other Comments" section, Paul added the following: "The half-brother of Mr. Yusuf Al-Rashid, the CEO of AMM, lives in the same house as the CEO (where AMM also has its offices). Mr. Efraim Al-Rashid, an imam in a mosque in Marrakech, preaches jihadist sermons, and rumour has it that he may have been connected to the bombings in Casablanca. We have drawn this matter to the attention of the authorities in Morocco."

He sent the revised report by e-mail to Roberta with a copy to Naomi. Late that afternoon, Roberta called him. "Thanks for the excellent, comprehensive report, Paul. I've added a couple of paragraphs of background material for the benefit of the Accreditation Board, and I'll send you a copy with my additions."

"I'm sure that'll be fine Roberta."

"There's just one other thing, Paul. I don't think we should include anything about Yusuf's brother. Don't forget; we normally send the CEO a copy of the actual report."

"Oh, I forgot about that! Naomi asked me to put it in. Maybe she forgot also."

"That's OK. I'll speak with her."

With the conference call with Yusuf scheduled for the following Wednesday, Paul had time available to look for new paid consultancy. He forced himself to make a dozen calls to prospects and to send out follow-up e-mails, but he felt restless. He knew what was missing, but there was nothing to fill the void. *I need to do something different!* His mind wandered back to Morocco, and since Naomi was off-limits, he began to reflect on Efraim, his fanaticism, the frequent calls to prayer and the sight of the faithful streaming into to mosques. *What is there about Islam?* he wondered. *I know almost nothing about it. Maybe I should have a look at the Qur'an.*

He logged onto the Amazon U.K. site and searched under books for 'Qur'an'. There were over seven thousand results, but at the top of the list, with a five-star rating and over sixty reviews, was a translation by Muhammad Abdel Haleem, an Egyptian by birth who learned the Qur'an by heart as a child. He was currently Professor of Islamic Studies at the University of London. Paul bought it with one click. "*But,*" he thought, "*I need something to put it in context.*" Searching further, he found *Understanding the Qur'an: Themes and Style* by the same Professor Haleem. Paul bought this, as well.

On Sunday morning, he went to the 9:30 service at his church near Parsons Green. He chose the earlier service because he and Sarah usually went to the 11:30 service, and he dreaded another meeting with her, particularly in the church where they had met. He chose to sit, not in the usual place, in the third pew on the left, but about halfway back on the right. Pushing the omnipresent thoughts from his mind, Paul gazed at the chancel with its white marble crucifixion on the rear wall, the altar shrouded in lace and the two huge candles standing like sentries. He began to feel suffused in the peace of the setting.

As the service began, two women hurried up the aisle to his left and took seats about ten pews in front of him. It was Sarah and her older daughter, Anne. Paul thought, *She probably didn't see me when she came in, but she'll probably see me when I go up to take communion. Maybe I shouldn't take communion. But I didn't do anything all that wrong. I'm just sorry for hurting Sarah. If I don't take communion, it means that I feel I have committed a sin.* Then he thought, *I'll take communion, but I'll be preoccupied within myself.*

He half listened to the priest's homily about forgiveness: "Seventy times seven times. Jesus has told us." Then, he thought, *Oh Lord, can you forgive me for the hurt I have caused to Sarah?*

At the conclusion of the service, Paul followed the crowd of people who were going downstairs for coffee. In the confusion, he lost track of Sarah, and when he stood to one side, coffee cup in hand, he saw that she and Anne had decided not to stay for coffee. *Was it because of me?* he wondered.

"Hey, Paul, how are you?" It was his friend Frank Portman, who, with his wife, Jennifer, had come over to stand beside him.

"Oh, hi, Frank. Fine thanks. Hi, Jennifer." The Portmans were an American couple, who retained their New York accents, but had otherwise gone native, even taking British citizenship. They were about ten years younger than Paul with no children. Frank, a vice president with Citibank, loved food and other good things in life, and was engaged in a constant battle to lose weight. It seemed to Paul that Frank's regular attendance at church served as a sincere counterweight to his good-humoured self-indulgence. Jennifer, tall and svelte, a classic beauty, her jet-black hair cut fashionably short, also worked at Debenhams. She lacked Frank's optimistic good humour, but her loving disposition meant that, in respect of her husband, she probably followed Jesus' instruction regularly.

Frank said, "I didn't expect to see you at this service, Paul. How come you decided to come early?"

"Well, I woke up early so I thought I might as well come along."

"I noticed that you and Sarah weren't sitting together," Frank continued. "Anything wrong?"

"We've had a little difficulty," Paul conceded.

"Oh, I'm sorry to hear it, Paul," Jennifer offered. "Anything we can do?"

"No, I don't think so, Jennifer. Thank you."

"Say, Paul, we're going fishing this afternoon. Want to come with us?"

"Yes. I'd like that."

"Well, we're going to leave home about eleven," Frank continued, "Why don't we meet you for lunch at the Green Trout at one?"

The Green Trout was at an intersection of two roads just north of Stockbridge in Hampshire. Being a Sunday, it was full of day-trippers from London, fishermen and local gentry. Frank, a regular and on friendly terms with the owner, Piero, who was also the chef, had a table waiting. "Tell Piero," Frank informed the waiter, "that he knows what I like, so I want him to choose for me."

"But tell him that I said small portions, please," Jennifer added. Frank frowned, but said nothing.

Over lunch, the Portmans wanted to hear about Paul's trip to Morocco, and he gave them a businessman's perspective with a few tourist attractions thrown it. Naomi was not mentioned.

"No dessert please, Frank," Jennifer instructed. I'm going to the ladies, and then I want to get fishing."

When she was out of sight, Frank beckoned the waiter. "Bring me a slice of that chocolate cake quick, will you?"

Paul added, "And bring me the bill."

"I don't suppose," Frank remarked, shoveling another forkful of cake into his mouth, "that Sarah caught you straying off the reservation, did she, Paul?"

"Something like that," Paul conceded.

Frank shrugged. "Oh, well, she'll get over it. Women always do."

"Not always, Frank."

Another shrug from Frank. "Well, the smart ones, like Jennifer, realise that we men aren't supposed to be monogamous. They realise that a little trip off the reservation now and then is good for the braves. Keeps up their fighting spirit."

In spite of himself, Paul had to chuckle at Frank's political incorrectness. "I don't think your philosophy would have worked very well with Catherine, Frank."

"God rest her soul," Frank said, wolfing down the last of the chocolate cake.

Immediately after lunch, Paul paid a visit to the Orvis shop in Stockbridge. He had brought all his fishing supplies with him, and there was nothing he knew he needed, but he always found the displays of hand-tied trout flies impossible to resist. He selected eighteen flies, including three that the store manager particularly recommended, and six, nine-foot, lightweight leaders, their barely visible strands coiled neatly in transparent envelopes.

Seventy-eight pounds seventy-four pence for this lot! he mused, gripping the box of flies and the six leaders between a thumb and forefinger.

The lakes where Paul and the Portmans fished were owned and stocked by a large U.K. corporation that had other real estate interests in the area. A small group of dedicated fishermen (and one fisherwoman) paid an annual subscription for the right to fish there. As it flowed through the flood plain north of Stockbridge, the River Test fragmented into various splits, one of which fed the two lakes. The lakes themselves were each about two hundred yards long and one hundred yards wide. They had been manmade years ago and were now surrounded by a wide grassy verge that melted into woodlands. The setting was serene and naturally beautiful: graceful old willows weeping down to the water's edge, clumps of wild flowers here and there, and the intense sky above pillowed with clouds. The only audible sounds were the squawking of ducks on the glassy water and the occasional whirr of a fishing reel being unwound.

Jennifer Portman was the real fisherperson. She had been taught fly-fishing as a child in New York's Adirondack Mountains by her father. Before assembling his rod, Paul sat on a bench and watched

Jennifer cast from the far side of the lower lake. Her intense gaze was fixed on a spot of water about twenty-five yards off shore. Her long composite rod was pointing at the same spot, and her right hand was slowly retrieving her line. After a few moments, she lifted the rod in a powerful fluid motion that sent the line hurtling over her head, behind her and forward again. Gently, the line straightened out and settled again on the water, causing barely a ripple.

Frank came and sat on the bench next to Paul. "It's a pleasure to watch her," Paul observed, "She's so damn good!"

"Yeah, I know. She puts me to shame." Then he added, slightly defensively, "But I get more fish than she does."

"Well, that's because she uses dry flies and you use nymphs." Paul was referring to dry flies that float on the surface of the water, and nymphs, which simulate the larva of an insect about to hatch and is trolled irresistibly through the water.

Good naturedly, Frank said, "What's the point of being a purist? We're here to catch fish, aren't we?"

Paul had heard this argument at least ten times before. "Jennifer enjoys luring the fish; you enjoy catching them. What's wrong with that?

Frank smiled. "Nothing at all. But let's not forget, I catch <u>bigger</u> fish!"

"That's because the bigger fish are too fat and lazy to come up to the surface to feed."

There was an unexpected splash from the lake, and they looked up to see Jennifer's rod bent at ninety degrees, her line pointing straight at the splashing. She was leaning backward slightly. The splashing stopped, but the line remained taught. Jennifer was concentrating her attention on the water, trying to see the submerged fish. Suddenly, her reel started to screech as the line paid out to the surging fish.

"Oh, she's got a good one!" Frank murmured. "Bring him in, baby!"

For the next ten minutes Paul and Frank watched the battle between Jennifer and the big trout, as it took line from her, and she repeatedly hauled it back.

The trout was clearly tiring as it flopped about on the surface near the shore. Finally, Jennifer scooped it into her net and held it up, all smiles, for them to see. Frank applauded. It turned out to be a female rainbow trout, just under four pounds in weight.

Paul fished both lakes but always within shouting distance of either Frank or Jennifer. He used only dry flies, and he changed them often, but none was consistently appealing to the trout below. Frequently, the surface would boil only a foot or two away from his fly as the trout expressed their preference for whatever nature was providing.

Catching fish was not Paul's objective; what he sought was the balm of the setting, being with old friends, the distraction of fishing and the absence of memories. As the sun began to set, Frank grilled steaks on the charcoal barbecue; Jennifer produced a salad and two bottles of Bordeaux. They fished until dusk, when the fish went into a kind of feeding frenzy, and one could no longer see the fly but had to strike at the sound of a splash. Paul took three fish home. The largest one he set aside for the priest. The two smaller fish, just over a pound, he planned for Cynthia and himself. He returned three other live fish to the lake.

"Thank you guys so much for including me," he said.

"Any time, Paul," Frank said, squeezing his shoulder.

Jennifer gazed at him for a long moment before kissing him on each cheek. "It'll work out, Paul. Somehow, it always does."

"Cindy, I caught a couple of nice trout yesterday, and one of them has your name on it. Want to come for dinner tonight or tomorrow?"

"I'd love to see you, Dad, but this is another hectic week. Any chance you could bring them to my place for a late dinner tomorrow, and I'll do the cooking?"

"OK. No problem. Is there anything the chef will need?"

"Umm . . . Let me think. . . . Parsley and a nice bottle of wine. I'm almost out of Sainsbury's Chardonnay."

When Paul had hung up, he thought, *Sainsbury's Chardonnay! Kids today have no taste! If she bought a vintage French wine, she would taste the difference, and it would be a rounding error on her bank account. Maybe it's my fault for not explaining what a good wine is when I served it.*

The following day, Paul paid a visit to the Connoisseur's Wine Shop in Earlsfield where after a careful browse, he found a 2007 Bernard Moreau Chassagne Montrachet. He decided to get two bottles. *That way she'll have an extra bottle to impress that James fellow.* He also decided not to reveal the price he paid: £42.50 per bottle.

Shortly after 9 p.m., Paul rang the bell of flat 5A, Mercury Court, Homer Drive, Isle of Dogs. Flat 5A had two bedrooms, two bathrooms, a large living/dining area, a balcony with views of the Thames River, access to a gym, sauna, and private parking. For Cynthia, it was a ten-minute walk to work at Canary Wharf. She had bought the flat four years ago with a bonus and a mortgage that she had probably since paid off. The furnishings were starkly modern but comfortable.

Cynthia considered the two fish Paul had unwrapped on her kitchen counter. "I don't think I've got a pan big enough for them, Dad."

"Have you got a roasting tin?"

"I'm not sure. If I do, it's in here." She peered into the recesses of a lower cabinet. "Yes! Here we go!" She produced a rectangular stainless steel container with the original manufacturer's labels still on it.

Paul smiled at his daughter, "Well, I see this has had good use."

"Daaad," was Cynthia's drawn out response, "I don't cook roasts. I do salads and omelettes— sometimes a steak."

"How are you going to impress James if you don't cook a nice joint?"

Cynthia took ingredients for a salad from the refrigerator. She gave her father a sidelong look.

"James gets the steak."

"Oh, I see. I hope you don't serve him Sainsbury's Beaujolais."

"No, he brings the wine."

"Sounds like this relationship is at an advanced stage."

She shrugged her shoulders slightly and busied herself with the salad. "It's progressing a bit."

"I brought you two bottles of wine. One for us tonight, and the second for you and James."

"Oh, thank you, Dad. What is it?"

"Something a little better than Sainsbury's Chardonnay." He opened a bottle and poured two glasses.

"Oh, that's good!" She announced after taking a sip; she studied the label. "Chassagne Montrachet. I'll have to remember that."

While the fish were grilling, she boiled some wild rice and talked about her work. They sat at her table that had a view of the river through the expansive glass windows.

"Tell me about Morocco, Dad."

Paul gave her the business and tourist summary of the trip. Then, he thought, *I might as well tell her—I can't keep this a secret from everybody.*

"The Operations Director of GYE was on the trip with me. She speaks fluent Arabic, which was a big help."

"Yes, I'm sure it was."

"Unexpectedly, we got involved."

Cynthia put her fork down and looked at her father. "You got involved with this woman?"

He nodded. She saw the tremors around his mouth. She said, "This is serious then."

There was a long pause while he reflected. "I haven't felt like this since I first met your mother. But . . ."

"But what, Dad?"

"I'm not sure it would work out."

"Why not, Dad?"

He sighed. "Lots of reasons. She's young, she's an Israeli, she's a musician, she speaks seven languages, and she's kind of an idealistic nomad."

"Oh, my gosh!" Cynthia searched her father's face. "Is she very pretty?" He nodded. "How old is she?"

"About thirty-five."

There was a long period of silence while Cynthia continued to study her father. "You say she's an idealistic nomad." He nodded. "But, Dad, what would an idealistic nomad want with a stable realist like you?"

He looked out at the river: black except for a shimmer of reflected moonlight. "I suppose it may be because opposite dispositions can find each other fascinating, particularly when there's a physical bond."

Cynthia moved her head slightly in acknowledgement. "You sure money's not a motivator?"

He shook his head. "Do you know of anyone who has spent the first fifteen years of their working life with charities who is money motivated?"

She shook her head. "Do you know anything about her family?"

"Never married. Her mother is a musician and lives in Jerusalem, where Naomi grew up. Her father is a Swede—also a musician—he's gone back to Sweden."

"She see much of him as a child?"

"He went back to Sweden when Naomi was twelve. I think she misses him, but can't get along with him."

Aha! she thought.

She asked, "Have you said anything to Sarah?" He nodded. "How did she take it?"

"Not very well."

"I can't say that I blame her. So what happens now, Dad? Are you going to see this Naomi? Where is she now?"

"I think she's in Bolivia."

"Doesn't she live in London?"

"She has a flat in Notting Hill, but she's seldom there."

"So you weren't exaggerating when you said she's a nomad." He shook his head. "Dad, I can see that you're hurting. I wish there was something I could do."

Again, he shook his head.

* * *

Efraim's Eye

Roberta had just finished placing the speakerphone sound module on the conference table when Andrew came in. He shook Paul's hand warmly. "Your report confirms my suspicions. Good piece of work, Paul."

"We haven't got any proof of wrong doing. Just a lot of opportunities for it."

"And the testimony of third parties," Andrew added.

"But they are aggrieved third parties, so I haven't put what they said in the report."

"I know. Naomi told me. By the way, how did you two get on?"

"Fine. She was a big help. I couldn't have done it without her."

Andrew nodded. "In terms of Yusuf today, what I suggest is that you start out with a summary of your findings. Then we give him a chance to comment on the individual conclusions. Following that, we can go through each section in detail if he wants."

"Is he the only other person on the call?" Paul asked.

Roberta said, "He's going to be the only one from AMM on the call. He said that the chairman will be in on the call with the Accreditation Board at the end of next week. Naomi's going to join the call. She's in Uruguay."

"What's your reading of Yusuf?" Andrew asked. "Do you think he's going to nitpick everything?"

Paul reflected for a moment. "No, I don't think so. His main concern will be retaining his accreditation." Andrew nodded. "Then, he'll be concerned about any major items that reflect on him personally."

"OK, Roberta, let's get him on the line," Andrew directed.

Naomi's voice was the first to come from the loudspeaker. "Hi, Paul. Hi, Andrew. Hi, Roberta. Naomi here. Calling you from Montevideo at the ungodly hour of 5 a.m."

Andrew smiled. "Sorry about the timing, Naomi, but for some reason, Yusuf couldn't manage an afternoon call. How are things in Uruguay?"

"Well, it's better than in Morocco in some ways. I mean, this chapter seems to be managed honestly and pretty well."

Paul was desperately trying to think of something he could say that would have meaning for her but would sound innocuous to Andrew and Roberta. He gave up when Yusuf's voice came on the line.

Andrew introduced the call. Then for about five minutes, Paul gave a summary of his findings and recommendations, glancing down occasionally at a hard copy of the report.

Andrew asked, "Do you have any general comments, Yusuf?"

"I certainly agree with most of Paul's findings, and I can assure you that AMM will make its very best efforts to implement the recommendations. I think it is essential for the survival of AMM and of GYE in Morocco that AMM retain its accreditation."

"Yes, I understand, but that's not a matter we can discuss today. In fact, that decision rests entirely with the Accreditation Board."

"But surely, you have considerable influence with your board."

"We discuss assessment reports with the board, but I leave the decision entirely in their hands. We have found that it is better to have an independent decision on accreditation. Otherwise, we could be seen as lowering our standards in the interests of promoting GYE. The only other point I would make, Yusuf, is that several items in this latest report are identical to issues raised in the previous report."

"As I have told you and your staff, Andrew, we are a small charity; we can't afford to pay a lot of staff to put a lot of bureaucratic measures in place."

"Yusuf, this is Naomi. I am currently in Montevideo, and the Uruguay chapter of GYE—which is smaller than AMM—has four full-time staff plus the CEO in their head office."

"Miss Evensen, please do not compare a modern Muslim state like Morocco to a backward colonial state like Uruguay!"

Paul interrupted, "Yusuf, can you tell me what percentage of your total income is spent on head office expense?"

"I would have to look it up," was the sour response.

Andrew asked, "Do you know what it is, Paul?"

"No, I can't tell from the information I have."

The jaw muscles in Andrew's cheeks were flexing. He said, "Yusuf, this is the kind of thing we're talking about. The chief executive of any charity should know that ratio, and he should be trying to optimise it, consistent with the service he provides."

Immediately, Yusuf asked, "What is your ratio?"

"For GYE headquarters, our office overheads last year were 28.7 percent of our grants, and the grants and loans we pass through to chapters."

Yusuf shot back, "Well you've got all those pro bonos to measure it for you."

Andrew was exasperated; he said, "If you don't measure something, Yusuf, you can't possibly control it."

There was silence on the line.

Andrew asked, "Are there any other points or corrections you'd like to make, Yusuf?"

"I have had the report only a few days. I will read through it carefully and send you any comments by e-mail." He dropped off the call.

"Naomi, are you still there?" Andrew asked.

"Yes, I'm here. That was typical Yusuf. He's always right and always has to have the last word."

Andrew continued, "On another subject, I wanted to ask if there's anything else we should be doing about this fellow Efraim."

"Well, as I mentioned to you, Paul and I went to see the military attaché at the U.K. embassy. Paul gave him some photos and a recording of the horrible sermon he preached. We also referred him to the Arabic website. The army major we met with talked to some Moroccan official, probably in the military."

"Anything new, Paul?"

"No, Major Bancroft sent me back my recorder without comment. I don't really expect to hear anything more from him."

* * *

Cynthia had spent the last several days thinking about her father. She mused, *This Naomi woman doesn't sound like the right choice for him. Exciting for a brief interlude, but for the longer term—living in London? With his friends? How would I feel about a stepmother who's four years older than me? I guess the age wouldn't matter to me, but what would we have in common?*

Feeling the need to do something, she thought briefly about calling Sarah or going to visit her. *I would try to convince her not to give up on Dad.*

But she realised *that would just be meddling in something that isn't my affair.*

So while things were relatively quiet at work, she decided to call John.

"John Winthorpe."

"Hi, John, it's Cindy. How are you?"

"I'm fine. What prompts a call from you on a Thursday morning? Have you got a rock on your left hand?"

Cynthia removed the handset from her ear and glared at it. "No, John! Have you talked to Dad lately?"

"He called last Saturday just to chat. What's going on?"

"He didn't mention a certain Naomi he's met?"

"No, but he didn't seem as cheerful as usual. What's with this Naomi?"

"She's with the charity— Global Youth Enterprise —Dad was working for in Morocco. She went with him to interpret. He says they got 'involved.'"

"Is she single?"

"Yes. Apparently, she's never married."

"Does Sarah know?"

"Yes."

"Oh, dear! . . . (there was a pause) OK. Operations Director, Naomi Evensen. She's rather pretty."

"John, what in the world are you looking at?"

"The website for Global Youth Enterprise. . . . About Us . . . then Our Staff. . . . She's an Israeli, Musician . . . Seven languages! My God, I can barely speak English! Fascinating! What's the problem, Cindy? I mean, apart from we may not get Sarah as a stepmother."

"Well, for one thing she's about thirty-five, and . . ."

John interrupted, "What's wrong with that? Are you concerned about getting a baby half-brother?"

Cynthia snapped: "No, John! I'm not concerned about that! I'm concerned that they're completely different kinds of people. Dad says she's an idealistic nomad, and he admits to being a stable realist. I don't see how that's going to work, but he says that opposites attract, particularly when there's a physical bond."

"I can't say that I blame him for forming a physical bond with her."

"John! Be serious for a minute, will you? This Naomi can't get along with her father; he left when she was twelve. I'm afraid that she sees Dad as a loving father figure."

"Maybe so. And if we look at it from his point of view, he doesn't really need another daughter. One Cynthia is enough for any man, but maybe . . ."

Cynthia was unable to keep the annoyance out of her voice. "Maybe what?"

"Maybe Dad just needs to be needed."

Cynthia was startled. "What do you mean, John?"

"Well, you and I don't really need him any more. We have our own lives and we're financially independent. Mom depended on Dad for a lot of things beyond companionship and financial security. Mom depended on him as a counterbalance to her emotional swings and impulsiveness—maybe not consciously, but she knew Dad was always there as a safe harbour. And Sarah? Well, Sarah's been on her own for the last five years, so as the saying goes, she probably needs a man like a fish needs a bicycle."

"Oh, God! This conversation is making me depressed."

"Why, Cindy? I think this girl—or this woman—would be good for Dad. She's just what he needs to spice up his life. Are you afraid she'll end up with your inheritance?"

"No, I'm not! I'm just concerned Dad's going to end up being hurt. He's suffering now that she's not here in London."

"Well, Cindy, Dad's a big boy. I'm sure he'll work it out. I'm going to have a look to see if Naomi's on Facebook."

"John!" Cynthia spluttered, "Don't you dare ask to be her friend!"

"I won't. I'm just going to look."

* * *

Paul arrived at the GYE conference room twenty minutes before the meeting was scheduled to begin. He did not want to keep the Accreditation Board waiting. Roberta got him a cup of tea and briefly re-summarised the board's membership and procedures. He had arranged his notebook, his file and the hard copy of his report in front of him. A handsome, grey-haired woman in a tailored dark blue suit, white blouse and pearls arrived. She set her briefcase down on the table and strode to where Paul was sitting.

"Hi! I'm Margaret Carpenter." Paul glanced at his notes and understood that she was the board chairperson. He introduced himself. "Oh, yes, Paul. We've all been reading your report with great interest. You've carried off a particularly difficult assignment very well indeed." She seated herself at the table, removed a file from her briefcase, and began to engage Andrew and Roberta in an energetic conversation. Paul looked at the business card she had given him "Margaret Carpenter, Partner, Damon & Struggles, Executive Recruitment."

Well, she's someone good to know! he thought.

Two other members of the board arrived and were introduced.

"All right. Roberta, if we can get Abigail and James on the line, we can get started," Mrs. Carpenter announced.

When a quorum had been established by telephone, the floor was turned over to Paul. "We've all read your excellent report, Paul, but if you would be kind enough to just summarise it for us, that would be most helpful."

"Well, for me," Paul began, "The most important point is that there has not been a complete financial audit of this chapter for some time."

Mrs. Carpenter interrupted, "Do you know when the last complete audit was done, Andrew?"

Andrew replied, "We thought the audits we received were complete, but Paul has discovered that they are incomplete. The problem for us at GYE headquarters, Margaret, is that the audit reports are in Arabic."

"Well, but can't Naomi read Arabic?"

"Yes, she can. But she has no financial training; it would have taken a major cooperative effort for Naomi and Richard, our financial controller, to figure out what was going on."

"But Paul seemed to find out pretty quickly, and he doesn't speak Arabic."

"I don't speak Arabic, Mrs. Carpenter, but the auditor speaks English, and I asked him."

"Oh, I see. OK. Well, it seems to me, Andrew, that somehow we've got to tighten up our procedures.

Dryly, Andrew replied, "I agree, Margaret."

She turned her attention back to Paul, who continued, "What I haven't said in the report is that Naomi and I met with two former employees, and . . ."

Mrs. Carpenter interrupted, "Oh, Naomi went with you. Isn't she a lovely girl?"

"Yes, she is. The employees alleged that there was fraud going on in the chapter. They told us that the records of the number of entrepreneurs receiving loans were falsified, and that Yusuf was embezzling the money. The reason that these allegations don't appear in the report is that the employees swore us to secrecy, and we were unable to find any independent confirmation of the allegations. That is why I feel a complete audit is so important."

There was a stunned silence in the conference room. A voice came over the loudspeaker: "Paul, this is James. In your report, you mention a number of other deficiencies: lack of proper governance, lack of management systems, and so on. Under these circumstances, wouldn't it be best if we just denied accreditation to AMM?"

Paul looked at Andrew, who took the lead. "I tend to agree with Paul on this, although the final decision is up to you, Margaret. AMM is a bellwether chapter in terms of our penetration into

Muslim countries. If we were to simply throw out a chapter that we've been touting as a leader, it might very well cause our start-ups in other Muslim countries to lose interest. If, on the other hand, we threw out a chapter because of actual fraud, it would be a signal that we are serious about our standards."

James said, "OK Andrew, I take your point, but what if AMM passes the audit. What are we going to do about the other major deficiencies?"

"I would suggest," Andrew said, "that we cross that bridge when we get to it. Whether you decide to suspend them or throw them out at that point will depend on what they've done in the meantime to address the other points Paul has raised."

Mrs. Carpenter said, "What I think I'm hearing is that we'll tell AMM that their accreditation is suspended pending the successful completion of a full audit, and that after successful completion, this committee will meet again to reconsider their accreditation status."

Andrew nodded. There were various voices expressing agreement.

"Motion carried," Mrs. Carpenter announced. "How much time are we going to give them to complete the audit? She was looking at Paul.

"I would say a maximum of six weeks. Two weeks to identify the auditor and a month to complete it."

"OK, Roberta, would you get the chairman and the chief executive of AMM on the line?" Mrs. Carpenter instructed.

While the call was being placed, Paul asked Andrew, "Have you heard anything from Yusuf since we last talked to him?"

Andrew shook his head.

A few minutes later, both Yusuf Al-Rashid and Hatim Al-Zahari were in the phone.

"Gentlemen," Mrs. Carpenter began, "I am Margaret Carpenter, the chairperson of the GYE Accreditation Board. Thank you very much for taking our call today. As I think you know, the committee has been reviewing and considering the report on AMM that was prepared by our independent consultant, Mr. Paul Winthorpe. First, may I ask, did you have any further comments on the report?"

"No."

"No. We don't."

"OK. Well the board has reached a decision as follows: we have decided to suspend the accreditation of AMM until the successful completion of an audit of AMM's books and bank accounts in their entirety. The audit is to be completed within six weeks, and if the audit is successful, the committee will meet again to review with you the implementation of Mr. Winthorpe's other recommendations and your accreditation status."

Mr. Al-Zahari asked, "Can you tell us, Mrs. Carpenter, what suspension of accreditation means?"

"It means that the status of AMM on our website will show as Accreditation Suspended. It also means that while your accreditation is suspended, GYE will not provide any services to AMM."

Mr. Al-Zahari asked, "But you don't notify our donors or the banks that our accreditation is suspended?"

"No. We do that only when accreditation is denied," Mrs. Carpenter replied.

There was a brief silence on the line. Then, Yusuf said, "I assume, Andrew, that GYE will reimburse us for the cost of the audit since it is requested by you."

Andrew shook his head. "GYE doesn't pay for any audit costs, except our own. And, if you look at the original accreditation agreement between GYE and AMM, it clearly states that each chapter is responsible for obtaining a complete and satisfactory audit."

"What is the position if we are unable to obtain a complete and satisfactory audit?" Yusuf asked.

Mrs. Carpenter responded, "In that case, your accreditation will be denied."

For about two minutes there was a heated discussion in Arabic at the far end of the line. Paul wrote a note to Andrew and passed it to him.

Finally, Mr. Al-Zahari said, "Yusuf tells me that he has asked Demoitte to conduct a complete audit on a pro bono basis, but he has not had a response."

Andrew said, "Paul has just offered to perform the audit on a pro bono basis. That would be satisfactory to us, if it is satisfactory to you. Alternatively, Demoitte or your regular auditors are satisfactory to us."

Yusuf asked, "Who would pay Mr. Winthorpe's expenses?"

Andrew tried to contain his exasperation, "AMM would. That is the proposition, gentlemen: Paul Winthorpe pro bono, or Demoitte pro bono, or PFC Maroc on whatever basis you arrange. Take it or leave it!"

There was another conversation in Arabic at the far end of the line, this time it was quite heated.

Suddenly, Mr. Al-Zahari announced, in English, "We'll take it!"

"OK. Good." Andrew said, "You have until two weeks from today to tell me who's going to do the audit, and within one month after that the audit has to be completed."

* * *

Paul had just finished reading the last, very brief sura (chapter) of the Qur'an: *People* (No. 114).

Fascinating! Absolutely fascinating, he thought, *and not at all what I expected. Instead, there's much that's familiar: Moses, Joseph, Noah, Adam, Eve, Satan, and Abraham.* He noticed some differences between the Qur'an and the Bible in the stories of these people, but he felt that was unimportant. What mattered was the significance that was attached to them.

He also noticed that Isaiah and Jeremiah were not mentioned but Elijah, Elisha, and Ezekiel were mentioned. *Well,* he thought, *that's fair enough. There's no point in confusing matters by quoting many prophets.*

He was surprised that Mary and Jesus are mentioned frequently, devoutly and favourably, as holy people, though not divine.

He re-read the first sura: *Al-Fatiha* (The Opening):

[1]In the name of God, the Lord of Mercy, the Giver of Mercy! [2]Praise belongs to God, Lord of the Worlds, [3]the Lord of Mercy,

the Giver of Mercy, ⁴Master of the Day of Judgement. ⁵It is You we worship; it is You we ask for help. ⁶Guide us to the straight path, ⁷the path of those You have blessed, those who incur no anger and who have not gone astray.

The translation Paul read explained that the above Fatiha is an obligatory part of daily prayer and is recited by the faithful several times a day. The first sura is therefore a brief summary of the Qur'an. *It is,* Paul thought, *in many respects like the Lord's Prayer.*

He found that the first aya (verse) of this sura is repeated at the beginning of every other sura, except one.

The emphasis on the mercy of God was very apparent. Confirmed disbelievers are to endure the fires of hell.

Some disbelievers' ears and hearts are sealed by God. Paul thought, *I've got to ask an Islamic scholar about that. How can a merciful God seal the ears and hearts of some people to the teachings of the Prophet and send those people to hell? And what about the billions of people who aren't Muslim, Jewish or Christian—many of whom are polytheistic—are they to be cast into the fires of hell? Also, what is the Islamic view of free will?*

The tone of the Qur'an struck Paul as being somewhat authoritarian. *But, why shouldn't it be authoritarian? After all, it is God who's speaking.* Nonetheless, he wondered whether the authoritarian tone might not carry over into the Muslim culture and into governance in the Muslim world.

A significant difference Paul noticed between the Qur'an and the New Testament was that the New Testament has two principle standards of behaviour: Jesus' two commandments to love God with all one's heart and soul and mind, and to love one's neighbour as oneself. The Qur'an has many specific instructions governing the behaviour of the faithful.

In thinking about Islam, Paul noted that four of the Five Pillars of Islam covered worship: worshiping only God and acknowledging his Prophet, performing the ritual prayer five times a day, fasting during Ramadan, and completing the hajj at least once. The fifth pillar is giving alms. Paul thought, *Well, maybe we*

Christians could benefit from more explicit instructions about the frequency of our worship.

Having read Professor Haleem's translation of the Qur'an and his related book, *Understanding the Qur'an,* Paul was pleased to learn that there are several misconceptions about the Muslim faith.

First, 2:228 says, "Husbands have a degree [of right] over them [their wives]". This has been interpreted by some to confirm that Islam relegates women to a lower status. But the reference is to husbands and wives, not men and women, and the context is divorce only.

Second, 3:85 has been interpreted as. "If anyone seeks a religion other than Islam, it will not be accepted from him; he will be one of the losers in the Hereafter." But Professor Haleem points out that the word Islam in the Arabic of the Qur'an means complete devotion to God, not the Islamic faith. In fact, Jews and Christians are frequently referred to as People of the Book. In 29:46, the Qur'an says "[Believers] argue only in the best way with the People of the Book, except with those who act unjustly. Say, we believe in what was revealed to us and in what was revealed to you; our God and your God is one [and the same]; we are devoted to Him."

Third, 2:191 says, "Kill them wherever you encounter them." This has been interpreted to mean kill non-Muslims wherever you find them. But it is clear from the context that 'them' refers to those who attack you [Meccan polytheists], and wherever you encounter them [in the city of Mecca]. Similarly, aya 9:5 reads, "When the [four] forbidden months are over, wherever you encounter the idolaters, kill them, besiege them, but if they repent, let them go on their way for God is most forgiving and merciful." This verse, too, is taken out of its context of the continual attacks by the polytheists, who wanted to banish from Mecca, kill or convert the Muslims, and who frequently ignored their treaties which required four months of grace. Paul noted Professor Haleem's summary: "The prevalent message of the Qur'an is one of peace and tolerance, but it allows self-defence."

I think, Paul reflected, *that I enjoyed reading the Qur'an, and it has caused me to reflect on my own faith, making it stronger.*

One week after the Accreditation Board's decision was taken, Paul received a phone call from Roberta. "Mr. Al-Zahari has decided that you will do the audit, Paul. Shall I book you a flight for next Sunday?"

"That's fine, but I'll need an interpreter. If Naomi isn't available, can you find me a local bookkeeper who speaks English?"

"Let me work on it. Paul."

Chapter 12

DISCOVERY

Abdul-Haqq Aboud's CV was quite impressive. He was 20 years old and studied at Institut des Hautes Etudes de Management (HEM) in Marrakech, where he was pursuing a degree in finance. He was the oldest of six children. His father was a Moroccan civil servant, and his mother was a high school French teacher. Abdul-Hagg also claimed to be fluent in Arabic, French, and English.

Roberta had contacted an employment agency in Marrakech and obtained six CV's for a qualified bookkeeper as a temporary position. Paul considered Abdul-Hagg the most promising of the six and had arranged to meet him at the Riad el Norj when he arrived on Tuesday in late July. In person, Abdul-Haqq looked more like sixteen years old than twenty. There was no sign of any impending facial hair, but he had a confident, friendly manner. He had a great shock of black hair that spilled down over his left eye and required frequent attention. He explained that he usually wore a white turban, but he felt was inappropriate attire for such an important interview. With dark eyes, prominent cheekbones, and expressive mouth, Abdul-Haqq was a handsome young man.

Paul found that, on examination, the young bookkeeper was fluent, also, in the language of finance with a good understanding of the construction of an income statement, the balance sheet, and a cash flow forecast. Moreover, Abdul-Haqq had an air of dedication and integrity about him.

"Would you be able to work with me for a week or two on a company audit?" Paul asked.

"Yes, of course. I am on the summer holiday, and I would like to audit a real company, not just a case study."

"This is not a company in the usual sense. It is a charity." Paul went on to explain what AMM did and its relationship to GYE.

Abdul-Haqq asked, "How are we going to audit this charity?"

"This is also not a usual audit. We are going to be checking for fraud."

Abdul-Haqq's eyes opened very wide. "We never had an example of fraud in the cases we studied at HEM!"

"Well, this may be quite an experience for you."

"Yes. It would also look very good on my CV to say that I worked with an auditor from England to discover a case of actual fraud in a Moroccan organisation!"

Paul then explained to Abdul-Haqq the procedure he had in mind for the audit, and he asked him to be at Riad el Norj the following morning at 8:30. .

The next morning, Mohammed drove them to AMM. The greeting they received from Yusuf was surly, bordering on rude. "This boy is going to conduct an audit of AMM?" He gave a derisive laugh.

Paul paused to control his irritation. "He is a qualified bookkeeper who will obtain a bachelor's degree in finance from HEM next year. He is also fluent in English. If you wish to test his financial knowledge, please ask." Paul gave a sweeping gesture toward Abdul-Haqq.

Yusuf ignored Paul's invitation. He said, "The office here is quite small. We have only one spare desk for you."

"That's all right. We'll be doing most of our work at my hotel."

Yusuf curled his lips in distain. "So you're going to do an audit by remote control?"

"No. We'd like to start with a copy of the list of entrepreneurs to whom you've made loans and your bank statements in dirhams."

"That would be eight sets of bank statements! Covering what period of time?"

"The last three years, please."

"I can't let you take all our bank statements away!"

"We can bring them back in the afternoon each day, if you wish. The alternative is for us to make copies of all the statements."

"Why is it necessary for you to take twenty-four years of statements?"

"Because one of our tasks is to verify that the one hundred and eighty-eight entrepreneurs actually received loans."

"That's ridiculous!" Yusuf fumed. "You'll have the list of one hundred and eighty-eight entrepreneurs: amount of loan, names, addresses, phone numbers, and so on!"

Paul looked at the ceiling briefly, "Yes, I know that, Yusuf, but I think you know that the purpose of an audit is to provide independent, factual verification."

Eventually, Paul and Abdul-Haqq had the bank statements. In Paul's room at Riad el Norj, they set up an improvised office, using the bedside tables as work stations for their laptops, which were connected into a local area network. They shared the Excel spreadsheet that showed the entrepreneurs who had been reported to the Inter-Sahara Development Bank as having received loans from AMM.

Abdul-Hagg's task was to go through the dirham loan disbursement account and match each disbursement to the entrepreneur who received it. Separate columns were added to the entrepreneurs' spreadsheet to show the actual amount of the loan and the date issued. These figures could be compared to those reported to ISDB. Since Paul could not read the bank statements, which of course were in Arabic, he contented himself with looking through the statements for patterns and inconsistencies. Every now and then, he would look at the spreadsheet to see the progress, which Abdul-Hagg was making. It was slow going. Frequently, the name on the spreadsheet was slightly different than the name on the disbursement account. For example, the nearest match for a loan of 25,000 dirhams to Barakah ben Farouq on April 10, 2009 was shown on the bank statement as "June 5, 2009; B B Farouq: 19,500."

To highlight these discrepancies, Abdul-Hagg added another column to include the name shown in the disbursement account.

By 4 p.m. on the first day, Abdul-Hagg had completed his review of the loan disbursement bank account. He had been able to match 92 of the 188 names shown on the spreadsheet. Strangely, there were three other names in the loan disbursement bank account that he was unable to match with any of the 188.

"What's the total amount of the three mystery loans?" Paul asked.

Abdul-Hagg paused to write a sum formula on the spreadsheet. "49,860 dirhams," he replied."

"OK. We'll give him credit for those three. That gives him a reporting accuracy of 95 out of 188 (Paul resorted to his calculator) or fifty percent. Tomorrow, we've got to check the other dirham accounts to see if any loans were disbursed from them by mistake."

Abdul-Hagg sat frowning at the bank statement. "What I don't understand," he said, "is why there are all these other disbursements. The bank calls them inter-account transfers."

"Are they to the same account number?"

"Yes, they seem to be."

"Can you figure out which account it is?"

Abdul-Hagg scanned the account numbers on the files that had been heaped on Paul's bed. "Yes. The money is being transferred to the AMM general expenses account."

Paul nodded. "And what is the total of the inter-account transfers?"

Abdul-Hagg opened a new spreadsheet and began typing numbers into it as he scanned down the loan disbursement account. He looked up at Paul. "5,977,000 dirhams!" There was a look of consternation on Abdul-Hagg's face. "Why would he transfer half of the money that was supposed to be used for loans into an account that's used for expenses?"

"To answer that question, you have to think like a suspicious auditor, and you have to remember that only the euro accounts have been properly audited."

Abdul-Hagg sat thinking for several moments. "Because," he began, "he wants to make it look like all the loan money has been spent, even though an audit would find that it hasn't been spent on what it was supposed to be spent on."

"Very good. And?"

"So he's transferred the money to an expenses account that isn't audited."

"Right. And then?"

"I suppose we're going to find that it's been spent on something else that it's not supposed to be spent on."

"Any idea what that might be?"

Abdul-Hagg frowned, thoughtful. "I was going to say, loose women, fast cars and good whiskey, but he doesn't seem like the type."

"Maybe we'll find out. For now, could you just check and see that what is transferred out of the loan disbursement account actually arrived in the expenses account?"

That evening as Paul was having dinner in the hotel, his mobile phone rang unexpectedly. "Paul Winthorpe."

"Hi, Paul, it's Naomi. How are you?"

Paul put his fork down so that he could concentrate better; he was conscious of his more rapid heartbeat. "I'm fine, Naomi. How are you, and where are you?"

"I'm in Miami about to catch a flight for London. I'm jet-lagged and a bit tired, but otherwise OK. How is it going? Roberta tells me you have an accomplice."

"Yes. Not as nice as the one I had before, but he's doing some good work."

There was a pause.

"Have you found anything juicy?"

"Well, so far, we've been able to find only 95 of the 188 loans he claims to have made. We may find a few more tomorrow, but I doubt it will be very many."

"Ooooh! That's interesting. What's happened to the unspent money?"

"It's been transferred to the AMM expenses bank account, and from there, it probably found its way into Yusuf's personal account. We're going to check that tomorrow."

"Very good! Found anything else?"

"No. It's been tedious work for Abdul-Hagg, because the names, amounts and dates frequently don't match exactly."

There was another pause.

"Paul, would you mind if I joined you in Marrakech? I'd like to be in on the kill."

Paul drew in a breath of sudden excitement. "Yes, please do! I'd like to have my accomplice back."

She giggled. "I should be there in time for dinner." And she hung up.

So she's going to arrive at Heathrow late tonight, go home for a rest and change of clothes, then journey to Gatwick tomorrow for a three hour flight to Marrakech. If she's tired and jet-lagged now, she'll be a wreck this time tomorrow—or at least I would be!

The following morning, Paul went to AMM alone to obtain the files on the private companies that had been supporting AMM. The previous evening he had asked Abdul-Hagg to return the bank statements that Yusuf insisted be returned to his office each afternoon. *I can't imagine what he does with the statements when he gets them back. Look through them page by page for any notations or any missing pages?*

Paul could have asked Abdul-Hagg to pick up the bank statements and the private company files on his way from home to the Riad el Norj on Thursday morning. But Paul was concerned that Yusuf would hassle the young bookkeeper, so he decided to go to AMM himself.

His concern was well-founded, and he became the butt of Yusuf's hassling. "You want the bank statements again?" the chief executive asked indignantly.

"Yes, please, we didn't finish with them yesterday."

"You're not very efficient, are you?"

"We don't intend to be efficient; we intend to be thorough."

Yusuf's tone was extremely sarcastic. "And what did your thorough approach reveal to you, Mr. Winthorpe?"

"Several things, but I don't think it's appropriate for me to comment until our work is completed. The other thing we would like to borrow today are the files on the private companies that have been supporting AMM."

"You don't need those files. They have nothing to do with the scope of your audit!"

"That is for me to decide, not you, Yusuf."

Yusuf folded his arms across his chest, and glared mutely and with hostility at Paul.

"I can tell you with great certainly," Paul began, slowly and evenly, "that if I don't get the files I want AMM will certainly lose its accreditation."

Paul got the files he wanted, but he stood next to Latifa, as she went through the file drawer, in order to make sure that no potentially interesting file was left behind.

Back at Riad el Norj, Abdul-Hagg was in a state of agitation, waiting for Paul. As soon as they were in Paul's room, the young bookkeeper's announcement burst out. "He tried to bribe me!"

"Sit down and tell me what happened."

Abdul-Hagg remained standing, he was gesturing wildly as his words came tumbling out. "When I got there last night, he offered me a green tea."

"Who offered you a tea?"

"Mr. Al-Rashid. And he said that I must be a very clever young man. He said that he would like to hire me too. He wanted to know how much I was being paid. So I told him. And he said that he would like to pay me twice as much. But I said I couldn't do that. So he said that my family would be disappointed in me for not taking up such a fine offer. And then he started talking about my family. And I got nervous, and . . ."

"Why did you get nervous, Abdul-Hagg?"

"Because in Morocco, when somebody talks like that about your family it's like a threat."

"What did he say?"

"He talked about my mother and father as if he knew them. He talked about their work and how important it is to the family. And then he said he knows powerful people in government.

And it would be a shame if my mother and father got fired because I refused an excellent job offer."

"What did you say?"

"I said that I would let him know this morning. What should I do Mr. Winthorpe?"

For some moments, Paul sat thinking.

"I think you should call him now and tell him that you have given me your notice, and . . ."

There was a groan of misery from Abdul-Hagg.

"Just a minute, Abdul-Hagg," Paul continued, "let me finish. You should tell him that a research assignment has suddenly come up at HEM, and you've decided to take it. So you won't be working any more for me, as you had expected to, and that, unfortunately, you won't be able to accept his very interesting and generous offer." Abdul-Hagg looked dejected.

"What I will do," Paul said, "is pay you one week's wages because the day before yesterday we talked of your assignment being a week or two, and because it's not your fault it's being cut short. Besides, at the end of today, you'll have done essentially what we wanted you to do."

Abdul-Hagg had tears in his eyes. "Mr. Winthorpe, will you write a letter of reference for me?"

"Yes, of course."

Abdul-Hagg completed the call to Yusuf.

"What did he say?" Paul wanted to know.

"He seemed to be pleased that I won't be working for you and pleased that he doesn't have to pay me."

"OK. That's good. Now, can you figure out to which account the extra funds are transferred from the AMM expenses account?"

Abdul-Hagg set to work, and Paul began to study the private company files.

An hour and a half later, the young bookkeeper reported that 7,654,900 dirhams had been transferred out of the AMM expenses account on inter-account transfers to account number AR490121376804.

That's about 640,000 *pounds!* Paul said, "That's not one of the other bank accounts we've got here, is it?"

"No, it isn't."

"Can you call the bank and ask who owns that account?"

"Yes, but I doubt if they'll tell me."

Abdul-Hagg called; he was right: the bank informed him that information about individual accounts could be given only to the actual account holder.

"All right. Did the 300,000 dirhams that were transferred out of the loan repayment account go into that same account?"

Abdul-Hagg leafed through the loan repayment bank statements. "Yes."

"How many other transfers were made out of the loan repayment account and into the same mystery account?"

Half an hour later, the response was, "Eight other transfers totaling 392,080 dirhams. The interesting thing is that each of those transfers is similar in size to an actual loan."

Paul commented, "All the better to mislead the casual observer. Now, Abdul-Hagg, I'd like you to go through the rest of the accounts here and see if you can find any loans which were made from them by mistake."

This took quite a while, but the bookkeeper could find none.

"OK," Paul said, "The last assignment I have for you, Abdul-Hagg, is to help me with these private company files. We're looking for instances of the same expense being recovered from multiple companies."

This task was complicated by the fact that the files Paul had obtained that morning from Yusuf contained no AMM invoices. There were, however, three instances of the same invoice to AMM appearing in two, three or four of the private company files. For example, there was an invoice for training of mentors from Training Maroc, LLC, dated 8 February 2008 in the amount of 129,000 dirhams. This appeared in the OilMaroc, Demoitt and Maroc Telecom files.

By examining the bank statement for the account into which Moroccan companies paid their contributions, Abdul-Hagg was able to find payments from OilMaroc on 10 March 2009, from Demoitt on 12 March 2008 and from Maroc Telecom on 28 March 2008, all in the amount of 129,000 dirhams. A similar result was found for the other two instances of duplicate invoices.

"This proves there was fraud, right, Mr. Winthorpe?" Abdul-Hagg suggested.

"I'm afraid that without the actual AMM invoices and specific reference to the supplier's invoice, it doesn't prove fraud, Abdul-Hagg, but it is pretty strong circumstantial evidence."

"Are you going to ask to see all their actual invoices, then?"

"I'd like to think about that. Now, before you go home would you help me make copies of all this stuff on which I've put yellow post-it notes? Paul had bought a printer/photocopier as being a far better option than trying to use the copier in the Riad el Norj office.

An hour and an half later, the photocopying was complete and Paul had packed the original AMM files in a box.

"Shall I drop these off at AMM?" Abdul-Hagg asked.

"No. I'll take care of it in the morning. I'm going to call a taxi for you, and I want you to go straight home."

"Why? I can take a bus."

"Because AMM may want to check that you weren't working with me today." Abdul-Hagg looked puzzled, a face Paul ignored. "Let me have your bank details, Abdul-Hagg, so I can get your money transferred tomorrow."

The old porter came to Paul's room to inform them that the taxi was outside. There was indeed a taxi waiting in the square. Paul noticed that there was another car parked just behind it, and as he and Abdul-Hagg moved toward the taxi, a man dressed in brown emerged from the rear of the car. The man strode meaningfully toward Abdul-Hagg, leaving the rear door of the car open. Paul pushed the young bookkeeper toward the taxi. At the same time, he placed himself in the path of the man. There was a yell from the brown man as he tried to get past Paul, who seized the shirt front of the oncoming man and shouted to the bookkeeper, "Go!"

Enraged, the brown man, who was smaller and younger, punched Paul in the stomach, still trying to get past him. He was too late; the taxi drove off. Deliberately and angrily, the man faced Paul, ready to exact revenge. There was a shout from the car that the man seemed to ignore. He readied himself to spring at Paul, but he paused, looking past Paul and hesitating. Then, he turned toward the car. Paul glanced quickly over his shoulder. There, just behind him, was the old porter, a cricket bat held high, ready to strike. Paul turned his attention to the car. There, next to the driver was Efraim, still yelling at the brown man, who finally got into the back seat of the car and closed the door. The porter shouted something to the occupants of the car as it drove off.

In the office of Riad el Norj, there was a three-way conversation between Paul, the porter, and Julian, the owner of the hotel—much of it in Arabic, some in English. After what had happened was explained to Julian, Paul expressed concern that the car would go to Abdul-Hagg's home and abduct him there.

The porter shook his head, and wrote something down on a piece of paper. Julian listened to the porter for a moment, then he picked up the phone, dialed and spoke to someone at the other end. He covered the mouthpiece and turned to Paul. "What's the bookkeeper's name and address?" he asked.

Paul ran upstairs and returned with Abdul-Hagg's CV, which he gave to Julian. Julian read from the CV, hung up and announced, "That's sorted!"

Paul asked, "Who was that you were speaking with?"

"The police. I gave them the license number of the car. Told them that the occupants of the car had tried to steal the money that had just been paid to Abdul-Hagg Aboud. I said that the people in the car would try again at Aboud's home. The police said they would take care of it."

In reflecting later on the incident, Paul concluded, *I doubt that Efraim would be so stupid as to try again to abduct Abdul-Hagg. There were several witnesses to the first attempt, and even if his connections were excellent, they wouldn't prevent him being detained by the police for a while. What I don't understand is why the brown man appeared to be so terrified of the porter. After all, he's quite an old man. But maybe he wasn't terrified of the old man;*

maybe he was terrified of Efraim, who was yelling bloody murder at him.

Paul decided to relax and consider his next steps in the hotel lounge. The old porter came in and asked, "Sir want drink?"

"Yes, please. What is your name?"

"My name Numair, but I called Rais, because I captain of cricket."

"You were captain of a cricket team in Morocco?"

"Yes. Moroccan team."

"That must have been some time ago."

"Thirty-three years, sir. Many good seasons."

"So, you're quite well-known."

"Yes, sir."

"And you were a good batsman?"

"One year, I have five centuries."

"So that's why the man in brown didn't want to fight with you!"

"Yes, sir. He not want hurt me. Very big shame!"

Paul had just tasted his gin and tonic when he heard French voices in the courtyard. Moments later, Naomi came into the lounge. He stood up to greet her, but she threw herself to him, kissing him soundly on the mouth. She held him at arms length for a moment, "How are you, Paul?"

He felt a surge of joy to be so close to her. "I'm fine. More importantly, how are you?"

"Oh, I'm fine. I sleep like a cat on airplanes. Tell me! What are the latest developments?" She perched herself expectantly on the edge of a couch opposite him.

For a moment, he took her in. The sleeveless Laura Ashley dress in a blue cornflower motif clung helplessly to her, and her gold hair hung lifeless, but her face was glowing with pleasure.

"Well, the evidence of fraud is convincing, but not conclusive in the sense that we know that about seven and a half million dirhams left the AMM accounts and went to one other account. We have no proof that the other account was Yusuf's."

"My goodness! That's about six hundred thousand pounds! A fortune in Morocco!"

Paul showed her the general list of the issues that they had prepared at the conclusion of their previous visit to Morocco.

AMM Problems:

1. Loans reported but were not made
2. Insufficient and inadequately trained mentors
3. Unfair contracts with entrepreneurs
4. Single expenses billed to multiple contributing organisations
5. Poor financial controls
6. Inadequate corporate governance
7. Future performance forecast in AMM 2015 overly optimistic
8. Inadequate financial audits
9. Attempts reportedly made to bribe GYE people
10. Excess funds embezzled

"We've got evidence to support all of these points except number ten. So removing their accreditation would be entirely justified, but at the moment, we can't get him for fraud. We have no proof that he got the money."

Naomi leaned forward; she was smiling to cover the intensity of her expression. "But, Paul, you promised that we would get him!"

"I know. If only, we could induce him to write a personal cheque for something! That will have his account number on it."

She sat back and thought. "OK. Let me think about it. That's my job for tomorrow."

Paul had decided not to tell her about the attempted abduction of Abdul-Hagg, but he told her that he had sent an e-mail to Roberta requesting that payment be made into the bookkeeper's account. For a few minutes they talked about the audit process and its findings.

Naomi said, "I've reserved the hammam. I need it! Are you going to join me?"

"Yes, of course." *I can't believe this girl! It's as if time apart doesn't count.*

Paul was dribbling water from a ladle onto the heated rocks and watching it bounce about before turning to steam. When the water was poured from the ladle, it was passive, utterly resigned to the force of gravity. But when the stream made contact with the rocks it was suddenly transformed into living, active spheroids of water, moving, jumping and shrinking into plumes of hissing steam.

"Are you playing?" she asked. She had come up beside him, one arm around his waist, and her body making light contact with his.

He looked over at her. "Yes, I am."

Feigning indignance, she said, "Well, it's time to get to work! I need a good scrubbing."

Suddenly she's the adult and I'm the child, well, whatever.

He reached for a hemp scrubber, doused it with soap, and began to brush her back, gradually sinking down until he was attending to her feet.

He stood, put the scrubber aside, and turned her around. Squeezing soap onto his hands, he began to massage her shoulders, arms and breasts.

"Don't I get a scrubbing on this side, too?" she asked, innocently.

"The back gets scrubbed, the front gets massaged. It's better that way."

"For whom?"

"Both of us."

She gave a soft giggle. As he glanced at her face now and then, her expression changed from contentment to erotic bliss to happy amusement.

"I'd like to wash your beautiful hair, but there's no shower in here."

"We can do it later. We won't be disturbed. I've spoken to Yvonne. OK, are you ready? Same rules as before? Scrub the back, massage the front?"

"The washer gets to choose the rules," he announced.

"OK, maybe I'll use this brush." She was brandishing a wooden-handled brush with nasty looking wire bristles.

"That's for cleaning the floor."

"But, you said I could make up the rules."

He suddenly swept her into his arms and began to kiss her. He heard the brush fall to the floor.

She washed him slowly, thoroughly and admiringly.

Holding him in her hand, she looked up at him. "Do you remember the first time I got you in this state?"

"Yes, very well."

"What did you think of me?"

"I thought you were a little naïve."

She gave a short chuckle. "And now?"

"I think you're an absolutely splendid woman."

Her lips were trembling, and she looked away to regain her composure. She pressed her face against his neck and whispered, "Lie down, Paul. On the bench."

Still holding him, she positioned herself above him and slowly lowered herself, her eyes holding his in intense communication. "Oh! That's good!" she breathed.

"It gets better."

"Show me, Paul!"

Naomi looked relaxed, alert and happy. Her feet, which were hidden under her floor-length green cotton skirt, were tucked up beside her on the sofa. She was wearing a high-necked white cotton blouse with puffy sleeves. Her hair, still slightly damp, was tied in a single green ribbon below her right ear. She took a sip of her sherry, "OK, I have to admit that you're not a bad hair washer. You just need to do a better job of rinsing."

"Right, I'll bear that in mind."

"Paul? . . ."

"Yes."

"Did you speak to Sarah when you went home?" She was leaning forward, waiting for his response.

"Yes, I did. I told her that I had met you and that I had fallen in love with you."

Naomi nodded, thinking. Nervously, she asked, "So is it over with you and Sarah?"

Paul nodded. "I guess so . . . for the time being. I told her that I wasn't sure how you felt about me, and . . ."

Naomi interrupted, "I love you, Paul." She said it with great fervour and conviction.

Paul moved to sit next to her on the couch. "That's wonderful, Naomi." He paused for a moment, looking at her. "I want a long-term relationship, Naomi."

She made a non-committal movement of her head, but said nothing.

"I couldn't be happy if my woman was gone over half the time."

"Why not?" she asked. There was something slightly childish about her tone.

"Because I'd be missing you too much, and I'd feel that part of me—the best part of me—was missing."

"Oh," she said. She looked down at her hands.

"Naomi, have you been in love before?"

She shrugged, then shook her head slightly. They sat in silence for a while. He asked, very gently, "Naomi, what are you running away from?"

Her face became contorted with grief. "Oh, God! I'm not running away from you Paul!"

He put his arms around her as she began to tremble. "From what, then?"

"Oh, God! I don't know. I just think of myself as a nomad, helping charities around the world. Perhaps . . . Perhaps that's my rationalisation. I don't know." She turned her stricken face toward him. "I don't know. What am I running away from, Paul?"

"Don't you ever get lonely when you're travelling?"

"Not particularly. I'm always with people." She sat thinking for a moment. "Except . . . except this last trip. I felt very lonely. It was terrible. What's the matter with me, Paul?"

"Nothing's the matter, Naomi. I think you've chosen the work you do to avoid a committed relationship. That may have something to do with your father and maybe your mother. And, I think that as a matter of self preservation, you see yourself as an adult child, rather than as a woman."

She gave a wry smile of acknowledgement. Then, wiping away a tear, she gazed at him ardently.

"God, when I'm with you, Paul, I feel like such a woman!"

"You are a splendid woman, Naomi, but I also rather enjoy your childish moments."

"So what's going to happen?"

"What would you like to see happen?"

She paused to reflect. "My fantasy—I invented this during the trip—is that I'll go to work in a charity in Israel. It doesn't much matter where—Tel Aviv, Jerusalem, the West Bank. I'll really work on my music—violin, I think—and try to get into a good orchestra. I'll marry you, and you'll work as a consultant. I'm sure you'll find good work. We'll have some babies and live happily ever after."

Paul smiled indulgently. "But," she continued with a touch of sadness, "I don't think it's right for you. You've spent all your life in England: your family, friends, and work are all there. You'd have to learn to speak Hebrew, and you'd have to learn a completely foreign culture. Israel is a benign police state where the Arabs are treated with suspicion, and religion, prosperity and land are the essential values."

"It doesn't sound like a good fit for me," Paul conceded.

"How about your fantasy?" she asked eagerly.

"Well, London, as you probably know has lots of two things that are important to you: charities and music. Apart from that . . ."

She interrupted, "No, Paul. No, I don't want to talk about London!"

"Why not?"

"Because I'm not ready." She shook her head vigorously. "Not ready to even think about it!"

They sat in silence for a time.

"Do your kids know about me?" she asked.

"I've told Cynthia; she's probably told John."

"What would they think?"

"Cynthia is mildly disapproving at the moment, but she's very fond of Sarah."

Naomi stared into her glass as if, hidden in it, was the secret of her future.

"If we," she began, "I mean, if we found a place in the world—maybe some kind of desert island —that was right for us. If we found such a place, would your kids be an obstacle?"

"No, I don't think so. I think you'd like them and they'd enjoy you. Oh, inevitably there would be unspoken frictions about half-brothers and -sisters, and about the allocation of time, resources and attention. But my kids are not the problem. We are the problem. I'm just afraid that you're a humming bird, and I'm asking you to leave the flowers alone because you'd be happier eating bugs."

She laughed aloud. "Well, I don't particularly like bugs, but I don't think I want to be a humming bird anymore."

At dinner, they left their serious discussion behind them. Naomi floated various ideas for getting one of Yusuf's cheques. Paul played the devil's advocate. With admiration, he thought, *She's a very inventive and persuasive girl!*

After a calvados in the lounge, Naomi said she was tired and went off to bed.

In the middle of the night, Paul was suddenly awake. Again, a large white butterfly was shedding its chrysalis. Naked, she slipped into bed beside him, pressing herself against him.

"I thought you were tired, sweetheart."

Dreamily she responded, "I slept for a while. Then I woke up. I thought about you. And, I thought, '*He's only on the other side of the atrium. Why shouldn't I be with him tonight?*' I love the feel of your warmth, Paul."

What started as a languid embrace became more and more fiery.

"Please be on top, Paul!"

* * *

They rang the bell at AMM. There was no answer. They rang again. No answer.

Paul said, "There must be somebody here." He knocked robustly on the door. A few moments later, the door opened slightly. The maid's face appeared in the opening. She said something in Arabic. Naomi replied, but the maid disappeared, and the door began to close. Paul shouldered the door open. The maid stood in the hallway, wringing her hands in distress.

"Tell her I promised to return these files to Mr. Al-Rashid," Paul announced.

There was a brief conversation in Arabic. "She says Mr. Al-Rashid has gone out. Only Latifa is here. Yaminah has the day off."

"We'll see Latifa, then," Paul confirmed.

Resignedly, the maid stepped aside.

Judging by the fondness of their greetings, Naomi and Latifa had become good friends. Latifa returned to her desk, Naomi sat beside her, and they began to talk. Naomi gestured toward the box Paul had placed on Yaminah's desk. Latifa nodded and asked a question. Naomi began to reply. Now and then, Latifa would interrupt with a question. Paul watched Latifa's face. It became apparent that whatever Naomi was telling her became more and more troubling to the young Moroccan girl. She made an appeal to Naomi. Naomi shook her head, and offered an explanation. Latifa was inclined toward Naomi, intent on catching every word. She asked several questions to which Naomi responded. Then, she sat back in her chair and gazed at the far wall.

Finally, she took a deep breath, rose from her chair and left the room. Two minutes later, she returned to the office carrying a hard, black file folder. She showed it to Naomi, who opened the cover to see the first page. Naomi nodded and gave a meaningful glance at Paul. The two women began to discuss something about the file, flipping through it and looking at various pages. They then went to the photocopier. Latifa handed one page at a time to Naomi, who put the page on the photocopier, pressed the copy button and returned the original to Latifa. They continued working like that for about fifteen minutes.

The maid came into the office. She whispered something loudly to Latifa, who slammed shut the file and ran out of the office.

Naomi scooped up the copies that had been made and stuffed them into her laptop case. In a panicked voice, she whispered to Paul, "Efraim's just arrived."

Latifa returned to the office just before Efraim entered. She was trying, unsuccessfully, to control her feelings of terror. Efraim regarded the three of them with acute suspicion. Paul gestured toward the box of files and said, "Naomi and I are here to return these files which I borrowed. You can tell Yusuf that all the files we borrowed have been returned. When we got here, we found that Latifa was feeling very ill. Perhaps she has the flu. So we're going to take her home."

Efraim said nothing. He continued to look from one to the other of them. He smiled when he saw the fearful faces of the women. Lifting a flap of the box of files, he peered inside, riffled through the contents and looked up again at the other three. "So you are going to miss my talk at the mosque this afternoon?"

Paul said, "We didn't know you were going to speak this afternoon."

"Yes, and if you understood what I have to say, you would doubtless find it very interesting."

"In that case, I should try to attend. My driver can translate for me. But right now, we have to take Latifa home."

Efraim leaned back against Yaminah's desk. He stared malevolently at the other three. "Yes, of course," he announced in a mixture of venom and false courtesy.

As the car pulled away, Paul could restrain himself no longer. "Were you guys copying Yusuf's bank statements?"

"Yes. Latifa thought he would keep them in his office. She found them in his desk."

"Could you see whether any of the numbers matched?"

"Yes, from a brief look, there were quite a few matches."

Paul turned to Latifa, "Thank you very much, Latifa!"

The girl was clearly very upset and worried. "I not know if I do right thing!"

Paul asked, "Wouldn't a cheque from his chequebook have been good enough?"

"I not find chequebook; I find bank statement."

"Latifa is worried about her job at AMM if it loses its accreditation," Naomi explained. "I told her that is a valid concern—that probably she'll be made redundant when it loses its accreditation. But I also told her that if fraud is proved, Yusuf will lose his job—maybe go to jail —and that GYE will restart AMM with honest people like her."

"I like very much see Mr. Al-Rashid go jail!" Latifa announced emphatically. "I am hating him!"

"Well," Paul responded, "You may have made your wish come true!"

Mohammed asked, "We are taking Miss Latifa home. Yes?"

"Yes, please Mohammed."

Naomi asked, "What are we going to do then?"

Paul replied, "I would like to do two things. I'd like to go and check out of the hotel, because, as of this morning, our work is done in Morocco. And then, I'd like to go hear what Efraim has to say at the mosque. Then, we can go to the airport to catch the afternoon flight."

Naomi groaned. "I can think of a lot better ways to spend the afternoon."

"Yes, OK," Paul said. "Women have their intuition. Something tells me that this is a talk we shouldn't miss."

"Miss Evensen," Latifa offered, "We go like before, and Mohammed go with Mr. Winthorpe."

Paul and Mohammed were seated about six rows from the front of the mosque. They were both wearing keffiyehs, but this time, Paul felt no need to cover his face. After all, he had been invited to hear Efraim speak. The women were on the far side of the partition, veiled as before, not wanting to reveal that Latifa was not sick. Paul started his pocket recorder as Efraim rose to speak. *Strange!* he thought, *I haven't seen Yusuf anywhere.*

It was not a long speech, but it was full of emotion and bombast. Several times, Efraim made explosive movements with his arms, positively shouting. At other times, he would shrink down and speak in a loud whisper. As theatre, it was positively riveting, but many of the male faces within Paul's field of vision clearly found the talk disturbing. Mohammed had his eyes fixed on his shoes; he was frowning, his lower lip protruding. He shook his head occasionally, as if he were being bothered by a fly.

At the conclusion, Mohammed took Paul's arm and pushed him forward, seeking the quickest exit.

"What's the hurry, Mohammed?"

"You not want to meet with Mr. Al-Rashid!"

"Why not?"

"I esplain later!"

As they left the little square, Mohammed whispered, "I think he planning set off bomb! He not say so, but I think!" This last pronouncement with an index finger pointing at his temple.

The women were almost to the car when the men caught up to them. They were both clearly shocked by what they had heard.

Naomi asked, "Did you understand any of it?"

"No. Mohammed says it was pretty awful."

"I think he's planning some kind of attack," Naomi announced.

"That's what Mohammed thinks. I have it all recorded."

Naomi motioned them together. "Let's go have lunch together and listen to the recording. That way we can make some notes."

Mohammed shrugged his acceptance. Latifa said that she didn't want to have lunch anywhere near the mosque.

"Mohammed," Naomi asked, "can you take us to a quiet hotel restaurant that's not very busy?"

"I not have very much money," Mohammed protested.

Paul spread his hands in a gesture that promised safety. "I'll take care of lunch."

They were seated in the corner of a Ramada Inn restaurant. It being Friday afternoon, the business guests had left, and the restaurant was nearly deserted. Paul put the recorder in the middle of the table, opened his notebook, and took out his pen. When the waiter had taken their orders and left, Naomi said, "Go ahead, Paul. When I raise a finger, stop it again."

Paul pressed the play button and Efraim's voice boomed out. Quickly, he turned the volume down. After a couple of minutes, Naomi raised a finger. "There, he says, 'I have spoken with The Prophet, and he has called on me to tell you this good news.'"

Paul wrote it down and glanced up at Naomi, who nodded. He pressed Play again. Almost immediately, she raised a finger. "He says, 'When you hear that what I promised you today has come true, your faith will increase, as you will know that the One True God has revealed His plan to you through me.'"

Continuing this procedure, Paul wrote additional points in his notebook:

- "It is time to strike at the heart of the infidels!"
- "They deserve to be punished for the slaughter of our Muslim brothers in Iraq, Afghanistan, Pakistan, Lebanon, and Gaza."
- "Vengeance will be in a pagan city, full of corrupt wealth and the worship of idols."
- "The infidels will fall screaming into hell."
- "We will strike them in the eye so that their blindness to the suffering they have caused will be repaid."
- "Near to their corrupt seat of government will the sufferings of the martyrs be repaid."
- "The hammer blow will strike on the wrong day they consider holy, thus exposing their folly in not worshiping the One True God."

Paul reviewed his notes. "Did he really say 'eye'—E-Y-E?" he asked.

Latifa nodded. Naomi said, "I know it doesn't make sense, but that's what he said. Let's listen to it again."

They listened to the recording again. Naomi, Latifa, and Mohammed all confirmed that the word he had used was 'eye'.

Paul said, "It does make sense if his target is the London Eye."

Naomi was horrified. "Is that possible?"

"I took my children and grandchildren for a ride on the Eye a couple of months ago. My son, who's a very imaginative mechanical engineer with Architectural Design Partnership in Manchester pointed out to me that it is possible."

"Oh, my God," Naomi exclaimed. "What should we do?"

"We should take Latifa home, go to the airport and catch the first flight to London."

"Should we call somebody?"

"Yes, we should do that, too."

Paul and Mohammed had been waiting in the car for some time for Naomi to return. She had gone in with Latifa to take off the black half niqab and to make sure that Latifa was all right. Twenty minutes passed. Twenty-five minutes. Paul picked up his mobile and called Naomi. The call went to voice mail. *Strange—very strange!* He was getting restless. He got out of the car and walked to the gate that the women had entered. His mobile buzzed and vibrated. He had just received a message. On the screen, the message read, "help @ amm." It was from Naomi. For some seconds, he stood, looking at the screen. *Such a short message. She didn't have time to write it—maybe she sent it surreptitiously, "help @ amm." My God, she's been abducted! That bastard Efraim's got her!*

He dashed to the car and ordered Mohammed: "Drive to AMM immediately! Naomi has been taken there!"

"How you know, sir?"

"I just received a message on my phone from her!"

"Very bad people at AMM," Mohammed announced. The car was hurtling through the streets of Marrakech. "You want gun, sir? I have." Mohammed flipped open the glove box, and with eyes still fixed on the road, he withdrew a small revolver. "I think is loaded, sir." He handed it over the back seat.

Paul examined the revolver—an old 32-calibre weapon. It was indeed loaded. Paul could see the blunt grey noses of five cartridges. "Thanks, Mohammed. I hope I don't need this!"

"You ever fire gun, sir?" Mohammed was looking at him in the rear view mirror.

"Yes. When I was in the army quite a while ago."

"I never fire. I have gun for ten, twelve years. Most drivers have guns."

They turned onto the street on which AMM was located. "Sir, I advise, not go to front door."

"OK. How do I get to the back door?"

"These kind of house have several back doors. Climb over roof." Paul began to have doubts.

Mohammed parked the car fifty metres from the house and got out. "Come, sir! I help. Then I in car. Ready for getaway!" He punched the air with his fist.

From the sidewalk, at the corner of the house, they looked up. At the edge of the garage roof, there was a triple strand of barbed wire, about 50 centimetres high, strung as a deterrent to any would be burglars. "Do you have wire cutters, Mohammed?"

The driver shook his head. *Well,* Paul thought, *they wouldn't have been much use anyway. How could you climb and cut wire at the same time? I'll just have to tough it.*

Just beyond the garage door, Mohammed made a step with his interlaced fingers. Putting his right foot into Mohammed's hands, Paul looked up. "One, two, three!" Paul was suddenly catapulted upward. His head was above the flat roof, and grasping the top strand of the wire, he was able to pull and lift himself up so that his waist was level with the roof. He pulled one knee up into the rain gutter, and then he flung himself against the wire. Suddenly, the wire collapsed and he was lying flat on the roof. Gingerly, he got up and appraised his injuries. His left hand was torn, and looking down at his shirt, there was blood seeping from puncture wounds.

"Pull me up, sir! We do again!"

The wooden post to which the wire was fastened had snapped off at its base. Paul took the post and dragged the wire out of the way. Then, lying on the garage roof, Paul reached down and grasped Mohammed's hands. Moments later they were both standing on the garage roof looking at the remaining story of the building. There were two small windows looking out onto the street; both were heavily curtained. *Bedrooms,* Paul thought.

They repeated the boosting process from the garage roof to the building roof, but this time, Mohammed didn't follow Paul. Instead, he dropped back to the ground.

Quietly, Paul walked to the rear of the roof and peered over the edge. One floor below, there was a terrace with a railing around it, and beyond that the house dropped another two floors into a sunken garden. Lying on the roof, he leaned over to see if there was a door leading into the house from the terrace. He saw a large, sliding glass door in the centre of the terrace. From one end of the roof, he eased himself down onto the terrace. There were curtains drawn most of the way across the inside of the doors, but through the opening, Paul could see the back of a large man dressed in black. *Probably Efraim.* Carefully, he tried to slide the door. There was some resistance; was it locked or unlocked?

Paul stopped to think. *If it is locked, I'll have to shoot my way in. Definitely to be avoided. Noise will alarm the neighbours. Take a chance that one of the women will be hit.* Suddenly there was a click. The door slid wide open, and with a roar, Efraim stepped out. He was carrying a club—a small baseball bat—in one hand, and he lunged at Paul. Paul stepped back and tried to pull the revolver from his pocket. There was a crash of breaking glass as one of the sliding doors shattered. Efraim's attention was diverted to the falling glass. Paul drew the revolver and pointed at Efraim. "Put the club down, Efraim!"

"You think I'm afraid of you and your toy gun!" the man in black roared. He raised the club menacingly, ready to strike. Paul stepped back, took careful aim and fired. The bullet struck the club, tearing it from Efraim's hand. Paul had already levelled the gun at Efraim's chest, ready for a fatal second shot, when Efraim slowly and incredulously raised his hands.

"We're in here, Paul!" It was Naomi.

In a gesture with the gun, Paul directed Efraim inside. The two women were tied, back-to-back, in wooden chairs. They had been stripped to the waist, and there were angry red welts on their faces and chests. Latifa, still terrified, was sobbing uncontrollably.

"Naomi, can you hold the gun on this thug while I untie you?"

"Yes. I got one hand free, and I threw that heavy mug at the door."

Paul gave the gun to Naomi. "Just go ahead and kill him if he moves."

She turned a look of pure venom on Efraim. "Go ahead, you Arab scum, make my day!"

Minutes later, the women had been released and had put on the remnants of their torn clothing. A defiant Efraim had been bound securely to the bedposts in another room. A sock had been stuffed in his mouth and secured with adhesive tape. Naomi left the room and returned with a braided leather lash; she ordered Latifa to do something. Efraim began to squeal and buck as his shirt was torn open. Using all her strength, Naomi slashed him savagely across the face and the chest with the lash.

Paul tried to intervene, "Naomi, the police will be here soon. We've got to go."

Reluctantly, Naomi passed the lash to Latifa, who let it fall to the floor. The young Moroccan girl approached Efraim, gave him a look of contempt, and spit in his face.

As they left the house, Paul locked the front door from the outside and threw the key onto the roof.

"Why did Efraim suddenly decide to abduct you?" Paul asked.

"Because," Naomi explained, "When Yusuf returned to the office shortly after we left, he found the last page of his bank statement on the photocopier. He guessed what happened, and he ordered Efraim to get back the copies."

"He didn't get the copies, did he?"

"No. Don't you remember? The copies are in my laptop case, which is here in the car. My goodness, Paul! Is that blood on your shirt and trousers?"

"Yes, I had a little altercation with some barbed wire on the roof."

"We ought to get you to a doctor!"

"No. I just need to wash up and get a bandage or two."

Latifa wanted to be dropped off at the central bus station. She was too frightened to return to her apartment. She wanted to take a bus to her mother's village. Naomi removed a dark, long-sleeved shirt from her suitcase and gave them to Latifa, who would change out of her torn garment in the women's rest room.

"Where we go now?" Mohammed asked, as they left the bus station.

Paul turned to Naomi. "We have three things to do: clean up, make some phone calls and catch a plane to London. But, I'm afraid we've missed the afternoon flights to London. We can go to a hotel at the airport, or we can go to a first class airport lounge."

"I vote for a hotel. I need some privacy and a proper shower."

"He didn't. . . . I mean I know he whipped you, but did he . . ." Paul was unable to utter the words.

"No. If he had, I would have shot him in the balls, and then after a while—probably quite a while —I would have shot him in the head."

Paul looked at her searchingly. She gave him a slight smile and turned away. "You don't understand," she began, "how your sweet little charity nomad could turn into such an unmerciful fury." Paul nodded.

She shrugged. "I don't know. The hate and anger just boiled up overwhelmingly inside me. Something snapped. I couldn't whimper and plead. I felt powerfully defiant. I was God's chained angel, and he was the devil incarnate! Besides, Israelis believe absolutely in the power of retribution."

"How did he manage to tie both of you up?"

"He beat both of us nearly senseless. I thought for a while, when Latifa had passed out, that he'd killed her."

At the hotel, they tended to each other's wounds. Naomi had a weal across her forehead and two on her left cheek. Both her breasts and her stomach were marked with raised livid welts.

Paul said, "God, it hurts me to see you like this!"

Tenderly she pressed a welt on her cheek. "I don't think the damage is permanent, but it certainly hurt like hell at the time. Let's look at you."

He removed his shirt. On his stomach were three puncture wounds. She cleaned them until there was a clean seepage of blood. The hotel first aid kit was raided for bandages.

"Let's see your hand." His left hand was clenched shut. "Open it, Paul." Slowly he complied to reveal a mass of coagulated blood, which she rinsed away under running water. There was one deep cut running parallel to his lifeline; blood still seeped from it. "Can you move all your fingers?" she asked. He demonstrated successfully. "I think this ought to have stitches, Paul."

"Later. Just do the best you can to prevent further bleeding."

"Who are you going to call, Paul?"

"I don't know who to call in MI5 or MI6 or even Scotland Yard. The trouble is I'll probably get connected to a duty officer whose first instinct is to evaluate me. So I think I'll call Major Bancroft, he'll know who to contact."

Major Bancroft was not in the office, but when Paul explained that it was an emergency—a matter of life and death—he was put through to his home phone. Major Bancroft listened, and asked several questions: "You have the latest recording?" and "Do you think he's still in this country?"

"Yes. He is right now, but he probably won't be for very long."

"Why do you say that?"

"Because of the reference to the infidel holy day. That would be Sunday. Today's Friday. Do you think after announcing this great event in the mosque today, he's going to wait a week or two?"

"OK. Let me make some calls. Give me the numbers where you can be reached."

Paul gave him his mobile phone number, Naomi's number, and the hotel's phone and room numbers.

While Naomi was in the shower, Paul searched the Internet for flights to London. There was an Iberia flight to Madrid leaving at 5:50 p.m., connecting with a flight to London that arrived at 10:05 p.m. It was already 4:35 p.m. Paul decided they should stay put to make sure the communications gap was closed.

The earliest arrival after 10:05 p.m. was at 8:25 the following morning, but that would involve a flight to Madrid at 9:30 that night, a layover in Madrid, and a 06:05 flight from Madrid on Saturday morning.

At 4:51 p.m., Paul's mobile phone rang. The man at the other end identified himself as Chief Inspector Clarkson of Scotland Yard. Paul went through the story again with him. "There was a Mr. Y Al-Rashid on easyJet flight 4723 from Marrakech to London this afternoon," the Chief Inspector said. "Is he the man you're talking about? We have no location on him presently."

"No, that's the man's half-brother. Do you have a passenger listing for a Mr. E Al-Rashid?"

"We don't get passenger lists until at least an hour after the flight departs."

"I suggest you check the passenger list on the British Airways flight that left at 4:10 p.m."

When Paul had hung up, he thought, *This is getting nowhere. I need a higher level connection* Suddenly, he thought of Miles Newcombe. *Yes!* Miles was the long-serving, Tory MP for Tooting and Wandsworth. Paul had campaigned for him during crucial elections, had attended his surgeries, had taken him to several Chelsea matches, and was generally regarded as a loyal constituent. Paul dialed his office number but got his voicemail. He dialed his private mobile number and again, got his voice mail. Paul left very urgent messages.

At 5:13 p.m., Paul's mobile rang again. It was Miles Newcombe. Paul went through the story yet again. Newcombe listened and asked several clarification questions. Then he asked, "Are you sure this isn't a wild goose chase, Paul?"

"I am absolutely sure this man means to hit the London Eye."

"OK," the MP said, "stick close."

At 5:31 p.m., Paul's mobile rang yet again. "This is Miles, Paul. I've spoken to the Prime Minister. We want you here. There will be an RAF aircraft picking you up within the hour at the business terminal Marrakech Airport."

"There are two of us, Miles."

"That's OK. Keep your phone on."

A Gulfstream jet pulled up to the ramp at the business terminal of Menara Airport at 6:37 p.m. The aircraft had no RAF markings, but its pilots wore RAF uniforms. Paul and Naomi got on board.

The plane accelerated down the runway and ascended in a steep climb.

When they reached a level altitude, the air force rating approached Naomi. "Would you like a drink, ma'am?"

"Yes, I'd like a dry sherry."

"I'm sorry, ma'am. We don't have sherry."

"In that case, I'd like a gin with some tonic."

Chapter 13

D-DAY

The approach to RAF Northolt was made to the west, so that the flight path took them over central London. The sun had set barely half an hour earlier, and Paul could clearly see the Houses of Parliament and the brightly lit London Eye below. Even at this hour, 9:12, on a Friday night in August, the Eye was still operating. *Probably packed with people,* he thought, *God, I hope we can stop this disaster!*

As they stepped off the plane, a tall, sandy-haired man in a somewhat rumpled blue suit, white shirt and regimental tie came forward to greet them. "Hello. I'm Chief Inspector Clarkson." As they shook hands, he added, "I hope you've had something to eat because we're going straight into London."

Paul said, "Yes, we had some rather good sandwiches on the plane."

There was a London taxi waiting for them outside the Northolt terminal building. "What we want to do in this briefing meeting is to get as much information as we can from the two of you. Then, we'll make an assessment and put an action plan into operation. You have everything with you?" They nodded.

Naomi asked, "Can you explain to me the difference between Scotland Yard, MI5 and MI6?"

"Yes, of course. That's a mystery to lots of British people."

"I'm not British. I'm an Israeli."

"Oh, I thought you worked for Global Youth Enterprise."

Naomi smiled. "I do, but I'm an Israeli."

"Oh, I see. Well you speak English like a native."

Naomi was clearly enjoying this. "Yes. That's probably because I studied English here. I have a degree in languages from City University."

"Yes. Well, that explains it. Now then to answer your question: Scotland Yard is another name for the London Metropolitan Police. Some years ago, the Metropolitan Police, or the Met as we call ourselves, had offices at numbers 8 and 9 Great Scotland Yard. And the organisation became associated, in the popular mind, with its location. So the Met is responsible for law enforcement in Greater London. MI5 is the security service. It is responsible for protecting the U.K. from threats to its national security. MI6 is the secret intelligence service, like the CIA or your Mossad. In this particular case, MI6 was contacted by a station officer in Marrakech about this man, Al-Rashid."

"Are all the services going to be in this meeting?" Naomi wanted to know.

"Yes, I expect so."

"And how do you keep people from stepping on each other's toes?"

Chief Inspector Clarkson frowned. "The situation doesn't really arise. The Met has the lead in this situation because a crime is threatened in London. At the same time, MI5 will want to listen in case a wider threat should emerge. And MI6 will want to assure themselves that there isn't a larger international dimension to the case."

Naomi persisted. "Do you know whether any MI6 agents are licensed to kill as James Bond was?"

At this point, Chief Inspector Clarkson realised that this Israeli girl was simply having fun. He considered his response carefully. "Well, I wouldn't want to be quoted on this, but I have heard that there are three agents with a double-O rating."

"Really?" Naomi feigned amazement. "I think there must be about twenty-five double-O-rated agents in Mossad."

It was Chief Inspector Clarkson's turn to feign amazement. "I had no idea it was so many!"

The taxi pulled up at the familiar rotating triangular sign in Victoria. In the entrance lobby, Paul and Naomi had to surrender their passports and were given visitors' badges. Their suitcases were passed through a scanner, tagged and held at the desk. Their laptop cases were carefully inspected. When the security checks were completed, Chief Inspector Clarkson led them onto an elevator to the ninth floor and into a large conference room full of people. Everyone present came forward and shook hands with the visitors. Names and roles were mentioned briefly, but it was impossible to remember the particulars.

There was one exception: Miles Newcombe, Paul's MP. Mr. Newcombe was a portly man in his sixties with near shoulder-length white hair, a kindly face and an effusive manner. Naomi liked him immediately, as he seemed to take it as his responsibility to look after her and Paul in the meeting.

In the centre of the room was a long, oak conference table with perhaps fifteen dark leather chairs around it. There were another dozen chairs against the interior wall; the exterior wall being floor to ceiling, blind-covered windows. In the centre of the interior wall, there was a large colour reproduction of a portrait of the Queen. Otherwise, the room was without decoration.

Chief Inspector Clarkson sat in the centre of the table, facing the windows. The visitors were invited to take seats opposite him. Paul sat on Mr. Newcombe's right, and Naomi on Paul's right.

The chief inspector made some introductory comments, and he invited Paul to begin the briefing.

Paul said, "Before I cover the matter which we're here to discuss, I'd like to point out that the marks on Miss Evensen's face are not birthmarks. They were inflicted with a whip earlier today by the man who we believe plans to attack the London Eye."

There was a murmur of consternation around the room. Mr. Newcombe was genuinely shocked. He leaned forward and to his right. "Miss Evensen, can you tell us please what happened?"

Naomi explained Paul's and her roles at GYE, and when they had completed an assessment of AMM two months ago, they suspected fraud.

There was an indignant response from Mr. Newcombe: "A charity committing fraud!"

"Unfortunately, Mr. Newcombe, it's not as uncommon as we all might like to believe." She went on to explain that Paul and a bookkeeper had very recently completed a proper audit of AMM's bank statements. They had found that the equivalent of about six hundred thousand pounds had been siphoned off to another account. They suspected that the other account was Yusuf Al-Rashid's personal account, but they had no proof of this. She explained Latifa's intervention, the sudden return of the half-brother Efraim, the trip to the mosque, the return to Latifa's apartment and their abduction by Efraim.

Chief Inspector Clarkson asked, "How did this fellow, Efraim, know that you had photocopied the bank statements?"

"In our hurry to return the originals to Yusuf's office, we left one page on the copier. Yusuf found it when he returned. He understood what we had done, and he ordered Efraim to get the copies from us."

"So he whipped you to try to get you to give back the photocopies?"

"No. We told him the copies were in the car with Paul. But he didn't know where Paul was. So, he just decided to punish us."

Another murmur of anger went round the room

"Have you reported all this to the Moroccan police?" Mr. Newcombe wanted to know.

Paul replied, "No, we were more concerned about the attack on the London Eye, and we wanted to get to London."

"Excuse me," a man seated against the wall had raised his hand, "but before we get to that, is there a possibility that some— or all—of the six hundred thousand you mentioned has been used to finance terrorism?"

"At this point, we don't know the answer to that," Paul said. "We have copies of Yusuf Al-Rashid's bank statements, but we haven't looked at them other than to determine that his account was the recipient of the money from the AMM accounts."

Someone seated at the end of the table asked, "Could we see copies of Mr. Al-Rashid's statements?"

"Yes," Paul put in, "but it's important to remember that Moroccan back statements are in Arabic."

"It will take some time for you to analyse the statements," Naomi added, "So I suggest that you make photocopies that we can use at GYE."

"I think we ought to listen to this tape you have," Chief Inspector Clarkson put in. "You have it with you?" Paul nodded. "I think we have all seen the translation of the previous sermon by Mr. Al-Rashid that MI6 prepared. Now I suggest that we let Mr. Shamoom, who is an Arabic translator with the Met, operate this latest recording. Mr. Shamoom, if you will play a little of the tape, stop it and tell us in English what is said."

She didn't say anything, but Paul was aware from her awkward shift in position that Naomi was not at all happy with this arrangement. Paul whispered to her, "We have to let them translate it. Otherwise, they'll be forever second-guessing your translation." She shrugged her understanding, but as Mr. Shamoom began his translation, she was paying very careful attention.

At the conclusion of Mr. Shamoom's short translations at several points, there were grunts and exclamations of consternation from around the room. Mr. Shamoom's translation continued, "We may strike them in the eye so that their blindness to the suffering they have caused may be repaid."

"No!" Naomi interjected. "Mr. Shamoom, the verb Mr. Al-Rashid used twice in that sentence is "will," not "may." There is no implication of conditionality. The correct translation is 'We will strike them in the eye so that their blindness to the suffering they have caused will be repaid.'"

Mr. Shamoom looked up, surprised. "Excuse me, but what do you know about Arabic?"

"I have been speaking Arabic for over thirty years, and I have studied it in school and at university."

Mr. Newcombe intervened, "Where are you from, Mr. Shamoom?"

"I am from Bradford, sir."

"And you learned your Arabic at home?"

"Yes, sir, from my parents. They are Tunisian."

Mr. Newcombe nodded. "With great respect, Mr. Shamoom, this lady is an Israeli citizen, and I'm sure you know that many Israelis speak fluent Arabic as a matter of survival."

"Yes, sir. Point taken, sir. I will look up the verb as soon as the tape is finished."

At the conclusion of the recording, Chief Inspector Clarkson looked around the room. "I think we can all understand now, Mr Winthorpe, why you are concerned."

"I agree," someone sitting down the table to Paul's left offered, "but how is this man Al-Rashid going to attack the Eye? With a bomb?"

"I think it could be more complicated than that," Paul said. "About three months ago, I took my two children and my grandchildren for a ride on the London Eye. My son, John is a very clever and imaginative mechanical engineer with Architectural Design Partnership in Manchester. ADP is designing the hundred and twenty storey Gulf Trade Centre in Doha. He pointed out to me in passing that it would be possible, with certain explosive charges to cut the cables that support the Eye. If that were to happen, the Eye would collapse into the river. And bear in mind, the doors of the capsules are secured from the outside. As the capsules filled with water, there would be no escape."

"Do you suppose we could speak to your son?" the chief inspector asked.

"Yes. I should think so. Shall I get him on the line?"

"Yes. If you could use this telephone here."

Paul dialed.

"Hello."

"Hi, Teresa, it's Paul. How are you?"

"I'm fine, but you sound like you're in a tunnel somewhere."

"Not exactly, but I need to speak to John quite urgently. Is he there?"

"Yes, I'll get him for you."

Efraim's Eye

"Hi, Dad."

"John, do you remember that conversation we had at the London Eye about how a terrorist could attack it?"

"Yes. Where are you, Dad? You sound like you're on a squawk box."

"I'm on a squawk box at Scotland Yard, and I'm trying to help the people here stop an attack on the London Eye."

There was a moment of silence. "How did you get that particular assignment, Dad?"

"I can explain that later, John. But right now I'm going to turn you over to Chief Inspector Clarkson, who'd like to hear from you how you felt an attack on the Eye could be done."

"OK. Good evening, Chief Inspector. Well to begin with, the London Eye is a cantilevered structure. That is to say, its hub supported by two rigid legs at one end of the hub, and it is prevented from falling over by cables that are anchored in the ground." There was a rustling sound as a large drawing was unfolded on the table. "Ah, do I hear the sound of a drawing being opened?"

"Yes, you do."

"Well, if memory serves me right, there are six cables which support the Eye. It would only be necessary to cut the cables with shaped charges for the Eye to fall over."

"I thought you said there are two rigid legs," the chief inspector commented. "Wouldn't the legs prevent it from falling?"

"No. Sorry. The legs are rigid only in the vertical direction. If you look carefully at the drawing, you'll see that they are hinged. This feature facilitated assembly of the Eye. The wheel was pulled up off a barge on the river. The hinged legs forced the wheel to swing through an arc in the vertical plane until the wheel itself was in the vertical plane."

"Oh, I see."

Someone else put in, "But with six cables to cut, it will either take a tremendous bomb or six individual explosions, and either way that would be difficult for terrorists to pull off."

"No, I don't think so. It would take six simultaneous shaped-charge explosions."

"But aren't you forgetting about the recoil from the explosions?"

"Think about it this way," John offered. "The shaped charges are tied together in a closed string, so that they are not allowed to recoil and all of their force is directed at the cables."

For some moments, there was stunned silence in the room.

"But on the drawing, it looks like there is a glass box around the bottom of the cables."

"Yes," John said, "I saw that. The box is about seven feet high, and it's flat on the top, where the cables are exposed again. Once a terrorist gets on top of the box, he has an excellent platform on which to work."

"How long would it take him to get the charges in place and ready to detonate?"

"That would depend on how well he has designed the string and how well rehearsed he is. Maybe a minute or two."

"A minute or two! My God, we'd have to have round the clock snipers ready to pick him off!"

"John," this is Chief Inspector Clarkson, "Are you able to comment at all on the design of the shaped charges?"

"No, Chief Inspector, that isn't my field. I'm sure you have contacts in the Army who can help you with that question. I just know from my time in the Army that a well-designed shaped charge can penetrate ten inches or more of steel armour plate."

The harmony in the meeting room decayed as small groups discussed what they had heard.

Mr. Shamoom returned to the room. He took the chief inspector and Naomi to one side. "I apologise. This lady was right. The correct verb is 'will,' not 'may.'

Chief Inspector Clarkson called the meeting to order and announced, "OK we're going to make a call to Army Ordinance."

The chief inspector was able to contact a Major Robbins at home, but while he said that anti-armour shaped charges came within his remit, he did not feel able to answer general questions on shaped-charge designs. He referred Scotland Yard to a Mr. Gottfried, the engineering director of Briscoe & Co., a supplier of specialised ordinance. Mr. Gottfried had just returned home from a performance of *Die Meistersinger* at the Royal Opera House, and he was apprehensive about a call from Scotland Yard at 11:32 p.m. After receiving assurances that the call had nothing to do with him or his company but rather to a terrorist plot that involved the cutting of steel cables, he was more forthcoming.

"Mr. Gottfried," the chief inspector began, "is it possible to use a shaped charge to sever a braided steel cable that is eight centimetres in diameter?"

"Yes, of course."

"How much explosive would be required?"

"That depends on the design of the charge. I would think that a well-formulated high explosive in the range of eight hundred grams would be more than sufficient."

"So little?"

"Yes. Do you remember the so-called underpants bomber? Well, he had three hundred grams in his Y-fronts. You may remember the pictures of that quantity of explosive being tested on an old aircraft. It blew a very large hole in the side of the airframe. And you must bear in mind, Chief Inspector, that that was not a shaped charge."

"Mr. Gottfried, would you remind us of the principles of a shaped charge?"

"Yes, of course. A shaped charge always has four components: the casing, the explosive, the liner and a detonator. The purpose of the casing is to focus the explosion in a certain direction, so that it is not just a spherical blast but a highly directional blast. The liner is the projectile. It does the work of the ordinance. But it is a rather special projectile, because it contains no explosive. Instead, it is made of a dense, heavy metal, like uranium, and it is accelerated to tremendous speed by the explosive. Bear in mind, if you will, that most high explosives burn at a rate of 5,000 to 9,000 metres per second! At that kind of acceleration, the liner is transformed into a solid-liquid state, and its power to penetrate is greatly increased."

"I see. And how large would a shaped charge be to sever an eight-centimetre cable?"

"Well, if I were going to design such a charge, I would configure it as an arc about a foot long. If you visualise a circle about two feet in diameter, I would cut out a sixty-degree arc to make my casing. The cross-section of the casing would be a deep C-shape with the opening of the C facing the centre of the circle. The explosive would fill the opening, and the liner would cover the explosive."

"Mr. Gottfried, how difficult would it be to get this shaped charge made?"

"I think the most difficult part would be the design. Then there is the question of how to get one's hands on the high explosive. Actual manufacturing and assembly work could be completed by any competent machine shop."

"Are there software design packages that can be used?"

"Yes, but they're not available on the Internet. Most ordinance suppliers and military special forces have proprietary software packages."

"You mentioned uranium. Wouldn't it be difficult to obtain uranium?"

"It could be, but what we're talking about is depleted uranium—U-238. You may know that it is commonly used as the projectile in shipboard anti-missile guns. But other metals can also be used: tungsten is a good alternative."

When the phone call was terminated, Chief Inspector Clarkson commented, "So I guess the question is: does this man Al-Rashid have the ability to get these shaped charges made?"

"But Chief Inspector," somebody toward the end of the table put in, "how do we know that Al-Rashid is planning to attack with shaped charges. Why not something simple and devastating, like a bomb?"

"Because in his little speech he says, the infidels will fall screaming into hell. To me that suggests he's planning for the riders on the Eye to fall. Can you think of a way for a bomb to make a large portion of the riders to fall?"

The man shook his head.

"Coming back to your question about the capability of Al-Rashid," Paul said, "I can tell you that both of the Al-Rashid brothers have connections to the Moroccan military. I don't know what the connections are. Yusuf was evasive about that."

A man seated along the wall spoke up. "Chief Inspector, we made inquiries about Efraim Al-Rashid's connections to the military when the subject first came to our attention two months ago. The response to our inquiries was that he was ex-army and that he was currently a contractor. We never got a response to our question: what sort of contractor?"

The chief inspector looked around the room. He had a sour expression on his face. "Now, where is this man Efraim Al-Rashid? We know that his half-brother was on easyJet flight 4723 from Marrakech to London this afternoon."

A woman in a grey suit who was sitting to the chief inspector's right said, "There was a Mr. E. Al-Rashid, traveling on a Moroccan passport to Madrid this afternoon on Iberia flight 296 that left Marrakech at 5:50 p.m. That flight was due to connect with Iberia 297 that was scheduled to arrive Heathrow at 10:05 p.m. But there was no E. Al-Rashid on the connecting flight."

"Isn't it possible," Paul suggested, "for someone to book a flight using one passport and then separately to book the connecting flight under a separate name and passport?"

"Damn it!" The chief inspector slammed his palm against the table. "Why didn't we have officers meeting that flight from Madrid?"

The woman responded nervously, "Because we don't know what this man E. Al-Rashid looks like."

The chief inspector could barely contain his exasperation. "His photograph is in the file, Mildred! It was sent to us by MI6 two months ago! Now, would you check everyone on that Iberia flight for a photo fit?"

Cowed, Mildred mumbled lamely, "We'll have to do a lot of hand-checking against the Schengen database."

"Do it! I want to see the results by 6 a.m.!" He turned to the group at large. "I think we have to assume that he's in the country."

Someone at the far end of the table said, "I wouldn't have thought he'd bring the explosives into the country aboard an Iberia flight."

"Good point," Chief Inspector Clarkson conceded. "Mildred, while you're at it, would you identify every previous entry by this man Efraim Al-Rashid in the last six months. Check both his Moroccan passport and whatever form of identity he used to get into the U.K. tonight."

Mr. Newcombe suggested, "That leaves us with the questions of timing and response."

The chief inspector nodded. "To me, the timing seems to be pretty clear. He refers to the infidel holy day. That's Sunday. He'll probably want to use tomorrow to get himself organised." He looked at his watch; it read 00:06. "Sorry, I should have said the rest of today to organise himself. And he'll want to attack at a time when the Eye is at full capacity between, say 11 a.m. and 8 p.m. That gives us a little time."

The man with the drawings of the Eye spoke up. "Chief Inspector, I suggest that we extend the glass enclosure around the cables, making it higher and a lot more difficult to climb."

"Good idea, Jason! Would you speak to the owner, Merlin Entertainments? OK. Now, police presence?"

A man wearing a senior police officer's uniform spoke up. "I think that on Sunday, from about 9 a.m. onward, we ought to position three snipers on the roof of the ticket office building. We'll need at least six armed police officers on the ground, a communications vehicle, a lock-down vehicle, and a dozen back-up officers in vans on Belvedere Road. This would be in addition to the normal foot patrols we have in the area."

"OK. Has Al-Rashid's photograph been circulated within the Met?"

"Yes, it's gone out."

It was 12:32 a.m. when Paul and Naomi finally got into a taxi. "Paul, I don't really want to go home alone with both Al-Rashids on the loose in London," Naomi had whispered. "Would it be OK if I stayed with you?"

"Yes, of course."

But as the taxi turned up Crieff Road, Paul had a sudden feeling of grim foreboding. There was no light on in his house.

Strange, he thought, *I always leave one light on upstairs and one downstairs. How could they have both burned out in a week?* As he approached the door, he saw that it had been forced open. He turned to Naomi, "Don't come in yet, Naomi. I want to check what's going on here."

It was then that he saw the telephone cable that served his house hanging down into a tree. Cautiously, he swung open the door. There was only the low ambient street lighting that relieved some of the gloom inside. He stopped to listen. The house was quiet. He could hear only the soft murmur of a television next door. His eyes were becoming accustomed to the dark. To his left, he peered into the living room. Papers from his desk were strewn all over the floor. *So he came here looking for the copies, and somehow, he silenced the alarm.* He returned to the hallway and bent down to look at the alarm panel that was located on the wall, under the stairs. The alarm panel had been ripped of the wall and lay amid some broken plaster on the floor. Four bare wires were protruding from an opening in the wall. He moved slightly to his left and examined the circuit breaker panel. The large red circuit breaker at the end of the row was switched off. He switched it on. Several lights came on, but the silence persisted. He went outside.

"The house has been searched. There are papers all over the floor in the living room." Naomi put a hand to her mouth, hiding her alarm. "I'm going to call Chief Inspector Clarkson. There could be somebody waiting for us in there."

Naomi stood next to him, shivering involuntarily as he made the call.

"They'll be a police car here shortly," he said.

Within five minutes, two police cars drove up, lights flashing but sirens silent. In the first car, there were two constables; in the second car, there were two officers carrying submachine guns. Briefly, Paul explained the situation.

"You wait here, please," one of the armed officers directed. He and his partner entered the house. Five minutes later they returned to the sidewalk. "There's no one in there," they reported. One of the armed officers made a call through his handset. "The chief inspector wants us to stay here tonight in case this suspect decides to come back. Is there somewhere you can go?"

"Yes, we can stay at my daughter's place. She lives in the city."

"Is her address known to this suspect?"

"No."

"We'll call a locksmith for you. He'll leave a message on your mobile phone. You should call your alarm company and BT (British Telecom) in the morning."

Paul nodded. Naomi asked, "If you're going to stay here tonight to catch the suspect, are you going to hide all these police cars?"

"Yes, ma'am. We'll take care of that."

"Hello." It was Cynthia's sleepy voice.

"Cindy, it's Dad. The house has been ransacked, and the police don't want us to stay there tonight. Can you put us up for the night?"

"Who is 'us'?"

"Naomi and me. We've just spent half the night at Scotland Yard helping them deal with a terrorist threat. We can tell you all about it when we see you."

"Doesn't she have a place of her own?"

"Yes, but she's quite understandably reluctant to go there when my place has been ransacked, she's not ex-directory, and there are two lunatics on the loose in London."

At 1:56 a.m. when they arrived at Cynthia's place, Paul's daughter had put on a green silk bathrobe, brushed her hair, and was prepared to be the hostess. Her first thought on seeing Naomi was, *My God, she's young—she's just a kid!*

She offered her father a gin and tonic, which he gratefully accepted. Naomi sipped a glass of white wine, as she gazed out the sliding doors at the silvery-black Thames. "This is wonderful!" she marveled. "Do you see ships going up and down the river?"

"No cruise ships or large cargo ships, but plenty of barges and yachts, and when it gets foggy, I can hear their horns."

Naomi's childish wonder at the river reinforced Cynthia's first impression, but when she heard Naomi tell parts of the story, particularly her beating of Efraim, she couldn't help but alter her appraisal, *My God, this girl has a backbone of steel!*

When the recounting was over, Cynthia said, "As to the sleeping arrangements: there is a bed in the second bedroom. I suggest that you, Naomi, take that, and, Dad, you'll have to make do with the couch out here."

Naomi protested, "Oh, no, Cynthia, that's very kind of you, but I'm like a cat. I can sleep anywhere. Paul, you take the bed, please."

Paul asked, "Are you sure, Naomi?"

"Yes. This couch looks very comfortable."

"In that case, I'm going to make myself another gin and tonic and turn in."

Naomi and Cynthia were sitting at opposite ends of the white sofa, half facing each other and in mirrored positions: legs drawn up beside them. There was openness and curiosity on each side.

Naomi gazed around the living room with its modern art on the walls and the collections of silver-framed photographs clustered on the walnut tables. "This apartment is very nice."

"Do you think so? It's quite comfortable for me, and only a ten-minute walk away from work. (she smiled) Or more often, a five-minute run."

"I think Paul said you work for a bank."

"Yes, an investment bank."

"And what do you do?"

"I help clients arrange mergers, acquisitions and financial restructurings."

"Oh, my goodness! I heard your brother talking on the phone today. He seems very bright also."

"Yes, he's the brains of the family. He went to Cambridge."

"Did you go there too?"

"No, I went to Oxford."

"I went to City University, but I managed to get a first."

"I understand you speak seven languages, and play the violin and the flute." Naomi gave a half nod. "And you're the operations director of one of the Duke's major charities."

"It's not such an important job."

Cynthia regarded Naomi skeptically. "I'll bet that if you asked a hundred people that you met in the street which job is more important to society in general, yours or mine, most of them would say yours."

"But that's just because people are mad at the banks."

"No, I don't think so, Naomi. I think people would recognise that helping young entrepreneurs get started is more important than helping rich people get richer."

Cynthia saw that Naomi's eyes were brimming and that she was biting the inside of her cheek.

"Don't get me wrong, Naomi. I love my job but I wish I had the disposition to do yours."

"I think I ought to let you get some sleep, Cynthia."

"No. Tomorrow's Saturday. I don't have to get up early, and it's pretty rare that I'd ever get a chance to talk to my Dad's girlfriend face-to-face."

Naomi's shy smile became alight with pleasure as she turned to face Cynthia. "You know, I don't think I've ever been in this part of London."

Cynthia turned to look out at the river. "Well, you know, this part of London is the docklands, where most of the cargo was handled, and many ships were built. It was bombed into rubble during the war, and for many years, it just lay here derelict. Then, about thirty years ago, the government started offering tax incentives for development. The Docklands Light Railway was built, construction started on Canary Wharf, and twenty years ago, the first big tenants moved here. It's seen tremendous growth ever since. If you like shopping, you'd love the huge underground mall at Canada Place."

Naomi was reflective, "It's strange how a war can change so many things."

"Has a war changed things for you, Naomi?"

"Yes. The First Intifada broke up my parents' marriage, but I was thinking about the Second World War."

"About the Holocaust?"

Naomi nodded. "My mother's parents came to Israel in 1946 from Buchenwald, when it was liberated by the U.S. Army." Her hatred for the camp was conveyed in her guttural pronunciation of its name. "They were barely alive, fortunate to be among the prisoners who weren't executed or dead of starvation or illness."

"Where were they from, Naomi?"

"They were German Jews. My mother was born in 1949, and I was born in 1976."

"I was born in 1979. Do you still have memories of your grandparents?"

"Yes. They were very sweet and very old-fashioned. They never liked my dad at all. They both died when I was about fifteen." There was a moment of reflection. "Do you have a boyfriend, Cynthia?"

Cynthia smiled. "Yes."

"Are you going to get married?"

"Maybe so. I'm not sure."

It was Naomi's turn to smile. "What's he like?"

"He's quite tall with sandy hair, brown eyes, and some freckles. He's a barrister, but he's quiet. I have to do most of the talking. He's very kind to me, and he's a good cook."

"Is he like your dad?"

"In some ways, he is: he's bright, kind and enjoys people. My dad is probably better looking, but James has a better sense of humour." She paused for a moment. "Is my dad like your dad, Naomi?"

"Yes. Except my dad is very blonde and very impatient."

"And you like my dad quite a lot."

Naomi took a deep breath and looked out at the river. "I love your dad. He's really wonderful." There was another pause. "But, I'm not sure we're right for each other."

Cynthia nodded gently. "I think I'll go to bed now, if you'll excuse me."

Both women rose from the sofa. There was an awkward moment as looked at each other. Then, magnetically, each of them stepped forward into an embrace.

"Dad, I've made an appointment for you to see my GP (general practioner) at 9:20. The surgery is open until noon on Saturday. I told him you cut your hand yesterday while you were helping my brother in Manchester. So don't let on that you live in Wandsworth and have your own GP."

Dr. Hammond looked down through his bifocals at Paul's left hand from which he had removed the adhesive tape and gauze pads. "Hmm, he said. Gently, he pressed the flesh on each side of the wound. "Hmm." He watched carefully as Paul responded to his requests to move each of his fingers in turn. "Hmm." The doctor sat back and scratched his head.

"There's still some seepage from the wound, but no sign of infection. I don't think a duty A&E surgeon would want to put stitches in this: too fiddly. Unless, of course, he were a specialist hand surgeon, in which case he would think he'd died and gone to heaven. So, Mr. Winthorpe, I'm going to turn you over to the practice nurse, who is extremely talented at protecting and immobilising wounds like this."

Twenty minutes later, Paul, Naomi and Cynthia were leaving the surgery with Paul looking as if he were wearing a white boxing glove on his left hand.

"Paul, do you mind coming with me to my flat? I'm sure it's been searched, and I'd be a lot happier if somebody were with me."

"OK. Then we'll go to my place, and afterwards we'll get some lunch."

Naomi's flat was in Chepstow Road, not far from the Westway and the main line railway. It was a third-floor walk-up. The door was slightly ajar. Naomi moaned softly, and hesitated. Paul pushed the door open and stepped inside. Papers and books were strewn on the living room/dining room floor. In the bedroom, the closet and chest of drawers had been emptied onto the floor and bed. Someone had swept the contents of the bathroom cabinet onto the floor. There were broken bottles and tablets scattered about. The refrigerator had been emptied of its meagre contents. There was a pile of broken crockery on the kitchen floor. Naomi wandered disconsolately from room to room. She stood by a pile of shattered books and began to weep.

"Oh, God!" she moaned. "What did I do to deserve this? They knew I didn't have the papers!"

Paul put his arms around her, and for some minutes she stood, clinging to him and sobbing. He said, "I guess whoever it was waited for you, but then he gave up, and, in his frustration, he trashed your flat."

Naomi, suddenly alert, looked up at him. "You think somebody was in here, waiting for me?"

"Yes."

"It was that bastard Efraim!"

"Maybe it was Yusuf or somebody he hired."

She disengaged herself from Paul, and looked critically around her: the sorrow was gone. "Shall we call the police?"

"Yes. I'll call Chief Inspector Clarkson."

"Paul, can I stay with you until this is over?"

He nodded. "Do you want to call a locksmith?"

Paul placed a call to the chief inspector. He moved a pile of papers out of the way, and sat on the couch. Idly, he looked around the small cluttered room. *It wasn't very homey to begin with. There are no personal touches: no photographs or decorations, no special mementos—just those two Israeli travel posters: one of the Wailing Wall, the other of the Masada fortress. It's as if she doesn't have a real home, just an idealised home in Israel.*

The chief inspector was on the phone. "Yes, I'll send a couple of guys over, but I'm not very hopeful. We found nothing at your place—not even the odd fingerprint. Is there the possibility that something was taken?"

"I'll check when I get home, but I doubt it. You have what he was looking for—copies of the bank statements."

"Oh, yes, and we did find something interesting in Y Al-Rashid's bank statement. There was a payment of $45,000 to E Rashid in early April of this year. The tag that goes with that payment is 'The Hammer.'"

There was silence on the line for a moment. "Do you suppose, Chief Inspector, that 'The Hammer' is the code name for a string of shaped charges?"

"That thought occurred to me, Mr. Winthorpe. We have also pretty well confirmed that E Al-Rashid is in the country. He came in from Madrid last night on a Greek national identity card—name of Mohammed Al-Buktar. The Greeks are checking, but we're pretty sure it's a forgery. Mr. E. Al-Rashid came to the U.K. on his Moroccan passport with a tourist visa—which we believe is valid—in early April and again two weeks ago."

The locksmith had finished his work. In addition to replacing the Yale key lock, he installed a Chubb five-lever deadlock. To Naomi, he said, "I think you'll be a lot safer now, ma'am."

On arrival at Paul's house, they found it locked securely with a locksmith's business card taped to the door. When Paul phoned, he was asked to come to the shop, where on presentation of his photo driver's license, he was given an invoice and his new keys.

Inside the house, it was evident that the intruder had a singular motivation—to find the bank statement copies and get out before the neighbours became suspicious. Paul's beautiful, walnut, leather-topped partners' desk had been ransacked. The drawers had been removed and unceremoniously dumped on the desktop. When the sought-after documents were not found, the piles were swept onto the floor. There were client files, tax returns and dozens of other business and personal files heaped on the floor. Drawers and closets throughout the house had been opened, but when no papers had been discovered, they had been maliciously dumped.

As Naomi followed Paul around the house, she thought the size of the home, its dark antique furniture, and its many cream brocade draperies were excessive. *Why does one man need all of this lavish space?"* she wondered. Then—much like Cynthia's flat, but more so—there were all the collections of silver picture frames on nearly every horizontal furniture surface. Every room had its share of paintings: landscapes and still lives in watercolours, portraits in oils. There were oriental carpets everywhere. The house spoke to her of tradition and of privilege. *This is Paul's heritage,* she thought. *It's so different than mine!* It made her somewhat uncomfortable.

"Naomi, I would really like to go to the London Eye now. I know I promised you lunch, and we'll have lunch, but I just feel the need to go and check."

"You're not going to take a ride on the Eye are you?"

"No. I just want to see what's going on there."

"OK. I can wait for lunch."

They got off the train at Waterloo and walked through Shell Centre toward the Eye, which was set against a clear blue sky. The lawn at Jubilee Gardens was crowded with people: picnicking, playing Frisbee, or just enjoying the sun. The walkway along the river was similarly populated with strollers who stopped to gawp at the silver- and gold-painted figures pretending to be statues.

"Oh, that cart has hot dogs!" Naomi announced.

Paul protested, "Sweetheart, I'll get you some proper lunch in just a little while!"

"No, no! I want one of those! They look like Nathan's hot dogs."

Paul followed her over to the cart where the proprietor was grilling hot dogs under a red and white umbrella. "What are Nathan's hot dogs?" Paul asked.

"They sell them in New York, and they're absolutely the best in the world!"

"Are they Kosher?"

"I don't know about Kosher, but they're all beef."

Ten minutes later, they each had a foot-long hot dog—Naomi's with mustard and relish, Paul's with catsup. Naomi held a paper cup full of Coke for them to share.

Naomi shook her head. "It's not Nathan's, but it's all right."

For a few minutes, they stood watching the long queue of people waiting to board the Eye, and as they looked up, they could see that each of the thirty-two capsules was full. The capacity of the London Eye is eight hundred people.

Paul said, "I'm looking for police. There is a pair of constables standing near the queue, and another pair down near Belvedere Road."

"There were also two policemen with machine guns on the river walk."

But the atmosphere was festive: hundreds of people were enjoying a beautiful August afternoon in London.

Naomi said, "I wonder what that gardening van is doing here on a Saturday afternoon. I don't see how they can do any proper gardening with all these people around." She was indicating a white Ford Escort van that had parked alongside the large rectangular stone bollards surrounding the glass enclosure around the support cables. They ambled idly toward the van. It had a green council logo painted on its side and below the logo "Westminster Council Gardening Services."

"But," Paul began, "this isn't Westminster, it's Lambeth . . ."

"My God!" Naomi exclaimed, "There's Efraim!"

"Where?"

"He's on top of the glass enclosure, and he's doing something up there!"

There was, indeed, a man in jeans and a green T-shirt on the enclosure, but he was bent over, arranging something.

"Are you sure it's him?"

"Yes, it's him! I'm sure!"

Paul thrust the remains of his hot dog at Naomi and began to run toward the van. He noticed two men sitting in the front seat, but he ignored them and leapt up onto the bonnet. With another leap, he was on the roof of the van. Swinging to his left, he saw the green T-shirt man, bent over and preoccupied with what he was arranging, less than ten feet away. There was a gap of about five feet between the van and the enclosure, which was about two feet higher. Paul gathered himself and sprang. He landed awkwardly and fell forward against the man. The man turned to see who or what had struck him, and tried to recover his balance at the same time. Desperately, Paul got his feet under him and pushed. This sudden momentum was transferred to the green T-shirt man, who lost his balance, and arms flailing in the air toppled over the edge of the enclosure opposite the van. There was a loud howl of pain as he struck one of the stone bollards.

Immediately, Paul turned his attention to the shaped charges that had been arranged neatly—each crescent charge seemed to be embracing a cable.

"Detonate!" screamed the green T-shirt man.

Paul scanned the array and spotted the links that closed the charges into a non-recoiling string.

There was another high-pitched scream: "Detonate!"

Paul uncoupled the links, holding one end down with his bandaged left hand while his right hand manipulated the clasp. With his right hand, he began to pull one end of the string. The charges were heavy.

"Where is the button?" Was the shouted question from the van.

Paul dragged the first four charges over the edge of the enclosure.

"On my seat!" came the agonised reply.

Paul kicked at two remaining charges that were still on the enclosure. With a rattle, they were dragged over the edge by the gravitational pull of the first four.

"No! No!" A desperate scream from below.

Paul began to turn away. He was struck by a tremendous shock wave. He hurtled forward, struck the edge of the van roof and landed, arms outstretched, on the pavement. There was nothingness.

Chapter 14

AFTERMATH

Kevin Bradshaw was enjoying his twelfth birthday party. He had his five good friends, his sisters Amy and Ella, and his parents on the London Eye with him as a special treat. They had all taken the train up from Portsmouth for the day, which had started with Madam Tussauds, and now the London Eye. Still to come were the Hard Rock Café for lunch and a 3D movie at the IMAX cinema. What a great day!

As Kevin looked down from his capsule on the Eye, it started to descend from its zenith, and he noticed something curious far below. One man had climbed up onto a van and had jumped up onto a big glass box down there on the ground. Kevin thought, *He's going to fight the other guy on the box!* He said, "Hey, look guys! They're having a fight down there!" And he pointed to the box. "One guy pushed the other guy off, and the guy who fell off looks like he's really hurt!"

"What's that guy doing?"

"He's taking something away."

"Do you think it's a robbery?"

"Nah, they keep the money in the ticket office."

Suddenly there was a blinding flash, and a boom that struck the capsule like a huge invisible hand.

"My God, what was that?" Kevin's father turned abruptly from his contemplation of the Houses of Parliament. The capsule and in fact, the whole Eye was rocking slightly from the impact. One could hear screams of terror from the other capsules. A middle-aged woman behind Kevin cried out, "My God! Someone's trying to kill us!" The Eye stopped rotating. "Oh, dear God! What's happening?" the woman exclaimed.

Kevin turned toward her. "Someone set off a bomb down there!" he told her breathlessly. "See, it was right there!"

Looking down, they could see pandemonium on the ground. A few people—those who had been nearest the blast—were lying on the ground. Others were running away from the Eye. A few hurried to help those who had been struck down. Many stood aimlessly in a kind of daze.

The screams of terror had stopped; there was a great deal of distant shouting. Two pairs of uniformed police were converging on the scene.

"Look!" Kevin said, "That van is trying to drive away!"

"The police are stopping it!"

Two of the policemen were pointing machine guns at the van that stopped. The doors opened. Two men got out and raised their hands.

One of the boys exclaimed, "They've captured two terrorists!"

The middle-aged woman had sat down on the bench in the centre of the capsule; she covered her face with her hands, moaning softly, and seemed to have been overtaken with ague.

"Dad, why aren't they handcuffing those guys?"

Kevin's father considered the scene below. The two men from the van had been herded into the centre of the grassy area at Jubilee Gardens by the police, who were keeping their distance. "Maybe they're afraid that they're wearing suicide vests."

"Did you hear that, guys? My dad says those guys are wearing suicide vests!"

"No, Kevin, I said they might be wearing suicide vests."

There was a soft lamentation from the centre of the capsule, "Oh, God! We're all going to die!"

Kevin's father said, "That's true, ma'am, but probably not today. The police seem to have the situation under control."

The sound of sirens could be heard coming from various directions.

"Look at the size of the hole that bomb made!" Kevin exclaimed, pointing, "and that glass box is gone! . . . I wonder what happened to the guy who was pushed off."

"Isn't that him there?" one of Kevin's friends said, also pointing.

"That's not a man."

"Well, it's legs and part of a man."

Kevin's mother attempted to intervene. "Boys look down here. People are helping that girl. She was lying on the ground before, but people have helped her up."

An ambulance was driving up the paved area from Belvedere Road.

"Yeah," Kevin said, "And that's the guy who pushed the other one off. They're putting him on a stretcher."

They continued to gaze down as more ambulances, and police vans converged on the area.

"Dad, how come the police are covering those people like that?"

"Because they're dead, Kevin, and they don't want people looking at them."

"But we saw them."

Kevin's mother intervened again. "Yes, I know, but you shouldn't have."

The 'why?' question surfaced in Kevin's mind, but he decided, after glancing at his mother, not to ask it. Instead, he whispered to his friends, "We saw two dead people today, guys!"

The loudspeaker inside the capsule announced. "We are starting the Eye once again. We have determined that it is safe to do so. We are sorry for the inconvenience, and we hope you enjoy the rest of your flight."

* * *

"Dad?"

"Unhhh." Paul struggled to make sense of his slowly returning consciousness. He knew he was in a bed. There were white walls, a white ceiling with unlit fluorescent lamps. *I haven't died, but I certainly feel horrible.* He turned his head to his right. A young woman was sitting there, leaning toward him.

"Cindy!"

"Yes." She was smiling. "How are you, Dad?"

"Pretty awful. Where am I?"

"In St. Thomas."

"Is Naomi all right?"

"I don't know, but I'll check. If she was hurt, she's probably here, too."

"The Eye didn't go down, did it?"

"No, but quite a few people were hurt on the ground. Apparently, there was a lot of flying glass."

He looked up at the clear bottle of liquid that was drip, dripping into a plastic tube. "Maybe that's why I feel like a pin cushion."

"The nurses said you have a broken collar bone and a concussion."

"That explains the head ache. That bastard, Efraim, didn't get away, did he?"

"Is he the one who planted the bomb?"

"Yeah."

"I don't know, Dad. I got a phone call, and I came straight here. I'm going to tell the nurses you're awake."

It's awful lying here in bed like this, he thought, *not knowing what happened. Except if I were dead I'd probably know exactly what happened unless I went straight to hell. Then I wouldn't know, either. But, I don't think I'd go straight to hell. . . . Maybe I'd meet Efraim . . . unless he went straight to hell . . . which is where he ought to be. . . . What would I say to him?*

"Hi, Mr. Winthorpe. My name is Diwata. I'll be looking after you for the next few hours. How are you feeling?" A young Filipino nurse with a blue starched cap was looking expectantly at him.

"Pretty terrible. I hurt all over."

She gave him a long sympathetic look. "Let me take your temperature and blood pressure, then, when the doctor comes around, we'll see about some more pain relief."

A few minutes later, Cynthia returned. "Dad, Naomi is in St. Thomas's, also. She was injured by flying glass, but apparently not badly. I understand she has a fractured wrist."

What could I have done to prevent her being hurt? he wondered. *She was the one who spotted Efraim just in time. And she was the one who persuaded Latifa to find the bank statements. If it weren't for her, the Eye might have gone down and Yusuf would have gotten away with his fraud. But, she is the one who gets punished.*

Cynthia saw the emotions flickering across his face. "What are you thinking, Dad?"

He told her.

She shrugged and said, "She'll have a couple of great, true stories for her grandchildren."

"Cindy, that's a terrible thing to say!"

"No, it's not!" Cynthia protested, "Dad, just think of all the people, like me, who've never taken a big risk for other people in their lives. What experiences have we had that we can pass on to our children to help shape their lives and their values?" She began to cry. "I'm so proud of you, Dad. But I was afraid we were going to lose you."

He smiled faintly and shook his head. "It takes more than a little high explosive to get rid of me!"

"You're incorrigible," she said, and then she laughed.

About half an hour later, a small, brown-skinned man wearing a blue dress shirt and blue silk tie came into the room. His dark eyes had an energetic sparkle, his moustache was neatly trimmed, and he spoke rapidly, fingering his stethoscope. "My name is Doctor Ramwaddy, and I have you in my care. How are you feeling, Mr. Winthorpe?"

"I have felt better, Doctor, but probably I shouldn't complain."

"Yes. Well, are you feeling discomfort in any particular area?"

"I have a pretty substantial headache, and my chest hurts, my left arm hurts, and the entire back of me, including my legs, is painful. Sorry, but you asked."

"Yes. Well, I think we can put you on a self-administered pain relief pump. We wanted to be sure you were fully awake before starting pain relief. Let me look in your eyes, Mr. Winthorpe. OK, now, follow my finger with your eyes. Good. Move your toes, please. Good. And your fingers now. Very good. I think just to be on the safe side we will do a brain scan. Judging by the abrasions on your forehead, you hit your head a pretty good knock. Somehow, you've broken your collarbone and your left forearm."

"What's wrong with the back of me? It's painful all over, even the back of my legs."

"Yes. Well, you have been hit with fragments of plexiglass. Fortunately, polycarbonate doesn't form sharp fragments like glass does when it is shattered. It forms odd-shaped pieces like a car window does when it is smashed. Because the pieces aren't sharp, most of them were stopped by your clothing. We had to remove about a dozen pieces that had penetrated your skin. No stitches required. Most of what you're feeling is like the pellets from a shotgun at a hundred metres. In fact, you'll probably be more comfortable sitting in a chair or standing up. I'm afraid that lying on your stomach is not possible because of the way we have your shoulder strapped up."

"How long am I going to be like this, doctor?"

"Well, the self-administered analgesia will make you a lot more comfortable. You won't need it any more in a day or two. Your back, arm and shoulder will be sore for about a week. The headache should be gone by tomorrow."

When the doctor had gone, Nurse Diwata fitted the analgesia pump and gave the small controller to Paul. He sat on the edge of the bed and began to smile. "Ah! Blessed morphine!"

"It's probably pethidine, not morphine, Dad."

He turned a teasing smile on Cynthia. "I could get accustomed to this."

"No, you won't! May I be the first to autograph your cast?"

"Sure. You got a pen?"

She produced one and scribbled: "Get well quick!" on the cast that covered most of his left arm.

"OK, Dad. I've got to go to work, but I'll be back tonight. I'm so glad you're going to be all right, and I'm really proud of you!"

She bent over, kissed him and disappeared.

For perhaps half an hour, Paul sat on his bed watching the traffic of nurses, visitors, patients and doctors. He was particularly interested in the small flocks of young doctors following a senior consultant as he (or she) made her rounds. The young medical students seemed well scrubbed, eager and attentive. Some were scribbling notes on clipboards; a few even dared to ask questions. He was half expecting that one of the flocks would descend on his bed, probing him with their eager eyes as they listened to Dr. Ranwaddy explain the intricacies of his case. He wondered what he would be asked about, and what he had done to sustain such a large collection of injuries? Then he hoped that Dr. Ranwaddy was not on the teaching staff and would not be shepherding a flock of hopeful young doctors. The idea of telling the world what had happened did not appeal to him.

But then the pressure increased. Nurse Diwata announced, "There's a young man here from the *Times* who would like to see you."

Good God! he thought, *how do they find me so quickly?* He shook his head. "Tell him that I'm only seeing family and friends for the time being, Nurse Diwata. You can refer him to Chief Inspector Clarkson at Scotland Yard."

As she turned to go, the young reporter brushed past her. "Hello, Mr. Winthorpe. I'm Eric Cotton-Davies from the *Times*, and I'd like to ask you just a few . . ."

"I'm sorry," Paul interrupted, "but I'm only seeing family and close friends now. I'm not feeling all that well. I suggest you speak to Chief Inspector Clarkson."

"I've already spoken to the chief inspector. He gave me your name, and I'd like to get your perspective on the terrorist attack."

"You can get all the information you need from the chief inspector. Now, if you don't mind, I'd like to get some rest."

"Mr. Winthorpe, our readers will be clamouring to hear from the hero's lips . . ."

"Young man!" Paul cut in with a flash of anger, "I'm not a hero! Now bug off and leave me alone!"

Nurse Diwata, somewhat forcibly, escorted Mr. Cotton-Davies out of the room. When she returned, she said, "I'm sorry, Mr. Winthorpe, I've asked the hospital switchboard to remove your name from their information sheets. If you have other family or friends that you'd like to see, you'll have to give them your room number."

"Paul?" It was a tentative female voice that woke him from a nap.

"Sarah! How nice of you to come."

"I almost didn't get here. The nurse out there said that only family and certain close friends were allowed to visit. I had to promise that I was a close friend."

"Of course you are!" Paul glanced toward the door, where he saw Nurse Diwata's inquiring face.

He nodded and she disappeared.

Sarah sat on a chair by the bed. "Cindy called me this morning. She told me some of what happened. And she . . . well, she said that maybe . . . maybe . . . I'd like to visit."

"I'm glad you did, Sarah. You look very well."

She gave a slight shrug, but she seemed to relax. "You're all bandaged up, except for your head. How are you feeling?"

"I'm feeling pretty well now that I have this heroin pump." He gestured toward the small black object on the bedside frame.

"Cindy said you're getting pethidine, Paul."

"What does she know? I haven't dared to look in a mirror. Is it pretty awful?"

"Well, you do have a pretty nasty scrape on your forehead."

He nodded and with his right hand he felt his forehead. "Lucky I have such a hard head. Otherwise, I might have ended up like Humpty-Dumpty."

For about twenty minutes, they talked about what had led up to the explosion. He didn't mention Naomi.

"Well, Paul, I should let you get some rest."

"Thanks so much for coming, Sarah. It was really nice to see you."

She was about to get up from the chair when a blonde girl with a cast on her right arm and several livid welts on her face approached the bed. She stretched out her left hand. "Hello. I'm Naomi Evensen."

"Oh!" Sarah uttered a gust of surprise. *It's her!* Then, she said, "I'm Sarah."

Naomi nodded and smiled; she pulled up a chair on the opposite side of the bed.

"Well, I really should go," Sarah announced.

Naomi said, "No, it's not necessary."

Sarah felt paralysed—unable to move. *I want to see this girl,* she thought, *just for a moment. Then I'll go.* But the moment turned into minutes as she watched Naomi and Paul talk. Sarah's focus was on their body language; she barely heard a word that passed between them. *But they're not like lovers!* she thought. *More like father and daughter.*

Sarah's eyes followed Naomi as the young girl left the room. She asked Paul: "Where's she going?"

"To Israel."

"Why is she going there? I wasn't listening."

"Well, she's going to work on a kibbutz in Galilee, try out for the violin section in the Israel Philharmonic, help with a charity for Palestinian children, and probably have some kids of her own."

"Oh! She's going to give up her job?"

Paul nodded. "I told her she was a nomad, but I think she realised that she was actually escaping her own potential."

"Why Israel? Why not London? Most of what you say she wants is in London."

"It's difficult to understand for those of us who love London, but Israel is different. Suffused in religion, history, tradition, conflict, and most of all, survival: all captured in one word: Masada."

"What's Masada?"

"It's a high mesa on the western shore of the Dead Sea, and it was turned into an ancient fortification. During the rebellion against Rome in the first century, what was left of the Hebrew rebels—less than a thousand men, women and children—held out there. They were besieged by about ten thousand Roman soldiers, who built a huge ramp against the mesa and breached the walls of the fortress. When the Romans entered the fortress, they found all of the Hebrews dead. They had killed each other in preference to becoming Roman slaves. Masada has become part of the Jewish conscientiousness, and Naomi holds some of that Masada ethic."

Sarah shook her head incredulously. "I don't get it."

"The short message of Masada is 'Live free or die.' But I think in the Jewish conscientiousness the message is more complex. It's more like, 'We, as a people, will do everything in our power to preserve the Jewish way of life in this land, or die trying.'"

Sarah nodded slowly. "OK. I get it. Paul, how do you feel about her leaving? You must be pretty disappointed."

Paul looked away for a moment. He shrugged, but there was a bittersweet expression on his face. "She's a lovely girl. In a way, I feel responsible for pushing her train off the nomad track and helping her train find the rails of the Israel-is-home track."

Hesitantly, Sarah suggested, "She's become like a second daughter to you."

Paul nodded. Wistfully, he said, "And, as it is with all young people, at a certain point they branch out on their own."

For a time, a companionable silence settled over Paul and Sarah.

Then he asked, "A piece of advice, Sarah."

She turned to face him. "What is it?"

"I'm going to be besieged by newspaper reporters. One has already been here, and I'm not keen on giving a lot of press interviews. But, at the same time I don't want to be rude, and, in a way, it's right for them to ask."

Sarah thought for a moment. "Why don't you pick out one for an exclusive interview? I think they'd pay you for it."

"But I'm not a celebrity, Sarah!"

"Oh, yes you are!"

"But I think getting paid to tell your secrets is kind of crass."

"I agree, but you can leave Naomi in client mode. Besides, you don't have to keep the money. You can give it to charity."

"Ohoo. That's a great idea. I could give the money to GYE. How much do you think I could get?"

"Well, I don't know. Maybe a hundred thousand."

"As much as that?"

"The man to ask is Mr. Clifford, and of course he'll take a cut. But there is one drawback, Paul."

"Which is?"

"It may not put you in the best light with Buckingham Palace."

"Do I care?"

"You might, if you fancy having the Queen pin one of her bravery medals on you. If you tell all to the *Sun,* the Palace may see you as a crass publicity seeker rather than a gentleman hero."

Paul laughed. "I'm neither one, and I think it might just be okay to give, say, seventy-five thousand to GYE while earning the distain of the Palace."

"Maybe if the Palace knew you were giving the *Sun's* money to the Duke's charity, they wouldn't be so harsh."

"I'll ask Cindy if she can get me Clifford's number."

Sarah drew her Blackberry from her handbag. "I'll get it for you in just a minute. I'll Google him." She pressed the small keys. "I can see the headline now: 'EXCLUSIVE! EYE HERO TELLS THE WHOLE STORY!'"

"Hello there, Paul. How are you feeling?" It was Chief Superintendent Clarkson.

"Doing better, thank you. How are you getting on?"

"Very well, indeed. Just a couple of notches below the top of the world category, and I wanted to thank you personally not only for knocking Efraim off his perch, but also for being so persistent in presenting your theory. It was just a theory, after all, and we policemen tend to be quite uncomfortable working on just one theory."

Paul smiled but said nothing.

"Tell me, Paul, why do you think that Efraim staged his attack today, rather than tomorrow, Sunday. You were there today. Did you have some premonition?"

"No premonition, Chief Inspector. Let's just call it Providence. I haven't any idea why he decided to attack a day earlier. Perhaps he was the one with the premonition that the net was closing on him, and I was just there out of compulsive curiosity."

The chief inspector nodded gravely. Then he offered, "You know there was a curious thing about his accomplices."

"No. What was it?"

"They were wearing suicide vests, except they weren't."

"What do you mean?"

"The garments they had on looked like suicide vests, and when they were apprehended, they seemed to be trying to detonate them. Unsuccessfully. When the bomb disposal unit arrived, it turned out that instead of explosive, the vests contained bars of soap, and, instead of ball bearings, glass marbles. Moreover, the accomplices claimed not to know they weren't wearing real suicide vests. Any theories on why that would be?"

"I haven't a clue, Chief Inspector. What did the accomplices say about the vests?"

"They said they thought they were real when they first tried them on."

"Maybe Efraim didn't have enough explosive, and he saved all he had for the shaped charges."

"They certainly made a big bang, as you know."

"What happened to him?"

"We had the disagreeable task of picking up the pieces of him."

"Couldn't have happened to a nicer guy, and what about his brother?"

"Disappeared. We wouldn't know if he left the country. The Moroccans say he hasn't come back there. We've also checked Iraq, but they say they haven't seen him. That country is hopelessly porous."

"I suspect he's somewhere in Basra."

The chief inspector shook his head. "We're not going back there to look for him. They can have him."

"Was anyone—apart from Efraim—seriously injured?"

"Two other people died. One was an elderly man who suffered a heart attack while on the Eye. By the time his capsule was unloaded, he had died. The other was a man who was on the grassy area, and he was apparently struck by a piece of metal. At this moment, I don't know whether the metal came from a charge or from the Plexiglas enclosure. There were also about fifteen people, including Naomi, who were treated in hospital for injuries—fortunately, none serious—and a couple of dozen more who were treated by ambulance crews on site for injuries. Even as it was, it could have been a lot worse."

"Hello, Grampa."

Paul opened his eyes. It was his grandson, David. In fact it was John, Teresa and both boys.

"Well, I didn't expect you guys."

John said, "Since I kind of started this mess, and you decisively finished it, I thought we ought to get together."

As the adults talked about what had happened, the two boys didn't know what to do with themselves. They had always respected and liked their grandfather, but now they wanted to get closer to somehow express their admiration and to be part of it all. From their parents' behaviour, they sensed that adulation was out of the question; it was difficult to know what to do. When there was a lull in the adult conversation, David said, "Grampa, can you help me with something?"

"I'll try, David, what is it?"

"I have a homework assignment to write a short play, and I've gotten most of it done, but I don't know how to finish it, and I thought you could help."

"What's the play about?"

"It's not very long. I can read it to you." He removed a neatly folded paper from the back pocket of his shorts. "It's called 'Saint Peter Decides.'"

Paul sat up, and turned toward his grandson. "OK. Go ahead."

David began to read: "Saint Peter is standing by the gate to heaven. Along comes a man named Barnaby who was a robber and a murderer. Barnaby says, 'Let me in Peter, I want to be in heaven now that I'm dead.' Saint Peter asks Jesus, 'What do you think about this man Barnaby?' Jesus says, 'He's not a friend of mine, and I don't think he belongs here.' So Saint Peter asks the Devil, 'What do you think about this man Barnaby?' The Devil says, 'I'll have him.' So Saint Peter gives Barnaby to the Devil. Barnaby screams a lot, but he has to go with the Devil.

Then along comes this nice old lady named Catherine. She says, 'Will you let me in, Saint Peter?' And Saint Peter asks the Devil, 'Is this lady a friend of yours?' The Devil says, 'No. She never did what I wanted her to.' So then Saint Peter asks Jesus, 'What do you think of this lady Catherine?' And Jesus says, 'She is a very good person. I think you should let her in.' So Saint Peter lets her into Heaven.

Then along comes this man named Geoffrey, and he asks Saint Peter, 'Will you let me into Heaven?' Saint Peter asks the Devil, 'What do you think of this man Geoffrey?' The Devil says, "I think he should come with me because sometimes he did what I wanted.' And then Saint Peter asked Jesus, 'What do you think of this man Geoffrey?' Jesus said, 'He is not perfect, but he has done many good things in his life. I think he would be all right here.'"

"Grampa, I don't know what Saint Peter should decide."

"I notice you don't have any Purgatory in the play."

"No, Grampa, I decided to leave Purgatory out of it."

"OK, David, if you were Saint Peter, where would you send Geoffrey?"

"That's the problem, Grampa. I think Geoffrey should be punished for doing bad things, but he also did plenty of good things."

"Who do you think Geoffrey likes better: the Devil or Jesus?"

"He likes Jesus better."

"How do you know that?"

"I just do."

"OK. Well, if Geoffrey is a friend of Jesus' don't you think that Jesus would want him in Heaven?"

"Yeah, but what about the Devil?"

Paul just shrugged.

"So maybe," David continued, "I could have Saint Peter ask Geoffrey who he likes better: the Devil of Jesus. And when he says 'Jesus', he gets into Heaven."

David looked at each of the adults in turn. They were either smiling or nodding. "OK, Grampa, thanks a lot."

When Paul was released from the hospital, he felt that one of his first priorities was to go and see Matthew Andrews at GYE. So arm in a cast, and his shoulder still strapped up, he passed through the security at Nine St. James's Place. Roberta met him and escorted him to the chief executive's office. On Matthew's desk was a copy of the *Sun* that featured the headline in three-inch high capitals.

"Goodness, Paul! I wasn't expecting you here. I thought you'd still be in the hospital under a security guard."

Paul shook his head. "There are a couple of things I wanted to see you about. First of all, I wanted to give you this."

He handed a cheque to Matthew, who looked at it and recoiled in surprise. "£66,450 for GYE." He looked up at Paul. "And it's signed by you. What's this all about?"

"It's my after-tax proceeds from the *Sun* for telling my story. If you apply Gift Aid to it, you'll get some of my taxes back from the government, and it should be worth nearly eighty thousand to GYE."

Matthew shook his head in wonder, still holding the cheque. "Paul, after all you've been through, I think you should keep this money."

"No. I couldn't keep the money, and I don't want anyone thinking that I did. So would you do me a favour?"

"Yes, of course."

"Would you put out a press release announcing that I've given the proceeds to GYE?"

"Yes. We'll do it right away. We're very grateful to you, Paul."

"And there's one other thing."

"Yes?"

"I'd like you to send me back to Marrakech for a couple of days."

"You certainly are a glutton for punishment. What do you have in mind?"

"Well, since Naomi isn't here, there are some loose ends to be tied up."

Matthew nodded. "I tried to get her to stay. I even offered her more money, but she's absolutely set on going back to Israel." He paused. "I was thinking of sending Roberta, but I know she wouldn't like the idea, and you know more about the situation in Morocco than anyone else. Still, it doesn't seem quite fair to ask you to go back after all you've been through."

"No, I want to go."

"What would be your agenda?"

"It would simply be to help the board get AMM restarted again, quickly, if possible. With Yusuf out of the way, I think the rest of the staff are capable of doing some good, honest work."

"OK. Keep me posted, will you?"

* * *

"Sarah, this is Cynthia Winthorpe. How are you?"

"I'm fine, Cindy. How are you, and how's your dad?"

"I'm fine, and he's definitely on the mend. Umm . . . Sarah, I was wondering if I could stop by and see you tonight?"

What's this all about? Has he actually taken a turn for the worse? Has Naomi decided not to go? flashed through Sarah's mind. She said, "Well, uhh, yes, I'll be home tonight. What time shall I expect you?"

"Is 8:30 too late?"

"No, that's fine. You know the address? It's 24 Horder Road in Fulham."

"Yes. Thank you, Sarah."

A nervous, but determined Cynthia sat across the coffee table from a nervous, but outwardly placid Sarah, as they sipped their tea and considered each other.

"First of all, Sarah, Dad doesn't know that I'm here, and he would be mad as hell at me if he knew." Sarah gave a wisp of a smile. "Secondly, I know this is none of my business." She took a deep breath. "I like you a lot, Sarah, and I know my dad likes you a lot." Sarah frowned, but Cynthia leaned forward earnestly. "I think he was very stupid getting mixed up with that Israeli girl, and I told him so, and I'm sure it felt very hurtful to you." Sarah gave a slight shrug.

Cynthia continued, "Fortunately, that's over now. Sarah, I love my dad, and I think, even though it's none of my business, that you two are right for each other."

"I don't know, Cindy."

"Sarah, you remind me a lot of my mom. They were very close: my mom and dad."

Sarah gave a slow exhalation of breath. "I don't know how I can trust him again."

Cynthia nodded. "I can only tell you that in thirty plus years, he's never let me down, and as far as I know, he never let my mom down."

"He let me down."

"Yes, and I think he's acutely aware of that. So much so that he's afraid to even ask you to go to the cinema. What I'm saying is that trust is very important to both of you—probably more important than for most people. And it would be a shame if that kept two people who really should be together, apart."

There were several moments of silence. Finally, Sarah asked, "What are you suggesting, Cindy?"

"That you invite him over for lunch—I'll make sure that he accepts. I'm only asking that you imply that you're willing to give him a second chance." Sarah sat mutely considering Cynthia.

"What do you think, Sarah?"

"I'm very flattered that you think so much of me that you're trying to catch me for your dad."

Cynthia put her head to one side as she looked at Sarah. "I'm sorry to be such a busy body, Sarah. . . No. Actually, I'm not sorry, and I meant everything I said."

* * *

Paul came early to church. He selected a seat in the third pew on the left, carefully leaving enough space for one and a half people on his right. He wanted to discourage any couples from sitting on his right, but he also created a pile of hymnal, church newsletter, and order of service on his left. That was so he could shift over to his left in the event that Sarah should happen to come with her daughter, Anne.

He very much wanted this after-church lunch at Sarah's to go well. He had bought some flowers: nothing grand—just a bouquet of white roses and jasmine. They were in the car. He was wearing his white linen suit, a blue dress shirt and loafers.

Why was Cindy such a busy body? he wondered. *Asking me if I've seen Sarah, and telling me that she reckoned Sarah would be willing to give me a second chance. Why doesn't she just look after James? She's the one who ought to worry about getting married! It's not my biological clock that's ticking! I guess she means well. I hope James doesn't mind if she's a bit of a control freak. What if Anne and/or her sister Paula are at the lunch? Possible but unlikely. Sarah's too straightforward for that. But if it happens, I'll just go with it.*

Somebody had just entered the pew to his right and had immediately knelt. It was Sarah. Alone. He glanced surreptitiously toward her. She was wearing a white, short-sleeved blouse with lace embroidery and a blue, knee-length, cotton skirt. Her hair was arranged in a neat bun at the back of her head.

When she sat up, she smiled and whispered, "You're looking very smart."

"Well," he whispered, "I'm meeting a very important person for lunch." There was that wisp of a smile on her face, but she looked straight ahead. He leaned toward her slightly, "You look very nice."

She confided, "I, also, have an important lunch."

He found it difficult to concentrate on the service, and several times he lost the thread of the priest's homily. His mind was busy with nervous speculation.

When the priest said, "Let us offer each other a sign of peace," Sarah turned toward him, and gave him a brief kiss on the cheek before turning to the pew behind her to shake hands with the people sitting there.

Well, he thought, *that's something. Not the usual kiss on the lips, but better than just a handshake.*

Sarah's home was a three-bedroom terraced house on a quiet street in Fulham. The ground floor was an open living-dining area, with hardwood flooring, modern pastel carpeting, and Italian furniture. The walls were decorated with colourful contemporary prints. At the rear of the ground floor was the kitchen: all beech and stainless steel, and beyond the kitchen, through sliding glass doors was a small private garden with vines, small cypresses, geraniums and a fountain to one side.

"Now, Paul, your job is to grill the prawns while I organise the chips." She removed a neatly wrapped package from the refrigerator, and upon opening it, Paul found it contained at least a dozen giant prawns.

"Shall I cook them with the shell on?" he asked.

"Yes, please. I think they're better that way. Do you like chips English style or American style?"

"I shouldn't admit it, but I love McDonald's chips."

Sarah grinned. She began slicing potatoes. "I thought so, and I'll have just a few."

Paul lit the barbecue and stood watching her. She said, over her shoulder, "I get nervous when people watch me cook. You can open the wine. It's in the door of the fridge."

"Wow! Chassagne Montrachet 2009. This is wonderful! Where did you get it?"

Sarah was amused. "They didn't have it at Waitrose, so I crossed the river and found it at that favourite little shop of yours on Garrett Lane."

"Well done, Sarah! Shall I pour it now?"

"Just a minute. Let me get out the smoked salmon."

They sat at the glass-topped table.

Sarah asked, "Have you heard anything from Naomi?"

Paul shook his head. "No. I'm not expecting to hear from her."

"Not even a Christmas card?"

"You mean a Hanukkah card. No, I don't think so. For her, it's like a change in identity. To go back and contact the people who were part of your old identity makes it that much more difficult to sustain the new identity. The salmon was very good, Sarah."

"I'm glad you liked it. Shall we get to cooking the prawns and the chips? I'm going to start a cherry clafoutis."

"What's a cherry clafoutis?"

"It's like a cherry pie except with cherries marinated in sugar and calvados baked in custard."

They sat down again; this time, Sarah had put finger bowls on the table. "I'm sure that the Queen would use a knife and fork to peel prawns and eat chips, but I think it's more fun to eat with your fingers."

Paul agreed. "This is so good, Sarah."

"Paul, tell me a little about Catherine."

"My late wife?"

"Yes."

"Well, she was a very positive, optimistic person with a wry sense of humour. She was bright and had lots of energy. She had her own PR business with about half a dozen clients and good connections in the media. We used to play bridge and tennis, but she was better than I at both. She was a very good looking woman—one would have called her beautiful when she was younger."

"Paul . . ." He looked over at Sarah, "did you ever cheat on her?"

Paul was stunned momentarily as if he had been physically struck. "No! Never!"

Sarah persisted. "Why not?"

"Because . . ." he began, "because . . . she was all I ever wanted."

"OK. But, Paul, you're an attractive man. Weren't there times when you were tempted?" He shook his head. Sarah gave him a sultry look, and she was leaning forward. Her décolletage was tempting. "By some good looking woman?"

"Well . . ."

"What?"

"There was one time . . . but nothing ever happened."

"Tell me about it."

Paul took a deep breath. "I was working for Boston Consulting at the time. There was a team of us working on a client's premises, so we were staying at a hotel nearby. One person on the team was a very good-looking young woman who prepared our PowerPoint presentations for us. She sat next to me at dinner one night and proceeded to tell me how she and her husband had an open marriage, that it was quite all right for her to have temporary liaisons, and that in fact she enjoyed such liaisons. She didn't actually say, 'Are you up for it?' but she had probably noticed my admiring glances, and it was pretty clear that she was up for it."

"So, what happened?"

"She gave me her room number, and said, 'Why don't we meet in the bar first?'"

"And then?"

"I made some non-committal statement, went to my room and went to bed."

"She didn't come pounding on your door?"

"No, but she was pretty pissed off the next day. She told me I could do my own PowerPoint presentations."

Sarah laughed. "Have you ever regretted not taking Ms. PowerPoint up on her offer?"

Paul smiled. "That's a good question. Yes and no. Yes, I have no doubt it would have been a thoroughly memorable evening. But no. Secrets have a way of coming out, or at least, of affecting the behaviour of the secret keeper, so in that case, my relationship with Catherine would have been affected. I had made a commitment to Catherine, and I wasn't going to risk changing it."

The cherry clafoutis arrived at the table; the burgundy tops of the cherries appeared to be floating in the lightly baked custard.

"This is really delicious, Sarah."

"It's Raymond Blanc's recipe, but I don't like kirsch, so I used calvados instead."

"The cherries in the calvados are marvelous."

"Thank you. What's going on with GYE?"

"I'm going down to Marrakech on Monday for a week to try to help the chairman of AMM restart the charity."

Efraim's Eye

"So you think with the old CEO out of the way, it's worth saving?"

"Yusuf and his brother are gone now, and, yes, the rest of the people are capable of good things."

Paul pushed his chair back and folded his napkin on his lap. "You know, Sarah, I really wonder what happens to the souls of people like Efraim when they die. When I was in the hospital, my grandson, David read me a play he had written on that subject."

He told her about David's play.

Sarah commented, "But that doesn't really answer your question about what hell is like."

"No, it doesn't. Do you have a theory?"

"Yes. I agree with David that people are selected for hell because they like the Devil better than Jesus, but I think the key point is that they enjoy hurting other people. So my theory is that the bad people are made to live through the pain they caused—or intended to cause—other people, over and over again. So those terrorists who smashed the airplanes into the World Trade Centre are, at the moment, living through all the terror, pain and suffering they caused each of their three thousand victims. And they are made to feel what each of their victims felt over and over. I don't really believe all that stuff about fire and brimstone."

"And is there no relief from this constant re-living the victims' terror?"

"I don't know, Paul. In my mind, there are three alternatives. For the recidivists, it can go on forever. For the truly repentant, there might be some form of reincarnation. For those in between, well maybe they get dropped into a black hole."

Paul smiled. "Do you believe in reincarnation for the good guys?"

"Probably not. Unless you volunteer."

They talked for about another hour. Paul helped Sarah clear the dishes. He thanked her for the lunch and said, "Sarah, you're not a great fan of ballet, but I believe you do like modern dance. Would you like to go to Sadler Wells next Friday? There's a

Spanish choreographer who has a show, and we could go to one of the restaurants on Upper Street for dinner either before or after."

"I'd like that very much, Paul."

* * *

Mr. Hatim Al-Zahari shook Paul's hand warmly. "I am glad to see you again, Paul. Matthew briefed me on what has happened, and he sent me an e-mail saying that you were coming to see me about AMM business." He retreated behind his desk. "I'm afraid there's not much to be done about AMM. It's finished, I suppose. Yusuf has disappeared, and well, he was AMM."

Paul looked out the window behind Mr. Al-Zahari to the grand palms in the park. He said, "AMM has some very good people with the right skills, the right attitude and values."

"Perhaps so. I've been traveling on OilMaroc business, and I haven't had the opportunity to call a board meeting or respond to the calls from the bookkeeper, Yaminah."

"Well, with your permission, sir, I'd like to see if AMM can be put back together. I can report back to you late tomorrow afternoon, if that's all right."

Al-Zahari consulted his computer monitor. "Tomorrow at six?"

"Yes, that's fine. I'll see you then."

"Good luck, Paul."

Mohammed knew from reading the Assabah newspaper that an attack on the London Eye had been thwarted, but no names were mentioned. The Assabah editor apparently did not read the *Sun*. Now, he heard the whole story from Paul, and he wanted to drive Paul immediately to the Assabah offices.

"No, Mohammed, I want you to take me to AMM right away."

"Is closed, Mr. Winthorpe. I hear Mr. Al-Rashid gone away."

"I want to contact Yaminah, Mohammed."

"I not know where she live."

"Well, let's try the AMM offices, first."

When the car pulled up to the familiar door, Paul did not get out. Instead, he dialed the AMM number on his cell phone. It rang. A female voice answered, "ash-Shbab Mshrw Maroc."

"Yaminah?"

There was a pause. "Is that you, Mr. Winthorpe?"

"Yes, it is, Yaminah. I'm outside. Can you let me in?"

"Mr. Al-Rashid is not here."

"I know he's not there, Yaminah. I want to talk to you about possibly re-starting AMM."

"I open door very soon."

Paul reached into his briefcase and took out a copy of the *Sun*. He handed it over the back seat. "Here, Mohammed, when we've finished for today, you can take this to Assabah."

There was no light on in Yusuf's office; in fact, the whole house seemed to be shrouded in darkness—except the AMM staff office where one light was burning.

"So, you're holding the fort by yourself, Yaminah?"

"What you mean holding fort, Mr. Winthorpe?"

"Sorry, Yaminah, I meant that you're here all alone."

"Yes. Mr. Al-Rashid call me from somewhere overseas. He ask me transfer money. I tell him I need him sign on paper. He say, you copy my signature. I tell him I not break law. He hang up. I not know where he is. Maid and gardener not here. I think Mr. Al-Rashid dismiss. Latifa not here. No work for her. I try reach Mr. Al-Zahari. He not return my calls."

"So, Yaminah, there is money in the AMM accounts?"

"Yes, is much money. I pay salaries."

"That's good. All the employees are still there?"

"Yes. Only Mr. Al-Rashid gone. His brother also gone."

Yaminah listened with intense attention as Paul told her the story of the Al-Rashid brothers. When it concluded, she nodded sadly. "I think something like that happen. Is all over now."

"No. I want you to help me get AMM restarted."

She shook her head. "Is impossible."

"Yaminah, do you remember Mosa Mitri?"

"Yes, he work for AMM. Mr. Al-Rashid dismiss, but he good person."

"Mosa Mitri is now a loan officer at Shahzad Rameel Bank. Do you think he could make a good CEO of AMM?"

Yaminah stared at Paul for a long moment. "I not know . . . I . . . Yes . . . Yes, he could be CEO . . . You think you hire?"

"No, I'm thinking of introducing him to the chairman, Mr. Al-Zahari. He would decide whether or not to hire him."

"I hope so."

"There's something I would like you and Latifa to do in the meantime, Yaminah."

"What is it?"

"I would like to ask you and Latifa to look for new offices for AMM. Not expensive or grand, but comfortable and convenient. If you and Latifa can pick out three or four possibilities, the new CEO can make the final decision."

"We move AMM away from here?"

Paul nodded.

"Is very, very good, Mr. Winthorpe." Yaminah was suddenly bubbling with positive energy. "I call Latifa. Then I send e-mail to Mr. Al-Zahari, telling him Mosa Mitri is good choice."

"I think you should wait on that e-mail, Yaminah, until after Mosa Mitri has had an interview, but if you can get him on the phone now, I'd like to meet with him."

At 10 the following morning, Mosa Mitri came to collect Paul at the reception desk of the Shahzad Rameel Bank, but instead of taking Paul into his small office, Mosa stood in the bank's bull pen, clapped his hands, and made an announcement in Arabic. Then he waved a newspaper, and made a further pronouncement for the benefit of his colleagues, who were standing and listening. His concluding flourish, indicating Paul, precipitated a burst of applause. The colleagues approached Paul, shook his hand. "Congratulations!" "Well done!" "Thank you!" "Very good!"

When Mosa finally escorted Paul to his office, there on the desk was a copy of a newspaper. The sophisticated Arabic script was unintelligible to Paul, but just above the Arabic title was one word in English, "Assabah." There, also on the first page was a colour photograph of Paul Winthorpe; it had been copied from his website.

Mosa announced, "One of the directors of the bank would like to have lunch with you."

"I don't think so, Mosa. You don't really know why I'm here."

"No. I just thought you were here to tell me about Efraim and Yusuf and the London Eye."

"No. Does the paper mention that Yusuf is missing?"

"No."

"Does it say anything about corruption at AMM?"

Mosa frowned, "No. In this country, the newspapers never print stories about corruption."

"That's probably just as well if we want AMM's reputation to be preserved. But the fact is that Yusuf passed AMM's funds to his brother for terrorist activities. The authorities in this country know that, so Yusuf is unlikely to return here. He's probably gone back to Iraq."

"So AMM has lost its CEO. Good riddance, I would say."

"You interested in the job?"

"What?"

"Would you be interested in being CEO of AMM?"

"Well . . ." Mosa looked around his office as if the answer could be found there. "Well . . . yes. There would be a lot of cleaning up to do."

"True. But if you were to get the job, I think you'd find you'd have the full support of the employees and the board."

Mosa gazed at Paul for a moment. "What would the job pay?"

"I don't really know, but I think it would pay more than you're making now."

"The offices are still in Al-Rashid's house."

"I've sent Yaminah and Latifa on an expedition to look for new offices."

"Oh, that's excellent. Yes, I would be interested."

"Good. I'd like you to e-mail me two copies of your CV: one in English and one in Arabic. I'll send the English version to the

CEO of GYE, and if he agrees, I'll take the Arabic version to the chairman of AMM tonight. If he likes what he sees, he'll arrange an interview, and if all goes well, you'll get the job."

"You don't want to have lunch with the director?"

"Under the circumstances, no."

Paul's mobile phone rang; it was Matthew, who said, "I've looked at the CV of this guy Mosa Mitri. He's worked for AMM before. Why did he leave?"

"Yusuf fired him. The usual story. He started to know too much."

"And you think he's honest?"

"He was one of the whistle blowers that Naomi and I met with, and he's working for a bank now. Even in Morocco, the banks seem to be pretty careful about who they hire."

"His CV has several good references, and he's a loan officer now. He knows what we do."

"Yaminah was quite positive about him becoming her boss."

"And Roberta remembers him quite favourably. I'd say go ahead and recommend him to Hatim."

"OK."

"If he does get hired, Paul, we still have the dilemma of what to do about the accreditation of AMM."

"Well, my view is that it would be pretty unfair to hire a new CEO and pull the accreditation of his charity. Can't we settle on something like 'accreditation under review—to be re-assessed in one year'?"

"OK. Let's take it up with the Accreditation Board when you get back."

Mr. Al-Zahari was relieved to hear that Yusuf had been unable to take the cash out of AMM. He said, "I made inquiries of the bank where his pay cheque was deposited, and they told me his account has been closed. That confirms to me that he's not coming back to Morocco."

The chairman also liked what he saw in Mosa's CV. "I'll call him tomorrow and ask him to come in for an interview," he said. "Then we'll probably get him to meet with some of the other directors."

Paul said, "There's just one other thing, sir."

"Yes?"

"I believe the board promised to be a governing board. That means that the board will set the strategy and approve the policies of AMM."

Mr. Al-Zahari smiled. "Yes. And it also means setting objectives for the CEO and holding his feet to the fire. We've got the message, Paul. I sincerely hope that GYE doesn't remove our accreditation."

"I'm going to recommend that they give you a year to get into compliance with GYE's standards."

"Thank you, Paul."

* * *

Something's definitely going on with Paul, Sarah thought. *There's a fire going in the fireplace: OK it's October, but it's not that cold outside. I can see candles on the table. He's serving champagne in his best glasses, and he seems nervous!* She said, "This is all very nice, Paul. What's the occasion?"

"Oh, I almost forgot," he said, "There's something in the refrigerator to go with the champagne."

When he returned to the living room, he placed a small, ziplocked plastic bag in front of her. There was something inside the bag, but because of condensation, she couldn't make out what it was.

"Is it something to eat?" she asked.

"Why don't you open it and see?"

Inside the bag was a small box wrapped in aluminum foil.

"Is this a special kind of caviar?" she inquired.

"You have to unwrap it to find out."

Inside the aluminum foil was a dark blue velvet jeweler's case. She looked up at Paul. "Is this something for me?"

"Yes."

Inside the case was a ring set with a large, brilliant-cut emerald, flanked by two baguette-cut diamonds. There was a sudden intake of her breath. "Oh, Paul!" She looked at him.

"Will you marry me, Sarah?"

"Oh! . . . Oh!" She saw the apprehension on his face, and she melted. "Yes, Paul. Yes, I will! When?"

"Whenever you want."

"This is really just beautiful!" She gazed at the flashes of bright green light emitted by the emerald. She slipped the ring on her left hand. "It's a little too big."

"That's all right. They'll re-size it for you. In fact, you can exchange it for something different if you'd prefer all diamonds."

"No. No. I love this emerald; it's so beautiful. Thank you, Paul!"

He sat next to her on the couch and kissed her. Then he kissed her again. And again. The mother of pearl buttons on her silk blouse came undone, as did the clasp at her back.

"You're so lovely, Sarah."

"Umm," she breathed. She cradled his head, closed her eyes, and leaned back. "Dinner will be delayed," she whispered between breaths. "The chef must attend . . . to an urgent . . . matter."

Later, when the oyster and lobster shells, and the plates with remnants of chips and salad had been cleared from the table, they sat gazing at each other across what little was left of the Crepe Suzettes.

"Where are you going to take us on our honeymoon, Paul?"

"I don't know." He paused to consider. "Maybe . . . maybe . . . the desert, the Atlas Mountains and Essaouira."

Lightning Source UK Ltd.
Milton Keynes UK
UKOW031546201112

202496UK00002B/23/P